Praise for Patri...

"When a historical romance [gets] ... ... treatment, the story line is pure action and excitement, and the characters are wonderful."   —Harriet Klausner

"One of the romance genre's finest talents."
                                                        —*Romantic Times*

"I couldn't put it down! This one is a keeper! Pat Potter writes romantic adventure like nobody else. *The Black Knave* will steal your heart! I loved this book! Delightful, daring, delicious—better than chocolate! Readers will love this book!"   —Joan Johnston

"Pat Potter proves herself a gifted writer as artisan, creating a rich fabric of strong characters whose wit and intellect will enthrall even as their adventures entertain."   —*BookPage*

"A master storyteller, a powerful weaver of romantic tales."
                                                        —Mary Jo Putney

"[Potter] has a special gift for giving an audience a first-class romantic story line."   —*Affaire de Coeur*

"Patricia Potter looks deeply into the human soul and finds the best and brightest in each character to help them face the challenges put before them with courage and love. This is what romance is all about."
                                                —Kathe Robin, *Romantic Times*

THE BLACK KNAVE

PATRICIA POTTER

JOVE BOOKS, NEW YORK

This is a work of fiction. Names, characters, places, and incidents are
either the product of the author's imagination or are used fictitiously,
and any resemblance to actual persons, living or dead, business
establishments, events, or locales is entirely coincidental.

THE BLACK KNAVE

A Jove Book / published by arrangement with
the author

PRINTING HISTORY
Jove edition / July 2000

All rights reserved.
Copyright © 2000 by Patricia Potter.
This book may not be reproduced in whole or in part,
by mimeograph or any other means, without permission.
For information address: The Berkley Publishing Group,
a division of Penguin Putnam Inc.,
375 Hudson Street, New York, New York 10014.

The Penguin Putnam Inc. World Wide Web site address is
http://www.penguinputnam.com

ISBN: 0-515-12864-3

A JOVE BOOK®
Jove Books are published by The Berkley Publishing Group,
a division of Penguin Putnam Inc.,
375 Hudson Street, New York, New York 10014.
JOVE and the "J" design
are trademarks belonging to Penguin Putnam Inc.

PRINTED IN THE UNITED STATES OF AMERICA

10 9 8 7 6 5 4 3 2

Prologue

Scotland, 1746

So much blood.

Rory Forbes would never again fear hell, for it was here now.

The thunder of cannon, the clash of swords, the screams. The moans. Dear God, the moans of the dying.

Except God had obviously deserted this stretch of moor and bog called Culloden. And the cries would haunt him until the day he died.

Only minutes after the afternoon assault, the heather moorland was soaked in blood. Wounded men on the ground were being systematically slaughtered, those limping off the battlefield struck down.

Rory had been trained well. He'd killed several men already, but *they* had been trying to kill *him*. Now—within an hour's time—the battle was all but over, but the killing continued. Brutal. Merciless. He wanted no part of it.

"No quarter!" He heard Cumberland's order passed from one man to another. "No quarter."

He dropped his blood-soaked sword and stood amidst death, then heard a moan behind him. A man in MacPherson plaid lay crumpled just feet from him. Blood poured from a wound in his chest, and a frothy pink bubbled from his lips. "Water," the MacPherson whispered.

He heard his father yelling at him. "Finish him."

Buy Rory couldn't. Instead, he stooped next to the man and offered his flagon to the man's lips, letting the water drip into the man's mouth. Several drops passed, then he was brushed aside by his brother, Donald, and before he could react, a sword plunged into the man's breast.

"No quarter!" His brother took up the call, the lust of killing darkening his eyes, flushing a face already red with blood.

With horror Rory looked at his older brother. Rory had been fostered by an English family and taught chivalry, but there was none this day. He heard the screams of women over the hill—the camp followers—and his heart constricted, even as he heard his brother's bitter word aimed at him. "Coward."

Rory turned away and walked from the moor, knowing he could do nothing to stop the slaughter but refusing any longer to be an accomplice in murder.

"Rory!" He heard his father's voice. "Damn your hide, come back."

The curses and threats of his father meant nothing. Nor did the taunt of coward from his brother. He was not going to be part of the continuing slaughter where whole clans fell before the king's artillery, where raw courage was met with something far less, and the tattered remains were struck down in retreat.

He had never seen such courage as that displayed by the Highlanders. He knew he was on the wrong side, had known it, in fact, since the message came to him in Edinburgh commanding him to return home to Braemoor.

But after his father's kinsman, Lord President Forbes, declared neutrality and stood against those who joined Prince Charles, Rory's father took his own branch of the family to join the Duke of Cumberland, who promised land and favors.

Rory had given precious little thought to loyalty and

honor. He'd hated Braemoor and all the cruelty he'd known there. He'd left the place, penniless, to make his way in Edinburgh, where quick hands and a ready wit had provided a fine income in gambling houses and a willing bed from ladies both high and low. His family had expected nothing of him. He lived up to their expectations. He had, in fact, courted his reputation of wastrel, the better to throw in his father's face.

But even he could not ignore the summons to battle. Not without being disinherited, not without being called coward. He'd not been ready to risk the first, and too proud the second. For a brief moment or so, mayhap he'd even thought honor was involved.

There was no honor today.

He still heard the clash of weapons. Small battles continued, but the result was clear. The Highlanders were being decimated, clan by clan, by overwhelmingly superior forces. He'd heard Cumberland's order to kill every Jacobite, and by God, he was not going to be one of Cumberland's executioners. He had supped and gambled and drunk with many of the Highlanders months ago when Prince Charlie had occupied Edinburgh. How many of them lay dead now?

Rory could barely breathe. He had thought he had no heart, that it had been hardened by years of abuse by his father. He had been excoriated for his worthlessness so long and so fervently that he had come to believe it. But now he thought his heart would break; it had only gone into hiding before.

"Rory, damn you, come back."

He heard the voices but kept walking away from his clan. He ignored their curses, their entreaties.

He reached a hill and looked down. Soldiers in red uniforms were everywhere. Some robbed the dead, others gave the coup de grace to the fallen. His tartan was stiff with blood, his arms—and probably his face— streaked with it. He took off his bonnet with its black cockade—the king's color, and fitting it was—and threw it to the ground. He continued to walk away, toward the horses held by several men in British uniforms.

He found his own mount, a large gray gelding.

"Going to run 'em down, sir?" one of the men asked.

"We crushed them Jacobite bastards," said another with pride, his eyes shining with blood lust even though his coat was unstained and his sword untested.

Rory didn't reply. He swung up into the saddle and guided the horse away from the sounds of the battlefield, toward a stream that he knew ran clear from the hills. He wanted to wash the blood from his hands. He knew he would never wash it from his soul.

He saw retreating Jacobites in the distance. He could still hear the screams and moans from the moor as he tightened his knees and urged his horse into a trot. He rode for an hour, perhaps more before nearing Forbes's land. He wound his way through the harsh landscape of scraggly brush and hard rock toward an unbloodied stream. There was a hunting hut there, one he used when he needed a sanctuary. It was a place where he could wash the blood from his body.

As he approached the stream, he heard a scream and cantered toward it, stopping his horse when he saw the three women and two bairns. Three British soldiers had obviously pulled them from the thatched hut. Before he could reach them, one of the soldiers plunged a bayonet into an older woman while a younger one leaned over a small child, covering its body with her own.

"Stay your hands!" Rory yelled as he galloped over.

The three soldiers looked up, their eyes going to his head to determine whether he was the king's man or a Jacobite. He was very aware of his absence of a bonnet as the soldiers braced for an attack. Suspicion darkened their faces.

He felt naked without the sword he'd abandoned on the battlefield. But he took his pistol from the belt, fully aware it had but one charge. He had that, and his dirk. Nothing more. Except fury.

"The enemy is over the hills," he said curtly.

"The duke said we was to kill any rebel—man or woman."

"I say otherwise," Rory said as he watched one woman huddle over the fallen one, the other cradling the children in her skirts.

"You a rebel showing your backside?"

"Nay," Rory said evenly. "But I suggest you return to the others."

"Not until I get a leg over," one of the men said, reaching out his arm and grabbing the youngest woman, pulling her to him.

Rory realized he was committing treason, that he could be tried and hung for interfering with Cumberland's orders. He didn't care. He still heard the sound of distant gunfire, and looked at the soldiers with contempt. These men weren't on a battlefield. They were slinking around, seeking to rape and pillage those weaker than themselves. He feared many more would scavenge these hills, indeed all the hills of Scotland, in the next weeks.

"Take your hands off her." Even he recognized the menace in his words. His knees tightened around the horse as he released the reins and his left hand reached to his side to take the dirk from his belt. He barely noticed his sporran slipping free, spilling its contents across the ground.

One of the soldiers backed up, aiming his own pistol as another took his sword from its scabbard. The third man continued to hold the woman, as the two children clung to her skirts.

Rory fired his pistol at the soldier holding the firearm, and watched with satisfaction as the man went down; he had no reservation about killing *these* men. He freed his legs from the stirrups and jumped the second soldier, aiming his dirk for the man's chest. The man dodged the blow, and with more agility than Rory thought possible swung his sword. The blade sliced through Rory's arm.

Ignoring the sudden pain, he tripped his attacker and

sent the man sprawling to the ground. His foot trapped the hand holding the sword. He reached down and took it just as he heard a woman's cry from behind him.

He whirled to see the third man release her and lunge at him with an upraised dirk. He swung the sword, ripped the man's chest open, and watched him fall, then turned back to the man on the ground.

Cursing, the second soldier tried to pull his dirk from his belt.

"I wouldna be doing that," Rory said, placing the tip of the sword at the man's throat. "Take your friend and get out of here." He knew he might be signing his own death warrant. He wore no bonnet signifying his allegiance, but he might well be identified later. He could only hope the blood and sweat and days-old beard might protect him. But he had no more stomach for killing.

The soldier looked at the sword tip that lingered near his throat, and nodded, but hate glistened in his eyes. He slowly, carefully, rose, his eyes obviously marking Rory's face; he would remember it.

Rory watched as the soldier's gaze rested on the man who had been shot and was quite obviously dead. Then he leaned down and helped pick up his wounded companion, and the two of them stumbled back toward the moor.

Rory waited until they were at a safe distance, moving away, then turned to the women. The older one regarded him with steady eyes. Her bairns still clutched at her skirts; one stared with great brown eyes, the other— a girl—cried quietly.

"God bless you, sir," she said.

The other woman kneeled next to the dead older woman. She stood. Her dark eyes blazed with fury. "They killed her."

"You must flee from here," Rory said.

"You're a Jacobite." 'Twas a statement, not a question. His tartan, he knew, was nondescript. It could have belonged to any number of clans.

"It doesna matter who I am. The Jacobites have lost. How did you happen to come here . . . ?"

"I am Kate McDonald. This is my sister-in-law, Jeannie. My husband and his brother are with Prince Charlie, and we came with them. But they sent us away at dawn. I think he feared . . . we might be in danger. Can you tell us anything about them?"

The blood on his clothes could well be her husband's. The knowledge weighed on him like a boulder. He wanted to reassure them, but he could not. Few men would live through the slaughter and its aftermath.

His silence seemed answer enough. The women wrung their hands, their faces aging with understanding.

"We have to go to them," Kate said.

"No," Rory said harshly. "Where is your home?"

"To the north."

He swore to himself as he looked around. "You have no horses?"

"We moved with the army."

He swallowed hard. He'd heard all the orders. Cumberland wanted every Jacobite killed. Women. Children. He didn't want one left to raise the Jacobite banner against his brother, the king, again.

Rory shook his head. "Do you have friends you can go to? Clansmen?"

The younger woman spoke up then. "I will stay and look for my husband."

"And the bairns? Do you wish to sacrifice them also, madam? Do you believe your husbands would want that?"

Kate's arms went around the children and she clutched them to her.

"You cannot stay here," he said. "Cumberland's troops will scour the countryside. It would be best if you went to a cave up in that hill. I'll show the way and send someone with food for you. When it is safe, we can find a way to get you back to your clan."

"Why do you do this?" The older woman looked at him suspiciously.

"Because it suits me," he said. "Do you wish my protection or not?" His answer was far more curt than he'd intended. He'd never intended this . . . involvement, either, but he couldn't let women and children be hunted like animals. He would surely lose his soul, then.

The two women looked at each other, then at the children. The mother nodded reluctantly.

The two soldiers were only specks now. They were moving with the speed of tortoises, but they *were* moving and would soon send someone after the Jacobites.

There was not much time.

He stooped down and picked up the sporran. A deck of cards had spilled out on the ground. He'd entertained himself with those cards during the endless wait for battle. He'd taken no small sums from his clansmen.

Rory picked up the cards. A knave of spades sat atop the deck.

"Who are you?" the older woman asked.

"That is something I would prefer to keep to myself," he replied.

"Then how . . ."

"Whoever I send will carry this," he said, his thumb sending the card flying up into the air and toward her.

She caught it, her eyes going to the face of it.

"The black knave," she observed quietly.

"Aye," he replied, then he caught the reins of his horse, led him to where the forlorn group stood.

"I canna leave her," the older woman said, looking down at the dead woman.

"I'll see to a decent burial," Rory said. "I give you my vow. But you must save yourself and your bairns now."

She hesitated, then allowed him to help her on the horse. He lifted the two children up. The older woman would have to walk, as would he. But the cave was not far. He moved quickly, but the older woman kept apace. Thirty minutes later they had reached a cave, and he saw them inside, then covered the opening with underbrush, left his flagon and the oatmeal he'd carried with him.

"No more than two days," he said. "Someone will come by for you. Do not forget . . ."

Through the dim light, the older woman smiled. "We will not, nor will we forget the Black Knave."

One

Rory had never wanted to be laird.

Today he wanted it even less.

But he stood at his father's grave on a cool, wet, dreary afternoon as members of the Forbes clan said farewells to their chieftain. Not even the bagpipes noted the burial of his father. After Culloden, their use had been frowned upon by Cumberland and King George, and there were rumors they would be outlawed completely.

He knew he should feel grief, but he didn't, only a mild regret that there was none. His father had hated him, and demonstrated it every day of Rory's life. If the estate and title had not been entailed, Rory had no doubt he would have been disinherited.

Nearly two months had passed since the battle at Culloden Moor. His brother, Donald, had died first, finally succumbing to a lingering fever after receiving a minor wound at Culloden. Ironically, it had been inflicted by his own sword when he had been chasing a Highlander and had tripped over a body. Rory's father died two weeks later during a wild, angry ride at night across the hills. He'd apparently been hit by a low branch and found early the next morning with a broken neck.

Rory knew the eyes of his clan were on him. None was happy that he was to become the new Marquis of Braemoor. His father had made his contempt for his younger son obvious, particularly after Culloden. He had not spoken a word to him after Donald fell ill.

And now Braemoor was Rory's. He dinna want it.

There were others who did, however, including his cousin Neil, who was glowering at him over the grave. Rory knew that Neil was wishing it was he in that grave, not the old chief.

Well, he would have to wait his turn. Rory had plans of his own at the moment. He rubbed his face, now cleanly shaven, as it had been since Culloden. He'd also cut his hair short and currently wore an English powdered wig, the hair tied neatly behind with a gaudy ribbon. In the past weeks he'd become even more the dandy, using his gambling winnings to purchase brightly colored trews and waistcoats. He was wearing a dark purple one this morning in honor of his father, whereas the other mourners— at least those who could afford it—wore black.

The new Marquis of Braemoor could do any bloody thing he wanted.

Up to a point.

He knew he would have been disowned after Culloden if he'd not reappeared on the battlefield in late afternoon with a wound and a tale of chasing some Highlanders. His father had not believed him, but neither could he call him a coward and liar without besmirching his own reputation, so he had allowed Rory to return home. Worried about his eldest son, the marquis had ignored the fact that his youngest son devoted most of his time to spending money and wenching with a tenant. Nothing had mattered but the heir.

Now *Rory* was the heir, and his father could do nothing about it.

The coffin was lowered into the grave, and a shovel thrust into his hands. He obediently shoveled dirt into the hole, hearing the thud of clumps on wood. Again, he felt a fleeting regret—not for the man, but for a small boy's hunger for acceptance, an acceptance never granted.

He turned and looked toward the Braemoor, its cold stones looking forlorn in the steady rain. Then he looked at the dissatisfied faces of the clansmen around him. Only one face looked even remotely friendly, and that belonged to a man who wasn't exactly of the clan. Alister Armstrong was the village smithy. He'd been orphaned as a boy, left to fend or starve as God willed. Rory had been but ten when he'd found him poaching, a hanging offense; but rather than turning him in, he'd convinced the blacksmith to take him on as an apprentice. Alister had been small as a lad, and the butt of jokes and pranks. Rory, another outsider, had taught him to read and write and had protected him; the friendship continued even after Rory was fostered to an English family.

Neil approached him. "Cumberland wants some of our men to help search the area for Jacobites."

Rory was only too aware of the request. Even his father had grumbled about it. Rory remembered his father's words now: *They took my lad,* he'd said. *No more. I willna give them any more.* "My father opposed sending any more men to him."

"There's been another request now that the man who calls himself the Black Knave is assisting Jacobites in their escape."

"A myth. A tale. Nothing more," Rory said. "If we send men after a phantom, then we give him credence."

"Some of our men wish to go. They believe your brother should be avenged."

Rory raised an eyebrow. "'Twas not an enemy sword that killed him."

Neil's face did not change. "It was in service of our king."

Rory was not prepared to get into an argument with his cousin, the content of which might well be misinterpreted and spread first among the clan, then to the Duke of Cumberland. "We obeyed Cumberland and fought at his side. I myself was wounded. Our obligation is over. If you feel one, then you must do as you will. But you will not take a Forbes's horse or weapon with you."

He turned away and walked toward the tower house. He knew fifty sets of eyes were on him, watching and weighing what he did. Some would like his edict. Not many wanted to leave their wives and fields to fight fellow Scots again. But others would call it cowardice.

His position as clan leader was precarious, though as marquis no one could take his title and lands except the king. And *he* could take Rory's head as well.

Activity in the tower house was humming. He had ordered a feast prepared for the mourners with copious amounts of ale and other spirits. He had need of muddled heads this evening, especially when the tower was so full.

He went into the tower house. The aroma of roasting meat permeated the lower floor and the huge banqueting hall. As the heir, he would give the toasts this night. He looked over the huge fireplace at the end of the room and the tapestries that hung on the side walls. The long table had already been set with goblets and pewter plates. He would sit at the head of the table for the first time.

And he would make a fool of himself.

He sensed, rather than heard, the presence of someone else. He turned.

"Alister," he acknowledged.

"Milord," Alister replied.

"I will be late tonight."

Alister nodded in understanding. "I'll let . . . our friends know."

Rory nodded. "Tell them the Black Knave himself will take them to Buckie."

"Is that wise?"

"I will be in disguise. They will never recognize the Marquis of Braemoor."

Alister continued to hesitate.

"Besides, when have I ever been wise?"

Alister grinned. "Now you have me there, milord."

"Our guests are a little skittish, and I canna blame them. Cumberland has offered a hefty reward for any of the McLeods. They willna trust a stranger."

"I can always wear . . ."

"Ah, but you do not have the knack of becoming other people, as I do. So I must leave tonight. Make certain our guests are content."

"I've added a wee bit of Mary's magic to the ale. They will have troublesome heads in the morn."

"Then you can tell them I have a worse one and wish them Godspeed."

Boots stomping down on the stone floor interrupted their speech. Men started to crowd into the large hall, each of them heading for the pitchers of ale.

Rory made sure the pitcher of ale next to him was untainted, and watered. He drank gloriously during the meal, his toasts growing more and more elaborate as the night wore on. He finally collapsed on the table, and Alister and another man dragged him up to his room.

Two hours later, the great hall was filled with snores. Rory slipped down the stairs unobserved. He had other, more important, business this night.

"Horsemen coming!"

Rory rolled out of bed at the warning and looked outside. *Noon. Or close to it.*

He had been marquis for three months now, the Black Knave for four. The double life was exhausting him. He spent half his time riding at night about the country, the other half appearing to be wenching, gambling and drinking. He had turned the day-to-day management of Braemoor over to his cousin Neil, who regarded him with contempt. Rory didna give a farthing about that, only about the fact that Neil had talents he did not.

He pulled on some breeches and a fancy coat and left the chamber, taking the steps two at a time. Rory strode quickly through the hall, then to the entrance. Three riders in British uniforms had already dismounted and were filing inside. "We have a message for the marquis."

Rory always felt more than a little unnerved at hearing his title. It still did not ring true. None of it seemed real. He'd been the outcast son. If not technically a bastard, then certainly he'd been treated as one these past thirty years.

"I am the Marquis of Braemoor," he said.

"The Duke of Cumberland sends ye this message. He asked that I wait for a reply."

Rory took the sealed piece of parchment. "You are welcome to wait inside. There is ale and food aplenty. I will have it sent into the hall."

The sergeant looked grateful. "Our thanks, milord," he said as they went into the great hall.

Neil was gone, and Rory went into the kitchen and ordered one of the kitchen servants to take food and drink to the troopers, then he went out to the stable. This was Alister's day at Braemoor. He had a blacksmith shop in the nearby village, but he spent one day a week at Braemoor, shoeing horses and repairing tack.

He was standing outside the barn when Rory entered. "I saw them ride in," he said.

"A personal message from Cumberland. Come with me and inspect the horses," Rory replied. The two of them walked into the barn. Rory looked around.

"No one is here now," Alister said. "Ned went to spy on the soldiers, pick up some gossip. Young Jamie's exercising a horse."

"Then let us see what the bloody bastard wants now." Rory leaned against a stall and broke the wax seal, then quickly read the contents. He felt his stomach clench. He was ordered to marry a Jacobite lass; as a dowry, he would receive two substantial properties and all their rents.

Wordlessly, he handed the message to Alister. His friend's eyebrows arched into question marks. "What are you going to do?"

"What would the Marquis of Braemoor do? The wastrel

who is always in need of money? Who thinks of no one but himself?"

Alister sighed heavily. "Do you know anything of her?"

"Nay, but if she is Jacobite, she will want this marriage as little as I do. I canna imagine how she would agree to it."

"She may have little choice."

"Damn. It says by order of the king. But Cumberland's behind this."

"He obviously believes he does you a favor. He's offering you a great deal of land and another title."

"In return for marrying a wench who is probably long in the tooth and ready to stab me in the back the first chance she has," Rory replied, unable to keep the anger from his voice.

"If you have been courting someone else . . ."

"Aye, but I ha' not. I had precious little to offer any woman until now. Now I have a hangman's noose, or worse." Rory took back the letter and read it again. "The bloody bastard wants an immediate answer."

"If you refuse, he will wonder why. 'Tis a more than generous dowry."

"What about wedding a woman who will probably despise me?"

"I think tha' is a matter of indifference to Cumberland. I am only surprised he has interest in a Jacobite lass, especially a MacDonell. He seems intent on wiping out any remnants of the rebels. There must be a personal interest we donna ken."

"Which makes her even more dangerous," Rory mused.

"You can always say you canna wed a Jacobite."

"Aye," Rory said. "I can do that. But if Cumberland presses me . . ."

"And with a dowry that large, and a request by the king through Cumberland, you canna say nay without rousing suspicions of being more than—"

"A wastrel and fool?"

"Aye, milord."

"Let us see how much he really wants this marriage. I will send a reply that I canna wed a rebel. They were responsible, after all, for the death of my father and brother. Mayhap that will satisfy him."

"Mayhap," Alister said doubtfully.

"Mary could be affected by this, too," Rory said. "My . . . dalliance with a tenant may not suit a new bride."

"Aye," Alister said carefully.

"Dammit," Rory said. "Why now?"

"Because you are one of the few unattached loyalists, I imagine, and this lass is important to the king for some reason. We may never know why."

Rory worried over that. Why would she be so important? Cumberland had certainly shown little mercy toward any Jacobite. A by-blow by some English favorite? He knew the lady's name, and he'd not heard scandal attached to it. If she'd been a great beauty, he would most certainly have heard of that, also, so he immediately eliminated that possibility. So what was so important about the lady that Cumberland wanted her protected by marriage to a family loyal to the English king?

It did not make sense, and he did not like things that made no sense. Not now.

And he certainly did not like the idea of wedding a stranger.

But could he afford to raise questions? Or Cumberland's wrath?

"I'll pen a reply. 'Tis possible I can show Cumberland this is not a good idea, that I could not accept a Jacobite in the household."

"It is worth a try," Alister said, but his expression did not hold much hope for the idea.

Neither did Rory.

Bethia MacDonell stood stunned before the intimidating presence of Cumberland.

"Marry?" She hated the tremble she heard in her voice. She hated it almost as much as she despised the man standing in front of her, trying to bend her to his will. "But I was betrothed—"

"To a dead man, milady," Cumberland said curtly and without sympathy. "He was a traitor. As you are a traitor. And your brother."

She did not shiver at this description of herself. But tremors ran down her back as she heard the threat for her brother. He had only eleven years, but he had the courage and mouth of a much older lad. He had already insulted Cumberland, calling him a scurvy dog before Bethia could get him out of the room. She had agreed with that assessment, but she knew their lives stood in the balance.

Bethia looked around the walls of the castle, which had become a prison. She'd been brought here to Rosemeare with her brother and held in a tower room to await Cumberland's pleasure. Her two oldest brothers had died at Culloden. Only her younger brother remained to carry on the name of their branch of the MacDonells. But there was little left remaining. Their estates had been confiscated, their clan members either killed or hunted.

Her betrothed, Angus MacIntosh, had been killed at Culloden. She thought of Angus: tall and fierce, even a little frightening, though he had always been kind to her. 'Twas not a love match, but she had been fond of him and had not objected to the betrothal which her older brother had arranged. Angus had been all warrior, all courage. A man—and leader—to admire.

She bit back her tears. She had not yet allowed one to fall, not when she'd heard about the deaths of her brothers, nor when Cumberland's men took them from their home and burned out all their clansmen. Not when she'd heard of Angus's death. She would be as strong as any of the men in her family. She would not, *could not*, show weakness.

"You are fortunate, Bethia," Cumberland said. "You have a friend at court who asked me to look after you. But the king's orders are quite clear. He wants no more Jacobite uprisings. Those who survive can do so only by submitting to his will." His dark eyes pierced her. "Do you understand?"

She swallowed the bile in her throat. She had to protect Dougal, no matter the cost to her.

"The king has chosen a husband for you," Cumberland said. "The Marquis of Braemoor. His family fought well at Culloden. I understand he is a pliable man."

Pliable. Weak. A traitor not to the king, but to all the braw men who fought for Prince Charlie.

"Does he approve of a bride he has never seen?" she asked, hoping against hope that he would not. She was not a beauty, nor had she any dowry now.

"The king is making it well worth his while," Cumberland said smugly. "He will receive confiscated estates. The Forbeses will guard them well from any additional uprisings."

She wondered if her own family's lands were among them. The bile grew even more bitter. She was not even to be sold. A man had to be bribed to take her, bribed most likely by her own property.

She searched her memory for any snatch of conversation about the Forbeses. She knew, of course, about Lord President Forbes. Because of his influence, several of the Highland clans refused to join the young prince. His name was an anathema to those Highland clans that *did* declare for the bonnie prince.

"I will tell the king you accept?"

She held her breath, her mind working feverishly. If she could take her brother and escape . . .

She knew there were people helping Jacobites escape. Prince Charlie was still free despite the huge reward offered for his capture. And there had been whispers lately of a man who helped fugitives. If she agreed, perhaps she and her brother could escape on the journey. She rode well; so did Dougal.

"I know nothing about the man," she said desperately, already forming her plan. She could not give up too easily.

"You do not have to know anything, other than he's loyal to the rightful crown and your king wishes it."

She had no other protests. She'd already voiced them all.

Cumberland apparently took her silence for surrender. "We leave for Braemoor within the hour."

"No." The word escaped her before she could take it back. She tried to modify it. "I must get my brother ready."

"Your brother will not be going. He will stay here, and Lord Creighton will convey your farewells."

She could only stare at him. "I must see him," she said after a moment's pause.

"He has already been taken to another room. You will gather what you wish to take, and be ready to travel in thirty minutes."

"Please. . . ." It was the hardest word she'd ever spoken. She'd sworn never to beg to her captors, but dear God, Dougal. How could she leave him alone after all he'd lost? How could she, too, disappear? The lord of this manor, the Earl of Creighton, was an Englishman. She'd been treated with the barest of courtesy, relegated to the meanest bedchamber. That did not matter to her, not after all her major losses, but it said a great deal about what her brother could expect. Especially if he was held hostage to her marriage.

Marriage. Her heart froze. Marriage to a traitor. To a weak man who would accept a wife in exchange for money.

But she did not matter. Her brother did.

She looked at Cumberland. "How will I know that my brother will be safe?"

"My word," he said.

His word meant nothing to her. She was only too aware of his butchery since Culloden. He'd hunted down every surviving Jacobite, including women and children. Whole families had been burned alive. She bent her head so he wouldn't see her hatred.

"You will be ready, then?"

"Aye," she said in a barely audible voice.

wo

Bethia despised herself for being so afraid. Yet tremors ran up and down her backbone as she—and her guards—approached Braemoor.

She had long ago understood that she was naught but an object to be sold at will. A woman in Scotland had little power unless her father or brother gave it to her, and she knew she'd been fortunate that her father had given her the choice to reject various suitors. He had loved her dearly; she'd always known that. He'd wanted her to make a love match. But when naught happened, he'd pressed her for a decision, putting forth one man, then another. As his impatience increased, she'd approved her brother's choice of Angus, a man she could respect.

Now her father was dead, as were her two brothers and Angus, and to protect the last of the male line she would have to heed the English king's command. God's teeth, but that fact galled her. The man who rode beside her, a stern-faced captain who had been assigned by Cumberland to accompany her, galled her as well. But the man who was to be her husband galled her most of all.

How could she, in all conscience, make vows with a Protestant? With an infidel? With the man who might well have killed one or more of her brothers? A cold chill permeated her.

The stark structure ahead did not allay her fears. A tower house rather than a sprawling castle, it rose vertically up toward the sky. She saw three towers but few windows, and it had none of the elaborate corbelled turreting of some tower houses. It looked cold and unwelcoming.

And how soon would she have to lie with the present lord in one of its chambers? She now knew a little more about him. She had listened to Cumberland's officers when they thought her asleep. The marquis was a misfit. A drunkard and gambler and womanizer. They even suspected that he'd slipped from the battlefield, and mayhap even injured himself to keep himself safe from the enemy.

That was the man they were commanding her to marry.

If it were not for her brother . . .

But she was a woman. Nothing but a woman. She wanted to fall to the earth and pound her hands against the ground. She wanted to scream. She wanted to protest the injustice of it all.

But her brothers had lost their lives, and wasn't that an even greater injustice?

She tried to keep her face expressionless as they approached the tower house. There were no walls around it, only a number of buildings: a large one that was obviously a stable, and several smaller ones. The grounds were unkempt, and there were no gardens. There was a lifelessness to Braemoor that conflicted with all the activity and warmth at her own castle. *Not her own.*

Not any longer.

God help her, this was now her home. Unless she could persuade the marquis that she would make a truly horrible wife. The sudden thought appealed to her. She knew she did not look well this day. She'd been traveling two days, sleeping out at night in the cold mist with no maid to do her hair. It was braided now for convenience. Since she'd had no mirror, she imagined it was a rather messy braid.

Her cheeks must be red from the sun and wind, and she knew her clothes were soiled and dirty. Mayhap the marquis would take one look at her and decline even the massive bribe offered him. And if she had a disposition to match . . .

Several men in plaids were engaged in swordplay. They turned and looked at her rudely as she rode amidst ten of Cumberland's army. Their scowls told her that the Forbes clan was probably not any happier about this alliance than she.

One headed for the massive door of the tower and slipped inside, obviously alerting the residents inside to the new arrivals. There were no soldiers standing guard on parapets, no watch. But then why would there be? The Forbeses had betrayed their heritage, Scotland's honor. *They* had nothing to fear from the king. Revulsion rose up in her throat for all those who had chosen the English king to save their own lives and their properties.

She was to be traded to a man without honor, a clan without principle. The prize for the king: insuring the MacDonells would not rise again against him. Her elderly mare, chosen by the English captain, stumbled, and she realized how tightly she'd clenched her hands on the reins.

Bethia leaned down and whispered apologies. The mare was as much a pawn as she. Then she straightened as a tall man in plaid appeared at the door and approached them as they came to a halt.

He was a well-formed man and, she had to admit, a handsome one. His hair was dark brown, his eyes dark, and he wore a Forbes plaid of green and black and purple.

The captain accompanying her rode up to him. "The Marquis of Braemoor?"

A pained look crossed the man's face. "Nay. He is not here. I am Neil Forbes."

The captain nodded toward Bethia. "I brought his bride. We sent word ahead. . . ."

"My cousin had other business."

Bethia didn't miss the contempt in his face, contempt for his own kinsman.

The captain's brows furrowed in anger. "But . . ."

Neil Forbes looked distressed. "He was told about your expected arrival. He left last night. We have not heard from him since."

The captain's frown deepened. "I was ordered to stay here until the vows were exchanged."

Neil Forbes's gaze went back to Bethia. "You must be weary, milady."

She was. She had slept little these past three days, and they'd ridden steadily the past two days. But she would not show these Forbeses any sign of weakness. She said nothing.

But he approached her and offered her his hand to dismount. Reluctantly she took it, knowing that if she did not, she might well fall. She could not afford to do that. Still, she snatched her hand away the second she reached the ground.

He merely looked amused and turned to the captain. "A room has been prepared for Lady Bethia and one for you. Your men can stay in the hall."

The captain hesitated. "His Grace wants the vows said immediately. He will be here next week."

"I am sure my cousin will arrive before long," Neil Forbes said.

Bethia stood there, her fists clenched. The insult was great. The bridegroom was missing. He thought so little of his bride-to-be that he didn't feel it was necessary to be present at her arrival. Well, she dinna want to see him any more than he wanted to see her. She hoped he never appeared. Mayhap he was hunting a boar. Mayhap if she were lucky enough, the boar would win.

But all she could do was clench her teeth as the Forbes clansman led the way inside the structure.

The interior was as unpromising as the exterior. Cobwebs and dust permeated the hall. Tapestries were faded and coated with dirt. Bethia had an overwhelming impression of gloom and neglect.

She involuntarily shivered, hoping no one saw it. She stiffened her spine, forced her fingers to relax from the tight fists her fingers had unconsciously formed.

Her home. She'd once thought her wedding day would be warm and wonderful, full of expectation and laughter and joy. Her family would be drinking to future bairns, her brothers offering toasts.

"Milady?" The handsome Forbes was openly staring at her, his eyes curious and . . . something more. Jealousy? Certainly not for her, not as she stood, her dress stained, her hair falling away from the braid in damp ringlets.

"I would like to retire to my room," she said, forcing her body to maintain a dignified posture.

The Forbes clansman nodded and said something to one of the men standing near him. In minutes, a girl appeared.

"This is Trilby. She will show you your chamber and fetch whatever you need."

The young girl—probably no more than fourteen—curtsied. "If you will be comin' wi' me, milady," she said.

Privacy. How much she wanted it. She had not been alone in the past two days except for humiliating moments when she'd had to ask permission to perform personal tasks. Even then, she was followed at a discreet distance. She never wanted to see another English uniform or a Forbes plaid. Dear God, how she wanted to hide from them all. She wanted to hide her anger, and the humiliation of being abandoned by her prospective bridegroom. He apparently wanted to show her how little he wanted the marriage, and how little value he gave to her feelings.

Well, she would not give him the pleasure of her anger.

She followed the girl up the winding stone stairs and down a long corridor to a room toward the end of the hall. The girl opened the thick wood door and stood aside while Bethia walked in. The room was as cheerless as the ones downstairs. Only the large feather bed looked comfortable.

Her small bundle of possessions arrived next. Two tunics, two overskirts made of sturdy wool, silk stockings, and several pairs of shoes were all that had been allowed her, in addition to the plain dark riding dress she currently wore, and that poor garment was travel-stained and dirty.

"May I have a bath?" she asked, not at all certain her request would be granted.

"Aye, milady. The marquis told us to do all in our power to make you comfortable."

She weighed that comment. Nothing had made her feel welcome. But, then, had she not dreaded meeting her bridegroom? Why, then, was she vexed that he had not been present for her arrival?

But she immediately knew the answer. The rude discourtesy boded ill.

"Where is the marquis?"

Her face turned red. "I canna say, milady."

Bethia knew immediately that the girl knew the lout's whereabouts, but was reluctant to say. She asked no more questions. She needed a friend, mayhap even an ally. This Trilby probably came as close to one that she could expect.

"Then a bath would be glorious," she said, forcing a smile to her lips.

The girl backed toward the door. "Aye, milady."

Then Bethia was alone. She went to the narrow window and looked down at the courtyard. This was to be her home, unless the damnable marquis decided he did not want a Jacobite bride. She would make it quite clear that she would not surrender her Catholic beliefs. She would let him know she did not wish this marriage.

But quite obviously he'd already agreed to it, and she

knew from experience that men did not care about love
and friendship in a marriage as women did.

If only she'd been born a man.

But she had not been. And all her "ifs" had dissolved
on a battlefield at Culloden Moor. Along with all her
dreams. She could only hope to be as braw as her brothers, and give whatever she must to save her remaining
brother.

"The lady is at Braemoor," Alister said as he met Rory
at Mary's cottage in the heavily forested area north of
Braemoor. "She arrived yesterday."

Rory swore. He had hoped to get back before the Mac-
Donell lass's arrival, but he'd had no choice. He'd hidden several Jacobites in an area about to be raided by
Cumberland's forces, and he'd had to spirit them to another place. Now he had to get them to a small fishing
village and out to a French ship. He had arranged for one
in two weeks.

His small group of fugitives was well disguised as
crofters returning home after being persecuted by the Jacobite army. A young earl had been turned into a sixty-
year-old, and his wife a maid. It had not been easy to
transform the autocratic couple into subservient peasants.

He still remembered the lady's plaintive plea. "But they
are filthy rags."

"That," he'd replied rather curtly, "is the idea."

The lady had said no more.

He said a brief thanks to Elizabeth McComb, an actress in Edinburgh who had given him instructions in
makeup. He was getting nearly as adept at it as she and,
indeed, had aged himself considerably several times.

But now he was exhausted. He'd had no sleep for the
last two days, while ostensibly spending time at Mary's
place in the wood where everyone thought he was playing and wenching. Alister had been sent to fetch him. No
one else had the courage, not after he'd informed his staff

that no one, absolutely no one, was to bother him when he was "occupied."

Probably, he thought wryly, even his wife-to-be had heard the gossip.

She was most certainly destined to be a problem. His absences had been explained easily enough in the past. But now . . .

He wished he could find a way to extricate himself from this wedding. Perhaps his behavior would be so obnoxious that the lady would refuse. He knew why *he* so reluctantly agreed. His character was considered so weak that he would most certainly jump at an opportunity to add so much wealth to his holdings. He supposed that she was also made an offer she could not refuse.

Damn Cumberland and his intrigues.

Mary left the room while he changed. Rory quickly rid himself of the makeup and fake beard that had aged him, then washed his face, scrubbing the heavy paint from his face and the gray powder from his hair. Alister helped him take off the ragged, dirty plaid he wore over the worn saffron shirt. Finally, he quickly pulled on colorful trews and a contrasting bright yellow doublet. His worn brogans were replaced by pointed slippers.

Rory shaved the dark stubble from his face and placed the heavy powdered wig on his head. He hated the bloody thing, hated the heavy doublet and trews. He'd far rather wear his kilt, but the Hanover disapproved of the plaids and kilts. There was even talk of outlawing them altogether, even among the loyalists. And he was, after all, a very loyal subject of the English king.

When he felt himself well enough prepared, he presented himself to Alister, who gave him a crooked grin. "A fine dandy you are, milord."

"Do you think my wife-to-be will be pleased?"

Alister remained silent.

"I am afraid I have blackened Mary's name even further," Rory said apologetically.

"'Twas her decision," Alister said, but this time the

smile was gone from his eyes. Rory knew Alister hated
the pretense they had created, and yet neither had been
able to discover another plausible reason for Rory's long
absences. And Mary Ferguson was already considered a
loose woman. Rory's brother had made quite sure of that.

Rory's fury rose whenever he thought of the day he'd
found his brother raping Mary. He'd flung himself on
Donald and warned him never again to touch the girl. But
it had not been the first time, and Donald had spread the
word that Mary had been quite willing. It was enough to
ruin the girl, who had been orphaned not long before.

Rory had threatened to run his brother through if he
had the girl evicted, and Donald had believed him. Rory
was far the better swordsman of the two, despite his reputation as a rake and wastrel. He'd been fostered with
one of the best swordsmen in England, and he'd learned
his lessons well. When he'd returned, his brother had been
humiliated at his defeat when he'd challenged Rory. Since
then, Rory had practiced little in public, preferring the
role of a lazy libertine, in part to provoke his father. But
Donald had been reminded every time he'd undressed and
saw the scar running up his side.

Donald had covered his anger over Mary's rescue by
telling everyone his brother could do no better then a slut.
But Mary had not been bothered again and she'd been
allowed to keep the thatched cottage in the woods, where
her mother, and her mother before her, had kept herb gardens and mixed medicines and potions. Some believed
her a witch and kept away from her.

But Rory had always liked her and her mother. Mary
was not particularly pretty in face, but she had lovely
gray eyes and long dark hair and a huge heart. She had
a way with beasts as well as plants, and Alister was head
over heels in love with her.

Rory had taken her to tend the first wretched group of
Jacobites when one of the children fell ill. She'd quickly
committed herself to their cause, to helping the innocent
escape the slaughter being committed through the coun-

try. As news of the Black Knave spread, more and more whispers came to her ears of fugitives and she, in turn, turned to Alister and Rory.

They had never expected their one act of compassion to turn into a huge network for escaping Jacobites. Nor that the Black Knave would become the second most wanted man in Scotland. Only Prince Charles himself carried a larger price on his head.

Now Rory was caught in a net of his own making.

And a wife would only complicate things. He certainly couldn't trust her, even if she were a Jacobite. He'd never had much faith in a woman's ability to keep secrets, with the rare exception of Mary and Elizabeth, both of whom had earned his trust. He could not endanger them now, or others he'd enlisted in his network that shepherded Jacobites to French ships. All their heads would be on the block.

If only Cumberland could have waited a few more months. . . .

But Rory had already used every excuse at his disposal: mourning, disloyalty to the crown by marrying a Jacobite, another woman he loved. All had been swept aside with the wave of a hand. The king wanted this marriage for some bloody reason, and he was going to get it, or know the reason why.

The best he could hope for was some arrangement with the woman, a marriage in name only. He would make damn sure she wanted nothing else. And with his current fashion, he was sure she would not. He looked like a dissipated peacock.

"Brandy?" he asked of Alister. Without a word, Alister handed him a flagon, and Rory took several deep droughts, making sure to spill some of it down his waistcoat, and then he wiped his hand across his lips so all of him smelled as if he'd spent the day in a keg.

Then, out of curiosity he really wished he didn't have, he asked, "Is she pretty?"

"She looked ill-used when I saw her. Bedraggled. Tired.

Her hair was straggling in her face. She did not look happy."

"Would you be if forced to marry an enemy, one you knew from reputation to be a libertine?" Rory asked softly. "I do not like this charade, but I will try not to make her suffer overmuch for it. I asked Trilby to attend her. She is a sweet, biddable girl."

"Aye, but you still have the wedding night."

Rory swore again. He'd thought of that, of course. Rape did not appeal to him. 'Twas not unusual for a husband and wife to have separate bedchambers, but occasional visits would be necessary. And he would have to maintain his role as fool and blusterer. It was a fine line to walk. Too much a fool and Neil would try to usurp him.

He leaned over and brushed Mary's brow with his lips. She had become as a sister to him in the past few months. "I don't know when I'll be back."

Mary nodded, her eyes showing worry. Worry for him. She and Alister were the only two people who'd ever given a damn whether he lived or died.

He touched her shoulder with what he hoped was assurance. "Mayhap we will have a slight lull in our business," he said.

He turned and watched Alister. The smithy was putting away Rory's sword and his dirk, even the pistol he carried. He wrapped them carefully in a plaid, then swept away dirt from a section of floor at the side of the fireplace. He and Rory had dug a hole there, lined it with cloth to keep the clothes and weapon clean, then fitted a board on top. Dirt would then be swept over it, matching the rest of the beaten earth floor. Finally, a table would cover it.

Rory's bay was kept in a makeshift corral in back of the house, obvious to those few who ventured to Mary's home for medicines. No effort was ever made to hide it, unlike the old swaybacked piebald secreted in a cave not far away, along with a sleek black stallion stolen from a careless British officer drinking in a wayside tavern.

Alister finished his task. Rory gave him his hand, and Alister took it in both of his. "You will be staying awhile?"

"Aye," Alister replied, his gaze going to Mary.

Rory grinned at him, then Mary. He knew she cared deeply for Alister, and the feeling was reciprocated. But Rory needed to continue the pretense of an affair, at least for a while. And then . . .

Well, *then*, nothing would make him happier than a union between Mary and Alister. She had suffered enough and, God knew, she had risked everything for him.

"I go and face the wench then," he said.

"She is not uncomely," Alister said. "Mayhap . . ."

"A wife, any wife, my friend, is most certainly a curse." Before either of his friends could debate the issue, he strode out the door and to the back. He quickly saddled his horse, and swung up onto its back.

A wife. He'd never intended on taking one. His mother's marriage had been made in hell, and he'd grown up amidst his mother's and father's hatred for each other. In Edinburgh he had seen few happy marriages; in truth he did not know of one. Faithful wives had been the exception, and nearly every man had a mistress. It had left him with a sour taste for the institution.

And to start with a reluctant bride blackmailed into marriage.

Bloody hell!

"The marquis is back," Trilby told her shyly. "He wishes you to meet him in his study. I came to help you dress."

A day had gone by. Pleading exhaustion, she had remained in her room despite invitations from Neil Forbes to join the clan for supper the night before. Now her hands felt icy and her heart thumped as erratically as the steps of a man being led to the gallows. She could no longer pretend that something might disrupt this godless marriage. She missed Dougal enormously, as she missed her older brothers. She could do nothing to help the latter, but at least she could save Dougal. With that thought, she allowed Trilby to brush her freshly washed hair and lace it with flowers.

She stared into the mirror. Her face was pale and thin. Food had been sparse since she'd been taken from her home, but even if it had not, she'd lost her appetite. She ate only enough to keep alive. How could she eat when she'd seen her clansmen killed as they'd tried to protect her? When her only surviving brother was imprisoned?

"You have lovely hair, milady," Trilby said.

Bethia tried to smile. The girl had tried to be kind, had tempted her last night with sweets, but hopelessness reached so far down into her soul, she felt her whole being dragged into a huge dark abyss. Then she looked at herself again. Where was the spirit that her brothers teased her about? Where was the courage they bragged about when she raced bareback across the moors?

No bloody Englishman or Scots traitor was going to defeat *her*. They would not see her bowed.

She stiffened her back as the girl finished her hair. "Thank you, Trilby."

"Do you wish me to help you dress?"

Bethia was wearing a linen tunic. She needed only to drape the overskirt and buckle the belt that held it in place. "No," she said. "You can tell . . . the marquis I will meet with him as soon as I have finished."

Trilby curtsied.

"You need not do that with me," Bethia said. "I'm naught but a prisoner in this place."

"But milady, ye are the new marchioness."

Such an exalted title. Bethia choked down a bitter laugh. Marchioness, indeed!

Instead, she asked the question that had been haunting her. "Can you tell me something about the marquis?"

The girl's face stilled. "What would ye be wanting to know?" she asked after a moment's pause.

"Is he . . . an older man?"

"Nay, he has but thirty years."

Bethia was not sure whether this was good or ill news. Part of her had hoped for an elderly man who was beyond the physical lust of marriage.

"Can you tell me something of . . . his character?" *He betrayed his own countrymen. What kind of character could he have?* Still . . .

The girl's face locked in indecision.

"I will tell no one what you say," she promised.

"In truth, milady, I do not know. He was fostered on the border and he rarely returned here until the . . . uprising. I heard . . ."

"You heard what?" Bethia prompted.

The young girl's eyes pleaded with her not to ask more questions.

"Trilby . . . I will know soon enough. Please."

"I do not know, milady. Truly I do not," Trilby said. "He has been gone frequently, even since he became the marquis. They say he is a gaming man and . . ." Her voice died away. "'Tis all I can say, milady. I should not have said that."

Bethia's throat grew dry. There was more. Much more, or the girl wouldn't look so miserable. What kind of man had Cumberland condemned her to?

Well, she would know soon enough. She turned away. "I will be down shortly. Tell me where to go."

"I will wait outside for ye," Trilby insisted, seeming to understand that she wanted several moments to herself.

Bethia swallowed. In truth, she did not want to go wandering about this huge pile of stones. "Thank you," she said. "I will not be long."

The girl disappeared out the door, closing it quietly behind her.

Bethia pulled on the overskirt, then defiantly positioned her tartan arisaid over her shoulder, fastening it with a plain broach. She gathered it with her lightly jeweled belt, the one possession of value left her. She had pride enough to wear the tartan, even though she knew it shouted her rebellion. She did not care. Let him know he was getting no meek maiden.

She pinched her cheeks, bringing some color into them. She did not want to look fearful or pale. Then she went to the door.

Think about Dougal.

With him, and only him in mind, she opened the door, tilted her head up proudly, and silently followed Trilby down the steps to meet her betrothed.

Three

Rory couldn't contain a certain uneasiness, even tension, as he awaited the MacDonell lass.

He would rather face a hangman, he thought, than a bride. Any bride. But especially a hostile one.

But mayhap she would be pliable, happy to have a title, even one granted by a Hanover.

A knock came at the door. What would the fop, Rory Forbes, do? Certainly not commit the courtesy of rising.

"Come in," he said loud enough to penetrate the door and half rose from the chair he occupied.

He immediately knew his betrothed was no meek maiden. The lass entered alone, her back rigid, a frown of disapproval on her face.

"Lady Bethia," he acknowledged.

He saw her gaze study him. Blue eyes. Dark like the Atlantic seas. And, at the moment, as angry as when a storm swept them.

He returned her weighing look. Obviously Trilby had taken great care with her hair which, along with her eyes, appeared to be her best feature. 'Twas the color of mahogany, dark and rich with just a sheen of red. A single braid, laced with flowers, fell nearly to her waist.

The face was too thin and angular to be considered pretty. Her chin was well defined and now it jutted out a mile in stubborn rebelliousness. His bride's mouth was wide, though her lips were pressed tightly together in a thin line. Her nose, sprinkled with a smattering of freckles, was the one regular feature.

It was difficult to imagine what a smile would do to the totality of that face. But still, 'twas an interesting face, illuminated by strength and intelligence. If she was frightened at the prospect of an unknown bridegroom, she didn't show it. He was immediately intrigued and that, he knew, was disastrous.

"I hope you find your new home satisfactory," he said after a long, stilted silence.

"No," she challenged him. "It is a pigsty."

She was quite right about that, and he could barely hold back a smile at her audacity. Instead, he merely raised an eyebrow in his most supercilious manner.

"Nor are the manners any better," she continued. "I observed how interested you were in my arrival." Her gaze rested on him with open contempt, and he knew she found him as unappealing as he'd hoped. Well, wasn't that what he wanted?

"Dare I hope that you were that eager to see me?"

Fury sparked in her eyes, making them really quite lovely. "Hardly," she said. "However, I did expect a modicum of courtesy."

He shrugged. "I had other business."

"Other business?"

"Aye," he said, waving a handkerchief under his nose as if he smelled something disagreeable. "I have many interests."

He saw distaste deepen in her dark blue eyes.

"You do not want this marriage?" he said.

"No." The reply was so quick and harsh, he nearly flinched. Why did he have such a reaction? Bloody hell, he didn't want it, either.

He stood and walked around her, ogling her, making

his possession obvious to her. "Then why did you consent?"

"Why did you?" she snapped back. "Could you not get a wife any other way?"

"My title and wealth insures a wife," he said, "and one of my own choosing. However, you come with a princely dowry."

He saw the enmity in her eyes. A shiver ran down his back. He'd thought he could finesse this marriage, give his bride dresses and comfort and forget about her, as he'd seen so many men do. But now he wondered whether anything would placate her.

"I answered your question," he said. "It is your turn now. Why did *you* agree?"

"My little brother would die if I did not."

He forced his eyes to remain blank. "A lot of people have died," he said emotionlessly.

"Including my other brothers," she said. "I will not lose Dougal."

"And so you consent to this marriage?"

"Out of necessity, aye," she said. "That should give you no pleasure."

He hesitated. He saw not only the anger in her eyes, but the anguish. Despite her harsh words, he saw her fear. If nothing else, he could do something about that.

"I am not enamored by you either," he said cruelly. "But I *am* interested in the lands you will bring to me. I have no desire to share a bed with you; I have other interests. So, madam, I will make a bargain with you. We will wed, because neither of us has a choice, but I will not interfere with you and you will not interfere with my life. Is that agreed?"

She stared at him. He saw her hands clasp one another, and he saw her face struggle for control. "*You* have a choice," she said bitterly.

He regarded his fingernails carefully. "You obviously do not know the Hanover. He wishes to gift me with lands and with your hand. One does not refuse a king."

Her eyes flickered with suspicion. "Why should I believe you?"

He flicked his lace handkerchief again in a gesture of complete disinterest. "I care not whether you believe me or not. I can do whatever I wish with you. Surely, you are aware of that. You are considered a traitor to the crown. You have been given a reprieve because Cumberland believes this alliance might benefit King George. You have little choice in the matter."

"Then . . . why?"

"Because I do not think we suit, madam, and I want something from you, also. I want the freedom to conduct my life as I have without questions or nagging or interference. Or copious tears. Therefore, I propose a truce beneficial to both of us." He leered at her. "Unless, of course, you feel compelled to consummate the wedding?"

"Will they not—"

"Check the sheets? Most certainly. However, blood these days is rather readily available."

She winced, and her face flooded with color. He suspected she'd never discussed such intimate things before.

"Madam?" he repeated the question.

"Can I ride? Leave the grounds?"

Amusement intermingled with admiration. She was in no position to bargain, and yet she was trying to do exactly that.

"Mayhap after a certain . . . adjustment," he said.

Her blue eyes narrowed. He wondered for a split second whether he had said too much, given her power he couldn't afford her to have. He had to smother it. "We will marry within the week. I have already invited other clans to the ceremony," he said. "And you will learn to do as I say. I merely wish to . . . make it as tolerable as possible for both of us."

"Tolerable," she said in a cold, furious voice. "Tolerable? Married to a traitor, a man who would kill his own countrymen, who . . . ." She stopped as her eyes raked him with contempt. "Or were you even there?"

"Oh, I was at Culloden, my lady, though it was not my wish. Battle is such a waste," he said with a flick of his wrist.

"My brothers didn't think so," she said in a low voice.

"We may have met," he said with indifference. He didn't like the way she was affecting him, the sympathy welling inside him. It was too dangerous.

The anger in her eyes turned to something akin to hate. "They died there. They were far better men than you," she said. "As was the man I *was* to marry."

He waved the handkerchief again, as if to shoo away an insect. "Did you love him?"

"Aye."

He felt the slightest twinge in his heart, then instantly berated himself. Why did he care whether she had loved before?

He shrugged, then fixed his gaze on her clothes again. "You will need better clothes, and a fine gown for the ceremony."

She looked at him with something like triumph. "This is all I have, this, and a faded riding costume."

"I will have dressmakers call upon you. They should have a dress ready in time for the ceremony. Lord Cumberland himself has said he will attend."

"Am I supposed to be pleased at that? What other fine gifts do you have for me?" she asked sarcastically.

"You have a tart tongue, my lady."

"You can always send me back," she tempted.

"Are you willing to risk the consequences?"

She hesitated, then he saw a wily look in her eyes. "I want my brother. Will you bring him here?"

Sympathy welled up in him. She was trying to bargain, even when her position was untenable. He wished he could accede, but he couldn't. He forced a harshness he didn't feel. "I'm told he is a ward of Cumberland. There is nothing I can do."

"You see nothing wrong with using an eleven-year-old boy as a weapon?"

"You do not understand Scotland, today, my lady. Everyone is using whatever—and whoever—they can to survive."

"There is honor left."

"Honor? Surely you must know that honor left this land long ago."

"It certainly left the Forbeses."

"I would not be saying those words at Braemoor," he said. "My brother died of a wound inflicted at Culloden."

Her chin went up. "I have heard of what you—and your fellow traitors—did after the battle. Did you, too, enjoy killing women and children? How can you even call yourself a Scot?"

"You had best watch your tongue. There is little tolerance for Jacobites here. Your beloved Prince Charles is no' one to be holding up as honorable. He ran, leaving all of his followers to die. 'Twas his lack of leadership that led to your defeat. Think not to find sympathy here."

"I did not expect to find *anything* here."

"Well, then, neither of us will be disappointed," he said. "Do we have a bargain?"

She hesitated. "What exactly would you have me do?"

"You will play the dutiful wife."

"And you the dutiful husband?"

"Nay. But you will not complain."

"No?" she said. "I find plenty for which to complain. This . . . house may be fit for those who ape the English, but no' for a self-respecting Scot."

He held back a smile. He'd wondered if she would get back to the condition of the tower house. He had to admire her spirit. And her powers of observation. Braemoor *was* in dismal condition. With no woman in charge, his father, never too fastidious in his personal habits, had allowed slovenliness to permeate the tower house.

He shrugged carelessly. "Then it is your duty to bring Braemoor up to your high standards."

She glared at him. "What do I care for Braemoor?

Cumberland . . . *and* his allies are savages. No wonder you live this way."

He sighed heavily. "I have no time for this. I can still tell Cumberland that I have no desire to marry a shrew. To hell with the estates. 'Tis not worth it."

"My . . . brother?" Her voice suddenly broke.

"He is not my concern." The sudden hopelessness in her eyes stabbed him. He wanted to gentle his tone, to tell her he would try to find a way to rescue her brother, but too many other lives were at risk. He could not deviate from a role he'd so carefully created.

"Is anything your concern?"

"Aye. My pleasure."

The look she cast his way would have quailed a dragon.

"You have not agreed to my . . . proposal," he said.

"But I have no choice, do I? Do you want an answer merely to enjoy my helplessness?"

"I do not believe you will ever be helpless," he responded without thinking. 'Twas not within his role to admit that. He should care nothing about other people, nor make thoughtful observations of them.

She narrowed her eyes and he realized she'd caught the inconsistency. She was no simpleton. He would have to be even more careful than he thought.

"I enjoy my life," he said with a yawn. "I want no lass complicating it with complaints."

"I will have no complaints if you stay away from me."

"Ah," he said, ignoring the insult. "Then we do agree. You manage Braemoor, and I will pursue my own pleasures."

He saw her tremble. He watched the spirit fade from the indigo blue. He had not wanted to humble her, but he'd had little choice. He didn't want her to look his way too closely. If she had even a hint of his activities, then might she not trade the price on his head for her own freedom? Or that of her brother?

"I will expect you to be ready for the wedding in a

week. I will send out messengers announcing the happy union."

It was a dismissal. Her face flushed red, then she turned and, her head held high, left him.

A marriage to that self-absorbed popinjay? Her heart froze at the prospect.

At least he wouldn't claim her in bed. *He said. Claimed. Promised.* The last thought lingered in her mind. His pledge meant nothing.

But then why would he make it? He held all the power. He'd accurately described her position.

Her hand clutched at her skirt. If only she could have stood beside her brothers on the battlefield. That was true courage.

Her mind went over the man she'd just left. She could tell little about him with that ridiculous wig. His eyes, though, had been hazel. Or had they? They had been chameleon, the color changing with the subtle variations of light. But they had been cold eyes. She knew that. Cold and emotionless. He had made it clear that his only interest in her was the wealth she could bring him.

Almost blindly, she stumbled toward the steps. She was completely trapped. At least he *said* he wouldn't force himself upon her. Or was that just a lie to make her more malleable? To keep her from fleeing before the ceremony? She had hoped against hope that she could find something worthy in her husband. But there had been nothing. Nothing at all. Not strength, or character, or humor, or understanding.

"Angus," she whispered desperately. "I need you."

Her wedding day was as cold and bleak and heartless as she'd known it was going to be.

Despite the number of guests, she soon realized her husband was not held in high regard by either his own clan or the visitors.

How was she ever going to get through the mockery of a ceremony?

She had never been so lonely, and so alone.

Trilby tried to cheer her up. She'd placed flowers in the room, and had chattered endlessly about "powerful folk" attending the wedding.

"The lord is handsome," the maid said hopefully, as she smoothed out the silk of Bethia's dress.

Handsome? He did not wear a beard as so many Scots did, but she had been unable to see much under the disdain and vacuousness he had displayed that day of their . . . interview. Mayhap his features were physically pleasing, but she'd been taught long ago that character created beauty, and this man obviously had little of the former.

Coward. She had heard that word expressed several times. His clansmen didn't even seem to care if anyone listened. He'd apparently disappeared during the battle at Culloden, only to appear much later with a slight wound.

Gambler. He had lost fortunes, according to the whispers.

Womanizer. He often visited some woman in the woods near the stream that ran through the property. Stayed for days doing God only knew what. Some even said the woman was a witch.

Husband. That was the worst description of all.

She also had learned in the week she'd been at Braemoor that his hereditary position of laird was in danger. The only thing that held the clan to him was his ownership of their lands, and they could do nothing about that. The grumbling was loud, however, and bitterness strong.

She understood why, too, as she listened to Trilby. The late marquis had started to move crofters from Forbes's lands, buying sheep and cattle to occupy what had been small farms. There had been hope that after the rebellion he would honor those clansmen who had fought with him and allow them to stay on the land.

They had no such hope for the new marquis, who

seemed interested only in his own pleasures. The fact that he'd seldom visited Braemoor before his father's death reinforced their fears that he would be naught but an absentee landlord. Everyone expected the young marquis to drain his lands of the people who had farmed it for centuries.

Rory Forbes had done nothing to allay their fears. Instead, he disappeared for days at a time.

And now all his efforts had apparently gone into providing a great feast—at great expense—for their wedding.

Three hundred guests or more had made themselves at home in the great hall and endless chambers at Braemoor. She'd heard their toasts and drunken laughter for the past two nights. She'd even had to avoid their overly active hands as she'd tried to move unnoticed the few times she had visited the spacious kitchens. She would soon be mistress, and she wanted to know the servants, the cook, the housekeeper. But all had turned their backs on her as if part of some vast conspiracy. "Jacobite." She heard the word whispered as if a curse. They may not care for their lord, but they seemed to dislike Jacobites even more.

She'd finally retreated. Temporarily. She would find a way to win their loyalty once she was married. She'd always had loyalty from those who had worked for her family. Kinsmen all, they were more family than servants. She remembered the mornings in the kitchens. The smell of pastries baking in the huge fireplace, the warm clucking of the cook, the blast of heat on a cold, wet day . . .

Family, warmth, safety.

She shivered, and Trilby's hands stilled.

"You look so bonny," Trilby tried desperately to comfort her.

But she was not bonny. She had never been pretty, though she'd been told she had pretty hair. She thought it too straight, too dark. Just as her lips were too wide and her chin too sharp. She didn't even care about that now. In truth, mayhap it had been her plain looks that had prompted the marquis to offer an arrangement that would keep him from her bed.

A knock came at the door. A man's voice filtered through the door. "The vicar is ready."

Bethia swallowed through the rock in her throat. She'd had no attendants other than Trilby. Rory's mother had died years earlier, and the marquis had not married again. Donald Forbes's wife had died in childbirth, as had the babe. So Rory Forbes had no women in his immediate family. And apparently because she was Jacobite, none of the guests had offered to help her.

But Trilby had provided all the help she needed. All she wanted. She did not think she could stand the ministrations of women who made no secret of their contempt. To them, she was a papist.

Trilby squeezed her arm. *Her one ally.*

Bethia tried to smile for Trilby's sake and went to the door, opening it.

She recognized the man who faced her. She had seen him about the courtyard.

"The marquis sent me to escort you," he said.

So his lord—and soon to be hers—was afraid she might flee after all. God knew how much she'd wanted to. Instead, she said steadily, "I am ready."

"You are not going to the gallows, my lady," the man said.

"Am I not?" she asked.

"Nay, I think not. I am Alister Armstrong, the blacksmith," he said offering his arm to her. The arm that should have belonged to her father.

For a moment, she wondered whether she should feel insulted. Instead, she felt a trifle reassured. The northern clans, including her own, paid little distinction to rank. Loyalty played a far stronger role as to who was the chief's confidants. Mayhap her bridegroom-to-be wasn't the fob she imagined if he had this man as friend.

He quickly destroyed the illusion.

"Lord Cumberland will escort you down the aisle," he said. "I was sent to bring you to him."

Why had he not sent a lady? Afraid the bride might run?

Her body stiffened. The last indignity. Instead of her father escorting her down the aisle, his murderer would do that deed. Instead of a host of friends sending her on her way, an enemy was sent to fetch her.

She glared at her captor, studying him as a trapped fox might study the huntsman. "And why were you given such an honor?"

"I was available," he said with the tiniest pull of his lips. "But I did try to make myself that way."

"Why?"

"I wanted you to know you have a friend here."

"A friend?" 'Twas scarcely credible. She narrowed her eyes. He looked too small for a blacksmith. Most men in that profession were huge, their arms as wide as most men's legs. But this Alister was lean and wiry with a merry little glint in his eyes.

"Did my . . . the marquis send you here?"

"He asked me to accompany you so you would not be alone."

"I *am* alone."

"Not quite so alone," he said in a soft tone.

She wanted to believe him. Alister Armstrong had warm brown eyes and an easy manner.

"It will be all right, milady. The marquis is no' a monster."

She wasn't sure she would agree with that assessment, but his attempt at kindness took away some of the chill from her heart.

She managed a small smile and nodded.

Almost blindly, she walked with him down the steps, past the great hall, then out the door to the chapel that was on the side of the tower house. She stopped the moment she saw Cumberland, who'd turned his gaze on her.

He approached her with a smile on his lips. 'Twas the coldest smile she'd ever seen, and his eyes were like the devil's own: dark and merciless. He offered his arm, but she ignored it, instead turning slightly away.

"Take it, madam," he said.

"Nay."

"Have you not learned yet that it is not *you* who will suffer if you do not do my bidding?" he asked in a low tone.

The threat went straight to her heart. Trembling, she slowly took his arm, and allowed him to escort her inside. She noticed the colorful profusion of plaids worn by the men and women sitting in the pews, saw their faces turn and look toward her. Curiosity as well as hostility radiated from those faces. She turned and looked straight ahead—directly at the bridegroom.

She had seen little of him these past few days. He had not asked her to join him at the evening meals in the great hall until last night. He had visited once, saying he'd thought she might prefer to take her meals in her room rather than join the rapidly expanding ranks of those attending the wedding. She had been grateful, even as she wondered whether he was that displeased with her appearance.

But now as she saw him standing at the altar waiting for her, she felt her heart pounding. She had no choice; yet she wanted to turn and run out the door. She wanted to grab the first horse and ride and ride until she was back home. *But there is no home left.* She tried to believe it was someone else inside this dress, but tonight she would be herself: Lady Forbes, the Marchioness of Braemoor. The man awaiting her would be her husband in fact, with all the rights associated with that state, regardless of his promises.

Her gaze met his. His hazel eyes were void of emotion. Unlike many of the guests who wore tartans or uniforms, he was dressed in a pale blue waistcoat and breeches trimmed with silver buttons. A frilled shirt and blue stock looked quite out of place, and the elegance of his costume made her feel righteously drab in a plain yellow gown she'd selected from those provided by the dressmaker. She sought his gaze, expected anger, but saw instead a glint of humor. It disappeared so quickly beneath a simpering smile that she doubted she had seen it at all.

He was wearing a wig, again, one even longer than the one he'd worn earlier. Marring his face was a small black patch, an affectation much fancied by the English. He looked the prancing English dandy.

And large. She'd not stood close to him before and had been unaware of how tall he was, how formidable, at least in size.

She took her place next to him, and Cumberland stepped away. She was standing next to the stranger who was to be her husband.

In a protective fog, she listened to the words that would change her life. She heard her toneless whispers in reply to the questions. She made her own answers in her mind.

No, she did not take this man.

No, she would not love him until death parted them.

No, she would not obey.

But she mouthed the opposite words and tried to keep the moisture in her eyes from spilling down her cheek. She would never let them see her cry. But when the vicar declared them man and wife, she felt her heart dying.

Bethia knew what came next, something neither of them could avoid, not with Cumberland sitting in the chapel. He had moved from her side to the front row where he sat surrounded by red-coated officers. She had the impression of a spider waiting to eat its prey.

Her husband took her hand and turned her toward him. His face was inches away, the black patch marring a face that was oddly attractive. Strange, she'd not noticed that before, nor the sudden intensity in his eyes. Then the curls from the wig brushed her face, as did the cambric of his stock, and she wanted to withdraw. But his hand captured hers with surprising strength and pulled her to him. His eyes glinted, then his lips pressed down on hers. The kiss was hard, without tenderness or consideration, his lips bruising hers before letting go.

His promise. Had it meant nothing?

He released her, and the two of them turned to face the congregation. She wanted to wipe the feel of him from her lips. Instead, she looked straight away and placed one foot in front of the other. She stumbled, but his hand reached out and righted her.

She looked around, but his face was as bland as before. His grip loosened but she felt his gloved hand around her elbow as they continued down the aisle and out the door. They led the crowd into the great hall where musicians started to play and tables were laden with food. Then he stopped just inside the door. "Time to greet our guests," he whispered into her ear. Surprisingly, he smelled pleasantly of soap, not the strong fragrances most of their guests used to disguise unwashed bodies.

But his hand snaked around her waist, and she froze. She barely managed a semblance of a smile as she was introduced to family after family, all of whom had either supported the Hanover or betrayed the prince when it became evident he might not succeed. She despised each of them to the bottom of her soul, even as she nodded or curtsied as the introductions went on and on and on. But if she played the role to the marquis's satisfaction, mayhap he would keep his promise.

Cumberland stepped up, no doubt silently congratulating himself. "You make a pretty bride, Marchioness," he lied.

She fought the bile rising up inside her. "You are leaving us now?" she said coolly.

"I must report back to King George that all is as he wished it. My brother does have your best interests at heart, Bethia."

Her fingers balled into a fist. The Hanover king. Her interests? She wanted to slap the smug look from his face. This was the man who had burned a barnful of women and children, the man who had ordered the death of wounded, unarmed men. He was the man who had killed her kinsmen and dragged her from all that was dear, and he had the gall . . .

"My wife must be quite weary," the marquis—her husband—said. "I think she needs some rest before the banquet tonight."

"Aye, and the bedding," Cumberland replied.

"Indeed." Her husband leered as he said the words and she caught the conspiratorial grin that passed between the two men.

Her heart dropped. So he *had* lied to her.

She dropped her eyes so neither the marquis nor Cumberland would see the hatred blazing there. She would find some way to escape this . . . travesty of a marriage.

In the past few days she'd overheard talk of a man called the Black Knave, who was helping Jacobites escape the crown's vengeance. Cumberland had posted a huge reward for his head. If only she could reach him, ask him to rescue her brother. Once that was done, then she could flee. But how could she contact him?

"Come, my dear," her new husband said, his hand again on her arm. She jerked away from his touch.

He leaned over and whispered, "I would not do that again, my marchioness."

His voice held a threat she'd not heard before. She whirled around. "You promised—"

"Only if you fill your own role as obedient wife," he said in a tone that made her skin crawl. His fingers tightened around her arm.

She wanted to believe him. Dear God, how she wanted to believe him, but that salacious look had not been her imagination.

Still, her only recourse was to pray he spoke the truth, that his interest lay elsewhere. At least for the moment.

And try to find the Black Knave.

She bit her lip, then gave him the barest of nods, and allowed him to guide her toward the table for the customary toast.

Four

"To many happy and . . . fruitful years."

Cumberland leered as he uttered the last words. He left no doubt in anyone's mind as to exactly what he meant.

Rory looked down and saw his wife's face pale. She looked as if a ravenous wolf was about to fall on her.

He wanted to reassure her, but he could not afford that luxury at the moment. Too many other lives were at stake. He could no' risk suspicion. He was already surrounded by a clan and neighboring families that doubted both his loyalties and his courage. Every one of them knew the marriage was not to the lass's liking. Any sudden change in her attitude could arouse suspicion. He'd tried his best to lessen her fears without giving anything away, but it had been important that Cumberland believe his role as a womanizer and scoundrel.

He could, however, give her a few moments of relief. He made excuses to other guests, saying the excitement had made his wife faint. They would return shortly for the wedding feast. His heart lurched as she glanced up at him with uncertain gratitude.

He kept his hand on her arm as they left the great hall.

It seemed as alien to him as it must seem to her. He'd always hated every square foot of Braemoor, and he would never feel like its master. He was a fraud. Even if he hadn't chosen to oppose the Hanover king, he still would have been a fraud. He'd never belonged here.

Bastard.

His father had uttered that word once in a drunken rage. He'd done it only once.

Rory had been in the room with his mother, and he had instinctively tried to protect her when his father entered. His rage was obvious.

"Whore," he'd said. "Daughter of Satan."

He'd reached out and slapped her, and Rory, despite his fear, had thrown himself on the man he feared most of all. A blow knocked him across the room as his father glared at him. "Bastard." He'd spit out the word.

His mother started laughing.

Rory closed his eyes for a moment at the bottom of the steps. He'd learned later what his father meant. And why his mother had laughed . . .

Rory became aware that the MacDonell lass—his wife—had stilled next to him. He swallowed all the doubts he felt and started up the stairs, aware of the smell of flowers that drifted about her, the softness of her skin. He was also aware of her fear. It was defiance, but it was also fear, and he hated himself for making her afraid.

Rory heard shouts from below. The great hall was filling rapidly, and obviously many of the guests had already sampled the kegs of wine, brandy and bowls of mead prepared for them. In an hour, they would be exchanging bawdy predictions. He hated to subject the lady to that, but there was no help for it. The guests—and his own clansmen—would be having their fun. He could only try to reassure her privately. But not enough to suspend that hostile look in her eyes. He needed the cloak of her hatred.

'Twas a fine line he would be walking.

They reached the top of the stone steps and walked

down the hall to her chamber. She turned and he knew she did not want him to enter. In truth, she stood bristling like one of the dogs downstairs.

He opened the door and waited while she walked inside. He saw her stiffen as he closed it.

She stood silently. *His wife.* Proud and rebellious and angry. Very angry.

"You swore you would not force yourself upon me," she said softly.

"A husband does not force himself," he corrected her. "'Tis the wife's duty to service him." He allowed the words to penetrate for a moment, then he continued in a cool voice, "Simply because I choose not to assume that right does not negate it. If you have heard any gossip, you must know that I frequent a cottage not far from here. The lady has far more . . . endowments than you, and a jealous heart. I do not fancy having a knife plunged into my own." He curled his lips in a half smile he hoped indicated fond remembrance. "As I said, I have no interest in your bedchamber, but Cumberland must not know that."

"Why? All he cares about is the nuptials." She obviously could not resist the question. It came reluctantly from her tongue. "That I am chained to you, a—Protestant."

He looked at her curiously. He knew that not all Jacobites were Catholic, though many were, especially the fierce northern clans. "You are Catholic?"

"Aye," she said proudly.

"You said nothing before the marriage."

She stood silent.

"Do you consider it a valid marriage?"

She said nothing again.

"It will not work, my lady. We are wed in accordance to the law of Scotland, and the king's law, whether or not either of us wants it."

Her face flushed.

"Cumberland and the king want this marriage. They

will want proof that it is valid. That means blood, my lady."

"Then why do you not give them what they want?" It was a direct challenge, a probing of his sincerity.

He frowned, trying to find a way to quiet her fears while revealing little. He was saying much more than he wanted to say, giving away more than he should.

He gave her the vacuous grin he'd perfected. "As I said, you do not suit my taste, madam. You are much too thin and your disposition too sour. So you may rest easy. Although I will join you this evening, I plan to spend my time playing cards."

"Cards?"

"Aye, madam wife. I play very well, particularly with myself." Rory knew he was good at playing the fool. "And I like Cumberland no more than you. It . . . pleases me to outfox him."

Her gaze bored into him, and he wondered whether she saw more than the fool he hoped she saw.

"What do you want in return?"

"I told you. I want my complete freedom. As well as the lands you bring with you."

"I pay for your freedom with my imprisonment."

"It is a silken imprisonment, and one many would not find difficult."

"I despise you. Does that mean nothing to you?"

"No, madam, it does not. I do not require your approval, only your obedience. I believe you swore to give it to me in the ceremony today."

"You are a traitor to Scotland!"

"Ah, but that is what the king calls you. And I believe our side has won. History tells us the victor is always right. And so you will do as you are told. You will attend the banquet tonight. You will be an obedient, if reluctant, wife. You will accept the toasts. You will accompany me up here tonight without discussion of previous conversations. And I will stay here, at least for several hours. Do you understand this?"

He spoke to her as if she were a child, and he saw the fury bank in her blue eyes. Her fingers clenched into fists at her side, and he knew how much she wanted to strike him.

"Will you at least consider trying to bring my brother here?" The words sounded forced from her throat.

Rory knew how difficult they were, how she must hate asking him for a favor, particularly after he had denied it once. He had to hold back his own desire to grant it, to tell her not to worry, that he would rescue her brother. But he knew the castle where the lad was held. He also knew from Cumberland's own mouth that he would not release the boy until the lass was safely with child. That was something he could not tell her. God only knew what she would do, or say, then.

"I cannot, madam."

"Will not," she corrected.

He turned. "I will come and fetch you in another hour. You will have time to change your dress. I rather like the blue one. And no MacDonell plaids, my lady." He turned and left the room.

Her husband had evidently told Trilby to attend her, for Bethia had no more than sat on the bed when the girl appeared.

"My lady," the girl said softly. "'Twas a fine wedding," she added, apparently at a loss of anything else to say.

Bethia ignored the comment. "Have you heard of the man they call the Black Knave?"

"Oh, yes, my lady. He and the price on his 'ead is all the soldiers talk about."

"What else have you heard? Is he thought to be around here?"

Trilby shrugged. "They say he is everywhere."

"Has anyone actually seen him?"

The maid shook her head. "Not as I heard. But they say . . ."

"Say what, Trilby?"

"That he rides a black horse. That he is very tall, and that he always wears a mask. But then I also heard . . ."

Bethia was growing impatient. Apparently Trilby wasn't quite sure what might get her into trouble. Should she be listening to so much gossip? Should she be showing some of the awe evident in her voice?

"That he is elderly. Or a gypsy. Some say he is the devil and can change form."

"Is that what you think?"

"That is what the soldiers say. That is why they canna catch him."

"I do not think the devil goes around rescuing people from those who want to hang them. Or worse," Bethia added.

Trilby shuddered. "I wouldna want to meet him."

Bethia sighed. She would get no useful information from the maid. But she decided then and there to end her isolation in this chamber and talk to others in the household. Mayhap someone knew more about this . . . Black Knave. And how to reach him.

"Come Trilby. Help me select a dress," she said, going to the huge dresser where her new gowns, all quickly sewn on demand by the marquis, lay in their obscene splendor. "Any but the blue one."

Rory played the amorous husband at the banquet. He played it well enough to see the alarm in her eyes.

He draped an arm around her, leered at her, even patted her backside as she sat down, all to the guffaws of the drunken guests. Only Cumberland seemed to remain sober, his cold gaze often resting on the new marchioness. Rory felt a chill go up his back. Cumberland's interest was more than a little odd. Did he suspect Rory of disloyalty? Or was the interest centered on the MacDonell lass?

He ate lightly of the endless courses necessary to entertain a duke: partridges stewed with celery in oyster sauce, pigeon pie, goose, salmon and numerous cheeses, eggs in their shell, and vegetable puddings. None of it, he noticed, was prepared very well. The fowl was raw, the vegetables too well done. His wife, he noted, ate even less, barely touching any of her food.

He joined in toast after toast—to fathering numerous children, to the night ahead, to King George. Bethia's face, he noticed, grew pale, her slender body more rigid. He wished he could reassure her even as he silently applauded her self-control. Though he thought he gave the appearance of drinking as much as the others, he really drank very little. He needed to keep his wits about him this evening. God's blood, he needed to keep them about him as long as Cumberland overstayed his welcome.

"Eat more, my lord," one of the Forbeses yelled from far down the table. "Ye will be needin' all your brawn t'night."

Rory heard the swift intake of his bride's breath, but there was nothing he could do but appear to be leering while a number of ribald comments followed the drunken observation.

"If ye need any help, milord . . ."

"Aye," came another voice. "Ye can count on me."

Other suggestions followed, some of them contemptuous of his own ability to perform. Rory looked toward Neil, who was silent. His cousin's dark eyes, however, watched him as closely as Cumberland's.

"I believe I can service my wife quite adequately," Rory said in a bored tone, taking a long drought from his tankard. She started to whisper something, but the sound was lost in the shouts. Instead, he felt a painful kick against his leg. He merely grinned at her and called for more wine, slinging his tankard so much of its contents spilled on the floor.

He allowed another few moments of false good wishes, then pushed back his chair. He staggered as he stood, then offered his wife his hand. She sat silently, not taking it. He leaned over, whispering in her ear. "Do as I say,

madam." Then he planted a kiss on that same ear to the
approving roar of his clansmen.

When he offered his hand again, she took it and stood
stiffly. She was rigid with fear and, he thought, humiliation. She had been the brunt of jokes all evening, and
even the few women present had eyed her with hostility.
There had been no sympathetic face in the hall this night.

He was used to disapproval, to scowls, to taunts, and
he'd long since ceased to let them bother him. But he
sensed she was from a far gentler background.

"Come," he said, as he feigned drunkenness, nearly
falling as they reached the door, then clumsily climbing
the steps. Some very descriptive comments followed them
all the way.

He stopped at her door, swinging it open.

She stood in the room, her blue eyes wide with apprehension.

"You will have to learn to believe me," he said curtly,
then went to the one table in the room. Trilby had done
as ordered. A bottle of fine French brandy had been
opened, and two silver goblets stood next to it.

Rory poured two glasses and offered one to her. " 'Tis
far better than what was served downstairs," he said. "It
will serve to relax you."

"Your departure will relax me."

"I think I explained that to you earlier," he said in a
tone he would use with a child. A simple one.

He saw the fury blaze in her eyes again, then they narrowed. "You are not as drunk as you seem."

"An apt observation, madam. I far prefer this brandy,
and I was not going to share it with Cumberland. Are you
sure you will not join me?"

"No." Suspicion darkened her eyes.

"Then I will help you undress."

She backed away.

"I think it might be considered strange if we stay in
these clothes all night."

"No one will . . ."

"Are you sure of that, madam? I am not."

He saw the suspicion deepening. "If indeed I wanted your body, my dear wife, I would not hesitate to take it. There is no one to stop me. In fact, I believe a scream or two might enhance my image."

"I . . . I want Trilby."

"I told her she could join the other clansmen and guests tonight. Surely, you would not want to deprive her of that."

"N . . . no."

Without additional words, he went to the large dresser and looked inside, pulling out a fine linen nightdress she'd received yesterday with the new dresses. He laid it on the bed, then went over to her. "Turn around, my dear."

Her mouth tightened, but she did so. She was learning. Reluctantly, but learning. He quickly undid the hooks and watched as the dress fell down over her shift. Her shoulders were smooth, creamy, and he suddenly ached to touch them, to run his fingers through her dark hair. She was . . . quite pretty, prettier than he'd first thought.

God's blood. He certainly couldn't afford such thoughts now. He turned back to the table, eying the two chairs, one on either side. He took the goblet he'd filled with brandy and took first one sip, then another. At least his father had had excellent taste in spirits, he thought bitterly. He tried not to hear her movements—the dull thud of slippers falling to the floor, the rustle of clothes.

He took another sip. He had not expected to be aroused by her. He had not anticipated the rush of hot blood when his finger had accidently brushed her skin, when her strands of dark hair grazed the back of his hand.

Rory turned. She was in the bed, the feather coverlet covering her far better than the fine material of the gown. He took off his own waistcoat, placing it neatly on one of the chairs. He then untied the stock and loosened the top of his linen shirt.

Next came his slippers, which he despised. He far preferred the soft leather boots he wore when riding. He looked back at his bride. The flickering light from the lamps cast shadows on the dark hair, made her face less stark. She was watching every move, though, much like a rabbit must watch a snake.

He sat in the empty chair that faced the door. By turning his head slightly, he could see his new wife. Keeping his eyes carefully from her, he dug around in his clothes for a deck of cards. He took it out, shuffled them neatly and started a game of solitaire. After several moments, he said, without looking at her, "Are you sure you would not care for the brandy? 'Tis very fine."

"Aye," she said suddenly, surprising him.

He raised an eyebrow, then picked up the second goblet and took it to the bed, watching as she sat up, still clutching the coverlet to her bosom. But something else was in her eyes now, something besides fear and dislike.

Curiosity?

God's toothache. The last thing he wanted from her was curiosity.

"You meant it?" she said with incredulity. "You will keep your bargain?"

"Aye," he said. "After tonight, you will see little of me except for brief appearances to assure the clan I am doing my duty in producing an heir."

"And when none comes?"

"'Tis God's will," he said lightly.

She wanted to believe him. He could see it in her eyes. He could also see a certain calculation there.

"You will not try to run away, my dear," he said, his voice becoming silky again. "My reputation will not bear that."

"Your reputation?"

"Such as it is," he admitted. "You will probably discover that my mother tried to escape once, and ended up imprisoned in one of the rooms upstairs. There is, in fact, some question rumored about my true lineage, but since my dear father would not admit to being cuckolded, I ended up with everything." His voice turned harsh. "I do not intend history to repeat itself or have old rumors revived. My cousin is waiting for just such an opportunity."

Comprehension spread over her face. "Is that why . . . ?"

"I agreed to this . . . marriage when I want another? Aye. My position is none too solid, and I do enjoy the fruits of my father's inheritance. I do not care much for the idea of actually laboring for my bread and drink."

She was silent. He prayed his tone had convinced her he was no more than a wastrel living off an inheritance.

"You said you were at Culloden Moor?" The question was little more than a whisper.

"Aye."

"Did you kill any MacDonells?"

"In truth, I did as little fighting as possible. I care naught for it. I far prefer my pleasures."

He saw a flash of contempt in her eyes. Thank God for that.

He turned back to his game. And silence.

Bethia had never been so aware of a man, but then she had never been undressed in a bedchamber with one, either.

She still expected him to leap on her at any second. 'Twas why she had tried to make conversation. She needed to know more about him. She *had* to know what to expect.

But she had learned little. He was a contradiction. Most of the time, he acted the fop, the pleasure seeker, the drunkard. But if he was all that, would he be faithful to a woman he could not, for some reason, wed?

Or was she really all that distasteful?

And then, despite his threats, there had been that effort to quell her fears and uncertainty. Did a complete rogue do that?

He still wore that ridiculous wig, yet without the bright frock and waistcoat, he did not look so much the dandy. His white shirt, without the stock, revealed a strong, lean body, not one that she would imagine belonged to a man who frittered his life in gambling hells and taverns. He also reflected a rare confidence that surprised her, she noticed as he shuffled cards with an expertise she'd never seen before. It wasn't quite arrogance, though he often retreated into that particularly unpleasant state.

She turned her head. She did not need to be thinking such thoughts. She needed to pretend a sleep she knew she could never achieve. Loneliness coursed through her, nearly drowning every other emotion. How was Dougal? He must feel every bit as alone as she. Except this was now her home, the guests downstairs her guests. And she despised each and every one of them.

Dougal was a prisoner, but one no less than she.

She lay still, hoping she would not draw attention. The more he drank, the more chance he might change his mind. She had seen the results of drunken soldiers, drunken men, happening on innocents. And she was no innocent to him. She was his wife. She shivered with the realization.

Think about something else. Think about racing across the highlands. Think about laughter, and teasing, and warmth. Think about the happy times. She swallowed hard, allowing tears to wander down her face for the first time, and she drew up the coverlet to cover them. She kept her sobs inside, though her body shook quietly with them.

Think of the gloaming, the sky over the jagged mountains. Think of the sea running strong against the cliffs. But, God, it was so painful. The loss was too great, the price too dear. She bit her lip, drawing herself smaller into the large bed. *Go.* She screamed it internally. She wanted him—her husband—to go, so she could scream and cry and release all the agony that had been building within the past twelve months.

Then she heard the sound of the door opening and closing, and she opened her eyes. It took a moment for them to adjust to the darkness.

He was gone.

She huddled in the bed and at long last let the tears flow.

As Rory shuffled the cards, he heard the quiet intake of breath. He ignored it, continuing to deal himself cards. Then, without will, he turned slightly and saw the small tremors of the large coverlet.

He knew little about her except that Cumberland was holding her brother hostage to the marriage and her two older brothers had died at Culloden. He wondered about the rest of the family, though he doubted any remained alive. Cumberland wanted no future uprising. He had killed, destroyed or transported every Highlander who survived Culloden, everyone he could find.

Rory knew he could give her little reassurance. He was astonished at how much he wanted to go to her, to comfort her. He wanted to tell her the truth, that he wanted this marriage no more than she, and that he would find a way to extract her brother from Cumberland's bloody hands. But he knew too little about her, about her ability to keep secrets or play a role. Or even whether she would trade knowledge about him for her brother.

So he could do nothing but give her the gift of leaving her alone.

He looked down at the cards on the table. He was winning; he nearly always won. He was extraordinarily lucky at cards, as much as he'd been unfortunate in family.

He felt the emotion of the woman in the bed. He sensed it down to the essence of his bones, and he empathized with it. He had been less than six when he'd understood that he had no champion, no one to love him. His father most certainly had not, and neither had his mother. Her whole concern had been her lovers and tweaking his father's nose. She'd turned to drink when, in essence, she'd been imprisoned by her husband. Once when he'd tried to comfort her, she shoved him, sending him crashing to the floor. "Little brat. If not for you . . ."

She'd never finished the sentence, but he'd always known that she blamed her misfortunes on him.

So he'd always been alone, and had learned to cope with it. Was it easier than having people you love taken away? Was love experienced and lost better than never knowing it at all? He did not know. He only knew that he had purposely kept people at a distance. He had learned to live that way and had found safety in it. He wasn't sure whether he could ever learn to live with the responsibilities and the tragedies of love.

He took off the bloody wig and ran his fingers through his hair, grateful for the sudden sense of freedom. He hesitated. Had he been here long enough? Several hours now. Certainly long enough to bed a wench. He tore his shirt open and untied, then sloppily retied, the thongs to his trews, missing one or two holes. He swore to himself, then opened the door and pasted a satisfied smirk on his face before launching himself drunkenly down the stairs in search of more spirits.

Now that was something everyone here would understand.

𝔉ive

Bethia sensed the light streaming through the windows before she opened her eyes. She groaned and stretched. Her head ached, and a sense of foreboding filled her. She had been plagued by nightmares all night. She tried to remember them now, but she could not. She only knew she had been frightened. Not merely frightened. Terrified.

She was tired of being terrified. It seemed she had been that way every day for the past six months, ever since she knew her brothers planned to join Prince Charles. She had felt disaster in her bones, even as she listened to their boasts and eager anticipation.

She looked around, her mind suddenly filled with the events of the last few days. Was that the source of her nightmare? The fact that she had changed? Her name had changed. Her public—if not her private—status had changed from maiden to wife. And she knew nothing of her husband.

Then her gaze found *him*. He was lounging against a wall as if he had no care in the world. He was still wearing what he had worn last night, only the garments looked far more mussed. He wore the hideous wig, and his face looked sharply edged under it, his eyes watchful but void of any other emotion. Even that wariness disappeared as if it never existed when his gaze met hers and his lips folded into a simper.

"I did not think you would ever wake," he said indifferently.

She saw his hand drop an object on the table. A book? That surprised her. He did not seem a man interested in books.

She tried to decide what to do. Her impulse was to move farther back into the bed, but she would not give him that satisfaction. Neither he nor Cumberland nor any of their minions.

"Will you send Trilby to me?"

"Of course, but first we must take care of a small matter."

His coldness sent chills down her back again. True, he had been good as his word. He had not touched her last night, but . . .

Then she saw the dirk in his hands.

The left side of his lips curved upward. "Do not worry, madam. If I did not take you on your wedding night, I most certainly have no such desire this morning. But if I know Cumberland, he might be asking your maid if she found blood on your bed."

"Why . . . would he do that?"

"He may not. But he *has* just shown a very unusual interest in our marriage. I went down last night for another bottle of brandy. He asked me whether you had been . . . cooperative."

She bit her lips. "What did you tell him?"

"That you were like any other virgin. Reluctant at first, then . . ." He spread out his hands expressively. "He appeared relieved and said the lands would be transferred to me. I do not want him to change his mind."

"So you can gamble away lands that have been in families for centuries? They must have belonged to—"

"Jacobites? Most certainly. They knew the risk they

were taking, and it is no concern of yours what I do with what is now mine." His voice was flat, emotionless.

She hated him, then. Any impressions she'd had of decency had been wishful thinking. He was using her to take lands that belonged to others. Just as her family's lands had been taken.

He didn't say anything else, merely rolled up his shirtsleeves. His right hand held the dirk lightly as he approached the bed and threw off the feather cover. "Move over," he commanded.

She reluctantly obeyed and watched as he made a shallow cut above his wrist and allowed the blood to drip on the bedclothes, then smeared it. Bethia watched his eyes as he did so; there was no indication of pain, or emotion. He looked at the stain with satisfaction, then tore off a piece of his shirt and bound his wound.

His hazel eyes cool, he pulled on the waistcoat he'd worn the night before.

"And now I leave you, madam." He hesitated. "Is there anything you would like?"

"My freedom."

"That, at the moment, is quite impossible." He paused. "Do you read?"

"Aye."

"There is a library downstairs. Take what you wish."

An unexpected kindness. In truth, inexplicable. "What is my role here?" she said.

He raised an eyebrow. "My wife," he said. "You are mistress of Braemoor."

"The servants?"

"They will take orders from you," he said. "Except for one thing. You will not be allowed to leave Braemoor."

She stood, feeling terribly vulnerable in her nightdress. "How can they be expected to take orders from me when they know I am naught but a prisoner here?"

"I expect you can find a way to convince them," he said indifferently.

And then he left her without any more words, but with a number of unanswered questions.

The guests departed during the afternoon.

Rory saw one of Cumberland's men approach young Trilby, saw her face turn red before whispering a few words. A report, no doubt, on the condition of Bethia's bed. She might well have protected her new mistress without Rory's contribution, but he hadn't been willing to take the chance.

Then Cumberland and his officers headed north, chasing rumors that Prince Charlie had been sighted in the northern Highlands. However, he left a garrison in a nearby town to continue seeking out Jacobites.

Alister found Rory shortly after Cumberland left. "Lord Ogilvy has been taken. He is naught but a twenty-one-year-old boy. Cumberland is said to favor hanging him."

"His grace is in favor of hanging everyone. There would not be a man left in Scotland had he his way."

"Jacobites, you mean?"

"Nay, he has contempt for all of us. You can see it in his manner. Well, we will tweak his nose a bit."

Alister groaned.

"How would you like to be an officer?"

"No' at all."

Rory grinned. "Nonetheless you will have the experience. We also need some men who look like soldiers."

"I can find a few. Some that donna like what's happening. And some that admire the Black Knave."

Rory nodded. It was Alister who had found the loyal Scot here and there, Scots—like himself—who were so offended by the aftermath of Culloden that they were willing to hide a Jacobite for a day or two, or act as lookouts, or give a ride in a wagonload of hay. And then there were the secret Jacobites, men who hadn't been able to leave their families to join the army. They were anxious to find some honor. "How long before they move Ogilvy to Edinburgh?"

"The end of the week. They hope to have a few more to take."

"We will try to disabuse them of that hope. And Alister, we will need five men at least."

"I can tell them the Black Knave will lead them?"

"Aye."

"I will be off, then. When should I tell them . . . ?"

"In three nights' time."

Alister nodded, then hesitated. "The lady . . . your wife?"

Rory stiffened. "What about her?"

"Will she be a problem?"

"I made a bargain with her."

Alister waited.

"She will not interfere with my activities, and I will restrain my licentious inclinations toward her," Rory said ruefully. "She believes I love—at least lust—after another and is bloody thankful for it."

"Mary?"

"Aye." He paused. "I am sorry, Alister. If you feel I should try to find another ruse, I shall."

Alister tried to smile. "It was Mary's decision, and her wish."

"When this is over, I will make it possible for you two to go wherever you wish."

"She has never indicated that she . . . favors me."

"Then you have not seen her eyes, my friend. Her feelings are quite clear."

Alister's brown eyes brightened, yet his voice remained matter-of-fact. "I'll have the men you need."

Rory nodded. "I will ride to Edinburgh. We need more stage paint and wigs from Elizabeth, and a few English uniforms. I prefer to steal them further north. I want no suspicion here. I also expect my new wife will be enormously relieved at my absence." He hesitated. "I think she must feel very alone. A friendly face might help."

"Aye, milord."

"You can regale her with tales of my decadence."

"Are you sure you wish to do that?"

Nay. In some ways, she appealed to him. She had courage and good sense and wit. She had not the beauty of many of the women he had bedded, though she had a certain attractiveness, the kind that would last through decades. But she also represented danger to him.

He must make himself as repugnant to her as possible. Already, he sensed, he had put more than a few doubts in her mind as to his bad character. Most men would have few scruples about taking a new wife to bed, regardless of the woman's own desires. And she knew it.

"Aye," he said. " 'Tis necessary."

"Ye know what the clan will say. That you were not pleased by her; that is why you are leaving so soon. It will make her position more difficult."

Rory sighed. He had already considered that. But he had little choice. He needed both information and theater props available only in Edinburgh. His frequent travels to Edinburgh—and debauchery, according to rumor—were part of his facade, one he did not want to destroy now. If he stayed here, he might well slip. He still remembered the fragrance of her, the feel of her skin against his fingers. Now *that* did frighten him.

"It cannot be helped," he said after several seconds. "Just . . . look after her as best you can. I will meet you three nights from now."

Alister nodded.

Rory looked at him for a moment. "Take care, my friend."

Alister grinned. "Always. But you . . . I do worry about you."

Bethia felt like a beggar child who did not belong, who might be snatched up and thrown outside at any moment. The irony was that she *wanted* to be thrown outside.

This would never be her home.

Her . . . husband had been gone two days, leaving without any more words than those he'd thrown at her the

morning after the wedding. *I expect you can find a way.*
But she hadn't. He'd also said the servants would obey
her. But when she offered a suggestion, they looked as if
they did not understand a word she said.

Then she had sought out Neil Forbes. He apparently
had kept the household accounts for the old marquis, and
the new marquis had shown complete indifference to them,
allowing Neil to continue. There was, however, apparently no love lost between them. She'd seen them both
bristle in the other's presence. Still, Trilby had told her
that the new marquis apparently didn't care enough about
Braemoor to take away the accounts or try to find a new
manager.

That fact obviously galled his cousin, and so did her
request to see the accounts. But she knew it was the place
to start if she were to run the household. She had kept
the accounts of her own home after her mother had died.

"Where is your husband?" he'd asked quite curtly.

She could only stare at him helplessly. She had no
idea. She suspected that most of the household did, however. "He did not inform me," she finally said, knowing
both the relief she felt that he was gone and the humiliation that she did not even know where.

Neil Forbes muttered something to himself, something
she suspected was a quite angry curse. "I handle the household accounts," he said in a slightly louder voice. "We
require no changes."

"I do not mean to usurp you, sir," she said as tactfully
as she could. "I just thought if I knew the tradespeople
that provide the goods to us, I would not make mistakes."

For a moment, his dark eyes seemed to soften as he
studied her. Then, he said rudely, "We need no new . . .
customs from Jacobites."

'Twas the last straw. She was tired of insolence and
disrespect that greeted her everywhere. Whether she
wanted it or not, she was mistress of Braemoor, and she'd
be no timid mouse about it. She straightened her back.
"Courtesy is one custom we value that you might well

benefit from," she said sharply. "The marquis said the household was to take orders from me. I assume that includes you."

"You assume wrong, madam. I take no orders from you. I did not approve of this wedding, and I do not approve of my cousin."

"Then why do you stay?"

"Because mayhap I can pick up the pieces after my cousin destroys everything."

She lifted her head defiantly. "I brought wealth to your family."

"To Rory, mayhap. To the gaming tables."

She recognized the anger—no, fury—in his voice. He and her new husband did not merely dislike each other. This man was obviously his cousin's enemy. Well, that was no concern of hers. Still, she wondered how aware her new husband was of the enmity toward him.

Bethia had thought that *she* had been the reason for her cold reception at Braemoor. Now she realized it might be for her husband as well.

'Twas none of her business if he received so little respect and liking from his own people. And yet . . .

She tried to make herself taller. "Nonetheless, it seems you must live with the fact that he is the marquis, not you, and I am his wife."

A flicker of admiration flashed through his eyes. "Temporarily," he mumbled.

"The only way you can change the situation is . . ." She stopped.

"My cousin's death? Not necessarily. The king's displeasure is an alternative. I know that you did not want this marriage. Mayhap you and I can—"

"You are right," she said with biting anger. "The marriage was not my choice. But unlike so many others in this country today, I do have a sense of honor. I may not want this marriage, but I am in it, and I will not betray my husband to another."

"To another? 'Tis a strange choice of words, my lady.

Do you mean to say *you* might do something yourself to betray him?"

Betrayal, she observed silently, was in the eye of the beholder. In truth, she felt no loyalty to her husband. If she had the chance to escape Scotland with her brother, she would do so. But she would not conspire with his enemies to destroy him.

She gave him what she hoped was a scathing look. "I have heard of families like this, but I chose not to believe the gossip. At least we Jacobites believe in loyalty. Another barbaric custom," she said bitingly.

"He is *not* a Forbes," Neil replied bitterly.

She must have looked startled.

"You will hear it sooner or later. His mother was a whore, an adulteress. He appears to have all her same weaknesses."

The insinuation was clear, and she felt a prickling down her back at the hatred behind it.

"I will not listen to such slander."

" 'Tis not slander. Every man and woman here will tell you the same. The old marquis had his doubts about Rory's birth. He said so. I have more claim. . . ." He stopped suddenly and turned away.

But Bethia wanted to know more. "Then why did he not disinherit him?"

After a moment, Neil turned back to her. "Because he had too much pride, and he thought his oldest son would beget other sons. He never thought—"

"And you believe *you* should be heir?" she said contemptuously.

"The Forbeses will follow me. They will not follow that popinjay."

"Are you looking toward another war?"

"Nay, but times are changing. We must have leadership," he said, his voice lowering. "Rory does not see that. He cares only about his own pursuits. To survive, we must change our ways. We have to put more land into

cattle and sheep, but still help our tenants use the remaining land more productively."

"You would have to clear some land. That means
removing your kinsmen from acres they've worked for
hundreds of years."

His gaze pierced her. "*I* would make provisions for
them. And why would a MacDonell care about that?"

"You obviously would not understand," she said. "I
am sorry I asked you about the books. I will look at them
when my husband returns."

"I would not hold my breath, milady. His trips are
often quite long, though not far. There is a cottage in the
woods not far from here—"

"I will not listen to gossip."

"I just think you should know what everyone knows."

"It is very kind of you," she replied. She turned without another word and left the room.

Now she had something else to ponder: Which of them
was most disliked? She or her husband?

And what might Neil Forbes do to acquire what he
obviously believed should be his?

Bethia inspected the tower house. It was not as large as
her home, but it was substantial. It was old, with a gate-
house extended into a form of the tower. The first floor
of the main tower included the great hall on one side; a
keeping or garrison room on the other. Beneath the keeping room was an unused area that looked like a dungeon
with its heavy doors leading to small cubicles. To the left
of that was an armament room.

A grand stairway led up to a hallway with rooms on
both the right and left. At the end of each corridor were
more staircases that led up to tower rooms. Many of the
rooms were sparsely furnished. The entire building looked
old, ill-kept and dusty.

Her husband's brother had been wed. She'd heard that.
She also knew the wife and his bairn had died in child-

birth. Had she tried to bring some warmth to Braemoor? Or had the cold, hostile atmosphere defeated her?

Well, it was not going to defeat Bethia. After Trilby had shown her the last room, Bethia decided to go to the stable. She might as well find out now whether her husband had indeed ordered her confined to the castle grounds.

The stable was far better kept than the human dwelling, and she wondered who was responsible for that. Neil Forbes? The marquis?

A stableman approached her as she went through the doors. He touched his fingers to his forelock. "Milady?"

"I would like to take a horse for a ride." she said.

The man, old and worn-looking, gazed at her with pale-blue eyes. "I am sorry, milady. The marquis told me I was no' to let you 'ave a 'orse."

She drew herself up for the second time that day. "I am Braemoor's mistress."

"Tha' may be, but the marquis . . ."

A second man in a dirty Forbes plaid moved to his side, as if to fortify him. He held a sack that was moving. A mewling sound came from within.

"What is that?" she asked.

The two men exchanged a glance. "A pup," the newcomer said. "The runt. The bitch canna feed it."

"Where are you taking it?"

"To the stream."

"No." Her horror must have been evident because the man paused.

" 'Tis the kindest thing," he said.

"Have you ever drowned?"

The man sputtered. "Why . . . no."

"Then how do you know?" She reached for the sack, and he handed it to her with a stricken look on his face.

She opened it and took out a terrier puppy. It was black and tiny, but active, its eyes obviously just opening. She swallowed hard as she felt its helplessness.

"We have a milk cow?"

"Aye."

"Then I want a cup of milk."

The stableman was obviously pleased she was not going to quarrel with the edict prohibiting her from riding. "Aye, milady. I will 'ave it sent to ye."

"Thank you," she said softly, her mind now completely occupied with saving the puppy. A glove with a small hole in one of its fingers would do. She had fed a calf that way once, when its mother had died, and had even nurtured a young hawk.

But the puppy was so very small. Yet it had snuggled into her hands as if finally finding the safety it sought.

Her heart turned over, or seemed to. A defenseless creature. In all the blood and strife in Scotland, here was one small life she might be able to save. Cuddling the puppy protectively, she hurried back to her room.

Trilby was dabbing her wedding gown with warm cow's milk to remove a wine stain spilled there by a drunken guest. As far as Bethia was concerned, she cared naught whether it was removed or not. She hated the garment. It was a reminder of events she'd rather forget.

"Ah, milady," Trilby said as she looked up. "And what do ye have there?"

"A puppy," Bethia said. "One of the stablemen said the mother could not feed it, and he was going to drown it. I thought to try to save it."

Trilby carefully laid the gown on the bed and went over to her, her right hand soothing the puppy's dark head. "'Tis a wee thing."

"Aye, but I saved a young hawk once, not much older than this."

"What do you need, milady?" Trilby asked, obviously as eager as she to try to save the pup.

"A glove and a pin. We will make a tiny hole where the little finger is. The stableman is sending some milk."

"I have some here. I was using it to clean your dress," Trilby said helpfully. "I will ready a glove." Then she stopped. "Ye only have but the one pair."

Bethia shrugged. "A glove against a life. 'Tis not a difficult decision."

Trilby looked at her, obviously stunned for a moment, then said warily, "It would be fer many ladies."

Bethia decided not to reply to that observation. Instead, she sat, still holding the puppy while Trilby found a glove, punctured it, then poured some of the warm milk she'd been using into it. The puppy wriggled, making little distress noises. It was obviously very hungry. But would it know how to use the glove?

Trilby sat next to her and held the glove as Bethia tried to guide the little finger into the pup's mouth. For a moment it refused to take it. Then the smell or the feel or the taste caused the pup to open its mouth, and Bethia gently squeezed milk into its mouth. In seconds the pup was eagerly sucking at the leather.

Bethia and Trilby smiled at each other.

"We will have to feed it every two or three hours," Bethia said.

"I'll feed it at night," Trilby offered.

"Nay, we will take turns," Bethia insisted.

Trilby watched the tiny mouth moving. "Will ye name it?"

Bethia had not thought of that, not yet. Mayhap if she gave the pup a name, it would give him the will to live. Not that it seemed to have a problem. Its tiny mouth was moving compulsively, eagerly.

She thought for a moment. The pup was the color of midnight. She had been thinking incessantly of the man named the Black Knave, the jack of spades.

"Jack," she said slowly. "Black Jack."

"Jack," Trilby said as one of her free fingers ran over the silky head. "I think Jack fits him well."

"Aye," Bethia said. "He's a gallant, smart little lad."

Trilby looked down, then looked up worriedly as if she were overstepping her bounds. "He is still very small, though. Do not get too attached, milady."

But the warning was too late. She was already attached.

Jack was the only living being here at Braemoor that depended on her, the only soul she could love. And animals
did have souls. She was convinced of it.

Her brother was in her heart, and she would try every
day of her life to make him safe, but now she had something she could help immediately and directly.

"He will live," she said. "I will not allow him to do
anything else."

Six

Edinburgh was bristling with British troops.

Rory had donned one of his most extravagant waist-coats, a bright blue garment embellished with gold lace and gold buttons, and a pair of plaid trews that fit his legs as if they were painted on them. Over the waistcoat, he wore a plaid of chequered tartan. On his feet, he wore a pair of shoes with gold buckles.

He hated the bloody shoes, just as he despised the heavy wig that decorated his head under a bright blue bonnet, also trimmed with gold. He'd much prefer the supple comfort of well-worn boots, but he looked much as he wanted: a foolish Scot aping a foolish English dandy

No soldier stopped him, no one asked for papers or the nature of his business. Some turned away with disgust in their eyes, some with contempt. Few took a second look.

He rode to the Fox and Hare, a tavern where he often stayed. Located near the Edinburgh Royal Theater, its patronage included a wide assortment, ranging from actors to British officers, who enjoyed the proximity of the latter, particularly the actresses. For the past five months,

Rory had maintained a permanent room over the tavern. Several British officers also kept rooms there.

He greeted the officers in the taproom, recognizing most, spotting one or two he'd not seen before.

"Ah, Captain Lehgrens," he said, swooping down on one of the officers as he waved his arm in an extravagant manner. "A game of hazard this evening?"

"My good fellow," Lehgrens replied, "you've been gone far too long. It's not good gamesmanship to win, then leave." He eyed Rory's clothing. "You've become quite a dandy."

"Since my father's . . . departure from this world, I can now indulge my tastes."

"I seem to recall you've always indulged them, but not quite as flamboyantly in dress."

"But now I have a bride to impress," Rory said with a grin. "The king's own choice."

"So we've heard. The notorious Rory Forbes a husband."

Rory wagged a lace handkerchief. "Braemoor, my dear captain. You keep forgetting I am now the Marquis of Braemoor."

Lehgrens gave him a mocking bow. "My lord."

"Ah, that's more like it," Rory said. "A little subservience."

Lehgrens stretched out. "You have it, as long as you lose. Now about this wife. Is that why we have not been graced recently with your presence?"

"Nay. No lass will ever tie me down."

Lehgrens frowned. "We were hoping your . . . marriage would open Elizabeth's door to us."

"Elizabeth can play with whomever she chooses."

"For some reason, she chooses you."

"Or she *doesn't* choose you," Rory said, leaning back with a smile pasted on his lips. If only they knew. As with Mary, Elizabeth was one of his couriers and, as important, supplier of the items he needed for disguise. She had also taught him to use them.

Elizabeth was fifteen years his senior. She had, in fact, initiated him in the ways of love when, as a seedling, he'd appeared backstage after one of her performances. He looked extraordinarily needy, she had teased him. She had become his friend in days when he'd had none, and because he'd been totally indifferent to politics, she'd confided in him about her Jacobite roots. When he'd become the Black Knave, he visited her in Edinburgh, trusting her with his deadly secret because he so badly needed her help. He needed to go places that Rory Forbes could not go; he needed the expertise to make himself into an old man, or a vicar, or even a woman.

Everyone believed he shared her bed, though that aspect of their relationship had ended years ago. He'd chosen to allow the myth to continue. It protected Elizabeth, and it suited him to have his father believe he was dissolute. So wags had him bedding Mary at Braemoor, and Elizabeth here. He was considered a cocksman of great repute.

A wife and two lovers.

If only the Brits knew the truth of it. . . .

He'd indulged in no lovemaking since before Culloden. 'Twas too dangerous for both him and the lady. He intended to take no one to the gallows with him if he were caught. His wife should be safe, since she was forced into the marriage by the king himself. Mary and Elizabeth knew the risks they were taking, but Mary's heart obviously belonged to Alister, and Elizabeth . . . well, he and Elizabeth had forged a friendship that no longer had a place for sex. He also suspected that her heart was already claimed.

"A tankard of rum?"

Rory looked at Lehgrens. "Rum? Have you sunk that low, my dear fellow?" He turned to the barmaid. "Claret, my love. The best."

"Your fortunes have indeed changed, my lord," Lehgrens said. "'Twas not so long that you bought your lodging with my money."

"Before you were run out of Edinburgh by Charlie," Rory retorted. The young prince had taken Edinburgh in September the previous year.

"I heard you stayed none too long yourself, Rory."

He shrugged. "My family's loyalties were well known."

"And where were you during the fighting?"

"Beside my father, of course. Earning the king's gratitude."

"I thought you were a lover, not a fighter."

Rory took out a snuffbox, took a sniff or two. "I can swing a sword. I fostered with the earl of Fallon."

The captain looked at his clothing dubiously. "I never would have guessed it."

Rory waved his handkerchief in Lehgren's face. "I avoid reminders as much as possible. You were quite right to observe I care little about the . . . discomforts of the battlefield."

"And now you have a wife, a battlefield of another kind, I trust. I've heard MacDonells were quite fierce."

Rory inwardly winced at the word "were." Outwardly, he shrugged. "She is tame enough."

"I heard she was plain."

Plain? Mayhap in some eyes. For a moment, he thought of the thin, determined face, recalled the desire that he felt when he'd touched her. She aroused something in him. He wished she didn't.

"The fortune she brings makes her quite presentable," he said. "Now about that game. I have a few errands first."

"The fair Elizabeth?"

"A gentleman never discusses a lady."

"Give her my best," Lehgrens said. "Tell her that if she ever gets bored with you, I would be more than happy to take your place."

"I will do that, my friend," he said, rising. "Ten o'clock tonight?"

"If you promise not to run off as I am winning."

"You have lost none of your optimism, Captain."

"I need some recreation. The Stuart bastard continues to allude us. Cumberland is not a happy man."

"I hear you've caught a number of Jacobites."

Lehgrens's face clouded. "Some. Not enough. That damned fellow called the Black Knave is smuggling them out of Scotland. Damned if I know how. The duke has put a five thousand pound price on his head."

Rory shrugged. "It's thirty thousand pounds for Charlie, is it not? No one has come forth yet."

"The Black Knave is no Charlie. They might protect their prince, but not an outlaw."

Rory brushed at his face with a lace handkerchief. "Mayhap you are right. Do you have any idea who he is?"

"Some Jacobite. They say he's a graybeard, but he's as agile as a fox."

Rory stood. "I am quite confident the king's forces are capable of finding the blackguard. Still, it's discomfiting knowing the brigand is running around free. He might well turn on honest citizens."

"He has protection. But we'll root out the traitor if we have to arrest every Scot in this damned country."

Rory raised an eyebrow.

"Excluding present company, of course."

"Thank you," Rory said, throwing several coins on the table. "I will see you in a few hours."

Elizabeth would be at the theater at this hour of the day. Rory, a frequent visitor, was allowed in a side door, then to her dressing room.

She was alone, applying cosmetics for her evening performance. She was an artist in the medium, able to transform a man into a woman, or a woman into a man, a young man into a graybeard.

She obviously saw him in her mirror and turned, a broad smile on her lovely face. The daughter of a dispossessed lord after the "Fifteen," the Jacobite rising in 1715, she was left penniless with naught but a pretty face and a talent for acting. She'd made her way to Edinburgh and, adopting an English surname, became a fashionable courtesan, then actress. She'd also been mistress to a number of English and Scottish lords. Now she had the funds to do exactly what she wanted, and that was mainly to tweak the noses of men who'd used her and destroyed her father.

"Rory. It is good to see you, even in that hideous coat."

Rory struck a pose. "'Tis the height of fashion."

She raised a haughty eyebrow.

"And as comfortable as striding barefoot across hell," he added drily.

"You should try some of the garments we women must wear."

"I might be doing that," he said. "How do you think I would look as an elderly woman?"

She looked at him critically. "A *very* tall elderly woman."

"I canna shrink," he said, "but I can bend a little."

"Hmm," she said, her gaze sharpening. "A challenge."

"And you love them."

"Some. But you risk much, my new lord."

"No more than you."

She turned back to the mirror. "I hear you have a wife."

"The whole of Scotland apparently has heard that."

"A Jacobite wed to a king's man? 'Tis news, Rory. And unexpected, at that."

"I was given little choice, and my new bride even less. If I did not marry her, God knows what fate Cumberland would have dealt her."

"Always the rescuer."

"I received land in exchange," he said defensively.

"But that is not why you did it, is it Rory?"

"I would have been suspect had I not. I am a wastrel, remember, and what wastrel would turn down the king's favor and new lands?"

"And how does the bride accept this?"

"My marriage seems to be the principal topic of conversation," Rory said irritably.

"Only because it is so out of character."

"'Tis true I have little faith in the institution. If you had known my mother, and my legal father, you would understand why. It is a marriage in name only, one that both the lass and I hope will end soon. But her younger brother is being held by Cumberland and you know my own precarious position."

"But does she?"

"Good God, no."

"Do you not trust her?"

"I do not want another life in danger. And she wants her brother freed. I am no' so sure what she would, or wouldn't, trade for it."

"Ah, Rory, sometimes I think you enjoy complicating your life."

"And you do not? But enough of this. Young Ogilvy has been taken, the last of his particular family. I wish to free him."

She stopped what she was doing and turned her body around. "You've only smuggled out fugitives before. Do you now intend to storm one of Cumberland's prisons?"

"Aye, that is exactly what I intend."

"You are daft."

"You've said that of me before."

"I've not changed my mind."

"I need some more cosmetics."

"Of course," she said wearily. "Can you tell me what you have in mind?"

"I know the gaol where they are keeping him. One of my men will instigate a fight and hopefully be thrown into one of the cells. Then his dear old mother will visit him, and on her way out ask to see the notorious Jacobite."

"And you are the dear old mother."

"Aye. Do you think you can do it?"

She eyed him far more carefully. "More to the point, *can you?*"

"I make a great greybeard," he said testily.

"A woman is a trifle different, my lord." Her hands touched him at his waist, bending him slightly. "If you bend, we will need to give you a hump. A cane would not hurt, either. I have a gray wig we used not long ago. A few handkerchiefs to give you a bosom, then a pillow some bulk. You will make an ugly woman, my lord, if you'll be forgiving me for saying so."

"I'd rather be ugly than fair," he said. "I donna fancy British hands on me."

"You will not have to worry about that, not when I finish with you."

"When?"

"When do you plan to return?"

"Day after tomorrow."

"Then come tomorrow night after the performance. I will have everything you need."

He took the several steps over to her, leaned over and planted a kiss on her cheek.

"Now you've ruined all my efforts" she fussed, even as she looked pleased. "I've missed you, Rory."

Bethia nursed the pup for the next few days, waking up several times during the night to give him another feeding.

She had fixed a soft bed for it, but its soft whimpering had struck a chord in her, and she allowed the pup up in the bed with her, its tiny little body snuggling next to hers. The comfort was not all the dog's.

On the second day of the marquis's absence, she decided to try to learn more about him. The place to begin, she thought, was the man who had been so kind to her the day of the wedding: the blacksmith. Alister.

She thought of sending for him, but felt he would be less prepared if she suddenly appeared. He came to Braemoor at least once a week to shoe horses and do whatever other chores were needed. The rest of the week, except for Sunday, he apparently kept a shop in a village not far away. Since she was not allowed freedom outside Braemoor's grounds, and he was apparently in residence this day, she planned a surprise visit.

Bethia again was surprised at his small stature, even as she noted the strength in his arms and shoulders. He grinned at her when she entered the hot, grimy building that served as the smithy.

"My lady. I am honored."

"Then you are the only one," she replied wryly. "My presence mostly instills resentment."

"It will be gone quick enough," he said. "Several of the servants had men killed by Jacobites at Culloden."

"My brothers were also killed," she said sharply.

"I am sorry," he said.

She bit her lip. She would not cry in front of these people.

"Did you have need of me?" he said in a gentler tone.

She fidgeted. She did not know how to ask the questions she wanted to ask. A lady dinna go to a blacksmith to ask questions about her husband. And yet . . .

"You said . . ." She hesitated.

"I said?" he prompted.

"On . . . before the wedding, you said something about my husband."

"Aye?" he replied carefully.

"No one else seems to . . ."

"Want to say anything good about him?"

"Aye," she said, relieved that she did not have to pose the question.

She watched indecision flitter over his face. "Has he been . . . unkind to you?"

"He has been nothing to me," she said flatly. "We have exchanged few words."

"He doesna' like to stay still."

"So I am told."

"Does that disturb you?"

"I think it is quite normal for a wife to want to know something about her husband."

"What he wishes to tell," the blacksmith said softly. "Not what others say about him."

"You are his friend." She had not been sure until this moment. His words now told her the truth of it. But she did not understand why the fop she knew as her husband would be friend to a hardworking blacksmith.

His lips thinned. "The marquis does not have friends such as I. I was sent by the duke of Cumberland to fetch you, and I said what you wanted to hear." He bent over the forge, his hands easily working the tools that turned a piece of iron into a shoe, bending it with such accomplished ease that she found herself fascinated, even as she realized he was trying to change the subject.

Bethia's heart constricted. She had thought, hoped . . .

After a moment, she tried again. "I . . . understand there is someone who grows herbs. I am in need of some."

The moving hands of the blacksmith stilled. "I will fetch what you need, my lady."

"I would like to see for myself what she has."

He didn't turn to her, nor did the expression on his face change. "It is dangerous, my lady, for a woman to travel these days. There are brigands about."

"The Black Knave, you mean?" There, she had said the words.

"Aye, and others."

"I heard he only goes about helping people."

The blacksmith turned then, his face red from the heat. "That is dangerous talk, my lady. I would suggest you not say it to anyone else. He is a rebel with the king's bounty on his head, and people here would not take kindly to any words said in his behalf. Your husband has just lost his father and brother to the Jacobites; he'll have little sympathy with your interest."

She drew herself up straight at the scolding. "You are among those who sanction having women and children burned out of their homes and innocent men hanged?"

"I do not sanction outlaws who defy the king," he said in a cold voice, "and I advise you, my lady, to ask no other about this matter."

She was going to receive no help from this source.

But even she had known what a flimsy hope it was. A kind word, and she had leaped upon it as if it were far more. It had been only a meaningless nicety, designed to disarm her and get her down to the altar.

She turned, her back rigid with shame that she had imagined she would receive anything from a member of this household, this clan that betrayed everything she'd been raised to respect and cherish.

"My lady?" His words followed her out the door, but she did not stop. She felt the mist of tears in her eyes, and she did not want anyone to see them. She would not show any of them, not one, the loneliness that clawed at her heart like some starving animal.

Her feet hurried toward the tower house, toward the sanctuary of her room.

Rory neared Braemoor, his pockets full of pound notes won from a churlish Lehgrens. Two kegs were tied down on a horse behind him. One of the kegs contained women's clothes, paints, a wig and two British uniforms; the other held a rather fine wine. He opened the tap, the better for a patrol to test. He'd been stopped by two patrols, but was immediately and with profuse apologies released as soon as his identity was known and the kegs explained as a gift for Cumberland.

Neither asked to sample the wine after that explanation, and his precaution was for naught; still, if an officer had been with them rather than a sergeant, the keg might well have been inspected.

Rory skirted the lane to the tower house. He wanted no one from Braemoor to see him, to report his homecoming to his wife. In fact, he fervently hoped everyone would believe him still in Edinburgh.

The very thought sobered him. He had thought about

her more than he'd wanted during the past several days. God knew he understood what it was to be alone, unwanted, even reviled. She would be all three, and he had no idea how to make her stay here more tolerable without putting both of them, and his friends, in mortal danger.

Damn Cumberland and his machinations. He would have to find out why it had been so important to the duke and to King George that Bethia MacDonell marry. They certainly cared little about the welfare of any other Jacobite woman, regardless of rank. What in the devil was it about the MacDonell lass? Not lass. His wife. That fact still astounded him every time he considered it.

He turned down the lane to Mary's cottage just as the sun set. Mayhap Alister would also be there, and he could sit back and enjoy a tankard of brandy and discuss plans for tonight. Tonight would be his most dangerous mission. Never before had he tried to take a man from British custody. Rory suspected the reward on his head might well double after this night's work. If he lived through it.

'Twas dusk when he rode up to Mary's cottage. He slipped his heels from the stirrups and slid down. He tied the horse's reins to a branch, then cut the rawhide strips binding the kegs in place. He lowered the first one to the ground, then the other. "You will be getting your reward soon," he whispered to the horse, a sad-looking bony mare he'd purchased in Edinburgh. But with a little fattening up, she would improve greatly. She might make a good mount for . . . his wife once he was satisfied that the lass would stay put.

He knocked lightly, and the door opened almost immediately.

Alister was indeed there. He grinned when he saw Rory. "I wasna sure you would make it."

"Neither was I. Patrols are heavy between here and Edinburgh."

"They are everywhere," Alister retorted. "I dinna know

there were so many Englishmen alive. And now, it seems, they are all in Scotland."

"Unfortunately."

Alister eyed the barrels. "Is that what it looks like?"

"One of them," Rory said. "The other includes some items of clothing. I think Mary will have to assist me with them."

Mary stepped out then. "Rory, thank God ye are safe."

"I'm far too wicked to die."

"Your brother managed it."

He looked at her face, suddenly tight and tense, and he remembered when he'd been riding past the cottage years ago, and heard the scream. He'd hesitated only a moment, then went bursting into the cottage, only to find his brother on top of her.

Mary's voice pierced his thought. "It is getting late."

"Aye, it is," he replied. "It will take me only a few moments." He turned to Alister. "Do you have a man who will not object to gaol for a few hours?"

Alister nodded. "We will have to take him to France with our next load, however. It will be too dangerous for him here."

Rory nodded. "Done. Now help me with these infernal garments."

"Your taste is not improving, my lord," Alister said with amusement. "And you might be interested to know your new wife paid a visit to the smithy."

Rory stilled. He should have known that she would look for friendship somewhere. Damn him for sending her in Alister's direction.

"She is lonely and she had questions about ye," Alister said.

"I imagined as much," Rory said. "But it is not wise for me to stay near her, even if I were more in residence at Braemoor. She cannot suspect anything."

"She *is* a Jacobite."

"Aye, but one that must stay in Scotland, at least until we can free her brother. Any change in her attitude toward me, a wrong word dropped, a whisper heard, could condemn us all. No, not until the time is right."

Alister nodded. So did Mary, who was standing next to him.

"Now help me get this bloody thing on. We have business this night."

Seven

"The bloody rogue struck again, this time the gaol in the village."

Bethia paused in the hallway. The voices from the great room were loud and angry. She'd heard the approach of horses a few minutes earlier, then the heavy trampling of boots in the hall, and she'd approached softly, wanting to hear. Her presence usually meant stilted silences.

She heard the marquis's cousin asking questions. The others, she suspected, were English soldiers.

"The sergeant swears the leader was an old woman," an unfamiliar voice said. "I know there are those who say the Black Knave is an old man, but a woman?"

"Are you sure it is the work of the Black Knave?" Neil Forbes's soft accent was distinctive among the more clipped ones.

"Aye, he left a jack of spades in the cell where Ogilvy was held."

"Arrogant bastard," Neil Forbes commented. Bethia thought she heard just a hint of admiration in it.

"Half my men believe he is a witch, or a devil, able to change his form whenever he wishes."

"That's pure nonsense."

"Some even claim it really *is* a woman."

Bethia heard Neil's laughter. "With that kind of audacity? I think not."

"You sound as if you admire him." The unfamiliar voice had taken on an edge.

"I admire courage, whatever the source. That does not mean I want this man running loose in our district. He might well turn from stealing Jacobites from Cumberland to taking something more dear."

"I want some of your tenants. We plan to search every hut, every barn or covey within fifty miles. The sergeant believes one of the attackers might be wounded. He found blood outside the gaol."

"The marquis is the only one who can authorize that. He is not here."

"When will he return?" The question was brusque, impatient.

"I do not know." Neil Forbes's voice was contemptuous. "No one ever knows. He does not bother himself with keeping anyone informed. I believe he's in Edinburgh, but he might well be in someone's bed."

"I thought he was just wed."

"A Jacobite," Neil said dismissively. "With a tart tongue and none of the attributes my cousin favors. 'Twas her fortune my cousin sought."

Resentment, anger and even shame ripped through Bethia. *None of the attributes.* "Plain" was what he meant. She told herself she didn't care what these English-lovers thought, but still the words stung.

And apparently her bridegroom shared that opinion, since he had no interest in her bed, nor, quite obviously, her company.

She should be pleased, but pride—the strong pride of the MacDonells—caused her to wince and left her feeling more alone than ever. No one in the MacDonell hold would ever have had such poor manners as to disparage the lord and his lady.

But then, these Forbeses had no honor.

She wanted to hear more, but she had no appetite now for being discovered lurking in the hall and overhearing their remarks. Mayhap she could learn more from the men being served mead in the great hall.

She was mistress here, but she knew the king's men were always welcomed at Braemoor, and their men fed and offered other refreshment. She flinched every time she saw a red coat. She knew them only too well.

Bethia entered the great hall. Weapons had been scattered along the walls, and already the sound of voices was growing louder with drink. Curses echoed in the hall. She caught bits and pieces.

"'E's a bloody phantom."

"Maltworm."

"We will be up all night, 'unting these bloody woods."

"Drink deep," said another.

"'Ow will we know the bloody bastard?"

"Someone will pay for lettin' that Jacobite go free."

"Aye, I would no' be in that sergeant's shoes. Be lucky if he ain't hung."

Bethia drank in all the comments, wishing that one might give her a clue as to how to find the Black Knave. Then one of the men looked her way, and punched another, and he a third until all of them turned toward her, their faces going red as they apparently remembered their language. One bowed. "Milady?"

"I just came to see if you had everything you need. Food? Drink?"

"Aye, milady," said the man who seemed to be the spokesman. "And we be thanking you for yer hospitality."

She inclined her head slightly in acknowledgment, then turned and left, relieved to be rid of their presence. The uniforms sickened her, as did their arrogance. They had so much blood on their hands, and they cared little.

But at least she knew the Black Knave was in the vicinity. If only she could get word to him.

And her husband? Where was he?

She wanted his support in looking over the accounts. She wanted more authority in this house. Mayhap it would eventually mean a loosening of the scrutiny she received, a better chance to escape. *Allies.* She needed a few allies.

Bethia went out the door into the courtyard. More English soldiers lingered there, seeing to horses or just walking about. If only she could take a horse. If only.

Horse thieving was not well regarded.

But she was tempted. So tempted. A short ride. Just long enough to get away from the sight of red uniforms. Just enough to breathe air unsullied by sweat and blood and arrogance. She sidled over to a large bay and ran her finger down the side of its neck. Cool.

The horse was still saddled, its reins tied to a post. Other soldiers were milling around, watering mounts, cooling them down. This one must belong to one of the officers who arrived earlier.

"I would not do that, milady."

She whirled around, afraid her face was reddening with guilt as she did so.

Her husband was standing there, his hazel eyes regarding her with interest. Why had she not seen him ride in? Where had he come from?

"I did not know you had returned."

"Obviously."

"I just needed some . . . air."

"Too many English soldiers?"

She knew her cheeks were darkening. Why did he always seem to know exactly what she was thinking?

"Aye," she said defiantly. "Far too many."

"I do not believe that stealing one of their horses would reduce the number of them around you," he said. "It would only serve to increase it."

Her gaze wandered over him. He was wearing a dandy's clothes, but there was a bulge underneath the sleeve of his brightly colored waistcoat and he held his arm stiffly. The sleeve was sliced and ruby-stained. His blank expression changed subtly as he saw her eyes rest on it. "A slight mishap," he explained.

Just then Neil and an English officer came out the door.

Bethia watched Neil's face change, darken with a frown. "I did not know you were back."

"I just arrived," her husband said, arching an eyebrow at the English officer. "I am late because I ran into a band of brigands. Could have been your outlaw. What, dear boy, do you call him? Some ridiculous name."

The officer's nostrils flared like those of a stallion who caught the scent of a mare.

"Where?"

"Halfway to Edinburgh. Must be near there by now. Saw Ogilvy with him. Recognized the young rounder. Tried to challenge them, but I was overwhelmed. Just barely escaped with my life."

"How many were there?"

"Six—no, seven, including Ogilvy."

"You are sure he's with them?"

"Aye, he was for certain."

"And the others? Come on, man. What of the others?"

Her husband shrugged. "They were dressed like peasants, though their leader could wield a sword well enough. I had engaged him when some villain struck me from the back. Ruined one of my best shirts and waistcoat," he complained plaintively.

The officer looked at him with contempt. "We had reports of a woman."

"A woman?" her husband said. "Nay, I saw no woman. There was Ogilvy and then a young man with reddish hair. Seemed to be their leader."

"Edinburgh, you say?" the officer said.

"Aye."

The officer turned to a sergeant who had accompanied him from Braemoor. "Get the men ready to ride. I'll turn the city upside down." He nodded at the Marquis of Braemoor. "What else about the leader? Age? Color of eyes? Mount he was riding?"

The marquis shrugged. "Ordinary. Red hair. Brown eyes. All, including Ogilvy, wore peasant clothing. And their horses? Damned near falling down," he added disdainfully.

"Why didn't you go into Edinburgh to report it?"

"I was already halfway home. I wished to return to my dear wife for comfort and attention."

The officer stared at him with disgust. "Do you not know there is a reward of five thousand pounds on the man?"

"I tried to stop him," Rory said querulously. "Got a slice for my efforts."

The officer looked at him contemptuously. "It was your duty to get to an officer of the king and run him down."

"My good fellow, it was my duty to return to my home and protect it. 'Tis not my fault you cannot catch this villain. There he was, bold as daylight, on the Edinburgh road."

"Are you sure it was him?"

"I am sure only that it was Ogilvy. I hear this . . . black rogue fellow is an old man, or, did I hear you right, a woman? You cannot find a woman or old man?" The marquis shook his head in obvious dismay.

The English officer pushed past him, muttering, "Knave. He calls himself the Black Knave."

"By God, but that fellow has no manners," her husband said as the officer directed his men to mount and moments later left the courtyard at a trot.

She had enjoyed the Englishman's consternation, even his revulsion at her husband's supercilious manner. But she worried about the man called the Black Knave. She looked at the man who had been her husband for a week. "The Black Knave . . . you said you struck him?"

His eyes suddenly pierced her. "You have interest in this matter?"

"Nothing. I just heard . . ."

"Well, madam," he said impatiently. "*What* have you heard?"

"That the Black Knave may have been wounded earlier. Did . . ."

Her husband's eyes narrowed. "Do you believe a wounded man could equal me?" he asked.

Her silence said volumes.

He decided to let that go for the moment. "Your concern for an outlaw does you no credit, madam. It should lie with your husband."

Bethia's gaze went back to his arm. "Is it . . . your wound . . . bad?"

"It requires a stitch or two. Are you up to that, wife?"

She lowered her eyes from his face, which towered over her. "Aye, I have mended wounds before."

"Then come with me." He strode ahead of her, past Neil, who was regarding them with a frown, through the passage that led to the great hall, then up the stairs to the room that she knew he used as his sleeping quarters. She had not been inside, had not been invited, and she'd been reluctant to pry. She even, perhaps, hoped he wouldn't return from wherever he'd been.

The room was dark and plain and far more Spartan than she'd expected for a man who dressed and spoke like a popinjay. It did, however, have a huge clothes press, along with a bed that looked too short for him, a plain table and two chairs. A table held a bottle of brandy and several glasses. That, at least, fit.

The fireplace had obviously been cleaned recently and new fresh wood had been placed in the hearth. He sat awkwardly in one of the chairs and sighed with obvious relief.

She hesitated for a moment, then asked, "If you will tell me where to find the herbs and bandages, I will fetch them."

His gaze was cold as it raked her. "There is no need. It has already been attended to."

"But . . ."

"I did not wish to humiliate you by revealing that I went elsewhere. However, Mistress Mary Ferguson saw to the wound quite nicely. She is a healer," he added.

She had already heard all the gossip, that the girl Mary was his mistress, and inexplicable anger coursed through her, even as she realized that he had made a small effort not to shame her publicly. Nonetheless, she did feel shamed. And inadequate.

Bethia told herself she wanted as little to do with this man as possible. Why, then, did she feel this odd disappointment?

She needed to feel needed. Even if the person was an enemy. And for the shortest possible time, she had.

But she wasn't wanted. No one wanted her. No one needed her. Not even the wretch who called himself her husband. No one.

Except, possibly, for Dougal. And she could not let him down.

She bit her lip. "If we are to preserve the pretense," she said as lightly as she could, "then I had best fetch the medicines and bandages. Perhaps some hot water?"

His gaze faltered for a moment, then he nodded.

She slipped out of the door.

Rory watched the door close, then closed his eyes. It had taken every bit of willpower he had to make it back to Braemoor.

He did not even know if he could make it to the bed. He'd lost so damn much blood before he'd reached Mary's cottage. A musket ball had lodged in his arm and Mary had dug it out, then sewn up the wound after Alister had sliced a bit more to make it look more like a sword than a pistol wound.

God's breath, but his arm hurt.

Bloody hell.

Everything had gone as planned. Up to a point. Feigning drunkenness, two of Alister's recruits had started a fight in front of the gaol the night before last; when one of the soldiers had come too close they had attacked *him*. Both men had been thrown into a cell. No one had questioned the bent and bowed old woman who appeared the next evening to see her only son. Rory had been able to slip both his supposed son and Ogilvy a pistol, and the latter a jack of spades. Unfortunately Ogilvy did not wait long enough to make his move, and Rory, moving slowly, had been in the line of fire of one of the more alert guards before he'd reached the waiting horses.

The four of them—Ogilvy, the two men and himself— had managed to escape only because Alister had earlier stuck thorns to the undersides of the English saddles. If Rory had not hurt so damnably, he would have enjoyed the sight of the bucking horses and English soldiers flying into the air.

They'd made it to a cave, where they left Ogilvy, then rode to Mary's croft.

It was decided then to manufacture another wound. Rory couldn't try to hide the one he had. His arm would be stiff for days. Explanations were needed, and not for a bullet wound. He and Alister had both decided on a sword wound as a plausible cause and a tale that would send the English on a false trail.

So Alister had carefully sliced the expensive—if atrocious—waistcoat as well as the linen shirt. They'd then bloodied both to make it look like a sword stroke.

He'd made little of the wound in front of Mary and Alister. He hadn't wanted them to worry. And it was odd how necessity blocked out pain, but now the pain was flooding him in wave after wave.

He had to make sure his wife never saw the wound. He hoped sincerely that she'd had little experience with them, but he knew that many women tended to their clan's wounded.

Had he really glimpsed a momentary disappointment in her eyes, even a flash of anger, when he'd said another woman had cared for him?

If so, he had not been harsh enough, arrogant enough, repulsive enough.

And yet something inside him yearned to see the flash of concern in her eyes again. Or had that brief sympathy been there at all?

He muttered a curse to himself. He had gone too long without a woman's soft touch, a touch meant for him alone. Mary's doctoring had been as gentle as possible, but there was naught but friendship between them. It was unfortunate that Rory was attracted to his own wife, especially since the attraction could mean the death of them both.

He would have to tamp down that yearning.

Damn, but he was weary. It had been more than a day since last he slept, and the letting of blood had not helped.

His hand pulled off the damnably heavy wig and let it drop to the floor. He opened the jacket of his waistcoat. Just for a few moments. Just a few . . .

Bethia tried to curb her anger as she confronted the cook and asked for the bandages and herbs she thought any wounded man would need. She suffered the woman's rude stare and hostile grunt as she waited for items she would not need because her . . . husband had received care elsewhere. Humiliation was being heaped upon humiliation. Still, she knew that any authority she hoped she would have was centered on the marquis. If the household felt he did not trust her, then she would never gain any respect. Without respect, she had no hope of escape.

Curse him!

She took the tray loaded with unneeded items and carried it back up to his room, knocking lightly before entering. Hearing no reply, she went in.

He looked asleep in the chair. He also looked different.

The powdered wig was on the floor, and for the first time she noticed he had dark hair, almost black, that curled slightly in thick sweat-damp clumps. Without the wig, the look of a dandy disappeared, and she noticed for the first time the handsome angular features of his face, the scar on his chin that somehow made him more . . . appealing. His mouth particularly looked vulnerable, the curve of his lips softer, less mocking.

His breathing was heavy. She touched his forehead and it was warm, warmer than it should be in the cold room. She finished unbuttoning his jacket and noticed that under the sleeve of his linen shirt, the bandage was a bright red.

He was still bleeding! She wondered for a moment how it was that he had seemed so unaffected minutes earlier when he was obviously far more seriously wounded than she had believed.

"My lord," she said, unsure of what else to call him. He did not answer.

She shook him slightly and called him again, her voice louder.

His lashes fluttered. How had she not noticed how thick they were?

"My lord," she said for the third time.

His eyes slowly opened and they looked glazed.

"Let me help you get into bed. Then I will look at your wound again. You are still bleeding."

He shook off her hand. "I can . . . manage myself."

She stepped back and watched as he struggled to his feet, then took the several steps to his bed, almost falling into it.

She approached, and he looked at her with hostile eyes. "I need no help from you, madam," he said, as if she were a particularly irritating mouse. "You would best please me by leaving."

She was not wanted here. She was not wanted anywhere. She took a step toward the door, strangely reluctant to open it. He had given her permission to leave, had even ordered it, so why did she linger?

She tried to tell herself it was what she would do for anyone, friend or foe. She stooped and picked up the wig, placing it on the table. 'Twas truly hideous and smelly. He would be rather presentable without it, and far more comfortable. But, then, she often did not understand the why and how of men's ways.

Bethia looked back at her husband. His eyes, still glazed with either weakness or pain, followed her. "You are not obedient," he said.

"I have been told that," she replied, twisting her hands together.

"I will have to do something about that," he said, closing his eyes. "But not now. Send for . . . Alister."

Alister. The blacksmith. The man who had tried to reassure her. It was something she could do, since the marquis did not want so much as her hands to touch him.

Why? Was he that repelled by her? She knew she was no beauty, but . . .

Or mayhap he believed she would do him harm. His death would free her.

She turned and left the room, intent—without knowing why—on helping the man she despised, the man who obviously felt the same about her.

The field was the color of blood. Rivulets of red ran like streams over the rough ground, covering the few struggling flowers, flowing to stain the clear, cold stream. Groans of dying men echoed across the moor. The world was red. The world was pain.

"Rory." He heard his name from some great distance. He did not want to heed it. He wanted the darkness again. He wanted . . .

"Rory!"

He tried to conquer the pain. God's breath, but he was hot. He felt that he was burning up.

"Can you hear me?" Alister's voice was pleading now.

He could not disappoint his friend. His friend. He willed himself to open his eyes, to force words from a mouth that felt like wool.

"Aye," he said, hearing the raspy quality of it.

"Thank God." Alister's voice was the breath of prayer.

Rory felt a wet cloth across his face. Felt good. So good.

"I thought we might lose you."

"How long . . . ?"

"Two days. I have been with you. Your new wife has tried to come several times but I told her that you had ordered that you be tended only by me, that you did not trust a Jacobite wife. I did not want her to hear your ravings."

He tried to understand. Why did she even try? He remembered several hours ago . . . days ago . . . she had hovered next to him. Now that she had been locked from her husband's own sickbed, she would have a more difficult time than ever at Braemoor.

"You should have stayed with Mary at the cottage," Alister said chidingly. "You had a fever even then, and that combined with loss of blood and no sleep . . ."

"Aye, but I needed to brag about my heroic deed."

"Aye, how you were bested by the Black Knave. Turned and ran, most say."

Rory tried to grin. He suspected it was more a grimace. "My poor blemished reputation."

"I know how you value it," Alister said wryly.

"Ogilvy?"

"Safe for the time being. He should be at the old Douglas hunting lodge by now."

"If he hasn't done something stupid again."

"After seeing the results of his impulsiveness, I think he will follow orders," Alister said, looking toward Rory's arm.

"And my tale. It is believed?"

"Aye. Neil has been seething quietly. He believes you are pretending a worse wound than you have. Mary and I have been encouraging that tale. You are mainly overwrought from such a death-defying experience."

"I should have died for the honor of the Forbeses?"

"Aye, and for Neil's advancement, I think," Alister said.

"And my wife. What does she believe?"

Alister looked at him keenly. "Do you care?"

"The situation was already difficult for her."

"I do not think she had very high expectations."

Rory muttered to himself, words he did not want Alister to hear. His wife's opinion did mean something. It should not, but it did.

"Mary was here twice," Alister said, ignoring the murmured curse. "She was with you all night the eve before last."

Rory closed his eyes and groaned. "My mistress."

"Aye, your cousin was not enthralled with having her here. I had to remind him that you are the master here, and that was your wish."

"And . . . the marchioness?"

"After the first visit, she retired to her room, apparently seething. Then she ordered the tower house cleaned from top to bottom."

"And . . ." Rory knew there was something more.

"No one obeyed at first, but then she got down on her hands and knees and started cleaning, and finally a servant joined her, then another. By her own will, she shamed them. Her husband may not allow her in his sickroom, but she made it clear *this* was *her* home."

Rory swallowed hard. He'd never wanted her to suffer for a marriage foisted upon her. That she had somehow triumphed in some small way did not make him feel better.

"She has courage and will," Alister said. "And she was asking about the Black Knave, seeking any information I might have. I believe she thinks he might assist her. Perhaps we should . . . tell her?"

Rory shook his head. He had made sure no one knew the identity of the Black Knave other than Alister, Mary and Elizabeth. He trusted them completely, and he trusted their silence. No one else. Not the messengers, or the occasional men Alister recruited through second parties, ever knew the man they followed was the Marquis of Braemoor. He was a faceless phantom and that was how it must remain.

"No," he said flatly. "I will not endanger her." He paused, then to change the subject as much as to relieve his torment, he muttered, "You are a damned poor provider. I am dry as a bone."

But the water Alister offered his parched throat nearly choked him as he thought of the lady down the passageway. Lumps filled his throat, lumps of guilt and regret. Still, he felt the stirrings of unwarranted pride in her, unwarranted because he'd certainly had nothing to do with her.

Still, in his mind's eye, he could see her face down the sullen servants who had been without supervision for far too long. There had been no mistress in residence since his brother's wife had died two years before, and Margaret had been none too immaculate herself. He doubted whether Braemoor had undergone a thorough cleaning in a decade. The floors were thick with dirt, the tapestries rotting from filth, the portraits dull with dust.

He moved slowly, then sat. For a moment, the room spun around, then it seemed to settle. His arm still hurt, but he knew Alister was right. He had gone without sleep too long, and that, and the loss of blood, had downed him. He would have to be more careful in the future.

Rory slowly rose to his feet. He swayed for a moment, caught the edge of the chair, then straightened. He took a few steps, then a few more, each time feeling strength flow into his body.

He turned to Alister. "Let us ruin Neil's day and show him I still live."

Eight

Bethia scrubbed a dirt-layered window, which had previously allowed little light to penetrate.

Two servants were scrubbing the great hall. It had been swept, probably for the first time in years, the prior day. She'd finally enlisted some assistance by remarking gently that mayhap she simply had not understood the customs of the Forbes clan. She'd failed to understand, she apologized, that Jacobites had higher standards and, thus, she most likely should adopt the slovenly ways of this household.

Since most of the Forbeses obviously considered Jacobites barbarians or worse, they were appalled at her comment and started to glance around at what they had not seen before. Neil gave tacit support to the effort, his gaze going to a floor slick with grease, the residue of thousands of bones being thrown to the dogs.

More important, the campaign gave her something to do and, for the first time, made her a part of the household. Her orders were now obeyed more often than not, although there were still ugly looks, and she heard their tittering when she approached. She suspected it concerned the visits of her husband's paramour. Bethia told herself

THE BLACK KNAVE   111

she did not care as long as those visits kept her husband away from *her* bed. And yet being locked out of her husband's sickroom had been an insult, as had the resulting explanation: he did not trust a Jacobite Highlander to nurse him.

He *should* be suspicious. At the moment, she could cheerfully drown him in her pail of dirty water.

She scrubbed harder, then felt a small body bouncing off her leg. She dropped her cloth in the pail and leaned down to pick up Black Jack, who had just rolled over and was trying to regain his feet. The pup now tried to follow her wherever she went.

She plopped him in her lap. "Still unsteady on your feet, are you, laddie?"

He snuggled down in her lap. His mouth caught her small finger and sucked on it. "'Tis greedy, you are," she said. "You are no' to be fed for another hour."

She lifted him up and placed his small, warm, silky body against her cheek. His tiny, rough tongue reached out and licked her skin.

"A charming picture."

She almost dropped the puppy, so startled was she at his voice.

Bethia slowly turned. The Marquis of Braemoor leaned against a wall, dressed, as usual, in gaily patterned trews and a scarlet waistcoat. Once more, he was wearing a wig, but this one was not as long, nor as elaborate as the others. Still, it subtly changed him. Days earlier, she'd seen another marquis: a vulnerable, wounded, attractive man charged with indefinable power. But now, as she looked at his arrogant pose, she realized that prior picture was merely a myth, something she wanted to see, not what she actually saw.

"You appear well, my lord," she responded acidly, though it was not altogether true. He looked pale and drawn. "I had thought you must be close to death."

He sniffed. "The other day was most upsetting. That . . . ruffian almost skewered me."

"It seems he *did* skewer you."

Her lord snorted. "Lucky blow. I dinna expect it. The man had no sense of honor."

"What did he look like?" she asked, knowing well she never should have asked.

"A peasant. Nothing but a peasant. I canna believe he was that Knave fellow."

Her gaze went to the bulge underneath his coat. "Your arm, my lord?"

"Wifely concern? How pleasant. It is well enough. A small fever of no moment."

"Then why did you feel the need of . . ." Her voice trailed off.

"Mistress Ferguson? She has herbs that soothe me. *She* soothes me. She understands my sensibilities."

"Better her than me," Bethia murmured in a low voice.

"What was that, wife?"

She met his gaze. "I am pleased someone looks after you," she said steadily, wondering whether he had the wit to understand her meaning.

"Other than you?"

"Aye," she said, feeling like a pawn on this man's chessboard. "Though I would prefer you did not flaunt it so openly. It . . . brings contempt for me."

"I am sorry for that. It was not my intent."

"Do you have an intent?" she asked ruefully. "You appear interested only in women and gaming."

"Aye, that paints the portrait well enough. I enjoy my vices, and until my father's unfortunate demise, I had little chance to indulge them."

"That is not what I heard."

"Ah, I was famous even in the far reaches of the Highlands?"

"Infamous is the word."

"That is even better," he said, a smug smile on his lips. "I have never liked being ordinary."

"Then rest assured, you are not," she said wryly.

His gaze went to the squirming puppy in her lap. "Where did you get *that*?"

"The stableman was going to drown him."

"He does not look like much."

Her hands went around the puppy protectively. No one was going to take this puppy from her. Too much else had been taken. "I am taking care of it."

" 'Tis too small to feed itself."

"I am feeding it with cow's milk."

She thought she saw a smile play around his lips for a moment, but then they firmed in a thin line. "As long as it does not get in the way."

She was not going to thank him. He had forced her into making this her home. She was not going to beg for something as small as taking a wee pet.

He continued to watch her under dark brows that appeared odd with the powdered wig. It did, in fact, make her feel as if he were a hawk and she a mouse.

He was a man who disappeared for days afer receiving a minor wound. He was a fool, a caricature of a man who sneered at everything noble. He was a wastrel who gambled and whored while brave men fought for their existence.

She turned back to her window.

"It appears you have won a victory, madam." His voice held neither approval or disapproval.

She didn't feel she had won a victory. "I do not discern your meaning."

"The hall. It is beginning to look respectable."

"I did not wish to live in a pigsty, although it seems to suit others."

"I was never here long enough to notice."

"So I am told."

Silence fell between them, and she looked up, just as Black Jack tumbled from her lap and squatted on the floor. "Jack," she scolded.

"Jack?" her husband said idly. " 'Tis an odd name for a runt."

"Black Jack," she said, wishing to prick the egotism of this man. It was a direct challenge, since everyone knew Black Jack was the same as the Black Knave.

"Ah, you admire the man?"

"I admire courage."

"He is a fool. He will be caught and hanged."

She bit her lip. It was a likely scenario, with every English soldier looking for him.

"And I would be very cautious about what I said around here if I were you," he added ominously. "Your title may not protect you."

"Do you think I care?" she challenged directly.

"For yourself, nay. But I remember talk of a brother . . ."

Her breath caught, and her heart plunged against her rib cage. Had she gone too far? "You are threatening him?"

"Nay. I care not about making war on children," he said, flicking a handkerchief as if at an imaginary piece of dirt. "In truth, I do not feel about them one way or another, certainly not enough to expend any energy on the subject. I am merely making an observation that you might well consider."

He looked at her critically then, and she felt the impact of his eyes. They were hazel, and she'd noticed they changed color according to light and the clothes he wore. Now they were a soft amber with flecks of green. Far deeper than she thought, clearer than she'd remembered. Intelligence seemed to leap from them, but then he turned slightly and when he looked back, his eyes had lost the brightness she thought she'd seen there. Imagination, she told herself. 'Twas just her imagination.

"I thought I had paid money for better garments," he said, his voice aloof, even indifferent. "I don't care to have my wife look like a kitchen wretch."

"I did not wish to ruin them."

"Then you should not be acting the maid. We have servants to do that."

"Your servants are used to doing precious little," she retorted.

"I believe that might be changing," he said with humor. "Alister told me what you said."

"Her back went rigid. "I will not apologize."

"I am not asking that of you. As you probably noticed, I have little interest in Braemoor other than to collect my rents. I do not care if it is a pigsty, as you so eloquently describe it. But neither will I interfere, as long as you play the role of lady."

"But you won't play one as gentleman?"

"I have never been one, and I am too old to change," he said. He looked at the puddle spreading next to her. "You might care for that puddle before it reaches your dress," he said, and her gaze followed his to the tiny puppy.

The size of the puddle was truly amazing. Her face reddened.

He raised an eyebrow and clucked. "And I thought you did not care for pigstys." He turned abruptly and walked away without another word.

Her gaze followed him as he disappeared out the door. He walked with arrogance, his tall, well-formed body moving with a grace she could scarcely equate with the bore she knew him to be. She tried to make herself relax but she felt as tight as the strings on a harp. He always affected her in odd ways, perhaps because she never knew what to expect. Every once in a while, his humor reached out and touched her, then it disappeared like a snowflake dropping into the flames of a fire. It was obscured by all the other colors and shades and moods.

She picked up the pup again, her gaze dropping to the puddle spreading next to her. How could such a wee animal . . .

Black Jack licked her hand, his gratitude obvious. At least her husband had not objected to having the pup in her room. There were others that wandered in and out of Braemoor, but they were all hunting, or ratting dogs.

Black Jack would be none of those. He would be hers
to love.

He was going to have to stay away from her. He did not
like whatever it was that pulled him toward her.

It had been the puppy today.

He'd already heard about the pup from the young stableboy who'd decided that perhaps the "lady" was not a
barbarian after all. He'd also heard from a disgruntled
cook who apparently was looking for any reason to complain, since dogs normally wandered in and out of the
tower. "Shouldn't be in the living areas," she said, her
chin wobbling with indignation.

"Why?" he'd asked.

"It messes."

"How can you tell?" he asked, looking about the
slovenly kitchen and hoping that might be Bethia's next
target.

"Isn't right that . . . Jacobite telling us what to do," the
woman mumbled.

"What isn't right is that no one has done so before,"
he snapped. "You can leave if you wish, but if you stay
you will remember she is mistress of Braemoor."

The cook's face reddened and her hands fingered her
dirty dress. "Aye, my lord," then muttered something
under her breath as she scurried from the room. Rory
heard his cousin's name mentioned and suspected the
woman was going straight to him.

She would receive precious little satisfaction there.

Then he had seen Bethia in the great hall, light streaming in from a newly cleaned window. A cap perched pre-
cariously on the dark hair and a smudge of dirt crossed
her nose. She looked wistful and charming, particularly
when she picked up the little black puppy. His heart had
caught at the sight, and he had found himself approaching her.

He had not been able to help himself, nor had he been
able to refrain from engaging her in conversation. He

liked the soft burr in her voice, one more pronounced than the clans in the middle and southern part of Scotland. He liked the challenges she threw at him, and even more the spirit behind them.

But even if his role hadn't needed to remain secret, he could never pay court to her.

He was nothing, would never be anything. The simple fact was he enjoyed playing a very dangerous game. He did it not out of valor or honor or good purpose. He did it because he enjoyed tweaking the noses of those with whom his father sided.

He hated the English because his father had become one.

And Bethia MacDonell? She was all honor, all courage. And all Scot.

He would leave Scotland one day. He would leave it either by a noose or to escape one. And he would have precious little to take with him except hatred, an ignoble burden that could no' be shared.

He left the room which she had brightened. He was restless, so damned restless, and yet still weak. A day of rest, then he could return to the saddle, and to the coast to make arrangements for his next shipment.

Yet he needed fresh air. Then he thought of the lady in the room just a few feet away. She had been a prisoner here for days. He wondered if she liked to ride.

A bloody poor idea.

A miserable idea.

A dangerous idea.

He retraced his steps back to the great hall, his soft leather shoes barely making a sound. Then she looked up, sensing his presence, and her face became wary.

"I wondered whether you would care to take a ride. You should know something of our property." He forced a cool note into his voice.

The wariness was suddenly eclipsed by something bright and wonderful, a small smile that, nonetheless, was like the sun emerging from storm clouds.

"Aye," she said simply.

"Then I suggest you put on something more suitable," he said, telling himself to act the arrogant fool rather than the sympathetic husband. "You *do* have something suitable?" he said with what he hoped was a sneer. He feared it was something else.

"Aye, the dress I arrived in. It is worn, but—"

"It will do. No one expects much of you."

Hurt dulled some of the brightness in her eyes. He felt like a bully pouncing on a child half his size. He turned before he said something kind.

She had been a prisoner inside the tower house for three weeks. She would have gone with the devil himself to escape it.

She asked Trilby, who had been cleaning her clothes, to help her change. The riding dress required another pair of hands.

Trilby's eyes grew large. "Riding dress?"

"Aye. The marquis is taking me out."

"He is?" She looked doubtful.

"Trilby, what was he like before he became marquis?"

Trilby shrugged. "He was not here much. He and the . . . his fa did not like each other. Jane told me he was a terrible lad. He even beat his brother nearly to a pulp before he was sent away the last time . . ."

She clasped her hand to her mouth as if she'd said too much.

"It is all right, Trilby. I will not tell anyone what you say."

Her face scrunched up in thought. "Well . . . no one knew much about the new lord. They say he ran away from Culloden Moor. His father threatened to kill him when he finally showed up. Lord Donald was wasting away then, and the old lord said the young lord would never get a penny of his money or an acre of land, but then he broke his neck and died and the young lord came home."

"He is not so young."

"Nay, but next to his fa, he is."

None of the information made her feel any better about her husband. He had said he fought at Culloden. Had he lied about that? A sudden chill ran down her spine, quenching the pleasure she'd felt at the prospect of riding, at being outside the walls of Braemoor. Her husband was a coward, a fop, a womanizer.

And he had just shown her a moment of kindness.

For a moment, she wondered whether she should accept that small act, but perhaps she could learn something about the land around her. She'd seen little the day she had first approached Braemoor. The rain had been drenching and she was overly tired; she had noticed very little in her misery.

Knowledge could be a weapon.

Knowledge about Braemoor. Knowledge about her husband.

Neil Forbes watched his cousin help the new marchioness mount a small mare. The lady herself held her head proudly, and with Rory's help mounted easily.

Envy coursed through him. He had wanted to marry years ago, but he had a heritage that had made it impossible to win the woman he wanted. If only the old marquis had lived long enough to change his will, as he planned, then Neil would have been heir. He could have made changes. He would have been his own man at last.

Instead, the least of them had become heir, a man who had left the battlefield. To be honest, however, Neil had been surprised in the first few moments of the fighting, when Rory had acquitted himself well. He had downed several Jacobites, had fought like a tiger. But then he'd just dropped his sword and walked away, deserting his father in midst of battle. He'd had no stomach for continuing. Neil hadn't liked it, either. And yet how many times could Scotland go through civil war? How many times could she tolerate periodic bloodletting?

To Neil, lack of resolve was as great a fault as cowardice.

Rory Forbes should have had no claim to the title, to Braemoor, to the hereditary leadership of the Forbes clan.

Neil had always been loyal. Loyalty was as much a part of him as his skill in fighting.

But Rory Forbes was a different matter altogether. Everyone conceded that Rory was not the marquis's seed. It had been only the old man's pride that he would not go to Parliament and say he'd been cuckolded. And so Rory had remained in the line of succession where he, Neil, had been left out, though he claimed far more Forbes blood than the current marquis.

If Rory had been worthy, it would be different. Neil would surrender his own needs to that of the clan's. But it was beyond his tolerance for a wastrel to usurp the title and estate. It was, in truth, a brand burning deep inside. As was his loss of Janet Leslie.

He had never harbored bitterness. He'd been born a bastard, a highborn one he'd been told, but a bastard all the same, the seed of an unmarried lady and a married lord. He'd not known his blood ties to the laird until he was ten and heard whispers. He'd vowed then to find his rightful place, and he realized the only way he could do that was through distinguishing himself in arms. The old marquis had seen him train one day, and had brought him to Braemoor as companion and protector to Donald.

Shortly after Neil had been installed at Braemoor, Rory had been fostered to an English family. When he returned, he'd had a fierce fight with his father, then virtually disappeared into Edinburgh's gaming rooms where he'd seemed determined to blacken the Forbes name. He'd been caught in a lady's bed and subsequently killed the husband in a duel. He'd won and lost vast sums. He'd mocked the king and mocked the clan.

But he had come home when called to join the English forces arrayed against the Scottish prince. Neil hadn't known why. He hadn't asked. He only knew he dinna trust the man and never would. Braemoor deserved more than a part-time landlord, a man who would gamble away the lands without a second thought.

And Neil was the next closest in line to inherit. He had no wish to claim the crumbs left by an irresponsible dandy.

Cumberland's gift of additional lands in exchange for marriage had only served to embitter Neil further. More bounty for one who did not take care of what was already his. The man's treatment of his wife galled him, even though he had always held little regard for Jacobites. They were troublemakers through and through.

And yet the new marchioness had a certain dignity that he appreciated. No woman should be treated as she had been treated, and his heart had softened as she had gradually tried to improve the condition of Braemoor. Even he had not realized how badly it had deteriorated in the past few years. Braemoor had always seemed to treat its women badly; few had lasted long before dying in childbirth, or of a fever shortly after. And each time Braemoor suffered.

He wondered whether the same would happen with the MacDonell bride. Cumberland had made it clear he expected a bairn within the year. Would it be the death of this lass, too?

Neil watched as his cousin and his bride disappeared down the lane, and he started wondering how he could bring down the Marquis of Braemoor.

Nine

The afternoon was cold and blustery, but it was the kind of day Rory loved best. It made him feel alive. He even enjoyed the chill that crept through the peacock-blue coat he wore. He only wished he weren't wearing one of his more obnoxious wigs. He had, however, indulged himself with a fine pair of boots.

He particularly enjoyed stealing glances at his riding partner. He did so, however, only when she was looking elsewhere, which she did far more than not. After her first disappointed look at his extravagant dress, she paid little attention to him. Instead, she focused on the road, on the woods beyond, on the small grouping of stone buildings that constituted the nearby village, and then on sheep huddled on a hillside. Her eyes went frequently to the woods that lined a river and climbed upward.

It all looked peaceful enough, even tranquil, except for the occasional men in red uniforms patrolling the road and searching each wagon that passed. Locking the door after the horses escaped. Ogilvy was long gone from these parts, but they might well be looking for a man with a new wound.

Which reminded him of his own arm. Alister would

disapprove if he knew what Rory was doing. And his own pain told him this was not wise. But he had seen the wistful look on Bethia's face. God in heaven, but he knew what it was like to be a pariah in one's own home. She needed some freedom, or she would wither like a piece of fruit left too long alone and neglected.

He looked at her, something inside responding to the blush on her cheeks, the way her hair escaped the neat cap she wore. Her back was straighter, her face relaxed for the first time since she'd come to Braemoor. She had done nothing to conceal the sprinkling of freckles across her nose, and that pleased him. Most other ladies would have powdered them over.

Rory found himself aching to reach out and touch them.

Even as he restrained himself from touching or even engaging her in conversation, he relished the simple companionship of riding next to someone who obviously also enjoyed the day . . . and riding. She radiated regal defiance in the way she sat her horse, in the sometimes disdainful look she gave him, her gaze flicking over his outrageous clothes.

She was an excellent rider. Not knowing her level of skill, he had selected a sedate but pretty mare. The mare he'd brought in earlier still had some mending to do. But from the second he helped her into the saddle, he knew she was a natural horsewoman. His respect had only increased as they quickened their pace. She looked as if she belonged on a horse, moving gracefully in the side-saddle.

And her touch? She was not wearing gloves, and the heat of her skin seemed to burn into his. It still did, and that told him more than any instruction from his brain that this was a very foolish thing to do. He knew his hand had lingered a moment too long on her leg once he had helped her up into the saddle. Yet she had not pulled away. Instead, her hands had jerked on the reins and the mare had quickly moved away. It had not been acciden-

tal, he knew, nor lack of control. She had not wanted his
hand on her.

His wife, and she obviously detested him. But was not
that what he wanted?

Despite such humbling thoughts, he quietly appreciated her obvious pleasure in the ride. Her dark-blue eyes
were alive with interest, and he sensed she was mentally
cataloguing every foot of the way for future reference.

As he watched her, he decided to make her brother's
freedom a priority. He would have to be careful, though,
and must be prepared for Cumberland's wrath when his
"wife" disappeared with the young hostage. And it must
all be done by the Black Knave.

She looked over at him when they slowed their horses
to a trot. "I would like to meet the woman who grows
the herbs."

The woman who grew the herbs was also the one who
was thought to be his mistress. "Why?" he asked after a
moment's surprise.

"Do you not believe a wife has the right to know her
husband's paramour?"

Surprised, he raised an eyebrow. "I did not think you
cared, my sweet."

Her face flushed. "You flatter yourself. I would like
to know about the herbs she used. I used to help with
healing at . . . my home."

He mulled that over in his mind. The last thing he
wanted was for Bethia to meet Mary. Women had a way
of gleaning information. She would probably know in a
moment there was little between him and Mary other than
friendship.

"My wife will not engage in such activities," he said
haughtily. "It is not fitting."

She glared at him rebelliously. "It *is* fitting, I assume,
to parade your mistress in front of your wife?"

"I am touched by your continuing interest in my . . .
affairs."

"I am not interested. I care not what you do. Just do not tell me *my* behavior is not *fitting*."

He arched an eyebrow. "I merely wish to help you, to instruct you in proper behavior. I understand some of the northern clans . . . are not well civilized."

Her eyes grew dark with fury. "And the Forbeses are? You lived in filth. And you, my lord, are . . . not admired. No such laird in the Highlands would last a fortnight."

"They do not exist at all now, my lady, or have you not looked recently? Their ways led them into extinction." He said the cold, cruel words even as they bit into his heart. They were among the hardest he'd ever said, but he needed the gauntlet between them. If he lowered his guard even a fraction of an inch, he suspected he would then be lost. He wanted her, damn it. He wanted her too much. Far too much. It was all, in fact, he could do not to snatch her from her saddle and hold her in his arms, to see whether she tasted as sweet as she smelled, whether she was as soft as she looked, whether the emotion that burned in her eyes could burn for him.

Bloody hell, but he sounded like a bleating poor poet.

He took her into town, to the butcher's, when she asked him. He helped her down from her mount just as the butcher ran out, his apron flapping as he noticed the visitors.

"My lord, my lady, what an honor." Then his mouth creased into a frown, and naked fear came into his eyes. "Is something wrong? The meat I sent?"

"It was very fine," Bethia said softly, with only the second smile Rory had seen. The first had been for the puppy she'd held earlier in the day. The smile lit her face, and suddenly the butcher was stammering. Rory had heard from Alister that villagers had been fuming about the wedding with a Jacobite, but the butcher was obviously melting under her smile.

He had a very sudden and intense need to have it shine on him.

"It was *adequate*," Rory corrected with pursed lips.

His bride did not look at him. "I wanted to thank you for such good service," she said.

The butcher puffed up with importance, but then he eyed Rory with hostility. "But payment is always late. Mayhap my lady . . ."

Rory glared down at him with all the haughty indignation a man of his character, or lack of it, should be able to muster. "You dare question our payment?"

The man took a step backward. "I . . . I . . ."

Bethia gave Rory a quelling look, then turned back to the butcher. "You will be paid promptly."

The butcher gave her a look of profound gratitude even as his gaze avoided Rory's.

"We must go, wife," Rory said, his tone hardening. She sent him a challenging look. She knew—or thought— he would have to honor her promise.

Ignoring the butcher, he took his wife's arm and led her back to her mare, helping her easily back into the saddle, then he mounted, too.

"I have learned one thing today," he said.

"Aye?"

"I must keep you away from butchers."

Her chin went up. "He and his family have to live, too."

"He is a bachelor, and he lives very well, thanks to overcharging us."

She shot a quick, searching look toward him. "How do you know? Neil said he kept the household books."

"I usually know more than people credit," he said. "I suggest you remember that." He allowed a shade of menace to shade the words. "And I would also suggest that you not try to enlist the support of my people to do me damage."

She was unimpressed. "I had no such intention," she said airily, the lie obvious in her face.

"Did you not, madam?"

"No. I wish merely to do my duty as the marchioness.

I asked Neil if I can do the household accounts. He appears very busy with other matters."

Rory said nothing. Neil had not mentioned it to him.

"I kept them at our home," she continued determinedly.

"Why do you want to do anything for the Forbes?"

"I am not used to being idle."

"Is that why you were scrubbing windows like a servant?"

"No one else would do it," she said tartly. "I am not accustomed to laziness as you seem to be."

"I did not marry a servant."

"Nay, you married an enemy," she retorted. " 'Tis quite obvious you consider me one, since you did not want me to attend your wound. I did not realize I terrorized you so."

"You are a Jacobite, are you not?" he said, and this time he could not keep a note of amusement from his voice.

She drew herself up proudly in the saddle. "Aye."

"I heard they were treacherous."

"You are assigning your own traits to those far nobler than yourself."

He almost laughed out loud at the fast retort. He enjoyed her wit and only wished he could see how far it went. However, he'd already stepped too far out of character. Elizabeth had warned him about that, about how careful he had to be in maintaining a role. Only *he* didn't have to worry about the disfavor of a theater audience; he had to worry about keeping his neck intact.

"I think it is time to return," he said, turning his horse back toward Braemoor.

"The truth is uncomfortable?"

" 'Tis your truth, not mine," he said, "and I would be most careful about bantering it around."

Her eyes narrowed. "Always threats, my lord. But I heard you ran from Culloden Moor."

He shrugged. "I care not what you heard. You are in my household and you will do as I order."

"You are a bully and coward."

"I am lord, and you will do well to remember that. I do have certain rights."

His meaning was clear, and he watched her mouth thin, the anger in her eyes grow more baleful. He watched as she struggled against her natural impulse to fight back.

He did not wish to prolong her agony. He tightened his legs around his mount and quickened into a trot, where no speech was possible. For a moment he was aware that he was alone.

Rory did not look back. He knew she would join him. She had no choice. Her brother's life was at risk.

But he was very aware of the cost to her.

He would make it up to her one day.

If he lived that long.

If she had a pistol, she would have used it.

He obviously enjoyed baiting her. Every time she thought there might be a thread of decency in him, he seemed to delight in trampling the notion, making her feel like a fool for ever thinking he had even one good quality.

She wondered now at his motives for bringing her today. Was it merely to demonstrate his power? His control? To show her it was impossible to try to escape his world?

If so, he had served only to fuel her determination to somehow get her brother and leave Scotland. As long as the marriage was never consummated, as long as it had not been officiated by a Catholic priest, she could get it annulled. She could not remain married to the arrogant popinjay. Still, she wondered why he had not demanded his husbandly rights. Despite his earlier words that he found her unattractive, she'd seen a gleam in his eyes several times when he'd looked at her. She recognized lust when she saw it. How long before he would break his word?

She had to get her brother and escape before that happened. For if he took her, and there was a babe, she would never have her freedom. She would be bound by honor to stay. She had no such bond now.

An idea had been playing around in her head. Everything she'd heard about the Black Knave had been contradictory. He was short. He was tall. He was old. He was young. He was a man. He was a woman. The only consistency was that he left a card after each of his feats. She did not know whether it was to taunt the authorities or give comfort to those who sought him out.

If no one knew who he was, or what he was, mayhap *she* could become the Black Knave.

'Twas a wild idea, and she knew it. How would she ever get out of the castle? Obtain a horse? Receive the help she needed? It was common knowledge that the Knave did have people helping him. But how to find them? Even a huge reward had not produced anyone willing to give him up.

She watched as her husband nearly disappeared from view. She looked toward the woods that would hide an army, then back toward the Marquis of Braemoor. Patience, she told herself. Patience. Wait and learn. And she would start gathering the items she needed.

With hope and even excitement churning inside her, she flicked her reins and trailed after her temporary lord.

Rory threw the reins of his horses to one of the stable hands. He went to help his wife dismount, but she had already slipped from the saddle, obviously reluctant to accept his assistance.

He wanted to take the horses inside the barn, to cool them himself, but once again that would go against his role as the lazy, arrogant new lord. He used to see to his own mount, but then no one offered to do it for him. His new wealth gave him a reason for an arrogance he'd never displayed before. He had been careless and undisciplined, but he'd not been irresponsible. There was, he hoped, a difference.

He had to convince his cousin now that he was all

three. He wanted to exert authority without Neil understanding that he was doing just that.

The current Marquis of Braemoor would care less
about his wife.

Rory strode into the tower house. He'd retained Neil as
estate manager, the position his cousin had held under Rory's
father. He knew exactly what Neil thought of him, and Rory
felt little better about his cousin. He was six years older
than Rory and had been Donald's friend. They had both
been contemptuous of the small, lonely boy and had alter-
nated between bullying and ignoring him. It was ironic that
now he was the marquis and Neil was dependent upon him.

At the same time, Rory was uncomfortably aware that
Neil had more claim to Braemoor than he. He had Forbes
blood where Rory had none, if the tales were true, and
nearly every family member knew it. Neil had also served
the Forbeses for years, whereas Rory had never served
them at all. He did not blame the man for despising him.

If Rory had his way, he would leave Braemoor with
all its bad memories to Neil. But there were too many
people still depending on him. He had not finished with
the good King George, or Cumberland.

Neil was in the office, as expected. He looked up as
Rory came in, sniffing disdainfully at the air in the room.

"Rory?" Neil seldom acknowledged Rory's title, and
then only in the presence of others outside the clan.

"My wife would like to start keeping the household
accounts."

Surprise flickered in Neil's dark brown eyes. "I did
not realize you cared what your wife thought." It was an
obvious reference to Mary's visit.

Rory struck an indolent pose and shrugged. "Cumberland wants her with child. A contented wife is more likely
to achieve that result, or so I am told."

"Contented?" Neil came out of his chair with a start.
"You would hand over these accounts to make her *content*?"

"Why not? 'Tis nothing important."

Neil's face grew red. "Mayhap you would like her to take over all my duties."

"Nay, I think not," Rory said mildly. "And why do you care? You still have the properties to manage, and that is a far larger duty," he said. "Anyone can keep the account books."

Neil settled back into the chair, a perplexed look on his face. "I do not understand you."

"That is not required," Rory said casually. "You know I have little interest in business matters. But 'tis only right that the marchioness take over her proper duties. You must admit she has already improved the tower house considerably."

"I never heard you complain."

"I avoided Braemoor for years. Its disrepair was one of the reasons."

"Too bad you do not continue to avoid it."

Rory smiled. "Do not vex me overmuch, cousin. You look after the estates well, and I have not interfered with that. But do not push me or question my activities."

Neil bristled with indignation. "Dear God, Rory. It is time for you to grow up."

Rory eyed him coldly. "And deprive you of the authority you enjoy so much? I would not dream of it."

Neil's mouth curled. "I have *no* authority when you can whisk it away at your whim."

"Aye, you are right," Rory replied. "So tread carefully."

Neil made a visible effort to control his temper in face of Rory's challenge. "I still do not understand why you wish to turn over the household accounts to . . . the marchioness. Has the lass bewitched you?"

"Hardly. She is as plain as a post, and those freckles . . . she takes no care at all in covering them." He shuddered with distaste. "Still, I want as much peace as possible, and it is little enough to let her busy her hands with the tower house." His voice grew colder. "And it is not your place to criticize her or question my motives."

Neil glowered at him. "How long can we anticipate

your presence this time . . . my lord." He made the title
an insult.

Rory decided to ignore it. He had dug in his spurs deep,
and he was ashamed of it. "My arm is still stiff from that
encounter with the brigand. Still, I promised a certain captain in Edinburgh a chance to win his money back."

"You seemed to have no trouble in helping the lady
mount."

"Ah, my dear cousin, 'tis all in the cause of being a
gentleman. I do not expect you believed such a day would
come."

Neil muttered something.

"I'm sorry, dear boy, I did not hear that. Would you
care to repeat it?"

Neil met his gaze directly, and the enmity between
them ran deep and dangerous. Rory knew he should not
bait Neil, and worse he did not even know why he did
it. His role as fool? Or the bitter memories of Neil's silence when Donald used to taunt him, "Bastard, bastard."
He wondered now whether Neil had been silent because
he himself had been a bastard.

"I know you will help my wife in every way," he said
after a moment's silence. Then he turned and walked out
the door.

Do not be impatient. Bethia repeated those words to herself as she lifted a wriggling Black Jack into her hands
for an adventure outside.

And yet it was hard not to be, as ideas tumbled through
her mind. She knew exactly what she had to do. Clothes,
cards, a weapon, a horse. If she could sneak out of Braemoor in a lad's clothes and mix with people in a tavern,
mayhap she could discover someone loyal to the Black
Knave.

She would have to be back by morning. The timing
would be everything. And if she could find someone with
information, she would leave word that a lass in trouble
needed him. In the meantime, she needed to find a place

so lonely and secret that she could go there on a regular
basis and await him.

If he did not show, mayhap she would learn of those
who might be sympathetic to his cause. She could then
pretend to be the Knave herself and ask for help in free-
ing her brother.

Dougal. The very thought of him alone in a cold, hostile place sent ripples of fear through her. He would not
be obedient. He had his brothers' own wild, bold courage.

Her fingers caught in a fist. She was a MacDonell. She
would free him. She would free them both.

She went down the stone staircase, the pup in hand.
Once outside, she went to the stable, flashing her smile at
one of the stablelads. "I would like to meet the horses,"
she said, still holding little Black Jack. She did not want
him to run under one of the stable doors and startle a horse.

The lad was looking at the pup curiously. "You be the
one who took the runt."

"Aye."

The boy's face split in a wide grin. "I wanted to take
'im, but my fa said we had no use for a weakling. But
he was my favorite."

Bethia knew instantly she had an ally, a friend. "You
can come and see him anytime you wish," she told him.

The boy's brows furrowed. "In the tower, my lady?"

"Aye."

"I do not think my fa would approve."

"Well, then, I will talk to him." She eyed him critically. His clothes were rough, worn and far too small. His
arms and legs stuck out like those of a scarecrow, like
sticks.

She knew how she was going to get the clothes she
needed.

All she needed was control of the household funds.

And then the cards. She knew how to get those, too.

"Now tell me," she said to the boy, "which are the
fastest horses?"

en

Rory gratefully took the heavy wig from his head and poured French brandy into a crystal goblet. The brandy was exceptional, a gift from the French sea captain who'd been smuggling his refugees to France. It had come through Elizabeth who, until now, had dealt with the man.

He stared at the rich color of the brandy. It was time to make a new bargain; he had at least two more cargoes for the man. Rory had decided to deal with him directly this time. He'd already involved Elizabeth far too deeply, and the risks to all of them had soared since his raid on the gaol. The Black Knave was wanted nearly as badly as Prince Charles.

Two more shipments would require a great deal of money. Until now, his gambling winnings had paid his costs. But they were running low. He may soon have to dip into Braemoor funds. Part of him found the idea ironic. Another part thought it thievery and he found himself loath to do so.

He had never wanted anything from Braemoor. If it had not been for the first tattered little group of refugees, he probably would have left Braemoor for good. The memories were too haunting.

He still didn't know why he had heeded his father's call to join his forces at Culloden. One last effort, he thought, to gain his father's approval. A final opportunity to prove himself a Forbes. But then the reality of the battlefield, the bloodthirsty savagery of his father and brother had drained any vestige of family loyalty, any longing to belong.

He ran his fingers through his hair. Damp with sweat from the bloody wig, it curled around his fingers. He undid the waistcoat, the stock, then jerked open the front of his shirt. He poured more brandy into the glass before sitting and sprawling over the chair.

His arm ached. But something else ached even more. He was not sure how many more encounters he could survive with his marchioness before grabbing her and making her truly his. He winced as he thought of her reaction.

The only solution was another absence.

He still had to get Ogilvy on that ship.

He was mulling over the afternoon with Bethia when he heard a knock on the door. He rose and went to answer it. All his servants had instructions never to enter without permission.

Rory opened it and saw his wife. He bowed slightly, keeping his surprise to himself. "My lady. You surprise me."

He watched her bite her lip. "I . . . I . . ."

He decided not to help her. He did not think the Marquis of Braemoor would care about her discomfort.

"They say . . . you are a gambler."

"Aye, an exceptional one," he replied with a lack of modesty.

"Would you teach me?"

"Women do not game." He said it with absolute authority.

She narrowed her eyes in disbelief.

"Not . . . ladies," he amended. *Of course, they gamed.* Elizabeth was really quite his own match.

"I have nothing to do here."

He looked down at the pup who was tottering around, investigating a pair of boots.

"You have the pup. And now, as you wished, you have the household accounts."

Something flashed in her eyes. It was not gratitude. Instead, it was almost sly.

She tried to cover it with a quick curtsey. "Thank you, my lord."

"You may have made an enemy. Neil was not pleased."

"Then why did you agree?"

"I enjoy watching him squirm."

"Why?"

He shrugged. "It does not matter now."

Her gaze seemed to pierce through him. "Will you teach me?"

He shrugged. He dug in a drawer and produced a pair of dice.

"I would rather use cards."

He would happily wager his new waistcoat that she had something more nefarious in mind than a simple game of cards.

Nonetheless, he returned to the wardrobe and opened the drawer again, taking out a deck of cards. He held out a chair for her, then dropped into one of his own.

"Do you have money, my lady?"

"Will you take my pledge?"

"Can you be trusted?"

"Nay."

"Ah, a quality I admire. Then this one time. Now, madam, this is casino . . ."

He dealt two cards at a time, four cards facedown for each of them, then four faceup. The jack of spades stared up at him. He looked up just in time to see quick interest in her eyes before she lowered them, thick, dark lashes shading indigo-blue eyes. Suddenly tension shimmered between them. Awareness.

Rory was only too aware that he was without wig or

obnoxious coat. He tired to make his eyes vapid, but he
did not think they quite reached that desirable effect.
How could they when she sat on the other side of the
table, her mouth pursed up in concentration and those
bloody freckles frosting her nose? Why were they so
damned fascinating?

He continued his explanation, wishing he had a handkerchief to flutter, or a wig to finger. He had never felt
so bloody naked in his life. Her frequent quick glances
did nothing to alleviate the feeling.

She was quick. Astonishingly quick. He won the first
game but she took the second. Her eyes were bright, her
movements sure, her decisions fast.

Bethia took the third game, then the fourth. He was
letting her win although she might have bested him at
least once on her own. He was supposed to be a boast-
ful lackwit, not a cardsharp. He allowed his frown to
deepen, even though he was pleased to find a way to give
her money.

Bethia did not understand it. She could barely take her
gaze from him.

She had previously noticed that without his wig and
dreadful clothes, he was not entirely unattractive. But her
own fear and grief had kept her from seeing, or retain-
ing, more.

Now her gaze was drawn to him. His dark, thick hair
was cropped shorter than custom, probably since he wore
a wig so often. But it was quite . . . pleasing the way one
lock fell over his forehead. Without the wig covering part
of the face, she could see the strong, angular lines of his
cheeks.

The room seemed smaller in some way. Much smaller.
She felt heat from across the table and she looked up to
see fire in his eyes. Not only fire, but intelligence. The
amber in them glowed, and the gray-green color seemed
to come alive. She felt her body reacting to the moment
of heat. She leaned forward, compelled by a fascination,

an attraction, that sent waves of uncertainty, then something of a more physical nature, through her. Bethia felt
mesmerized, swept into a force she did not understand.

She could not be attracted to this . . . fop, this gambler,
this man many called coward. And yet she could not tear
her gaze away from him.

Then his lips moved, curving into the supercilious smile
she hated. The light—the fire—faded, yet this time she
knew she had seen it. It had not been her imagination.
There was far more behind that facade than he wanted
anyone to know.

Why?

And what was it? Calculation? Greed? Or did he just
delight in irritating everyone, using a jester's tricks to
protect his real motives? But what were they?

They were suspect, whatever they were. Still, she ached
in places that had never ached before and the cool room
felt overheated. She suspected that when she stood, her
legs would not work properly.

Remember why you are here.

"I have something to ask of you," she finally said with
a voice that didn't sound like hers.

He cocked one of those dark, bushy eyebrows.

"Some of your servants appear very poorly clothed.
I . . . I . . . would like to purchase some material for new
clothes." She was stammering. She never stammered.

He looked at her for a moment, his gaze weighing her.
She could not determine what his conclusion was. "You
care about how the Forbeses are dressed?"

"The boy who works in the stable looks like a beggar. So do others. It does no honor to Braemoor any more
than the filth I found here."

"And now you care about our honor?"

"I care about the boy." She heard the passion in her
voice and was immediately shamed by it. It should be
there for the lad; instead, it was there for her own benefit. The boy will benefit, too, she told herself. As would
others.

"What other improvements would you make?" he asked silkily.

"The crofts looked in need of repair," she said heedlessly. "You could use a better cook."

"Aye, but then what would we do with the present one? She has a family."

Astonishment struck her. 'Twas the last thing she suspected him to say. She was surprised he even knew the cook had a family, much less cared.

"I can find her something else."

"'Tis done, then. Do what you will. I will tell Neil to give you whatever funds you need."

"For the boy, too, and others who need clothing?"

His gaze met hers. "Aye, as long as you do not bother me with it. I have more important matters."

"Like gaming?"

"Aye."

"And your paramour?"

"That, too," he said, challenging her.

"I may have to go into the village for material."

"Do I have your word you will not try to run away?"

"How could I? I am your wife."

"And I am your lord, and of course you will obey me in all things."

It was not a question, but a statement. She chose not to reply.

"Do I have your word? The word of a MacDonell?" he persisted.

"About what?" She wriggled around the question.

"If I give you freedom of movement, the freedom to go into the village, will you behave as the Marchioness of Braemoor should? You will not try to leave . . . the marriage?"

"Where would I go? You still have my brother as hostage."

"Cumberland has him. Not I. And you are skating around the question."

A lie? An oath taken but never meant to be observed?
Where did honor lie?

"I see the question gives you pause, my wife. Does
that mean that you have plans I should know about?"

She felt red creeping into her cheeks. She had always
been a poor liar, and this fool, this Scottish traitor, obviously saw right through her. His suspicions could destroy
everything.

Your brother's life is at stake.

She would willingly stay if she could free her brother,
get him out of Scotland and into France where other Jacobites would care for him. She would not be violating
her oath then, and her own happiness would be a small
price to pay. Happiness was, in fact, a rare commodity in
Scotland today.

"Aye," she said finally. "You have my word. For now."

His eyes narrowed as if he were gauging her credi-
bility. "Now?"

"That is all I can give you."

He suddenly smiled, an ironic twist of his lips. "Fair
enough. I trust you will give me warning when you consider the bargain over."

"I swear," she added. She was surprised at the smile;
even more so at his concession.

"I'll tell the stable hands that you are allowed to ride
the mare you rode today," he said. "I would suggest, however, that you ride with someone. Jacobites are not pop-
ular these days."

Excitement surged through Bethia. It was even more
than she'd ever imagined. She lowered her eyes. "Thank
you."

"Do not abuse my good nature," he said, yawning. He
stood as if weary of the conversation, and scooped up
the cards.

"My lord?"

"Something else?" he said with exasperation, his mouth
pursed in annoyance.

"The cards. I would like to practice."

"You have already bested me," he said. "I do not believe you need practice."

"It will help pass time."

He looked down at Black Jack, who had been sleeping but who had clumsily stumbled to his feet when Rory had scraped back his chair. The pup was busy watering the leg of the table. "Between runts and stableboys, you seem to find much to occupy yourself."

"The evenings are often long."

He tossed the deck down, and she scooped them up, then stood.

"Are you not going to take your winnings?"

She looked down at the coins lying on the table. "I had no money of my own."

"The first rule of a gambler, my lady, is always take your winnings regardless of how you came about them."

She did not know what she saw in his eyes. Amusement? Speculation? He might well be laughing at her.

But money was power, and she had precious little of either. She scooped up the money, hoping there would not be an unexpected consequence accompanying it.

"Madam?"

She turned.

"Good night," he said with a mocking bow.

Her stomach turned inside out. She suddenly had the terrible feeling she had made a bargain with the devil, and she had no comprehension of the price he would exact.

Rory watched her go and wondered what in the hell she was thinking.

No good.

He knew that. He knew it by the rush of blood in her cheeks. He knew it by the cordiality she'd tried so hard to maintain.

His new wife certainly hadn't come to his bedroom to learn how to play a game of chance. He just wasn't quite sure exactly what she wanted.

Was it only more control of Braemoor? More freedom? Better clothing for his kinsmen?

He doubted all of those. He had seen something deep
in her eyes. He was well used to reading emotions. All
good gamblers were, and he was a very good gambler.
He could tell by the movement of a body whether someone was bluffing. Or lying.

His lady wife was lying.

God's breath, but he wearied of lies, his own as well
as those of others. He wondered how long he could keep
up the masquerade—not that he had kept it very well this
evening. He'd let his guard down several times, and he
suspected that she realized there was more to Rory Forbes,
the Marquis of Braemoor, than he'd ever intended her to
know.

Still, he felt quite proud of himself that he had kept
his hands to himself when she'd smiled with delight at
winning at casino, when she'd pleaded for a young lad,
when she'd demonstrated her mettle in warring with Neil.

He also remembered her hesitation before she gave
him her oath. She was making a mental reservation.

He would have to keep a close eye on her. But that
might be even more dangerous than letting her run loose
to spread havoc.

She had looked so appealing, so enticing. The fact that
she did not realize it made her appeal that much stronger.
He sighed. He had wanted to run his fingers through her
dark hair. Even worse, his gaze had kept going to the
nape of her neck. He wondered how it tasted. He wondered how she would react.

Emotion ran rampant in her. He saw it in her eagerness today on horseback, in the pleasure with which she
sniffed the air and cared little whether her hair tumbled
down. He saw it in the way she'd rested her head on her
hands as she considered her choices in casino and when
he'd allowed her to win. He often lost several hands purposely before plucking his opponent. He was as skilled
at losing as he was at winning.

He wondered now, though, who had been plucked tonight. He took another sip of brandy, stirred the coals in the fireplace and sat staring at the flames.

Alister greeted him cordially when Rory stopped by the village smithy the next day.

"Two of our horses need shoeing."

"Aye, my lord," he said, using the pump to fan the flames. He picked up a piece of metal with tongs and easily twisted it into the shape of a shoe.

Rory leaned against a wall and watched his quick, competent movements. Alister would be valuable anywhere. He had a quick mind as well as quick hands.

"How is the marchioness?" Alister asked, as if he knew exactly what was on Rory's mind.

"Fair enough."

"Are you speaking of her health or her physical features?"

"Both," Rory admitted wryly. "Like most bridegrooms, I had no idea what I was getting into."

"John told me about her visit to the shop. Fairly bursting with pride, he was."

"She appears to have that effect on people. Braemoor is actually being swept."

Alister opened his eyes in mock alarm. "Swept?"

"Aye. The food has already improved; she has washed the windows, and we can actually see from them again. And her latest crusade, after saving a runt puppy, is clothing my clansmen."

"And how does Neil feel about this?"

"He resents it mightily, as he resents anything about me and mine."

"Mine?"

"A figure of speech."

Alister gave him a crooked grin. "So you say." Then his expression sobered. "You will have to make a trip to the coast near Portsoy. A ship will be there in three days for Ogilvy and others. They will be wanting payment. Unless, of course, you want me to go."

"I fear your absence would be noted far more than mine," Rory said. "You are too good a smith."

"Your arm?"

"Sore, nothing more."

"You have never . . . quite collapsed like that before. You worried us both."

"I will try not to go three days without sleep again."

"You cannot keep this up forever."

"I know," Rory said. "Mayhap the hunt for Jacobites will lessen."

Alister looked dubious. "You canna save them all."

"No, but there is still Ogilvy and others waiting passage, and a young lad imprisoned by Cumberland."

"Have you said anything to the lady about him?"

"Nay. 'Tis best that she know nothing."

"When will you go to the coast?"

"On the morn. Try to watch the marchioness. I think she might be planning some mischief."

"But she is staying inside Braemoor."

"I gave her permission to leave."

Alister bent over his forge. "Was that wise?"

"I could not keep her prisoner forever. I think as long as the boy is in Cumberland's hands, she will not do anything to risk his safety."

"Then . . . ?"

"I *think*. I cannot be sure. But I saw the pleasure on her face today when we were riding. I could not deprive her of it."

"You have a soft heart."

Rory groaned. "Nay. I merely want—"

"I know. To pull the tiger's tail. Trouble is, you always hang on too long."

"You are always in back of me," Rory said with warm affection.

"All the way to the scaffold, I think."

"I will not let that happen."

Alister leaned over the forge rather than answering. They both knew that Rory might not have a choice in the matter.

Terror. Terror greater than she'd ever known before thundered through Bethia.

She and Dougal were running, fleeing from some unknown evil along a bank. 'Twas night, and clouds masked the moon and stars. She could see little, but she heard the sound of hoofbeats behind her and it spurred both of them to quicken their pace.

Then Dougal fell, rolling down the bank into something dark and forbidding. A bog. When she reached for him, she fell down, and they were both sucked into its quicksand. Terror seized her as they sank deeper and deeper. She cried for help, over and over again. But there was no one, not even the hoofbeats that had followed them. There were only the shadows of a moonless night and forbidding sight of bare branches bending in a strong wind.

She sank lower and lower as she struggled to keep her brother's head above water. Then, when she believed they both would surely die, a man appeared. His face was masked and he was dressed totally in black. He tied a rope around a tree, then around himself, and he used it to approach them. He reached out to her, but she could not touch him. He was an inch away, only an inch, but she could not reach him. . . .

She woke. Her body was wet, her hair tangled and damp. The bedclothes were twisted around her. Her breathing was swift and hard. She forced herself to relax. There was no bog. No stranger. Dougal was safe, although miles away.

Or was he? Was that what the nightmare had tried to tell her?

And the stranger. Had he been the pursuer? Or the savior?

She looked toward the window. Light was streaming

into the room. It must be late, much later than she usually slept.

Bethia looked into the basket next to the bed. Black Jack was squirming around, whimpering. Probably for food.

She picked up the puppy, running her fingers over the soft fuzz of his skin. Just that gesture slowed the beat of her heart, the pounding in her head. The overwhelming sense of panic slowly faded from her.

She stood and went over to the table where Trilby had placed a bowl of fresh water the evening before. Using a piece of linen cloth, she washed her face, hoping to wash away the remnants of the nightmare.

Did dreams have meanings?

She usually did not dream at all, or at least none she remembered. So what had brought this one on?

And where was Trilby?

As if her very thought had summoned the girl, a light, tentative knock came at the door.

Bethia went over and opened it. Trilby held a tray, laden with fresh pastries, a tankard of chocolate, and a small pitcher of milk intended, Bethia knew, for the puppy.

"I looked in on you earlier," Trilby said, "but you were so deep in sleep I thought to wait."

"Wait?"

"The marquis has left Braemoor," Trilby said apologetically with a sly grin. "He left this note for you."

Her maid had expressed no surprise that the marquis seldom shared her bed, but obviously Bethia's presence in his room had been noted, and Trilby's eyes were openly curious.

He was gone. Again. Bethia did not understand the sudden sense of loss that she felt. Even disappointment. In her mind's eye, she recalled how appealing he'd looked last night without the wig, without the frilled, brightly colored waistcoats.

But that was who he was. A popinjay and libertine who sought out the company of other women.

She slowly looked at the note. *"As I promised, Madam, I have given instructions to John, the head groom, that you be allowed to take out Miss Fancy. I have also talked to Neil about your authority over the household accounts."*

He'd signed it with an extravagant brandish, *"Your husband."* Not his name. Not Rory, or Rory, Lord Forbes. Or Braemoor. For a moment she thought that strange, as if he were denying the title or his own position.

It was her imagination. He was merely asserting his authority, flouting his power in her face, even while giving her only a breath of freedom. As long as Cumberland held her brother, she had no real freedom.

"A love note?" Trilby said hopefully.

Bethia shook her head. "Just . . . some instructions."

Trilby's face fell. In just a few weeks, Trilby had become dear to Bethia. She had an unflagging optimism that usually lit the room, and she was humbly grateful to make the extra money that came with being a lady's maid.

"Here, help me feed Jack," she said, trying to take her maid's mind, and her own, away from the enigmatic man who was her husband.

Jack had progressed from the glove to lapping milk from a small saucer. Trilby filled the saucer with milk, and together they watched the little terrier greedily lap it up. It would not be long before he could have gruel or cereal.

"I did not believe you could save the wee creature," Trilby said with admiration.

"He has a will to live."

"Aye," Trilby said. "Would you like me to leave while you eat?"

"Will you join me? There is far too much food."

"It would not be proper, milady."

"I do not care about proper. I care about good company."

Trilby flushed with pride.

"Sit then," Bethia said, watching as the maid self-consciously sat across from her and hesitantly picked up a sweet. Bethia had not realized how pretty the girl was. In the past several weeks, she had transformed herself, picking up some of Bethia's own habits. She now washed her hair, and it had lightened the color to the shade of wheat. Bethia had had two dresses made for her, and she kept them clean. The girl's posture was straight, her eyes lively now with pride.

"It is good," she said, licking sugar from her lips.

Not very, Bethia thought. But better than when she'd first arrived. The servants were beginning to take care, even pride, in their duties.

Bethia only nibbled on hers, though she enjoyed the hot chocolate. Her mind kept reliving the dream, then the hours she'd spent with her husband. Did one thing have to do with the other? Had she been running from the marquis?

Yet he seemed the last person to run from. Ineffective. Careless. Indifferent to Braemoor and his people. She surmised that the reason he'd allowed her to dress the servants better was simply to keep her occupied, not out of any deep concern for his own people.

Where had he gone this time?

And why did she care?

Eleven

The Sail and Wheel Tavern in Aberdeen was dark, moldy and dirty. The candles were smoky, the ale poor and the tables stained and scarred.

Rory paused at the door, adjusting his eyes to the dim interior. He had been here several previous times, each in a different disguise. Now he wore an English captain's uniform, and a bushy dark mustache perched over his lips. The English had been looking for an old man, a young man in peasant's clothes, and even a woman. As far as he knew, they were not yet looking for an English captain.

All heads turned. Their whiskey-fogged eyes stared at him dully as he walked in. Some of the patrons spat on the floor as he passed them. He went up to one of the barmaids, patted her bottom and leered, then asked whether a gentleman was awaiting a Mister Smythe.

The woman looked at his captain's insignia, then tucked her arm into his.

"There be a man waitin' in a room upstairs."

"The private room?"

She widened her eyes. The room was usually meant for assignations, and few but regulars knew of it. Her gaze became more curious, more greedy. "Would you like a bit of a tumble after yer business?" She was eyeing him with a great deal more interest now. If he were meeting with a French sailor, it meant smuggling. It meant money.

"We will see," he said.

"Do ye need me tae show the way?"

"I think not," he said in his best English accent. Since he had frequented the tavern previously, Rory knew of the private room upstairs. The tavern was one of those places where few questions were asked and few faces remembered. It was perfect for a French smuggler or an English officer if they were trying to arrange an assignation, a bit of smuggling or some other nefarious activity.

He went up the stairs and found the room on his right. He knocked lightly and the door opened, revealing a tall man with a strong build, dressed carelessly in the nondescript garb of a ship's mate.

His eyes widened at the uniform, and his hand went toward a table with a sword lying on it.

But Rory was quicker. He moved swiftly, pulling a pistol from inside his coat.

"I would not advise that, Captain Renard."

The captain's gaze studied him, then dropped his arm to his side. "You know who I am."

"Ah, yes. Rene Renard. At least, that is the name you use." Rory flipped a card in his direction.

Renard caught it easily, glanced at it, then back to Rory, before showing a wide smile. "Monsieur. I did not expect the Black Knave himself. Especially in that uniform."

"'Tis only borrowed," Rory said.

Renard started to laugh. "And how, monsieur, did you know I am Renard?"

"Our mutual acquaintance described you well," Rory said, not wanting the man to know he had actually seen him earlier. Renard had been Elizabeth's suggestion. She'd once been his mistress and had retained him as a friend as she had Rory. She had once pointed him out to Rory when both were in a tavern.

Renard was reliable, she'd said, and even more important, he had sympathy for the Jacobite refugees. His honor was involved, and he would fight before sacrificing his human cargo.

But he *was* rather insistent on receiving his fee.

This time Rory had wanted to meet him in person, to judge his mettle.

"Ah, the lovely lady. She is well?"

"Very." Rory tucked the pistol back under his coat.

"She plays dangerous games."

"So do you, Captain." Rory felt immensely reassured that the man knew not to mention names. "My last shipment?"

"Safe," the French captain said. "I expect they are in Paris now." He hesitated, then added, "You are the *true* Black Knave?"

Rory shrugged.

"You speak like an English aristocrat."

"I can play one as well as an old fisherman."

"And a woman, I heard."

At Rory's frown, he shrugged. "I do hear gossip, monsieur. Rest assured, I wish to know nothing more. Now, do you have the money?"

"Aye. One thousand pounds. Five hundred for this trip, five hundred for another next month."

"And the cargo on this trip?"

"Four men, three women, six children."

The Frenchman pulled out a map and spread it on the table. He pointed out a spot on the coast between Portsoy and Cullen. "Tomorrow night. Two hours after midnight. I will have a boat already ashore. I will not wait more than an hour."

Rory nodded. "Done."

"And now the money."

Rory took out a wrapped package from under his shirt.

He watched as the captain counted it, then nodded. "I want you to pick up another load the same time next month. Same place."

"I enjoy doing business with you, monsieur. Would you care for some fine French brandy?"

"Aye," Rory said. "The same you gave to our friend?"

Renard nodded. "She was to keep that for herself."

"She knows how much I enjoy it," Rory said. "If you have any aboard ship, I would like to purchase a keg."

"Ah, a man of fine taste."

"Nay, it's for Cumberland."

The Frenchman raised an eyebrow. "Cumberland?"

"He likes fine wine."

The Frenchman roared with laughter. "I do not know your game, monsieur, but I think I like you."

Rory shrugged, though he was pleased. The Frenchman was obviously a rogue and a rebel, much like him. And Rory instinctively trusted him, perhaps because of Elizabeth's appraisal. Trust came to him rarely.

He took a quick gulp from the goblet, and he and Renard talked about the dangers of the voyage. Smuggling had become far more difficult since the English wanted to ensure that Prince Charles did not escape to France. Renard's ship was sleek and fast, dependent on speed and stealth rather than arms. But every voyage carrying Jacobites was dangerous, though smuggling other goods was generally overlooked.

"Why do you do it?" Rory asked.

The Frenchman shrugged. "I do not like the English," he said simply. "Some of my best customers have been hanged, or worse." He grinned. "And it pays well."

Rory finished the brandy. "I have a cargo to fetch. Tomorrow night."

The Frenchman nodded. "I will not wait," he warned. Then he picked up the card Rory had given him. "You might be needing this, monsieur."

• • •

Bethia considered how to go about what she wanted to accomplish.

She was more than a little disgruntled that her bridegroom had disappeared again for an unknown period of time. He now intrigued her more than a little. Not, in any romantic way, she hurried to reassure herself, but as a puzzle she wanted to solve.

She also had to admit deep in her heart that she had enjoyed their exchange several nights ago. He might be a dandy and a traitor to Scotland, but he was no' a lackwit. So why did he so often play that role?

But finding the answer to that question could wait. She had a goal—namely, one of getting her brother away from Cumberland. Then perhaps they could both flee Scotland. They would have friends in France, fellow refugees. Fellow Catholics. She could earn their way as a governess. That would be far preferable than being amidst the slayers of her family, this next of traitors.

Then she remembered her oath. But didn't her brother's life and well-being mean more, much more than her word to her family's enemies? Her country's enemies? He had no safety now with the MacDonell name.

She tried to silence her conscience. Smother it off with plans. First she needed clothes, then a way to sneak away from Braemoor.

And money. They would need passage money. At least she had a few coins now, her winnings from the other night. She also had the household accounts, but thievery had never appealed to her. Not even from the king's Scottish lackies.

A few more games with her husband and she might have enough.

But for now . . .

She dressed in a comfortable but comely gown. She had seven now. Four new ones, and three cut from dresses formerly owned by the Forbes women. Bethia did not like the idea of wearing dead women's clothing, and the marquis had told her she could order new ones. Still, it was a waste not to use the fine materials, especially since she did not plan to be here long.

The dress was blue, a color that had always flattered her. She meant to visit Alister, the one person who had been friendly and sympathetic. She'd received little information when she had asked him about the Black Knave. But perhaps he would be more helpful in finding new clothes for the stablelad. Then she could take the boy's present clothes without anyone noticing it.

The Black Knave had been described as an old woman, a young man, even a devil capable of changing shape. Why not a lad?

She may even aid the real Black Knave by further confusing the authorities.

Trilby dressed her hair, pulling it back with a plain silver clasp, allowing it to tumble down her back in curls. Then the maid pinned a cap on her head and studied her handiwork with pride. "Ye look lovely, my lady."

Bethia squinted at herself in the mirror, trying to see what Trilby had seen. It had always hurt to be plain, and time had not changed that. The others in her family had all been handsome or beautiful. Only she had those terrible freckles, a too-wide mouth, and too-thin face.

Loneliness overwhelmed her. She missed her family, especially her fa, who had always called her his bonny lass, and her mother, who had loved her ugly duckling. Her brothers who had protected and teased her. All were gone now. Her mother had died after a long illness; her father had followed within five months. The physician said his heart stopped, but Bethia knew it was because it had also been broken. She had never seen two people more in love.

She'd once hoped . . .

She thrust that thought aside. She would never have what they had. She might escape this marriage by running away, but she would never marry again. Even though her vows were not witnessed by a priest, nor had the mar-

riage been consummated, she knew she would never be
able to recite them again without believing it a sin.

"My lady?"

Trilby's voice shook her from her musings.

Bethia stood, so quickly that the stool fell over. The
noise made her cry out, and she bit her lip. The memories were too strong, the hurt too deep, the loneliness too
pervasive.

Which was why she had to do *something*. Otherwise
she would be consumed by guilt, by surviving when so
many others had died.

"Fetch my cloak," she said.

Trilby's eyes questioned her, but she didn't voice them.
It was obviously not her place to do so.

"I am going for a ride into the village to see about
getting some new clothes for the lads who work here,"
she said.

"Would you like me to go with ye?"

"Do you ride?"

Trilby dropped her gaze. "No, my lady."

"Then I shall teach you if you wish."

"Oh, yes, my lady." She hesitated. "Would ye teach
me to read, too?"

Bethia hesitated. She was not at all sure she would be
here that long, and she tried not to make promises she
could not keep.

But Trilby's face fell at the silence.

"We will get started tomorrow," Bethia said gently, and
Trilby's lips broke into a huge smile.

It would be good, Bethia knew, to keep herself occupied, particularly in the evenings. She usually had supper in her room, feeling awkward in the great hall without
the marquis at her side. Although she knew she had won
over a few members of the household, the tacksmen were
still hostile, and she realized she was the object of any
number of jests. The woman unwanted by her husband.

She did not feel it her duty to suffer their insolence,
although she had supped with them on several occasions,

not wanting it to appear that she feared them, or any Forbeses, for that matter. She *was* mistress of Braemoor. She refused to allow anyone to forget that.

And today she would discover whether her husband spoke truthfully. Whether, indeed, she was to have freedom of movement.

Moments later, she arrived at the stable. The stable-boy greeted her with a broad smile that warmed her. She had at least two friends here now.

"I would like to take a horse into the village," she said.

The tall, thin figure who had been taking out the puppy to drown suddenly appeared out of the shadows. He did not touch his forelock as many of the servants did.

Instead, he just stared at her.

She held his gaze until finally he was the one to lower it.

"The mare, please," she said.

"Ye should be takin' an escort," he said.

"I believe the marquis made his orders quite clear," she replied, hoping that he had indeed instructed the man as he'd said in his letter.

The man muttered under his breath. "'Tis dangerous for a lady tae ride alone."

"That is my concern. I do not intend to go far."

He muttered again.

"What is your name?"

"Ned."

"And the boy's?"

"Jamie."

"Can Jamie ride?"

"Aye, like a lord," the man said, some of the scowl leaving his face.

"Perhaps he can come with me, then."

Ned looked as if he would refuse, then realized that he could not do so. Though he had little apparent liking, or respect, for a Jacobite, he could not refuse the lady of the house.

"Jamie," he said, "saddle the small chestnut for yerself. *I* will saddle the mare fer the marchioness."

Bethia's heart lightened. Not only would she have companionship, but small lads seemed to hear more than adults ever believed. She also knew that her ride would draw less comment with a groom in tow, regardless of the fact that the lad would be useless as a protector.

She waited until they were well outside the walls of Braemoor. She slowed the horse and waited for the lad, who was riding a respectful distance behind her, to catch up. He hesitated, then, at her smile, guided his horse alongside.

"Tell me about Braemoor," she said, knowing that in a few moments she would change the subject to far more important topics.

Rory traveled late into the night, then stopped at the edge of a dense forest. It had not been an easy night.

He worried over Bethia, whether he'd made the right decision to give her a measure of freedom. After all, what trouble could she possibly create? She was busy transforming Braemoor into something livable. And he refused to be someone's jailer. It went against his grain. He'd felt a prisoner in Braemoor far too long to wish it on anyone, particularly an innocent like Bethia.

So with her distinctively stubborn face in his mind, he drifted in and out of sleep, and finally started at dawn for the place Ogilvy was secreted. This would be a long day if he were to deliver his charges to Renard in less than twenty-four hours.

Still wearing his English uniform, he left before dawn and rode into the forest. Though it was cool, he'd taken off his coat at midday. He suspected other fugitives might be hiding in the forests, and he did not want his coat to flag attention.

He was looking for a hunting lodge where Ogilvy had intended to hide. Once owned by the Gordons, it had been abandoned years ago. Now that family was nearly extinct, few remembered the old lodge. Ogilvy, though, had visited it as a boy and thought it the best place to hide. He'd been safely accompanied there by Alister, who'd drawn a map for Rory. The lodge would be his first stop, then a cave where more Jacobites waited, and finally a small farm where the last of his fugitives waited.

The path seemed to end, and Rory cursed. He looked at the scribbled map, then searched the dense woods for an opening. Finally he gave his horse its head, and the animal found an opening he'd not been able to see. An hour later, he approached a larger building than he'd expected. It was made of dark stone and blended into the equally dark forest.

He whistled once, then again. A head cautiously poked out the door, and Rory sighed with relief. He dismounted, led his horse to a tree and tied the reins to a low-hanging branch. He turned and saw a pistol aimed at his heart.

"Ah, you do not want to shoot me," he said, spinning the card with the black jack toward him. "You will never get to France."

The hand wavered for a moment, then lowered the weapon as weary eyes studied him. "That uniform . . ."

"It is easier to move about as a soldier," Rory said. "You will have to wear one yourself." He looked at Ogilvy, who was still wearing his clan's tartan. It was filthy and bloodied.

Ogilvy, little more than a boy, shook his head stubbornly. "I will not wear that bloody uniform."

"Then I have wasted my time," Rory said. "There is no other way of getting you to the coast, and the ship leaves tonight. I have other passengers to pick up along the way."

Ogilvy looked both hunted and haunted. He hesitated, then nodded reluctantly. "When do we leave?"

"As soon as you change clothes and clean up." Rory went back to his horse and fetched a bundle. He threw it to the young Ogilvy. "There is a corporal's uniform in there, along with a knife for shaving. Your beard comes off."

Ogilvy's hand went up to the red bush that ran from cheek to below chin. He hesitated.

"I do not believe the French ladies care as much for beards as the Scottish ones," Rory said. "And they prefer bodies with heads to those without them."

Ogilvy scowled at him, but then his gaze went to Rory's arm. "Is your arm all right?"

"A pretty girl fixed it for me," Rory said lightly.

Ogilvy hesitated a moment. "Who *are* you?"

Rory shrugged. "No one special. Now get on with it."

Minutes later, they were riding toward the coast to collect the other refugees. The earl and his lady, whom Rory had found several days before his marriage, as well as one other man who had fought with the Jacobite cause, were staying in a small farm near the coast. The farmer was one of many who had come to Rory's attention as one willing to help stop the bloodshed. The earl and his wife—and their demanding ways and many complaints— had probably changed the farmer's mind by now. The other group, now staying in a cave, included two women and four children. They'd reminded him of that first forlorn group of women and children who were now in France. These women were also new widows, members of prominent Jacobite families marked for extinction by Cumberland.

Rory and Ogilvy moved swiftly, Ogilvy riding a horse Alister had supplied earlier. Noon became late afternoon. They reached the cave just as the sun was descending.

Both men took off their red coats, since the children particularly were terrified of English uniforms. Rory whistled.

A face appeared from underbrush that hid the cave, a small one. Rory tossed him a card, and he emerged, eyeing both men suspiciously.

"Aye, but ye are a foine lad," Rory said, aging his voice.

The lad's eyes widened, then he grinned. "You are the old man."

"Aye. I have been drinking from the fountain of youth," Rory said, chuckling. "And this gentleman with me is Andrew Ogilvy, who is wanted nearly as badly by the English as you." He reached the lad and put his hand on his shoulder. He was thirteen, the son of a Cameron who had been one of Prince Charlie's earliest supporters. That made him a particular target of Cumberland. Cumberland had sworn to hunt down and kill every Cameron over the age of twelve. With him was his mother, now a widow, and her sister, who'd been wed to a Stewart who'd been hanged after Culloden. Because the boy had a price on his head, Rory had thought it wise to separate him from the other refugees. If one group was discovered, at least the other would have a chance.

"And where are the rest of your people?"

"In the back of the cave. 'Twas decided I was the swiftest of them, and if any soldiers came I could lead them away from here. I already planned my trail," he said proudly, his body seeming to gain two inches in height.

"Ah, you are a brave lad to risk your life for the others," Rory said.

"Are you the Black Knave?" the lad asked.

"Nay, I am only one of his helpers. But we must hurry. A French ship will meet us in a few hours and you will be safely on your way to France."

The boy disappeared into the cave. Several moments later two women and a gaggle of children emerged. Where there had been six souls, there were now at least twelve, some as young as four or five. All were ragged.

Rory's heart dropped. How could he get so many, and some so young, to the coast without notice?

He looked at the two women, one the widow of an earl, the other her daughter.

"They kept coming," she explained. "It was as if they knew they would find safety around here." She looked at

Rory anxiously. "We canna leave them. Several are Mac-Donalds."

Rory knew what she was saying. Cumberland was also a particular enemy of the MacDonalds. Once in France, he thought, the children would be cared for by refugee societies, or by earlier Jacobite arrivals.

He turned to Ogilvy, who still sat his horse. "If I give you directions, can you gather up others at a farmhouse on the way?"

"Aye," Ogilvy said, his gaze still on the children. "I can take at least one of the lads with me."

Rory shook his head. "No. You have to move fast, and I do not want you stopped."

"What about you? Good God, man, you canna do it alone."

"I will manage," Rory said, adding a prayer under his breath. He took out a card from a pocket in the uniform. "Give this to the farmer. You will be the Black Knave."

Ogilvy gazed at the card for a moment, then took it. "I will do honor to him."

"That would be different," Rory said with a grin. "Now get along. If we do not make the rendezvous, you get the others aboard. The passage has already been paid."

Ogilvy nodded and turned the horse around, and headed out the way they had approached.

Rory dismounted. He regarded the children. Three of them were probably under six. He judged three to be between six and eight, two between eight and ten, and two—a girl and the boy who had impudently stuck out his head—over twelve.

Some wore fine garments that were now torn and soiled; results, he supposed, of running for their lives, or being dragged along by older siblings. Their faces, though, were clean, probably thanks to the two women.

He spoke to the older woman. "We will put the three younger ones on the horse until we are out of the woods." He reached out and ruffled the hair of the older boy. "Per-

haps you can be our scout. Run ahead and make sure we
do not run into any patrols."

The boy's face reddened with pleasure. "Aye," he said,
and without more instruction started moving down the
path. Rory lifted one child into the saddle. In minutes
three children sat on the horse's back, two in the saddle
and one behind it.

"Have you had any food?" Rory asked. He had previously provided provisions but only enough for six.

"Timothy caught several rabbits in his snares," the older
woman said.

Rory took out a loaf of bread from his saddlebags.
He'd suspected that some of his charges would be hungry and had purchased it at the last inn. He broke it up,
giving a large piece to each of the travelers and saving
one for the boy.

"You can eat as we travel," he said. "We do not have
much time."

He took the reins of the horse and started walking at
a fast rate. They would be extremely lucky if they reached
the coast by midnight.

Twelve

Bethia had milked as much information as possible from young Jamie. According to him, the Black Knave was nine feet tall. He was part devil, part hero.

The boy obviously knew he was to despise the man, and yet the Black Knave's adventures had inspired awe as well as fear in him. No, he did not know anyone who had actually seen the fellow. But Jamie knew he was behind every shadow at night, lurking in the woods to take honest boys like himself. And, he added, in a confidential whisper, the Knave had actually murdered people in their beds. His father had told him that while warning him not to wander out alone.

Bethia suspected that the older man had concocted that story to keep Jamie by his side, and working.

They had gone into the village. She studied each building. There was a kirk, a smithy, a butcher's shop, alehouse and weaver. Nothing more.

She eyed the alehouse enviously. She did not care about the spirits, but she knew there would be talk there. She saw several horses tethered and decided they must be English soldiers, since few peasants could afford such luxuries. She'd often wished she were a man. There was no sadder lot than a woman who could do little while her husband, brother, son went to war. Women could inherit only in rare instances, and they were bartered like cattle.

That thought reminded her of her own marriage, and her spirits plunged.

She spent the afternoon purchasing wool for new clothes. She'd already located a servant who could sew the garments, the same one who had fitted her own dresses.

The blacksmith was outside the weaver's shop. He gave her a broad smile and lifted her purchases up in front of the saddle. "I hear you are making converts."

"Not Neil," she said wryly. "Nor most of his tacksmen."

"They are worried about their future. They lease the land from the marquis, then parcel it to tenants. They are afraid he might evict them and turn the hills over to sheep."

"Do you think he would do so?"

"Nay," the blacksmith said.

"Why?"

"Because he does care about Braemoor in his own way."

She looked at him dubiously, but said nothing. She accepted his help in mounting. Jamie looked disappointed, but he was far too small to offer a boost. "Thank you," she told Alister, wishing she could exact more information from him. But she'd already learned it was futile.

Instead, she urged her horse into a canter until they reached a split in the road. She stopped and turned to her young escort. "I need some herbs," she said. "I understand Mary Ferguson lives nearby." She'd heard the name whispered in hallways.

His small face went crimson, and she knew that even this stableboy knew that Mary was her husband's mistress.

"I believe we should be gettin' back, milady," he said.

"Mary Ferguson," she said.

He looked stricken, but she would not relent.

"The marquis will beat me," he said, obviously very much believing it.

But the one thing she had come to believe was that her husband, the Marquis of Braemoor, might be capable of many things, but no' the beating of a child doing her bidding. Had he not given her freedom? Though, she thought, probably not if he knew where she was heading. Yet she was driven to meet this woman and talk to her. Bethia had seen her only fleetingly when Alister, apparently at her husband's directions, had demanded that Mary Ferguson attend him, rather than his wife. The woman's face had been pleasant enough, but Bethia had noted she did little to enhance her appearance. That had seemed strange to her at the time, that her husband would be so attached to a woman with no appreciable beauty. She felt fair in so judging since she was no beauty herself.

She wanted to meet the woman.

Bethia gave Jamie an encouraging grin. "I willna tell anyone."

"But *she* will. She be a witch."

"Now who told you that?"

"My fa says so. He says she has bewitched the marquis."

"There is no such thing as witches."

"But my fa—"

"Your fa is mistaken," she said sternly. "Now will you lead the way or must I try to find it on my own?"

She felt guilt at his miserable face. "Just tell me how to get there," she said gently. "You can go home."

He sat straighter in his saddle. "I willna leave ye. Ye are my responsibility." His lips trembled for a moment, then he said bravely, "I will take ye."

She should have felt triumph but, to be truthful, she felt a bit of a bully. She would make up for it with the new set of clothes. She had not told him yet that the bolt of cloth was partly for him.

He led the way off the road and through a stand of

trees toward a stream, then followed it upstream a short distance before leaving it and ending up in front of a simple hut. It was plain, but roses climbed its side and the adjacent land was neatly planted.

The door opened and a young woman stepped out, her body stiffening as she identified the riders. But she did not avert her gaze, nor did her eyes indicate anything but curiosity as Bethia slipped from the horse.

The woman curtsied. "My lady?"

"I need some herbs for the kitchen," Bethia said.

The woman smiled and Bethia realized she was quite pretty. It was the smile that did it. A tentative shy smile.

"And I wanted to thank you for caring for my . . . the marquis," she added, her gaze searching for something in the woman's face. Bethia still did not know what had driven her here, why she had become obsessed with this woman. She told herself it was only to learn more about her husband. Knowledge was a weapon. Did he just . . . use Mary Ferguson? Did he love her?

"Come in," the young woman said. " 'Tis very . . . simple, but I have tea. You can tell me what you need."

Mary Ferguson spoke very well, far better than many of the other Forbes tenants. And she had a calm, quiet grace about her. Still, she did not seem at all the type of woman who would attract, and hold, a man of the marquis's reputation. Bethia did not know what she had expected, but certainly no one like this woman.

Jamie stayed with the horses, his face twisted with concern.

"I willna be long," Bethia said, then followed the woman inside.

Mary Ferguson looked as awkward as Bethia felt, and she wondered why she had come here. "Marchioness, would you like to sit down?"

"Thank you," Bethia said as if she were being invited to sit in the parlor of her best friend rather than the small cottage of her husband's mistress. She selected a chair at the table and sat.

She looked around. The sides of the cottage were lined with shelves, each filled with small bottles of powder, or leaves or petals. The smell of herbs mixed with that of peat from the fireplace, producing an oddly attractive aroma. Though it was quite dark inside, Bethia saw that it was clean and well-maintained.

She watched as the woman stooped and hung a kettle on an iron hook above the fire.

Then she came to stand next to Bethia. "What is it you would like?" she asked in a soft, almost musical voice.

"Fennel," Bethia said, her gaze moving along the shelves. She recognized some of the herbs, but not all. "Scented geranium, savory and marjoram. And some rose petals," she added.

Mary Ferguson nodded and efficiently took several small bottles from her cache and carefully placed them on the table.

"Please sit with me," Bethia said, knowing that her title precluded the woman sitting in her own house without permission.

Mary nodded and looked at her steadily, but without the curiosity Bethia knew she herself must be displaying. "You live here alone?"

"Aye, except for Catherine."

"Catherine?" Bethia looked around, expecting some small face to appear out of the shadows.

"My cat," Mary explained. "She does not care for strangers. She has found a hiding place."

"I wish I could do that," Bethia said wistfully.

"You miss your home?"

"Aye, and my family."

Mary asked no questions, but her gray eyes seemed to encourage confidences. How very strange it was to sit in a room with your husband's mistress. Of course, she cared nothing about him, less than nothing. She was grateful that this woman took care of his needs so she was not required to do so.

Why, then, did she feel a ripple of jealousy?

Had she expected to find him here?

And yet there was no sign of him. No horse. No clothes.

Mary Ferguson apparently saw her look around. "He is not here," she said quietly.

Bethia flushed, then rose. "I am sorry. I should not have come here, but—"

"You are lonely."

Something in Mary Ferguson's voice stopped her. Understanding. Empathy. Again, Bethia wondered about the woman's appeal to her husband, an appeal strong enough that he had eschewed his wife's bed even under orders from Cumberland. It was a loyalty she'd rarely seen between man and woman, even when married. And totally unexpected in a man everyone considered a libertine, fool and dandy.

Bethia made a move toward the door. "I should go. I am sorry to intrude."

"Do not be. I welcome the company. I get few visitors."

Except for the marquis.

"How much are the herbs?"

The woman shrugged gracefully. "Two pence."

"I will have it sent over."

"There is no hurry."

Bethia found herself liking the woman, liking the easy, comfortable way she had, despite the awkward circumstances. "I must go."

"You have not had your tea."

Bethia hesitated, then smiled. "Jamie will believe you have cooked me."

Mary suddenly looked wistful. "Aye, the witch."

There was a flash of movement behind her, then something furry rubbed against Bethia's ankle.

"Catherine," Mary said, shock evident in her voice. "She never does that."

"Perhaps she smells Black Jack on me."

Alarm suddenly flashed through the woman's eyes, and they seemed to narrow. "Black Jack?"

"A puppy. The stableman was going to drown him."

"Then he and Catherine have something in common," Mary said, but her body was rigid. "Why did you name him Black Jack?"

But Bethia could not say. Mary Ferguson was her husband's mistress, no matter how warm she appeared to be. The marquis must not learn that she was looking for the Black Knave. He must not know she had any interest in him.

"He is small and black," she finally said.

Mary went to the kettle and poured a portion into a plain white cup, then into a second cup. She looked expectantly at Bethia, who took several sips, then stood.

"Please stay awhile."

Bethia was lured by the pleasant warmth in the woman's voice. She felt more at home in this humble room than she ever had at Braemoor. She was suddenly very envious of a woman who apparently was free to love whom she wished, who had a freedom that Bethia could never have.

"I cannot today," she said, "but I thank you." She hesitated. "I saw a path go upward. Does anyone live further up in the woods?"

The warmth in the woman's eyes faded. "No," she said. "I just walk up there."

The room seemed to chill, and Bethia wrapped her cloak tighter around her. "I thank you for the tea."

The woman merely nodded.

Bethia escaped, wondering why her comment about the woods above seemed to upset Mary Ferguson when the unexpected visit of her lover's wife did not.

Rory tried to turn the walk into a game as rain started to fall. 'Twas cold and uncomfortable, but he hoped it would keep Cumberland's soldiers around a fire. They had passed through ruined fields, by burned crofts, always keeping away from the roads. Timothy would run ahead, drop back occasionally, and leave markings to point the safe way. Two of the older children would run ahead trying to find them.

Timothy was indeed a good scout. They reached the coast not long after dark. They still had two miles to go, though, before reaching the point chosen by the French captain. Rory could only hope that Ogilvy was also able to avoid any English patrols.

The children took turns riding the horse as they moved toward the sea, finally arriving there after several hours. Rory carried a small girl, as did one of the women. They walked across the great dunes to the beach, then continued toward the rendezvous site.

He prayed that Ogilvy had also reached the site with the other refugees. They didn't have much time now.

The rain had stopped and a piece of the moon occasionally emerged from behind clouds. It provided just enough light that he could see shadows and keep the children together.

He heard a whistle of a bird. *Ogilvy.* They had practiced several calls as they'd rode from the lodge to the cave. The young nobleman suddenly appeared as if out of nowhere. He was on foot.

"An English patrol," he said, his voice buffered by the sound of the ocean. "Right behind me."

Rory turned toward the women. "Take the children into the dunes," he said. Ogilvy grabbed several of the children, and Rory took his horse up over the dunes. The children huddled down while Rory placed his hands over the horse's mouth to quiet him. Minutes later, he heard the sound of hooves thudding along the sand, the sound of jangling spurs. They were coming from the direction in which Rory and his small band were headed.

Rory held his breath as the troop continued down the beach, thanking God once more for a dark night. He only hoped that the French captain was as skilled a navigator as Elizabeth claimed.

After the last sound of horses faded, he tried to get his small party moving again. Their terror was palpable. He ruffled the wet hair of one of the boys. "Brave boy," he said approvingly, then turned to a girl who whimpered ever so quietly. "Soon you will have blankets and hot food," he promised. "It will not take long now."

Ogilvy was reassuring another child. He looked toward Rory. "The others are hidden in the dunes near the rendezvous spot," he said. "I came down to meet you, then heard the patrol."

Ogilvy, Rory thought, had been worth saving after all. "My thanks," he said.

"No, mine," Ogilvy said quietly.

Ogilvy led the way this time, Rory taking up the rear. An hour passed, then they reached a great cliff that jutted into the North Sea. They were to wait on the southern side.

Ogilvy disappeared, then reappeared, this time with the others he'd collected. No one said anything, although the men took the children in their arms, sharing the plaids with them for warmth. An hour went by, then another. No one said anything, although a woman sang a soft lullaby to the children.

Then they heard the sound of oars, a low whistle. Rory carried two of the youngest children, and the others ran down to the sea. A long boat danced on the incoming tide, and two large sailors jumped out and pulled it up almost to the beach. One held the rope while the other started helping the passengers inside.

"Too many," one of the men said. "We were told fourteen."

"Tell your captain I will settle with him later," Rory said.

The sailor hesitated.

"Eight of the children make four adults."

The sailor still hesitated.

"Do you wish to throw them into the sea? You might

as well, for all the future they will have if you leave them on this beach."

The man made a barely visible shrug, waited for the last passengers to be seated, then hopped into the boat, hauling in the rope behind him. The oarsmen pulled at their oars, and the boat disappeared into the rain, leaving Rory alone.

Feeling as if a tremendous load had been lifted from his shoulders, he made his way back to where his tired horse waited. He would ride along the coast until he found a village, then rest both the horse and himself. He would start home tomorrow.

Home. For the first time, the word seemed to have meaning. He felt an eagerness he'd never known before. He did not want to think it was caused by the woman who so unwillingly lived there.

A week. The marquis had been gone more than a week. Nearly nine days, in fact. His absence was longer than any other time since their marriage two months earlier. Bethia frowned at the thought as she watched two newly employed maids polish silver that was black with tarnish. They had, with her assistance, pounded dust from tapestries and dusted off the huge paintings of generations of the Forbes family. Their dark, beady eyes seemed to follow her wherever she went.

Strange that they all had dark eyes. The marquis had hazel eyes, changeable eyes. Rather remarkable eyes, in truth. Surprising eyes. He should have the dull, lifeless eyes of a wastrel, of a man who drank too much. But instead . . . they sometimes shimmered with intelligence and . . . secrets.

Nonsense.

A wife for two months now, and she'd spent two days with the man she called husband.

All to the good, she told herself.

She'd put the last week to good use. Jamie now had a new pair of britches and a new shirt, as well as a pair of shoes. His father had frowned at first, but she'd told him that new shirts were being made for all those who worked in the tower house and in the stables, and his scowl had faded. A new shirt was a prize of great value.

She'd taken Jamie's old clothes, saying they would be mended. She would give them to the kirk for the poor. And she would. Later. Much, much later.

She washed them late one night after Trilby had gone to bed, and had spread them out in front of the fire to dry. Then she'd folded and tucked them away in a drawer. They represented a means of escape, though she had not yet exactly determined how or when.

Jamie and his father slept in back of the stable, ready to take in the horses of any late or early guests. They would immediately miss one of their charges. She had to find another horse, buy one, and keep it somewhere else. But how? Her small winnings from her game with the marquis would not begin to buy a serviceable mount and tack. Still, she had no intentions of giving up.

She debated something she'd thought about for several days. The tower house was becoming more and more respectable, but what about his room? What might she learn about him there?

Invading his privacy, or anyone else's, was abhorrent to her. Still, his room needed cleaning. She'd noticed that the other night. It had been neat, far neater than she would have expected, but the floors had been dusty and the windows as dirty as those in the great hall. No wonder he apparently did not notice. He was seldom there.

She also wondered about the choice of his room. It was small, not nearly as large as the huge room down the hallway. That room had evidently belonged to the former marquis, and was unused at the moment. Cumberland had stayed there when they were wed, but her husband had never moved from what was apparently his old room. Neither did he have a personal servant to look after him.

Another paradox. For a man who claimed to love lux-

ury and elaborate clothing, his own room had few trap-
pings of privilege. Was it just laziness?

None of it made any sense to her.

But perhaps in exchange for his giving her some freedom and the power to run the household, she would clean
the room, mayhap even take a carpet from another room
and use it to replace the worn, threadbare cloth that now
covered the floor.

In transforming the room, she might learn more about
her elusive husband.

With renewed interest, she went up the stone stairs,
the dog close on her heels. Little Black Jack followed her
everywhere now. He could manage the stairs now, though
it took a little effort. She looked down as he made an indignant yelp when she went too fast for him. She slowed
down, waited as he gained the stone steps, then went to
the marquis's chamber. She opened the door. A bottle of
spirits and an empty glass sat on a table.

She remembered that table. She remembered the crackling attraction that had flickered between them. She felt
it now. A warmness invaded her lower regions as she
thought of his touch.

How could she?

He *was* her husband.

He was a traitor and a wastrel.

She leaned against the wall of his room, aware that
her breaths were coming faster. Her eyes went to his
wardrobe in the corner. She hesitated for a moment, then,
as if a compulsion had taken over her body, she opened
it.

A gaudy parade of colors met her eyes. Waistcoats of
the very best materials, shirts of silk, brightly colored
trews made of the finest wool. A stand held several wigs,
each one elaborate. She found herself looking for something else, for something simple. Her mind's eye kept seeing him that night they'd played cards. He'd been wearing
a full white shirt open at the neck and a pair of deerskin

britches that had fit him well. He *did* have fine legs, even in the dreadful trews.

Her face flamed at the thought, at the warmth pooling in her belly.

She touched one of the shirts, and felt something hard under it. She lifted it up and found a number of decks of cards. The gambler's tools.

"Marchioness?"

She whirled around and saw the object of her musings standing in the doorway, a quizzical look on his face.

He was dressed in a bright green waistcoat, purple and yellow trews and a wig that was slightly askew. His eyes narrowed as his gaze roamed up and down her, then rested on her face.

"I did not know you had returned."

"Obviously," he said lazily.

"I thought to clean in here."

"Amidst my clothes?"

"To see whether any needed cleaning or repair. Is that not a wife's duty?"

"I think I would prefer her other duties if she sincerely believes in fulfilling a wife's function." His voice was silky, his lips turned upward in a suggestive smile. She saw a sudden cruelty in that smile. A calculated cruelty.

"You did not say I could not come into your room," she said, closing the door to the wardrobe.

"No," he agreed pleasantly. "I did not."

He seemed to be viewing her as a spider might ogle its web-trapped prey.

"You were gone a long while. I really thought your room might need a thorough dusting." She realized she was repeating herself, even babbling.

The corner of his mouth crooked up. "A long while," he repeated. "You missed me, then?"

"No." It took all her courage not to make a fast dash for the door. She did not like the odd speculation on his face.

"You just had a sudden desire to clean my room?"

"I wondered why you did not move into the marquis's room."

"This *is* the marquis's room," he said.

"I mean . . ." She bit her lip.

"Ah, the old marquis's room."

"Aye," she said.

"Then you have no' heard the rumors."

She looked at him curiously.

"My father did not much care for me. He did not, in fact, believe I was his son. He hated me, and quite frankly I returned the favor. I ha' no wish to live in his room." His voice was suddenly hard, cold.

Trilby had told her that he and his father had not cared for one another. She had not dreamed, however, that the enmity had run so deep. She remembered her own mother and father, the love they had showered upon her. She felt an instant sympathy for the marquis, for the man who was her husband.

"Your mother?"

He emitted a short laugh, more like a bark. "She made his life as much a hell as he made hers."

"And you?"

He shrugged. "It does not matter. She died years ago. It was my father's misfortune that he did not have time to disown me after my . . . brother died at Culloden. I am sure he is rolling about in his grave that I now own Braemoor." He smiled, but there was no humor in the ironic twist of his mouth. "And that a Jacobite is the marchioness."

She felt a sudden chill. She had thought he was as much a reluctant bridegroom as she was a bride. Now she wondered whether this was not his ultimate revenge against his father. That idea did not appeal to her.

"You must have had a long journey if you came from Edinburgh," she said. "I will have water sent up, and some food."

"I believe I would prefer to eat in the great hall with my wife at my side."

She looked up into his face. "Why?"

"I do not want any rumors that we do not . . . suit."

"I would think your absences would make that clear."

"Business, lass. I took a keg of fine French brandy to Cumberland, among other things. He asked how you were."

She stiffened. "Did he say anything about my brother?"

"Nay."

She chewed on her lip for a moment. He seemed in good humor, for some reason. She did not know, though, if that bade well or poorly for her. But she would try to use it.

"I would like to send my brother a letter, but I do not know if Lord Creighton will give it to him."

"Write it, and I will try to get it to him," he said unexpectedly. She searched his face, but the mask was in place. He gave away nothing.

"Why would you do that?"

"You are my wife," he said lightly. "And I am impressed. Braemoor has improved considerably since you became its mistress. And now I would like to bathe. Will you order hot water? You may stay and scrub me if you wish."

Her face reddened again, and she was mortified that he saw her confusion. She never quite knew exactly what he intended by his words.

"Or not," he said mercifully. "I will come to your room when I am ready for supper."

She left quickly, unwilling to take a chance that he might change his mind and wish her to attend him during his bath.

Yet even as she hurried to her room, to safety, she tried to understand why her nerves all tingled from the thought of him naked.

Nor why she always felt so confused after each and every one of their encounters.

And why she felt he wanted something unsaid from her. And, God help her, why she felt she needed something from him.

She just did not know what it was.

Thirteen

Rory knew he would have to be more careful. He had almost brushed a lock of hair from her forehead. He had almost kissed her.

Damn, but the lass sent his senses reeling.

He poured himself a glass of brandy, welcoming the warmth as it slid down his throat. God's fury, but he was weary. He still felt the chill of riding days through cold rain. He'd stopped at Mary's, changed clothes from the uniform into a bright waistcoat and had stripped the mustache from his face. He'd changed from the mud-splattered boots to nearly useless shoes that were little more than slippers.

Mary had told him about Bethia's visit, about her request for herbs, which seemed little more than an excuse. Her real intent, Mary had surmised, had been to learn more about the marquis. "She is canny," Mary said. "I think she can be trusted."

"What would you have done to save your mother?" Rory asked. "Wha' would you do to save your bairn?"

Her eyes met his, and she did not answer.

"Her brother is her last living kin. She has no reason to have loyalty to me."

"I donna think she would betray the Black Knave," Mary said.

"She may not mean to," Rory replied. "But I will not draw more people into this circle. It is dangerous not only to me but for you and Alister as well."

"She is lonely, my lord. And desperate. I could see it in her eyes. She might well do something . . . reckless on her own."

"I will try to give her hope, then, without being specific." And that had ended the discussion. Still Rory did not like the idea that his new wife was looking into matters he preferred to be his alone.

As she'd apparently been looking through his belongings.

Rory looked around the room. It did need tending. But he used it so seldom, he'd cared little about its upkeep.

He'd turned down Neil's offer of a servant. He wanted no one snooping among his belongings, no one keeping abreast of his comings and goings.

That thought made him check the wardrobe where the lass had been looking. He looked under the shirts. The decks of cards were still there. 'Twas unlikely that she had checked them and found most of them missing the jack of spades. He would rid himself of the remaining cards in the fireplace this night. He should have done it earlier.

He slipped off the heavy, soaked wig, then took off his waistcoat and loosened his shirt at the neck. Rory then checked the fireplace. He'd brought a candle from downstairs to light the fire, but there was no wood. He supposed then that he did need a servant. He was just too damnably tired to do more than sprawl across the chair and think again of his small group of refugees aboard the French ship.

It was three months now since the battle at Culloden Moor. Some of the families that had fought with Cumberland were becoming more and more disturbed by his excesses. He was called "the butcher," and obviously someone—more than one or two—was helping Prince

Charles who, despite the reward of thirty thousand pounds, remained at large.

There were also grumblings now about men and women killed, transported or pushed into gaols in flat defiance of the Act of Union which guaranteed the integrity of Scottish law courts. Still, the devastation of the Highlands was tolerated, even applauded, by a number of Presbyterian Scots who hated Highlanders more for their stubborn adherence to the Roman Catholic faith than their loyalty to the Stewarts. The cauldron would continue to boil for years to come, especially with Cumberland's new edicts banning the wearing of tartans and kilts, the playing of pipes and the owning of weapons. Even the speaking of Gaelic was prohibited.

As much as he wished for a more peaceful existence at times, he knew there were still Jacobite clans marked by Cumberland; any of their members still in Scotland remained at risk. And as much as he despised any suggestion that his small efforts were anything more than a game to him, he knew that if the Black Knave was called, he would answer. His guilt over Culloden was too overwhelming to do anything else.

Bloody hell, he muttered to himself just as a knock came at the door, and in came several servants with a tub and pails of hot water.

He asked for wood, and a fire, and soon small flames were eating along a large oak log. A lass, who brought several more pails of water, cast interested eyes at him and lingered when the others left.

"Would ye be likin' me to tend ye?"

Strangely enough, the thought of the MacDonell lass tending him held a great deal of appeal, but this lass's offer did not, though she was bonny enough. He'd always had a taste for pretty faces and fetching bodies. What in the bloody hell was happening to him? Why did he feel a need to be faithful to a woman who was his wife in name only, and then, he hoped, not for long?

He wriggled uncomfortably under the thought, dismissed the girl, and sank gratefully into the cramped tub.

He thought of Bethia just a few doors down the hallway. He thought how appealing she'd been, standing in his room. He thought about the way his heart had thumped faster when, for a second, he felt as if she were there to greet him, that she really had wanted to mend his shirts, to make this damp, cold tower house a home. A home he'd never had. Something he'd never even considered having.

And then he'd seen the guilt in her face and knew that she was not there in a wifely role. That was like a splash of cold seawater.

What in the hell had he expected? She was here as a prisoner. Their bargain had been a cold, empty one.

He gulped down the rest of the brandy.

Then he washed thoroughly. He knew the others in the house thought he was addlepated for requesting a bath so often. It was well known that too many baths caused illnesses, and it was an indication of his popularity—or lack of it—that no one reminded him of that sad fact.

He washed his hair, then finally rose and dressed. He had shaved himself at Mary's cottage. Now he merely had to get dressed. The thought depressed him. He longed for simple garments, for a pair of britches and a comfortable shirt.

A damnable trade. He'd once told his father he wanted to go to the University of Edinburgh where he could read law or become a physician. But his father had merely roared with laughter at the idea. He would not spend a pence on a bastard. And in any event, Rory was too stupid to do anything but be a stable hand. His one value to Braemoor would be marriage, to bring about an advantageous alliance.

Rory didn't know why he had come back to Braemoor when his father had called him to fight with Cumberland. Perhaps it had been a boy's need for acceptance, one that

had never quite died. And so he had done what he would
never have normally done. He had killed good men.

He swore to himself, then picked out a particularly
hideous waistcoat and trews and hurriedly dressed. If he
could not keep away from his bride, then he would have
to make himself as unappealing as possible.

But before he left, he fueled the fire with the decks of
cards that lacked one jack.

Bethia dressed with Trilby's assistance. She'd selected a
dress of dark-blue velvet, one that had been newly made.
She tried to tell herself it did not matter, but she knew
the dress showed her eyes—her one good feature—to best
advantage.

Mayhap the marquis had learned something during his
travels. He might have learned something about the Black
Knave. He might have heard something about the prince,
who had disappeared. And, most important, he said he
would help with her brother.

She held onto that. She held onto it with all strength.
Dougal. I will get you out of there. I swear.

Trilby dressed her hair, brushing it back and holding
it there with silver clasps. Bethia wished she had one of
those elegant faces that looked truly wonderful when one's
hair was drawn back. But her face had no elegance, particularly with the freckles that brushed her nose. Her
mother had tried any number of concoctions to make them
fade, but nothing had worked, and Bethia refused to hide
them under layer upon layer of powder.

Utterly dissatisfied with her appearance, and confused
as to why she even cared, she dismissed Trilby. She sat
and waited for the man the king called her husband. Did
God also believe that, even if they had been married by
a Protestant vicar rather than a Catholic priest?

She went to the narrow window and looked out over
the hills and the forest beyond, the forest where her husband's mistress lived. A mist was falling, turning the hills
to a soft green. It seemed so peaceful, so far away from

what she knew was happening across the Highlands. The thought saddened her, and she wiped a tear from her eyes.

She could not bring back her family. She could only try to save Dougal.

Then she was suddenly aware of another presence. She'd been so wrapped up in her own misery that she had not heard him. She did not turn. She did not want him to see her tears. She was a MacDonell, proud and strong.

The carpet covered his footfalls. She knew he had neared only by the scent of soap. Bethia swallowed deeply, trying to gulp down those tears that wanted to rush from her eyes.

"My lady?"

She turned, hoping her eyes were not red. She knew she failed when she saw something flicker in his eyes. Sympathy?

Bethia did not want it. He had fought alongside Cumberland at Culloden. He might even have killed one of her brothers. He was a Scots traitor, a renegade. And yet despite all those things she told herself, she could not tear her gaze away from his.

His eyes were mesmerizing. They had depths, just as he had layers to him. Layers she did not understand. She just knew they existed. She did not know why he acted the fool so many times, but looking into those eyes, she knew he was no fool.

"Are you ready, lass?" He took a lacy handkerchief from his pocket and dabbed at her face. "Some rain must have seeped inside."

The words were extraordinarily kind and gentle, and they served not to stop the tears but to spur them on. She'd had no comfort since she'd learned of her brothers' deaths, the same day Cumberland's forces took Mac-Donell's land and dragged Dougal and her away. She'd had no arms around her, no words of sympathy, no kindness. And that had been her strength.

Now a kind word made her blubber like some child.

A kind word from an enemy.

Forcing her gaze away from his, she turned away from him again. But it did no good. She was so very aware of his presence. Heat wrapped around them like an invisible cloak. Every nerve in her body was aware of him. The air hummed like the lingering sound of a harp.

It could not be. She could not be attracted to her husband, to a man she'd hated. A member of a clan which had taken up arms against their own countrymen, who held the life of her brother as hostage to her own behavior.

"Your brother will be safe."

It was as if he knew her every thought. It was . . . unsettling. Confounding.

She lifted her hand and wiped away the dampness from her eyes.

He was silent, so silent that if it had not been for the lingering smell of soap, she might have believed him gone, but then, perhaps not. There were no more words, no handkerchief dabbing at her eyes, and yet she felt strength.

She slowly turned. So did he. But not before she saw his face, saw something flicker again in his eyes, saw a muscle clench in his cheek.

"We had better go down to supper, madam. My cousin will already be there along with some of our tacksmen." He hesitated, then handed her a box that she had not noticed earlier.

She stared at it.

"Take it," he ordered in an arrogant voice.

Bethia slowly opened the package. A glittering necklace of sapphire and diamonds lay on a velvet background. It was one of the most beautiful pieces of jewelry she had ever seen.

"It matches your dress," he said. "And your eyes."

She could do naught but stare at it. "I . . . canna . . ."

"It belonged to the previous marchioness. It would be expected."

"Your mother?" she asked, wondering at the detached, dispassionate description.

"She called herself that," her husband said. Bitterness accented the words.

Bethia still did not take them. She wanted nothing of the enemy's. She wanted nothing that seemed to make this marriage real and unbreakable.

He took it from her and moved to stand behind her back, placing the necklace around her neck. She felt his fingers against her skin, contrasting with the chill of the metal. For a moment, they hesitated, then she felt the clasp close and the necklace hung heavily about her neck. A noose. A lovely noose, but a noose just the same. A tremor went through her, and his hands moved to her shoulders.

She liked the feel of them. Surprisingly, they were hard, callused, and they felt right.

Then they left her, and she felt the weight of the necklace. It carried with it the legacy of the Forbeses, a family she believed traitors.

But also she knew that with it, Rory Forbes was declaring her authority over Braemoor. She suspected he knew that she was having a difficult time at Braemoor both because of who she was, and also for his own derelictions. This necklace, and the supper tonight, were meant to assert her authority. She was no longer a prisoner but the mistress of Braemoor, a title of dubious honor.

Still, it would mean more freedom for her. She gritted her teeth. "Thank you," she said.

"I've heard the words spoken with more emotion."

"From prisoners?"

"You are no longer a prisoner. Now are you ready?"

She nodded. She was not, but she would not let him know it. She hated eating down in the great hall. Usually there were more than a few English soldiers who had stopped in for Forbes hospitality.

He said nothing else, until Black Jack yelped as the puppy suddenly realized he was going to be left behind.

He growled and ran over to the marquis, snapping at his ankle. Her heart stopped. She knew he'd tolerated the puppy, but it had never gone after him before.

The marquis leaned over and the wig went tumbling over. The puppy grabbed at it, snared one of the great curls in sharp little puppy teeth and tried to drag the wig over to the bed. When that was unsuccessful, he tumbled in the midst of it, growling and attacking it, stumbling over it, falling as little legs caught in the curls.

"Jack," she said, horrified.

The marquis had turned to watch the puppy's contortions. Then she saw his shoulders start to shake. She feared it was in anger, then she heard the chuckles. The chortles turned into great bursts of laughter.

Bethia stood there. Stunned. She moved to where she could see his face. She was astounded. She had never heard him laugh before. Or even seen a smile. Oh, there had been a supercilious twist of his lips, but not actually a smile. And it had never, ever touched his eyes. But now they seemed to dance with merriment.

His wig. His very, very expensive wig. She giggled as the pup became more and more enmeshed in the hair, the powder turning him partially white.

"I'm . . . sorry," she managed between giggles.

He leaned down and disentangled the puppy from the wig, then picked up the hairpiece. It was totally destroyed. He glanced at it ruefully.

"I like you better without it," she said, her reserve with him broken.

"Ah, but my cousin and his friends expect my . . . excesses. I would not like to disappoint them."

She'd been reluctant minutes earlier to take her gaze from him. Now it was impossible. His dark hair was mussed, and his hazel eyes were bright with amusement. Without the wig, his face seemed sharper.

That image of strength, again.

How had she ever thought him a weakling?

For some reason, though, he wished others to believe

him a fool, a dolt, a dandy. Now she remembered how strange she'd thought his friendship with a blacksmith. Stranger still to be faithful to a village girl.

She thought of the girl's serenity, her quiet competency, and now she understood more of the apparent commitment between them. Envy nibbled at her, though. Took a big bite, in truth. She did not understand anything now except the pull she felt toward Rory Forbes, the Marquis of Braemoor.

"I feel naked," he said. "I must return to my room and find another headpiece."

"Why?"

He lifted an eyebrow.

"Why do you pretend to be something you are not?"

"And you know what I am?"

"I know you are no fool."

"I would not take a wager on that, my lady."

"You did not answer me. I have seen enough of you to know . . ."

He waited, his mouth curved in that supercilious smile that she disliked. But now she knew there was something under it. "Know what, my love?"

"That you have honor."

"You flatter me, madam. I care naught for honor. 'Tis just a word that men toss around to impress their ladies, and I want none of it. I am a gambler who would take the devil's hand to win a wager."

His voice was cool, though she saw the lingering flicker of desire in his eyes.

"Your clothes do not . . . suit you."

"That is your opinion, lass. They suit me very well."

"Why?"

"You know something of my family now. My legal father never wished to spend a ha'pence on me. I rather enjoy tweaking his memory."

"You have said that before. Do you live only to gain revenge on him?"

"Aye. 'Tis as good a reason as any."

As lightly as the words were said, they carried a bitterness and even an odd insincerity. Yet she knew she was going to get nothing else from him. She went to the door.

His hand caught her arm. "You are very bonny," he said. "You do Braemoor proud."

She did not care whether she did Braemoor proud or not. Yet it was the first compliment she had received from him, and she blushed. She also felt inordinately pleased. Far more pleased than she should. She reminded herself that, fool or not, he was still the enemy. He had fought with Cumberland against her brothers, against her betrothed, against her friends and her family's friends.

His fingers seemed to burn through her, and though she wanted to brush away from the branding heat of his touch, she seemed unable to move. Her legs simply would not work.

He lowered his head, and she felt the soft sigh of his breath as his lips—no longer supercilious but tempting as they curved into a sensual smile—touched hers. The kiss was not violent as it had been before, but exploring. Even tender. Sensation washed through her and her body pressed against his, reacting to his hard body. Heat radiated between them. She felt it to the essence of her soul. It surged in the deepest, most private part of her. Her entire body felt like fluid fire.

His kiss deepened. No longer exploratory, his lips searched and demanded. And she felt herself respond, her lips mating with his as fervently as his with her.

Then suddenly he let go, and she heard him curse under his breath. Her stomach twisted into a knot. He did not want her, and God help her, she wanted him. An enemy, and *she* wanted *him*.

She backed away, tripping over little Black Jack.

He yelped, and she started to fall, her body twisting in an effort to protect herself. Her husband's arms caught her, straightening her with easy strength. But the fall seemed to continue. She felt as if she were whirling down some hole to disaster. Her senses were swirling, and she felt both protected and threatened.

"Bethia." It was the first time he had ever said her name, and it sounded strange on his lips. She'd always been "my lady" to him, or "madam" or some word designed to keep a distance. But now intimacy danced between them like flames.

"Are you all right?" he asked, his voice hoarser than usual. Or was that her imagination?

"Yes." Her voice was lower than usual, even faltering.

His gaze held hers, and again she saw the depths he usually tried so successfully to hide. "I am your enemy," he said reluctantly, as if feeling the need to remind her.

"Aye."

"I love another."

"Aye."

He still did not leave, nor did he take his hand from her arm. "I ha' not changed."

"Nay."

"Nor will I."

He was reciting a list of reasons for both of them to leave, and yet neither made the slightest movement to do so. The room was even more heated. Smaller. Pushing them closer together.

"You are my wife."

"Aye."

He smiled then. "I did not know you were so agreeable."

"Nor I."

"Ah, lass, I am sorely tempted to take what should be mine."

She said nothing. She already heard the rejection in the words. She bit her lower lip. *'Tis just as well,* she tried to tell herself. He *was* indeed the enemy. To her. To Scotland.

"They will be waiting in the hall," she said, trying to keep her voice under control. "They cannot eat until you arrive."

"They are used to waiting for me."

"And that is admirable?"

Another raised eyebrow. "You care about the feelings of the Forbeses?"

"The law says they are now my people."

"Are you instructing me on my duty?" he asked, amusement in his voice.

"Aye."

"That infernal affability again. I think I preferred the asp's tongue."

The room was cooling. A wee bit.

Yet they were still linked by some strange magic.

She sought to break it. "How is your arm?"

"Well enough."

"And your mistress?"

He smiled slowly. "Also well enough. She said you stopped by to see her."

"I needed herbs."

"Trilby could not fetch them? Or cook?"

"I wanted to see what she had," she said defiantly. In truth, she did not know herself why she had visited that cottage.

"Did you satisfy your curiosity?"

"Aye." She saw the amusement flicker again on his face and she had the strangest desire to kiss *him*, to touch his face and get a measure of it.

"Aye," he mocked, and his finger touched her cheek, just as if he had read her mind. She felt the breath in her lungs leave them as the fingers traced a trail across her face. Then he dropped his hand with obvious reluctance and took the several steps to the door, opened it, and swept out his arm for her to go first. He stopped at his room, donned a new wig, then returned to her side.

She started for the staircase, stopping only when he said, "I would prefer, madam, that you do not go back to Mary's cottage."

She turned. "Is that an order?"

"Aye."

The magic disappeared, but the aching inside her did not as she allowed him to lead her down the steps to sup with the Forbeses.

He almost had taken her to his bed. They were married; there was no impediment except his own conscience, and it had been a long time since his conscience had guided his actions. He refused to believe that his current actions on behalf of the Jacobites had anything to do with conscience. Guilt, perhaps. Conscience, nay. One was a motive of convenience, the other one of nobility, and God knew, that was the last quality he wished to claim.

He had been perfectly honest with the lass when he'd said honor was naught but a word without meaning. He heard the word bandied about before Culloden, and then he'd watched the worst kind of murder, pillage and inhumanity following it. Nay, he had no use for so-called virtues.

But, he told himself, bedding the lass would mean nothing but trouble. A new and . . . affectionate relationship between the two of them would certainly cause comment, and he would lose his excuse to visit Mary. And the cottage was vital to his various roles.

Yet he'd revealed far more than he'd intended, and now he would have to give her a reason, one she might believe, for playing the fool.

He put his hand on her as they went into the great hall. The sound of laughter ceased as he entered, and he wondered whether the talk had been about him.

They all rose, however, as he led his wife to the head table where Neil already sat. He, too, stood until Bethia was seated.

Rory remained standing, noting all the curious faces. Many of them were hostile, some suspicious. But he nodded in what he hoped was an arrogant pose of graciousness, and sat.

"We are not often graced with your presence," Neil observed dryly as he speared a pigeon from a tray being carried by a servant. "Should I inquire as to where you have been?"

"Edinburgh," Rory said airily. "A few other places."

"I would like several hours with you tomorrow. Decisions must be made about some land."

"You do what you think best," Rory said. "I have no head for such matters."

He saw several scowls from men sitting closest to him. In truth, he did have faith in Neil as far as property management went. His cousin had obviously tried to protect the tacksmen who leased land from the lord, then rented it out to smaller farmers. Rory agreed with Neil's attempt to help the tenants, most of whom were clansmen, rather than simply evicting them and turning the land into grazing for sheep as so many other landowners were doing.

But he did not particularly wish to communicate that concern, or interest. Not when Neil was taking care of it. He saw, though, his bride's blue eyes darken with disapproval. She obviously wanted him to care more for the people who were, in many ways, his responsibility.

He would leave that to her and Neil. She was already winning a few hearts at Braemoor. That much was obvious. It was he they disliked, and that suited him also.

He took a long sip of strong ale that had been poured into his cup. Then he leaned over and kissed his bride. His lips had none of the finesse of his earlier, spontaneous kiss; this one was planned, deliberate, an open declaration of ownership. And where she had melted earlier in his arms, he saw surprise, disgust, outrage at his public assault.

"What do you think of my bride, Neil?" he said when he finished, pulling out a lace handkerchief and dabbing at his mouth.

Neil scowled, obviously uncomfortable at his lord's behavior. "You are fortunate," he said in a cool tone.

"Aye, I am. I am missing only a bairn, but that should soon be remedied." His tone left no question as to exactly what he meant, and he saw Bethia's face pale. The softness he'd seen in her eyes earlier was gone. Distaste, even horror, had replaced it. Well, wasn't that what he wanted? For both their sakes.

He leered at his wife, which, unfortunately, was not at all difficult. Her eyes widened, and her back stiffened with outrage.

He ignored her and drank some more, eating heavily from the food on the table. It *was* better than it had been. Much better. She was obviously making the best of a very bad game.

Rory hated what he was doing, but a doting husband just didn't fit his needs at the moment, nor did the appearance of a chaste one. He did not doubt for a moment that Cumberland had a spy somewhere about, and Rory had been warned about the need for a babe. He still wondered why the girl meant so much to someone, but the Marquis of Braemoor would never inquire into such matters.

The meal seemed endless to him. The role of fool had once appealed to him. It no longer did. And the reason was sitting next to him, stiff and withdrawn. She had barely touched her food while he had sat at the head of the table, smirking like some half-wit. For the first time, he did not enjoy his role. He did not like his game. For the first time, he wanted to be . . . respected.

Hell and damnation. She had him in knots. He took another long drought, then pushed his chair out. " 'Tis time for my bride and me to retire."

He nodded to the men and two ladies sitting at the table. They all stood as he did. He felt their eyes on him as he took Bethia's arm and led her from the room toward the stairs. She said nothing as they climbed them, but then at the door of the room, she paused, her eyes as angry as any he had ever seen.

With no warning, she swung her hand up. It connected with his cheek in a loud crack. His face stung. Hell, it hurt. He stepped back and regarded her cautiously. One hand went up and fingered his cheek. Even his jaw ached.

"*You* should have been at Culloden," he said.

'Twas the wrong thing to say, and he regretted it the moment the words were out of his mouth. He was accustomed to making sharp retorts, particularly when attacked.

Her face clouded, and he saw the hurt he had just imposed.

"I am sorry, madam. I should not have said that."

She stood even stiffer. 'Twas as if a steel rod had been inserted in her back. "You purposely humiliated me," she said.

He had no answer for that, no explanation.

He saw her swallow as if a stone was caught in her throat. "I was wrong earlier, when I thought . . ."

"I do not ken your meaning."

"I thought you were actually human." She turned around and opened the door, starting to slam it behind her.

But he caught it. "Oh, no, madam. That will not do. That will not do at all."

Fourteen

She despised him. She had lowered her guard, and he'd swooped in with his sword and plunged it into a vulnerable place.

She had never been so angry.

She was, in fact, trembling with that anger. And she hated that even more. She did not want him to see it. She could not stop him from entering her chamber, but she certainly could make it unpleasant for him.

"You plan to break your promise?"

"It was a bargain, not a promise."

"You play with words as you play with cards," she said bitterly. "Lives mean no more to you than the next wager."

"You are right, my marchioness. However, I must warn you that Cumberland wants a bairn, and your brother's life could depend on whether or not he believes that one might be in the making."

She stared at him in horror. "What do you mean?"

"Surely you must have suspected he had something more than a simple marriage in mind. Why do you think he wanted proof of consummation? His goal has always been a bairn, a child. He is waiting very impatiently," he said, his gaze raking her. "He stressed that to me days ago when I delivered a small gift of brandy to him. I told him I was well pleased with my bride."

"Why did you not tell me that earlier?"

He shrugged. "I did not wish to spoil my homecoming."

"You are truly loathsome," she said, her voice breaking slightly.

"That is probably among the mildest adjectives applied to me," he replied mildly.

"What do you want? Tell me and end the torment."

"Is marriage to me torment?"

"Your incessant games are."

He bowed. "Then I apologize."

He entered and closed the door behind him. Black Jack stirred from his basket where he had dragged the wig and made a nest of it. He ran over and started nipping at her slippers, asking to be picked up.

The marquis looked at the wig ruefully.

"You can have it now," she said helpfully.

"Ah, he has taken possession, and that gives him the legal right to it."

She was fascinated at those fleeting instants of whimsy he allowed himself. But then, they were always so very fleeting.

"You care about legality?"

"When I have nothing at stake." He took a step toward her.

She leaned down and picked up Black Jack, using the squirming black puppy as a shield.

"It will not work, Bethia." He took a step toward her.

"I do not ken your meaning."

"Distraction. I do not believe I wish to be distracted."

She backed up, uncertain. He had an odd gleam in his eyes, and he smelled of strong ale. And yet . . . yet he seemed to have complete control of his actions.

"What *do* you want?"

"I want the Forbeses to see a husband and wife together, doing what God intended to be done, creating new life."

"I do not understand why that is so important to you."

"It might well mean my neck as well as yours and your brother's."

"I do not understand."

"Cumberland has only one lord, Bethia, and that is the king. I do not think Cumberland has a personal interest in you, which means the king does. Would you know why?"

Bethia drew in her breath. Her husband was most definitely not a fool now. She remembered Cumberland's words when he'd pressured her into this marriage. *You have a friend at court who asked me to look after you.*

Not her. Her mother. Her mother had been born on the English side of the border, and she'd been very beautiful. Bethia had heard she'd been promised to a highly placed English lord, when her father had won her heart and whisked her off to Scotland. She'd always thought the tale very romantic, but now she wondered. She had never known her mother's family; her mother had been disowned when she had married a Catholic Highlander, and she never spoke of her family. But Bethia knew the name.

She was reluctant, however, to discuss it with a man she dinna trust. In fact, she had dismissed Cumberland's reference when he'd said it. Her grief, her despair, had been too great to question exactly why she'd been singled out from other women torn from their homes and often imprisoned because of their family's loyalties.

The marquis was watching her closely. Why did he even care as long as he received the lands he had wanted?

"Why do you always act the fool?" she said, deciding attack was the best defense.

"I like low expectations," he replied.

"So you will not disappoint, as you feel you did as a boy?"

His gaze grew sharper. "An astute theory."

"But not true?"

He shrugged. "You may think what you will."

She tried to look inside him, to go beyond the various masks he wore. Whenever she thought she was reaching behind one, another appeared.

Was the cause really as shallow as not wanting expectations? Indifference? A reason not to involve himself in the difficult business of running an estate?

The contradictions kept piling up, one upon another. He had fought at Culloden. He was said to be a good swordsman. But he apparently had left the field before the end. She'd heard "coward" whispered. She heard it whispered louder after his encounter with Ogilvy and the Black Knave.

Why did she not believe it? Even as he threatened in various ways, she'd never really feared him. Nor could she think of him as a coward. Or mayhap, despite his protestations, he did have some honor. Mayhap he could not stomach the butchering Cumberland had ordered.

If so, she might have an ally. Dare she hope?

"You wish to play cards again, my lord?"

His eyes narrowed, then he seemed to relax.

"Do you still have those I gave you the other night?"

"Aye."

"Then why not?" he asked carelessly.

Relieved he'd dropped the subject of a child even temporarily, she quickly fetched the deck of cards while he brought a second chair to the table. She studied him as he shuffled the cards with extraordinary dexterity.

She thought she was beginning to understand something about him now. Although just a little. He was a master at holding people at a distance, at keeping them from knowing him or anything about him. As angry as she had been about his behavior at supper, she realized now that there was a purpose behind it. Just as she sensed there was a purpose behind many things he did.

Now that her temper had dissolved under his wry good

humor about her dog, she remembered what it was this afternoon that had so drawn her to him.

She looked at him curiously. "Do you really like gaming so much?"

He shrugged. "My father sent me to foster with an English family. He included no funds. I learned to game to purchase weapons and found it to be one of my rare talents. Then there were other things I wanted. I knew . . . thought . . . I would never inherit a pence from my father. Gaming was as good a way as any to earn my way."

"Was there nothing you wanted to do?"

"At one time, I thought . . . I might enjoy the study of medicine. But my father, such as he was, was right. I had no temperament for it."

"I disagree."

"Only because you want to win this game."

"I have a sweep," she said, proclaiming her win as she claimed all the table cards.

"Do you cheat?" The marquis raised an eyebrow as he posed the question.

Black Jack whined.

"He really does not know," she defended herself, her lips curving into a small piece of a smile.

The marquis stood and took off his coat, but he left his wig on. She ached to take it off. She wanted to reach over and touch him. She wanted to hear that rare, rich chuckle.

He won the next game, and that pleased her. She did not want anyone to pretend to lose for her sake.

She looked up and his eyes met hers. "Why do you not take off that wig?" she said.

"Must you ask? Your small protector might appropriate that one, too. After playing with you, I cannot afford to lose another one."

"*You* are winning."

"Aye, but you have far too quick a mind."

For the first time in months, Bethia felt a rush of pleasure. She had loved her brothers; they had been her life

after her mother died, then her father months later. But
they had seen no reason for her to read, had teased her
about the way she had begged their tutor to teach her.
Lasses, they had said, had no need to learn such things.

She had never been praised for her wit or mind. It felt
very, very fine.

The game continued. As it had before, the room became smaller, closer, hotter, despite the cold wind that
blew outside the tower house and the damp, cool air that
penetrated it. And then when he gathered up the cards,
his hand touched hers. She felt as if her skin sizzled.

Her gaze met his. His hazel eyes shimmered with something she believed was desire. Heat crept through her body
and lodged in the core of her.

He rose, kicking the chair away with a violence that
would have shaken her earlier. "All of Braemoor will be
sleeping. 'Tis time I returned to my room, lass, before I
break my bargain."

She knew for certain, then, that all his earlier baiting
had indeed been meant to widen the gulf between them,
not narrow it. He'd wanted her angry. He'd wanted to
pierce that fragile intimacy that had spun a web around
them earlier. But she no longer cared what he wanted.
She only knew that she needed to feel his lips again. Not
that mocking, careless kiss at supper, but the earlier tender touching.

*He is still Cumberland's man. He might have killed
one of my brothers. He is a gambler with no care for the
people who depend on him.* She thought all that and more.
*Just because he kept a bargain doesna change that. Just
because he has a mistress he prefers . . .*

She balled her fingers into a fist. For a few moments,
a few hours, she had not been so lonely.

*Do not forget about Dougal. He needs you. You
promised to get him out of Scotland. You have to keep
your wits about you.*

"My brother," she said. "You said you might be able
to get word to him."

"Write your letter, madam," he said, and just that last word reestablished the distance he had kept between them. "I will get it to him."

"Thank you."

He hesitated, then reached out and touched her cheek. A sweet aching awareness filtered through her.

He swore under his breath. After a long second, he leaned down. His lips met hers with a hungry longing she felt down to the marrow of her bones.

A whisper in the back of her mind warned her that he was still so many things she disliked, but it was like chaff in a furious storm of so many other feelings. She felt shivery and shaken and altogether confused at the attraction between them, the desire that even now seemed to burn out of control.

His lips moved on hers, searching, teasing. Swirling eddies of sensations enveloped her, tumbling her along in a vortex that eclipsed every caution, every warning. She wanted to touch, to feel, to explore the man behind the many masks. She wanted to feel him close to her. She wanted to prolong the dizzying, warm feelings that rocked her practical world.

The kiss deepened, his lips hard and demanding. His arms pressed her against him until she felt the hard changing of his body. She had never felt anything like it before, and she was stunned by the answering response of her own. She found herself moving into him, wanting more of those strange, compelling, glorious sensations that seemed to arc from her body.

Her arms went around him, her fingers playing in his hair and along his neck with an instinct she'd never realized she had. Her body, her hands, her mouth were all reacting completely on their own. Warm, irresistible feelings flowed through her body like a surging tide. Swelling and ebbing, then swelling again with renewed energy.

And she sensed the greatest wave was yet to come.

She felt the tension in his body, the barely restrained passion in his hands. They started moving at the small of her back, each subtle touch igniting new fires. His lips released hers, and they moved softly, seductively along the line of her cheek, down to her throat where they lingered. She thought she might explode with the growing need inside her. At the same time, she recognized his skill, his experience, and was reminded of his reputation, of his mistress.

Yet there was so much want. So much feeling. So much need. She felt a bewildering pain, a longing for something she did not understand. The strength of that need terrified her.

She trembled with the rush of unfamiliar emotions. She heard a small cry rip from her throat. Her hands fell from around his neck.

He hesitated, his body going still. Then he lifted one of her hands and brought it to his mouth, kissing each finger. She had not thought such gestures could bring about such havoc, could make her forget all the grief and loss and anger of the past year. But there was a gentleness, a tenderness to the gesture that made her heart ache.

He *did* make her forget.

She stood up on tiptoes, and this time she was the aggressor. Her lips pressed against his, and they clung together, savoring the intimacy of warmth and belonging, her body melding to his again. She opened her mouth to his with an awakening longing of her own. His hands moved over her body with poignant slowness as if exploring—and memorizing—every moment.

"Bonny lass," he whispered as his hands caressed and aroused, their gentleness sensual and inviting.

Magic wrapped around them, a seductive, drugging sorcery. Her heart bounced against the edge of its cage, and her body tingled with anticipation, the need inside growing as his hands heated every inch they touched.

Then his hands went to the laces in front of her dress. They fumbled, and she sensed that was unusual. Her gaze met his, and the green gold in his eyes was so tumultuous, so turbulent they reminded her of the rough seas not far from home. Her fingers went up to his face, touched the small cleft in his chin and watched as his mouth widened, the ends turning upward. Then her hands took the wig from his head, and her hand caught in the short, thick strands of his dark hair.

He stilled, as if frozen, then with a groan his lips seized hers again. This time there was no hesitancy, no restraint. This time their lips met in an explosion as bright as lightning striking the earth.

It was foolish, and dangerous and destructive. Rory knew all that and yet he could not keep his hands off her. Her eyes, which had once regarded him with contempt, were soft and wistful and longing. She needed this . . . affection as much as he did. He would not, could not, call it love. Love was too dangerous a word, too precarious an emotion.

They were wed. They were husband and wife in the sight of God. Not, he corrected, that he really believed in God. Not after the past few months. But they were also wed in the sight of the church and state.

She had been a good facade for his activities. She was, after all, the king's choice for him, and he had cooperated. But now he regretted his compliance. Or did he?

That was the hell of it. He stood a foot away from the gallows. Or worse.

"Rory?"

It was the first time she had said his name. It was naught more than a hoarse whisper, but it echoed throughout him. What in the hell was he doing?

Yet he could not stop. Her eyes were so very blue, so serious, so full of roiling emotions. He saw uncertainty, but he also saw desire. A desire that matched his own. He leaned down and kissed the tip of her nose, the freckles that amused and delighted and intrigued him. She truly did not understand how appealing she was, and that was an aphrodisiac. She was brave and stubborn and yet had a strong and generous heart.

He couldn't help himself. His hand went up to her

cheek, softly touching it with a tenderness he didn't know
he had. He wanted to know her thoughts, her very soul.
He brushed away a curl that had fallen over her right eye,
and he cherished the silken feel of it. No more anger in
her eyes. No more fear. Only wonder. A wonder more seductive than the accomplished wiles of a courtesan.

Rory savored that wonder. He felt it himself. For the
first time in his life, he felt no bitterness, no anger. He
felt he needed to be no one but himself. For he knew it
was Rory Forbes that she wanted, not the marquis of
Braemoor. She already had sensed more about him than
anyone ever had, including Alister and Elizabeth. He had
seen that knowledge in her eyes.

Then he had no more time to think, because his mouth
was moving toward her, his lips reaching down for hers.

They touched, gently at first, then with fierce need. He
disregarded the familiar call of caution. He heard only
his heart, greedy for what she was offering. His body
heated, his blood running hot and his heart beating rapidly.

"This is not wise, lass." His voice was a hoarse whisper.

"We are wed."

'Twas her agreement, plain and simple. How could he
not take something offered so sweetly?

"Are you sure? I fought with your enemies."

She stiffened slightly. "They said you walked from the
field."

"They say I am a coward."

"I do not believe that."

"Such faith," he whispered. His arms wrapped around
her, fusing her body to his, exploring every curve, feeling the heat radiate between them. Then he picked her
up and carried her to the bed. He leaned over her. Impatiently but gently, he stripped her garments from her—
the dress, then the petticoat, her laced shoes, her stockings
held in place by silk garters.

She was lovely in the light of the candle. It flickered
across her face, casting a glow over her dark hair. And

he realized he had never wanted a woman as badly as he wanted this one.

Bethia felt the oddest sense of freedom as he relieved her, piece by piece, of her clothes. She should feel wanton, she knew, but she felt no such thing. Instead, her body trembled with expectation.

He leaned down and kissed her. She felt the wistful yearning of his lips, the quiet searching, and her heart hammered, her breathing growing ragged. His hand covered her lower stomach, his fingers caressing. His lips moved down to one of her breasts, his tongue making circles, leaving hot wakes in its path.

Sorcery. It could not be anything but sorcery. Her body hummed. She was feeling sensations she had never even imagined.

She did not know how it happened, but his trews were gone, and he was naked except for his linen shirt. Bethia found herself shamelessly reaching for him, running her fingers against the fine symmetry of his chest, then his flat stomach. He was heavily muscled, something she'd not noticed under layers of flamboyant clothes. Again, she wondered why he so favored them when he would look so fine in simple britches and shirt, or a plaid.

Her hands caressed him, shyly at first, then more aggressively.

In retaliation, he kissed her throat and she was immediately engulfed in a maelstrom. Just as she thought she might explode with delicious heat, he licked the sensitive skin of her left breast, then its taut nipple. His tongue played with it, creating a string of fires that ran through her body like lightning.

He slipped off his shirt, and she stared at him in wonder. He was beautiful. The scar on his arm was new and raw and ugly, and there were several other thin scars, but his body was all hard angles and intriguing bulges. She felt the heat inside rise.

He kissed her again, his tongue moving inside her mouth, caressing and loving, awakening each sensitive nerve. Then, his lips still on hers, he arched himself over her, his body touching and teasing.

For a moment, she felt fear, but then she heard only her heart, and it was greedy for what he was offering, a sweetness that turned her blood to honey, a need that made her body tingle and come alive in the most wondrous ways.

His kiss deepened, became voracious. Bethia had never known a kiss could have such power, could melt her down to her bones. An elemental force raged between them now . . . as primitive and potent as the sea pounding against cliffs. Shamelessly she explored his taut body, her fingers lingering in forbidden places, then instinctively guiding him into her.

Still, he hesitated. His lips left hers and his gaze studied hers. "Are you quite sure, marchioness?"

She was not sure at all. She still knew little about this man who was her husband. But she needed him more than she had ever needed anything in her life. She was on fire, and she knew he was the only one who could extinguish the flames.

She nodded, unable to talk, to say the words.

He lowered himself and she felt a strange sensation as he started to enter her, then a sharp pain. She could not help but cry out, and he immediately stilled. She felt the taut control of his body, watched a muscle flick in his cheek.

Then, slowly, the unexpected pain receded, and hunger filled her. She put her arms around him.

"Bethia."

In answer, her hands urged him down, and he entered her again, slowly, moving unhurriedly, allowing her to adjust to him, to the new feelings that dazzled her. With her first uncertain compulsive movement, he went deeper within her, moving unhurriedly but with obvious purpose. She felt the first jolt of pleasure, and her own body moved against his, seeking more than the hint of rapture. He moved faster, rhythmically, each time thrusting deeper and deeper.

Bethia felt a glorious conflagration, a soaring splendor that eclipsed all previous sensation, everything she had ever known or thought she'd known. A profound pleasure grew and grew and grew until she thought she could stand no more.

She could. Every feeling intensified, whirling her into something splendid and indescribable, a dizzying, dazzling world of exquisite sensations.

Bethia clung to him, savoring the intimacy, the warm aftershocks that continued to bring rushes of pleasure, of contentment.

He lay still, then rolled over, carrying her with him. He looked at her through eyes lazy with satisfaction. His hand took hers and his fingers played along her palm.

"You are . . . lovely," he said.

Not just bonny. Lovely. And she felt lovely. She felt lovely and loved and cherished and wonderfully satisfied.

She snuggled into his arms and she felt safe for the first time in a very long time.

Fifteen

Bethia woke to a soft but persistent knocking. It took her a minute to grasp where she was. She felt different. Sore, yet complete in a way she'd never known before.

The sun streamed into her room, and she heard the plaintive cries of the little black terrier.

The knock came again and with it a shrill puppy bark. She looked around, trying to find evidence of her husband. She had gone to sleep in his arms last night.

He was not in the room. And he wouldn't be knocking this morning.

She wondered what time it was. Long past her usual rising hour, she thought.

She looked down. Black Jack's claws were all entangled in the wig, which he'd made into a nest. She smiled at the great curls all in disarray. "Where did he go?" she asked him. "And when?"

Her wistful question brought forth no answer. Reluctantly she left the bed, and the lingering scent of her husband. Then she looked down and saw a red stain on the bedclothes. Somehow she had to hide it. That stain supposedly had already been on the bedclothes.

She pushed the coverlet over it, then looked around

the room. No signs of Rory Forbes remained other than Jack's possession. The other wig was gone, as well as the waistcoat and shirt. And trews. 'Twas as if he had never been there at all. Except for the blood on the bed.

As before, Jack had no answers. He looked at her with an expression as bewildered as she felt.

Why did she feel so disappointed? Why did she miss him so?

She should be thinking about her brother, about getting him away from Cumberland and his minions.

Shame and self-disgust filled her. Yet there was a hint of glory there, too, pushing those other feelings aside.

Feeling a bit lost and uncertain, she left the bed, untangled the puppy, then wrapped a nightdress about her and went to the door.

Trilby stood there, laden with a tray of hot chocolate and pastries. "The marquis said to send this up to ye," she said, her eyes bright with inquisitive interest.

"Where is he?"

"He received a message, then left abruptly."

Disappointment was like a sword slitting her in two. Nor could she believe she had slept so long.

"How long ago?"

"No' verra' long."

"And he did not say how long he would be?"

"Nay."

Bethia ruffled the fur of the little terrier as her thoughts pillaged any remaining pleasure lingering from last night.

Why had she expected more? Why had she expected the magic to last?

He had never said he loved her or even cared for her. Indeed, even as she gave herself to him so wantonly, she knew he had a mistress. He'd never denied it. Never tried to hide it. Had he gone to her this morning? Had the woman in the woods sent for him? That hurt beyond bearing.

Trilby set the tray on the table, the table where a deck of cards remained. So there *was* something physical left of his presence. She turned one over. The jack of spades.

She bit back an exclamation. 'Twas as if some phantom was trying to remind her. Even if the marquis cared for her, which at the moment seemed unlikely since he'd not even bothered to say "good morn" to her, how could she have forgotten her brother? Even a moment?

"I will be back with water," Trilby said, watching her with a strange expression.

"Aye," she said softly. She sat down at the table and looked at the pastries. She had never felt less like eating. She tore off a tiny piece and gave it to Jack, who regarded it suspiciously before taking it daintily in his mouth.

She looked across the table, seeing the marquis in her mind's eye as he'd curved his lips into an unexpectedly whimsical smile. Why had she insisted on seeing more in him than probably existed? Just because he saw humor in a small dog?

Just because his practiced hands had been gentle?

She bit her lower lip, wishing she had been stronger last night, that she had remained cold and aloof. He'd said Cumberland had wanted a child. Was that why he had come to her last night? Why he had seduced her?

Or had she seduced him?

He could have just taken her.

But the marquis was a man who enjoyed games, who enjoyed playing with people's lives. He'd said as much last night.

Why, then, had she allowed him into her bed and into her heart?

She fed another small piece to the dog, then took a sip of the chocolate. Then with renewed determination, she rose and gathered the lower sheet on the bed, folding it as small as she could, and placed it in the bottom of the wardrobe. Trilby would not ask about it. Trilby asked about little.

In tucking it away, she touched the torn britches and shirt she had collected from the stableboy. Mayhap tonight she would make use of them. She would try to find the

Black Knave. And if she could not find him, she would become the symbol herself.

After last night, she knew she could not delay.

Rory rode as if the devil trailed him. In fact, he'd already decided that particular fiend was indeed riding his shoulders.

He'd never had a great deal of respect for himself. He'd never commended himself for honor or valor or strength of will.

But he had miserably failed himself and, God help him, Bethia last night. He'd had no right to do what he'd done. By taking her to bed, he'd made promises he'd had no right to make. He'd placed her in danger. He'd made sure that he would, in one way or another, betray her. She'd had enough tragedy in her life. She needed no more.

He'd lain awake most of the night, his arms around her. He'd determined then he could do one thing for her. Retrieve her brother and get the both of them out of Scotland as soon as possible. It did not matter what happened to him.

But getting her brother would be dangerous, and he would not raise her hopes.

He'd left the bed at dawn, fearing that seeing her in the morning might further erode what small will he had. Then he'd received a message from Alister that he was needed immediately.

He almost did not go. He did not want her to wake believing he'd cared nothing about her. But neither could he build false hope, let her think that he was anyone with whom she could build a life. He could not compound the damage he'd just inflicted.

He arrived at Mary's cottage, the place he and Alister usually met since his own home and blacksmith shop were far too visible. Their friendship had always been private. He doubted any suspected its strength. He was thought incapable of honest feeling. He'd worked hard at fostering that idea, even before his guise as the Knave. For a while, he'd even wanted it to be true.

There were no horses in front of Mary's cottage, which meant Alister had not yet arrived or had hidden his horse somewhere in the woods. Rory quickly dismounted and tied his horse in front of the cottage, hoping deep inside that his wife never heard that he had visited Mary the morning after sleeping with her.

But perhaps that would be best. Bethia *must* think the worst of him.

He knocked. Mary opened the door to him, then closed it sharply behind him.

"James Drummond is near Buckie, trying to find a ship, and the English know about it. They are planning a trap, passing along word that a certain fisherman might be agreeable to smuggling out a Jacobite. A barmaid overheard the planning and word was passed."

"Alister?"

"He went up there to try to find and warn him."

"It could well be a trap for the Black Knave, too," Rory said. "'Twould be just like the devious English: Set a trap and allow information to leak out, then prepare an altogether different one."

"He thought of that. He will be careful."

"He'll be stopping by the Flying Lady, then," Rory said. 'Twas a tavern near Buckie that they had visited together. The owner was sympathetic to the Jacobites and had previously passed on information to Rory via various routes. Rory had been there, had judged the man before trusting his words, but the tavern owner had not recognized the elderly English gentleman with the supercilious air.

"He said he would meet you there."

"The traitorous fisherman. Do we know who he is?"

"Aye. The word is he would betray his own mither for a half pence."

"And Drummond is most likely too young to know better."

"Or too desperate."

Rory knew a lot about desperation. He had seen enough of it these past few months. The Highlanders were braw and brave in battle, but they had no guile. They had little patience with stealth and duplicity.

She nodded, fear in her eyes.

He touched her cheek. "Alister will be fine. He is as slippery as an eel."

She did not answer, but her eyes remained troubled.

"I will bring him home," Rory said, trying to think what might be best. Should he go as himself, or in some other disguise? He needed to ride fast, which meant he should disguise himself as an English officer again. He disliked using the same disguise twice in a row, but he had few options.

"The English uniform?" He looked at Mary with a question in his voice.

"I cleaned it the best I could. It is dry."

He nodded. "I'll take the black and leave my horse here. If anyone comes by, I am in the woods hunting and will not be back until late."

"Including the marchioness?"

"Aye."

"Someone might see your horse here."

"Most likely."

"She will not object?"

"It is not for her to object." His voice was harsh, harsher than he intended. He didn't want this. Yet he did not want anyone to know that both he and the blacksmith were gone from the area at the same time. Far better that they think he had taken back up with his mistress.

Far better for whom? The demon whispered in his head.

He didn't waste more time. He took what he needed from Mary's hidden compartment under the floor and folded them into a blanket. Too many people knew him around here. He would wait to change until it would be unlikely that anyone would recognize him.

"Do not worry," he said. "I will send Alister back as soon as I find him."

Rumors abounded in the tower house. So many, in fact, that Bethia wondered whether she had been meant to hear them.

Whisper, whisper, whisper.

"The marquis is at the whore's cottage."

"He's been there two days."

"The Drummond lad is on the run."

"They say it is a trap for the Black Knave."

The Black Knave and the marquis's whore. Every time she approached a door, passed servants in the hall, went by the great hall at suppertime, she heard the voices pause, but their echoes ate a hole in her soul.

A trap.

The marquis and the woman.

A trap for the Black Knave.

She could not allow it to happen. He was her only hope to save Dougal. And herself.

She had to warn him.

Buckie. The whispers said the trap was being set at Buckie. 'Twas many miles away. How could she possibly reach it in time? How could she find him?

When would her husband return?

His frequent absences almost always lasted at least two or three days and often a week or more.

Bethia remembered the warmth she'd felt in his arms, the passion, even the gentleness. Now he had gone to the home of his mistress. To laugh about how he seduced his wife? How he had charmed and duped her?

How could she have been so fooled by the man? He had jumped from her bed into that of a loose woman. Had she been that inadequate? That unappealing?

Her heart felt hollow, her throat thick.

She went into his room, closed the door firmly behind her, and positioned herself so she could search his wardrobe as well as watch the door. She would not be surprised this time. She looked for the deck of cards. Surely he would not miss one or two.

They were gone. All of them!

She had the one jack from the deck of cards he'd given her. No more.

He had given her permission to ride alone, but if she took a horse and did not return it before nightfall, she was sure an alarm would be raised. The Black Knave was said to be a horse thief as well as a Jacobite. She could steal a horse.

What would happen to Dougal if she were caught? The thought sent shivers of terror through her.

But she had to do something.

Could she trust Trilby?

Her mind kept jumping from subject to subject. Did she dare take a chance?

The Black Knave had repeatedly risked his life for her friends, for Scotland's patriots. How could she do less for him?

She replaced the marquis's clothes and left his stark room.

'Twas midday.

Bethia went to her room, Black Jack anxiously tagging after her. He whined as if he knew what she was thinking and didn't care for it at all.

She regarded her face carefully in the mirror. It was pale, but not pale enough. Mayhap it would be easier to put color into it. An unhealthy color. A very unhealthy color.

But what kind of illness would keep people away, unwilling to go into her room? The pox? That would terrify everyone but it would also bring attention to Braemoor. That would not do.

Fainting spells? Everyone would suspect a child. It had been three months since their wedding.

That was it. She could go into seclusion. She remembered hearing tales of women who swooned when they were with child, who became deathly ill. Her mother, who had seven bairns, four of which survived childbirth, had always voiced contempt for such behavior. It was a woman's lot to bear children with dignity.

Would Trilby cooperate? Would she risk the marquis's wrath?

She would tell Trilby she was faint and ill with an uncertain stomach, that she was not well enough to see anyone. They would draw their own conclusions. Then she would slip out tonight, leaving a note for Trilby, telling her she had to make sure her brother was safe, that she had heard he was not. Would she please tell everyone the marchioness was still fragile? But then would Trilby be blamed?

She immediately dismissed that plan because of the last factor. She could not be responsible for Trilby being caught in such a lie.

Mayhap the direct route was best. The marquis had given her freedom to ride. He had left her bed and gone to his mistress. She would just take a horse and ride away, leaving a note to him or to anyone who asked that she was going to visit her brother. She had promised not to leave the marriage. She had not promised she would not try to visit her brother.

Many things could happen along the way. She could take the wrong road and become lost. For days.

She was certain there would be a price to pay, but if she would be able to warn the Black Knave it did not matter. Especially if she could earn his gratitude—and his help.

And if her husband was dismayed, she could counter accusation with accusation. Her husband had left her bed without so much as a word. Probably for the bed of his mistress. His anger could be no greater than her own.

Bethia planned her escape carefully. She had to leave during daylight hours or there would be questions. She knew that Jamie's father stayed in the stable at night, and he would well question a midnight ride.

She dressed in her riding costume, then carefully

wrapped Jamie's old clothes along with a bonnet in a piece of cloth. She planned to say, if anyone asked, that she was taking the bolt for a shirt to be made for her husband. As an afterthought, she took out the necklace her husband had given her. She might need a bribe. It had held some meaning for a fraction of time, but now it held none.

She carefully sewed it inside one of the trouser legs, then sewed another piece of cloth over it. It would be uncomfortable and complicate her walking, but it might well be necessary. It gave her some bit of satisfaction that she might be using his gift to thwart his patron.

She then wrote a note saying that she had gone to see her brother. Hopefully, Neil would not care enough to send someone after her, especially without orders from the marquis.

Bethia planned to get lost along the way. She would take the road to Rosemeare where her brother was imprisoned, then cut down toward Buckie on the coast. It would be a most unusual thing for a woman to take such a trip without an escort, but after all, she was a Jacobite. If her husband could disappear for days, she did not know why she could not.

More important, she would be taking action, becoming a part of events that affected her, not just a pawn in someone else's game. In numerous games. Cumberland's. Her husband's.

Neither cared about her or Dougal.

She'd never felt so alone. And yet she also felt a sense of purpose.

Bethia hurried down the stairs. Neil and some of his men were out looking for the young Ogilvy and now probably Drummond, and any other Jacobite they could locate. They would be back tonight, and all they would care about would be the casks of wine and hot food.

Jamie was in the stable, and he saddled her horse. He asked to go with her, but she said she now knew the way, and would be safe by herself. He looked at her doubtfully, but then his fa came in, and told him to mind "the lady."

'Twas obvious that no one but Jamie really cared about her safety.

She mounted with his help, then walked the mare down the lane and out of sight of the tower house. Bethia then urged the mare into a canter until they reached a cross-roads. She took the road that led to the mountains and the coast, the one away from Lord Creighton and her brother.

She was free.

The rumor was indeed a trap for the Black Knave rather than Drummond. If Drummond, however, was also apprehended, so much the better.

Rory discovered that fact very quickly.

His uniform gained him entrance to a tavern frequented by English officers. They were thankfully well into their cups and accepted him without question, especially since he seemed as rollicking drunk as they.

They were not discreet. Several of them had just come off patrol. Every approach to the fisherman's house was well watched. Any stranger, no matter how old, or which sex, was stopped. Drummond would probably hear of the fisherman shortly, and he would make his way to him.

The Black Knave would undoubtedly try to save him from his own foolishness.

The English were not exactly sure where Drummond was, except they believed he was hiding in the Grampians. He had been sighted near a village, and later a village lad had been heard asking whether anyone knew a fisherman willing to risk sailing him south to a port where he might find passage out of the country. He would be well-paid.

The word was out that a Geordie Grant would be interested. Geordie, it was said, would do anything for a coin or cask of ale. 'Twas expected that Drummond would approach him either tonight or the next. The soldiers had apparently been part of the patrol watching the fisher-man's house for the past two days, and were weary of inaction. They also wearied of the incessant cold rain, and complained bitterly that the Scottish weather was as cold and treacherous as many of the country's inhabitants.

Still, the thought of trapping the Black Knave was an enticing one. The reward was large.

Rory affected his best English accent. Since he'd fostered with an English family, he could talk about nearly anyone with some knowledge. He soon had his companions roaring with laughter with imitations of several highly placed officials in King George's government. Then, thoroughly accepted, he sat back with a brandy, faked a drunkenness and listened as a plan fermented in his mind.

He'd next have to find Alister or make sure warnings had been delivered.

He suspected Alister might already have found Drummond. His friend had built several strong networks of spies, using information from those they had already helped. Spurred by his own dismal childhood, Alister had quite actively and enthusiastically turned into a protector of the weak and hunted. He had, in fact, a genius for names and organization.

Rory wished the other officers luck in finding the black-hearted villain who had made fools of them. He discreetly left the latter part of the sentence unspoken, and lurched uncertainly toward the door and his horse.

Fifteen minutes later he approached the Flying Lady. It was a tavern frequented by local fisherman, many of whom hated the English, and was therefore avoided by soldiers of the crown. Rory would be thoroughly obnoxious, obnoxious enough to bring attention to himself.

The Flying Lady was part of an inn and was far quieter than one frequented by the English. Scots huddled around the tables in bleak and sullen silence, their expressions bitter and hostile as he entered the public room. Their fishing had been curtailed in large measure by the

English who worried about Jacobites escaping. Boats were repeatedly searched and often confiscated by the English who claimed their owners were Jacobite sympathizers.

A man approached him, a burly individual with a deep frown. "I am thinkin' ye are in the wrong place," he said.

"*I* think not," Rory said and took a chair. "I will have your best brandy."

Moments later he was drinking what must be the worst brandy in all of Scotland.

All eyes were on him. He ignored them, raised his feet to the table and leaned comfortably back in the chair and regarded the others with equanimity. An hour went by, then another.

His tavern mates muttered. He grinned at them.

One by one they left, leaving the owner glowering at him. "Closing time," he said.

"I had hoped for a friendly game of cards."

The tavern keeper looked at him as if he had grown a set of fangs and was breathing fire. He knew he could not force an English officer to leave.

"Sit down and play with me," Rory said.

The man glowered.

Rory paid no attention to the scowl. Instead he took out a deck of cards and facilely shuffled them. Then he split the deck and turned one side up to a black jack.

The tavern keeper's scowl deepened. He turned and started to walk away.

"Brodie said you could be trusted." Brodie was the name Alister used on his travels.

The man stopped. "'Ow is Mr. Brodie?"

"Sick in soul."

The tavern keeper's gaze bored into him, accepting the agreed upon words with a lingering doubt. He was still being cautious, and Rory approved of that.

"What do ye want?"

"Has Brodie been here?"

"He has."

"When?"

"This morning." The tavern keeper continued to regard him suspiciously. "He left a warning."

"For Drummond?"

"Aye," the man said cautiously.

"You know where he is, then?"

"Mayhap." He looked at the card again. "Anyone could have tha' card."

Rory took his feet from the table. "True," he said amiably, "but we needed something people could trust. It might well have outworn its purpose. I knew the words, though, too."

The tavern keeper's eyes narrowed. "Are ye 'im? The Knave?"

"Nay. Just a messenger."

The man did not look as if he believed Rory, but then he appeared a naturally suspicious man. Rory approved of that, too.

"I must get in touch with Drummond."

Cool blue eyes appraised him. "Ye look and talk like an English officer."

"It is helpful at times."

"Aye," the man said grudgingly. "But I can take a message." He bristled. "Or am I not trusted?"

"I would not be here if you were not." Rory dropped the English accent. "But Drummond is headstrong, and he may not believe you."

The innkeeper hesitated, then slowly relented. "I will take ye to him. I was planning to take Brodie's message to him later tonight. First I will have to get my brother to take over the inn."

"Do you have some other clothes? This uniform is rather conspicuous. I do not fancy being shot as an Englishman."

The innkeeper finally smiled. "Our Father may not let ye enter His gates."

"I should hope not," Rory agreed.

"He sees into their black hearts."

"Aye," Rory said.

He was suddenly accepted. He did not know why or how, but the man gestured him up a narrow set of steps and opened a door to usher him inside.

In another few moments, Rory was dressed in plain ragged breeches made of drugget. It was coarse and undyed and exactly what he needed. He selected a used and somewhat smelly shirt of similarly rough material, then some shoes with a thin sole nearly worn through. The innkeeper added a worn jacket.

The man watched with curiosity as Rory stripped the well-manicured mustache from above his lips. He was, Rory knew, reconsidering Rory's denial that he was the Black Knave. But Rory had no intention to debate the point. Let him wonder.

He stuffed some cotton in his cheeks, then darkened his teeth with a substance Elizabeth had given him. The cotton also changed his voice.

The innkeeper stared with amazement. "I nev'r would 'ave believed it." He struck out his hand. "I am Kerry."

Rory gave him a crooked, toothy grin. "I know."

Sixteen

Every bone in Bethia's body ached. Every muscle, every part of her body. The cold crept inside the thin clothing she wore, and the wind lashed at the worn bonnet. She prayed the too-large bonnet would keep her hair inside. She'd disciplined it into a tight braid and pinned it tightly to the back of her head.

She'd also bound her breasts with a piece torn from a sheet, and she *thought* she looked like a luckless lad. The problem was, of course, the horse. It was much too fine for one of a lad's obvious station. Yet she needed it to get to Buckie in time to warn those intended for the English net.

So she rode through woods and fields and the Grampians. At night she risked the roads, listening carefully for the sound of hoofbeats and drawing into the shadows at any sound.

Had she been a complete fool?

She was beginning to think so.

Trilby would be missing her by now. Would she sound the alarm, or would she simply believe she was with the marquis? They might be searching for her at this very moment. Perhaps the marquis had arrived home. She had tasted his cynicism, his irritation, but never yet his anger. What would he do?

She thought of Black Jack in his basket at Braemoor. Trilby would see to him, Bethia knew that. The maid was as captivated with the pup as she was.

And what could she really do? Relay word? She had thought about trying to become the Black Knave, but whoever would believe such a scrawny lad could be the valiant and fearless hero? Master of disguises or not, he could never fit into so small a form as hers.

Feeling more and more useless, she nonetheless kept riding through the night until she reached the Innes lands. The Innes clan had always been Jacobites. Their land lay not far from Buckie. She had visited there several times with her brothers. One brother, in fact, had courted Anne Innes.

Had any of them survived the bloodbath? Their branch of the clan was small, with no title, only a laird. Had they managed to hold on to any of their property? She remembered one of the grooms. He had openly flirted with her. That had only been eighteen months ago. It seemed a lifetime.

She thought of the house party she'd attended, the dancing and merriment. Most of the guests were dead now. Her betrothed, Angus, had been there, as had her two brothers. All had talked of nothing else but the imminent arrival of Prince Charles and how they would chase the British from Scotland once and for all. They had boasted and drunk and danced and had been so very young. She bit her lip to keep the tears from coming, to hold back the feeling of loss and emptiness.

All were gone now. All of them.

And gone for a cause that never really had a chance. She knew that now. She knew about the clans that had deserted the prince, about the mistakes, all the warnings he'd disregarded. And yet she, like so many Scots, wished him speedy and safe passage to France.

There would never be another uprising, though. Cumberland had done his job well.

Nearly numb with cold and echoes of a past that could never be reborn, she tied her horse to a bush, then approached the tower house where she'd once danced so gaily. The first gray glimmers of dawn were appearing over the hills. She would approach the stable first and try to learn whether Anne Innes was still in residence. Perhaps Anne could find her a less conspicuous horse.

The door to the barn was closed. She opened it and slipped inside. It was only a wee bit warmer than outside, and she shivered. She stilled until her eyes gradually adjusted to the darkness. The first morning light crept through, enabling her to see objects, then the animals.

One of the horses neighed, then several others joined the chorus. She did not know if they were voicing disapproval at being disturbed or hope that food was coming. She counted only five; the Inneses once had one of the largest and finest stables in the Highlands.

She looked to see whether anyone stayed within the barn as did John and Jamie at Braemoor. There was no one.

Bethia then studied the horses. Her own was very tired. If Anne was in residence, or any of her family, she felt certain she could borrow a mount. One of them, an older mare, appeared a possibility.

She considered approaching the back door as a beggar. But better yet, she thought, to wait here and see if the same groom she'd met months ago appeared. She could discover from him the fate of Anne and her family. By virtue of the fact that Anne's father had been too old to join the rebellion and Anne had no brothers, they may have escaped the fate of so many other Jacobite families. And perhaps they had heard something of the Black Knave.

She went into an empty stall. Clean hay absorbed the chill from the dirt floor. She curled up in a ball. She would sleep for a few moments. Just a few . . .

• • •

Bethia woke to a sharp kick to her chest.

Consciousness was swift and painful. So was immediate comprehension. She grabbed for her bonnet, making sure it had stayed in place, then glared up at her attacker.

It was not the groom she had seen months ago.

"Beggars go to the back of the tower house," the man said.

Bethia tried to sit up, but her chest hurt. She glared at the man, trying to remember how to speak. "Ye 'ad no need to do tha'. I dinna hurt anything."

"What do ye want?"

"Miss Innes. I wanted to see Miss Innes."

The man looked at her suspiciously. "What's the likes of ye want with the mistress?"

She was here, then. Bethia silently said a prayer of thanks.

"She said she would gi' me a 'elping hand."

"Then why did ye not go to the house?"

"I dinna want to wake anyone," she said indignantly.

"Ye donna look like much."

Bethia gave him an indignant stare.

He scowled at her. "Mistress Anne will not be up this early."

She looked at him slyly. "I can be helpin' wi' the 'orses while I wait."

Some of his truculence faded. He nodded curtly.

Bethia cleaned out a stall, then helped with another. By the time she was through, she was odorous, blistered and weary again. And her chest still hurt from the stableman's blow. But she had managed to engage the man in conversation.

"They say the Black 'Nave's been aboot," she said as they cleaned out a stall together.

The man shrugged. "None of my business, 'cept I wouldna mind 'aving some of that reward."

Bethia looked at him with horror. "You would turn 'im in?"

" 'E's nothing to me. Trouble, tha's all 'e is."

She held her tongue. She could not betray her interest.

"Has the mistress wed?"

"Nay. Her fa is ill. And 'tis said the man she was to marry died at Culloden."

Her brother. So Anne had been loyal to him even after death.

"The laird is ill?"

"Aye. The butcher took 'is cattle and sheep, even 'is best horses."

So Anne had known her bad times, too. At least, though, she had not been forced into a detestable marriage. She felt blood rush to her face at the thought of Rory Forbes, at how she had responded to him, to those moments of tenderness. They had all been part of some game, or, even worse, a ploy to get her with child. He could have just taken her at the beginning, of course. It was his right. Now she almost wished he had. It would have been preferable than to be taken so lightly, to be used so mindlessly.

Her gruff companion finished cleaning the last stall, then said, "I will go tell the mistress ye are here." He hesitated. "I will tell 'er ye are a good worker." He paused at the door. "My name is John. Yer name is . . . ?"

Bethia had not thought of that. The whole idea had occurred so suddenly. Her brother's name. Anne's betrothed. *Coinneach.* Gaelic for Kenneth. "Kenny," she said after a brief pause. "She said more than a year ago tha' if I ever needed a position . . ."

John looked at her strangely. "A year ago."

"Or more," she added helpfully.

He went to the door, then looked back. "Donna ye be taking anything."

Bethia shook her head as earnestly as she could. "Sirrah," she said. "The lad who used to work here . . . would ye be knowing anything of 'im?"

John shrugged. "He joined the Prince. 'E was never seen again."

The burden on Bethia's heart grew weightier. How many more were gone? She sighed as the groom left the barn and went to the door, waiting.

Would Anne understand? Would she come out or ask to see the ragged lad? Bethia could have gone to the door when she first arrived, and probably would have, had it not been for the early hour. She was depending on Anne's curiosity if not her immediate recognition.

Minutes went by. She didn't know how many, and her anxiety grew. Then she saw Anne at the door, and the groom came trotting back to the barn. "She will see ye," he said, his gaze regarding her with new respect.

Bethia swaggered out the door with what she hoped was a street lad's arrogance.

When she reached the steps to the door of the tower house, Anne's eyes grew increasingly large. She did not say anything, though, until Bethia came within several feet of her.

"Bethia?"

Bethia grinned. "Aye. But I dinna think anyone would know me under this dirt."

Anne looked away from her. The groom was watching. She turned and opened the door and went inside, indicating Bethia should follow her. Once the door was closed, she turned on Bethia and embraced her. "Holy Mother, Bethia." She squeezed Bethia's hand. "I have worried about you so. And now you turn up looking like this. What is going on?"

"The Black Knave. He is walking into a trap. I had to find someone who might reach him."

Anne's nose wrinkled. "I thought you had married—"

"The butcher forced me into a marriage with the Marquis of Braemoor. Cumberland holds Dougal as hostage to my obedience."

"Then it was nothing you wanted?"

" 'Tis the last thing I wanted. He is a . . . profligate. A traitor. I despise him."

"He allowed you to come here?"

"Nay. He is away, probably with his mistress. I left a note telling him I was going to see Dougal. Lord Creighton is holding him at Rosemeare."

A chill suddenly racked her, and Anne regarded her damp clothes worriedly. "You must have warmer clothes."

"I have to get to Buckie. A lad can visit the taverns and mayhap hear something of the Black Knave. You have not heard anything, have you?" she asked hopefully.

"Nay, but I wish him Godspeed."

"I need a horse, Anne. I took one from Braemoor's stable, but it is far too fine for someone dressed as I am. I had hoped you could provide me with a less conspicuous animal."

Anne hesitated. "There is an old mare . . . she is more a pet now."

"I would take very good care of her."

Anne looked at her wistfully. "I wish I could go, but Father—"

"John told me he was ill."

"His heart broke when Cumberland took our sheep and cattle. We have no way to feed our people now. Some have already left to try to find jobs in Glasgow or Edinburgh. I think he has willed himself to die."

"Perhaps I can help."

"You were always one of his favorites," Anne said, "but you cannot see him like that and if you change clothes, someone might recognize you."

Bethia leaned over and hugged her. "Then you might be blamed. I will try to come back."

Tears glistened in Anne's eyes. "I will never stop missing your brother." She paused, then went to a desk and sat down, taking a quill and paper. She quickly wrote out something, scribbled a name on it and sealed it.

"It is a letter to my sister, inviting her to visit," she said. "If anyone stops you, tell them you are employed

by me and delivering the letter to Jane Grant. It will give
you a reason to have a horse."

"Thank you," Bethia said gratefully. "And now I must
go. It might already be too late."

Anne nodded. In minutes she had found a worn jacket
that Bethia could wear over her still damp clothing, then
she walked with her to the stables.

Once there, she confronted John. "Saddle Sadie. The
lad here is going to take a message to my sister."

John looked surprised but obeyed quickly; faster, in
fact, than Bethia would have believed. She remembered
Anne's comment that many of their people had had to
leave. Why had *he* stayed? Loyalty to Anne. Or loyalty
to someone else?

Bethia mounted easily, noting again how much easier
it was to mount a man's saddle rather than the sidesaddle to which she was accustomed. Anne walked out with
her, then out of sight of the groom, seized her hand and
held it tightly. "Godspeed," she said.

"My horse is just beyond that hill. You might take a
ride that way and find her."

"Aye, I will do that. And hold her for you."

"Thank you."

"No need for that. Just be careful. I do not wish to
lose another MacDonell to the butcher."

Bethia reached Buckie in late afternoon. Afraid someone
might see through her disguise, she avoided one tavern
that seemed to host numerous English soldiers, and
stopped at a small alehouse. She sidled in, found a seat
in the shadows where she could overhear without at-
tracting attention. She hesitantly spent coin for a glass of
ale, which she barely sipped. And she listened.

The coins came from her wagers with the marquis. She
had resumed thinking of him that way. 'Twas altogether
too disturbing to think of him as her husband.

She dismissed thoughts of him and instead tried to listen to the several conversations going on. But after sev-

eral wary glances at her, talk centered on fishing and the interference of the English. Beginning to feel that her mission was hopeless, she left the tavern.

Bethia made her way to where she had left the mare. She'd learned of another tavern, one connected to an inn. She could stable Sadie there and feed her. Then she would decide what to do next.

She led the tired horse down the street, ducking into shadows as she heard a detail of soldiers come down the road, stopping at the earlier tavern that served the English. Two went inside, apparently searching for one of its members.

"Damn me if I know where Robbie's gone," said one of the remaining men in the street.

"The colonel's going to flay him. He wants every man in those hills."

Bethia put her hand over the mare's mouth, urging its silence as she tried to slink ever further into the shadows.

She strained to hear snatches of conversation.

"Damn me, but it appears that the colonel's plan worked."

"If Dan'l and Jock can keep up wi' 'em."

She did not hear the answer, but she did hear another voice. "At least we know the innkeeper and another man went up into the forest. To meet Drummond, no doubt. The colonel's blocking every path, using every mon in these parts."

"Wha' if it is not the Knave?"

"Do not be suggestin' that to the colonel. He is convinced the Flying Lady is a nest of traitors. 'E's had them watched for days now, then two men slipped out before dawn. No doubt it is the Knave."

"Why dinna they not arrest them?"

"The colonel wants Drummond, too. Good for a promotion."

"And the reward. He won't be sharing it, either."

"What about Geordie?" Another voice, but they were moving farther away now and she could barely hear.

" 'E was a fool to believe he'd ever get his thirty pieces of silver."

Their voices trailed away completely as they moved down the lane.

Geordie. He must be the fisherman set to betray the Black Knave. A name. She had a name. It should be worth something.

But how could she warn the Black Knave now? The paths were obviously watched by the English, and she had no idea where they were.

An idea started to form in her head. If they thought the Black Knave was somewhere else. If they thought he was about to get Drummond out of Scotland, then they would leave the hills.

But how would anyone mistake her for the Black Knave, the tall giant on a black horse, or for an old woman, which disguise he was rumored to adopt? Or even an old man?

She needed help, and the people at the Flying Lady had to be warned. They would all be hanged if it were proven any had helped the Black Knave.

The Flying Lady.

She led her horse out into the open and walked away from the soldiers. She saw a boy spit at where they had walked. She approached him.

"Can ye tell me where the Flying Lady is?"

"Aye. Down on the waterfront. Take the road to the sea. Ye can see it from there." He looked at Bethia curiously. "Ye ha' business there?"

"Nay. I was told I could rest and feed my horse."

"I would go somewhere else. The English have spies watchin' it."

"I ha' no' money. The owner is said to be kind with feed."

He shrugged. " 'Tis your neck, not mine."

Bethia led the mare down the road to the sea. It was past dusk, but the rain had stopped. A bright moon lit the sky, although an occasional heavy cloud blotted it. She peered first one way, then another. She saw a weather-beaten sign creaking in the wind. An outline of a ship perched above carved letters.

So it had been named after a ship. She looked around. If English soldiers remained to spy, she could not see any. But then the soldier had said every man had been sent to comb the roads and paths down from the forest. She could only hope.

Bethia reached for the deck of cards buried in her clothes. The jack was on the top. Then she approached the door. No sound came from within, no raucous noise as there had been at the other two establishments. She tried the door. It was open. She went inside.

One man was inside, sitting forlornly in a chair. He was of huge size. Half of his face was buried by a red, untamed beard.

"We are closed, lad," he said.

"The door is open."

"It is always open, but now 'tis not wise to be here."

She started. "Then you know?"

He rose with startling speed and in three large steps, stood next to her, clasping her arm tightly. "What do ye mean?"

Bethia held out the jack of spades with her free hand and placed it on a table next to them.

His beard wriggled and his eyes narrowed. "Wha' does a slip of a lad know about cards?"

She drew herself up to her full height, disregarding the pain from his hold.

"You know the . . . Knave has many disguises."

The man's head jerked back. "What's your game, lad?"

The pressure on her arm was like a vise. It was all she could do to keep from screaming.

"Are you the innkeeper?"

"My brother is. He asked me to stay here for him."

"He is in danger. The English knows he has left with another man, one they suspect is the Knave."

"But he is not, because you are," the man replied sarcastically. "I ask you again, what game do you play?"

"I play none," she said, and she knew her accent had slipped from a stableboy to the more precise diction of royalty.

"What are the words?"

She closed her eyes. She knew no words. Bethia felt sick. How could she ever have thought she might fool anyone?"

"I am not the Knave," she admitted.

"Obviously" the man muttered.

"I am a friend in desperate need of his services. I was looking for him when I overheard some British soldiers saying that they had been watching your inn, and that two men left early this morn. They were followed into the forest but then they disappeared. But the English have every path covered." She paused. "And anyone who comes here is in danger."

His deep sunken eyes took on a fierce glare. "I think ye are the danger. How much are the English paying you to snoop?" His hands did not release their hold. "I think I should just drown ye."

"Then everyone will die," she said defiantly, glaring at him. "Do you not see? The Black Knave has to appear elsewhere. At Geordie's house."

His brow furrowed.

Bethia rushed on at his hesitation. "It's a double trap. The English let it be known that a man named Geordie— I do not know the last name—would sail Drummond south. But they really want the Black Knave. They believe that if the Knave learned about the trap, he would try to reach Drummond. They must have suspected your . . . inn."

"The English are no' that clever," he replied suspiciously.

"They are sly." She stamped her feet anxiously. "There is no time to waste. Another Black Knave must visit Geordie, convince him that his life is no' worth a pence if he does the crown's bidding, then take his boat. He will go running to the English, and they will send their men to watch the beaches instead."

"Ye are sure of tha'?"

"Nay," she admitted. "But it was the only thing I could think of. They will believe then that your brother went on some other errand, that he had nothing to do with the Black Knave."

The man released his hold on her arm, and scratched his beard with his other hand. "What do ye want from me?"

"Some men you trust. The English obviously think the two men are in the Grampians, not on the coast. Most of the patrols have been sent into the mountains. Geordie will be lightly guarded. We—you—can take him easily. And his boat." She wanted him to start thinking it was his idea.

Tired, pale blue eyes stared out at her. "I 'ave only my brother left. If you betray him, I'll kill ye."

"This may be the only chance he has."

"It might be tae late," the innkeeper said despondently, obviously reluctant to put his faith in a slip of a boy.

"The Knave is cautious," she said. "The Brits will not easily catch him."

"Ye know him?"

"Aye," she lied.

"I told my brother no' to get involved, but he dinna listen." He released her arm. "There are a few men I trust."

Relief flooded her. She'd won. "Do you have any black clothing? Something I can use to mask my face? The others will need them, too, but none must speak but me. Their voices might be recognized."

His eyes were dubious as he gazed up and down her body. But then he seemed to make a decision. "My brother 'as a black cloak. It might make you look more . . ." He stopped, obviously at a loss of a description.

"Substantial?" She asked helpfully.

"Aye," he said. "'Ow old are ye, lad?"

"Old enough to have lost my entire family."

He frowned. "I canna trust—"

"You have no choice. 'Tis your brother's only hope."

The man muttered that they were all doomed.

She waited, her throat tightening.

"Are ye sure there are not spies outside?"

"I did not see any, and I looked."

He seemed to be fighting an internal battle, then he puckered his mouth. "All right," he finally said. "But if ye are lying to me. . . ."

She was. But only partly. And all for a good cause. She said a silent prayer for forgiveness to the Holy Mother.

"I will get ye a cloak. Ye stay here until I can find some men to help. But I doona know if they will follow ye."

"They will follow *you*," she said.

His face cleared slightly. He obviously felt more comfortable putting his fate in his own hands rather than those of a young unknown stranger.

He told her where to find the cloak and black material for masks. Then he slipped out the door.

"Hell and damnation." The oath came spilling from Rory Forbes's lips.

He'd had a plan.

He always had a plan.

They just dinna always work. And this, apparently, was one of those times.

That was exactly what he got for trying to be clever.

They had been here two days. Cooped up in a wet, cold cave like chickens awaiting the fox.

He had doubled back on the trek up into the forested hills and had spied someone following. He and Kerry, who was half Irish and had a hatred for English greater than any full-blooded Scot, had managed to lose the men trailing them. They reached Drummond in a well-hidden cave just after dawn.

But when Rory had scouted several hours later, he'd discovered English soldiers everywhere. He had barely made it back. Now they were trapped with very little food and even less water.

Rory knew where he'd made his mistake. He'd apparently missed the spies who had watched the tavern. He had not expected that the Flying Lady was suspect.

He would never be that careless again. If he had the chance.

His main regret was that he might have irreparably damaged Kerry. The innkeeper's life could be as tenuous as young Drummond's. At that thought, he turned his attention back to the young lord. Drummond shivered in a corner with a fever that came, Rory suspected, from both lack of food and exposure. They had to get him to safety if he were to live.

They could not even build a fire for fear that the smell of smoke might reach the searchers. Both he and Kerry had given him their cloaks, but still he shivered and still his face burned with heat. In the past few hours, their charge had been growing progressively worse.

He turned to Kerry. "If we can get past them, we can always say that I came to you as guide, that I wanted to hunt the Black Knave, to earn the five thousand pounds. 'Tis enough of a princely sum."

"It might be tae late for that."

It might, indeed. It might send both of them to the gallows. And yet it was the beginning of a plausible story. That depended, however, on getting Drummond out of here and on a boat. If found with the man, all three would be swinging. He just might have the added pleasure of being drawn and quartered for committing treason.

Yet, he would never abandon Drummond. Nor, he sensed, would Kerry. The man thrived on hatred.

To save Kerry, he had to save Drummond. Right now he had absolutely no idea of how to do that. The English were as thick as the underbrush.

Rory knew he needed a miracle this time. He turned

toward Kerry, who was barely visible in the dark cave. "I am sorry for involving you."

"No one forced me," Kerry said gruffly. "I will take a few of the bastards out wi' us." He patted the pistol next to him. A deadly looking knife hung from his belt, and Rory knew a second one was tied to his leg inside the trousers.

Drummond, who was no more than twenty, coughed, a succession of spasms that alarmed Rory. The sound could alert any nearby soldiers.

He took his flask and offered the lad the last of his water. Drummond took it gratefully, then sunk back on the damp floor. Rory exchanged worried looks with Kerry.

"I will go out and check again," Rory said. "Mayhap they have given up."

Kerry looked at him dubiously, but did not express his thoughts. Neither of them wanted Drummond to know how serious the situation really was.

Rory went to the front of the cave and listened for several moments before squirming under the barrier he and Kerry had built after discovering they'd been followed part of the way. He continued to crawl along the ground.

It was dawn. Gray colored the sky, but there was no sun yet. Wind blew through the trees, and the ground was damp. He had taken the cotton out of his cheeks when they'd first arrived, but now his clothes were nearly black with dried mud. The new moisture seeped through the dried mud and cloth and clung clammily to his skin.

He'd also pasted some mud on his face to keep the white of his face from showing and he wore a worn dark bonnet over his dark hair. He scooted like a crab some distance from the cave, then, in the shadow of trees, listened for the sound of boots against leaves, the rustle of bodies against branches, a flight of birds that had been disturbed.

Nothing.

He moved further down the hill to a spot where he'd

heard, and seen the fires, of an English detail hours earlier. Nothing. He kept moving until he reached their campsite. The remnants of a fire remained, but the ashes were cold.

The ground looked as if they had slept here last night. When had they left? And why?

Another trap?

He would not underestimate the English again. He moved on until he found a place that overlooked a trail below. Clear. He listened carefully again. Every sense was aware. No smell of fire. No discordant sound. Birds were singing their usual greeting to dawn. Squirrels jumped playfully from tree to tree, chattering playfully.

He shivered in the cold dawn. Where in the bloody hell did they go? And why?

Rory stood, trying to blend his dark shape with that of a large oak tree. Still nothing. No red uniforms breaking the grayish green and brown of the forest. He descended through the woods, avoiding the path worn by numerous hunters. Most of the game was gone now, killed by the two armies that had gathered at Culloden Moor.

Hunters now looked for human prey.

He had never enjoyed hunting animals and had avoided the large hunting parties held each fall. He had killed for meat as one did to survive, but he had never thought it should be cause for a festive event. Now that he knew exactly how the quarry felt, he would be many times more respectful of life.

He went more than a mile. Once he saw a group of English below him, but they were retreating in orderly fashion. For some reason the search was being abandoned. They would wait until tonight and try to make the coast. Kerry had said he knew a fisherman he could trust. The man lived on the far side of Buckie, far from the man said to be involved with the British. If young Drummond could be moved by boat to the other side of Nairn, then he could stay with the same farmer who had helped others until the Frenchman returned on the tenth of the next month.

Rory carefully made his way back to the cave. "The soldiers are gone."

Kerry frowned his brows in worry. "Are ye sure?"

"Aye. Nothing within a mile of us. I saw some English soldiers moving back down the trail. They are retreating."

"Should we go down now?"

Rory lowered his voice. "I think we should wait until dusk. We may have to carry Drummond part of the way. How far to your friend?"

"We ca' make it before dawn if we leave in late afternoon."

"I will look again about midday. We will take turns sleeping. You go first."

Kerry started to protest. "Ye've had none at all."

"I will have all afternoon. 'Tis all I need."

Kerry started to look as if he'd protest, then looked at the shivering Drummond. "Do ye think we can start a fire?"

"Aye," Rory said. "We will build it deep inside."

Kerry grinned, a snaggletoothed grin if ever did Rory see one. "We'll outwit them bastards yet."

Seventeen

Bethia had never been so physically frightened in her life.

She had been frightened for her brothers when they joined Prince Charlie's army, and particularly after she heard of the slaughter. She had been frightened for herself when she'd been married to a man she did not know. But she'd never experienced anything like this pounding in her heart.

For the first time she understood the male predilection for battle. She had never been so terrified; neither had she ever felt so alive.

She'd had to hide her uncertainty well. If she'd shown one second of fear, she would have lost every one of the small group the innkeeper's brother had found. They had been dubious enough about her size, but her plan had changed their minds. 'Twas a fine plan, everyone agreed. A plan worthy of the Black Knave.

Each also wanted Geordie Grant to receive his due. He gave them all a bad name. To scare the life from him, and also to take his boat, seemed suitable repayment, enough to gag other potential traitors.

Miraculously, it had all gone as planned. There were six of them, all masked, including Bethia. The five local

men easily captured the three English soldiers still watching Geordie's small stone house while Bethia remained
in the shadows. 'Twas important that she not be injured,
since she was the only one to talk. He might recognize
the voices of the others.

Heavy, dark clouds blotted any moon or starlight, and
a light fog made visibility impossible. Her heart beat faster
than it ever had before, and once—when she heard a
grunt, then a heavy thump—her breath caught in her
throat. Her entire body tensed, shivers of apprehension
running through her. What right had she to endanger these
men? She, who had no skill at any of this?

A great hulking form dressed in dark oil cloth materialized over her. "It is done, lad. None of 'em will be
botherin' us this night."

They approached the house and Bethia, clad in the
black cloak and a piece of cloth masking all but her eyes,
drew herself as tall as she could and entered with the
rest. With pistols trained on Geordie Grant, Bethia threw
down the jack of spades and watched the man's face pale
with terror.

With more confidence than she thought she possessed,
she castigated him in a husky voice for turning on his
countrymen. Then she told him they were taking his boat,
that Drummond was waiting outside.

She watched as he was tied loosely, while three other
men ran down and pushed the boat into the sea, holding
it there until Bethia had finished her part, making Grant
believe he was indeed talking to the Black Knave. Leaving the card on the table, she ran down to the beach with
the innkeeper's brother. He helped her into the boat, and
the small craft swept out into the sea as its sails were un-
furled.

The sea scared her witless. The small fishing boat
plunged and lifted with the heavy seas; she nearly tumbled off before she learned to keep a good hold. Spray
drenched her bonnet and clothes. One particularly hard
wind caught her bonnet and it went flying off. One of

her braids fell from where she had pinned it, and first one fisherman, then another, stared at her.

"Jesu," uttered one.

"A lass!"

"Bloody hell."

She could only stand there, holding tightly to the side, as frowns and furrowed brows stared at her disbelievingly.

"Damn me, but we followed a lassie."

"Remember the tale that the Knave was an old woman."

They all looked at her as if she had grown a second head, even as the boat plunged once more, then seemed to rise on a wave, riding over it as water smashed down on her.

One man snatched the wheel from one who stood stunned at the wheel.

"Are ye *he*?"

"She didna 'ave the words," the innkeeper's brother reminded them. "The real Knave is in the forest with my brother."

"Still, it were a plan worthy of 'im," said another.

"But it could still fail if you do not pay attention," she said sharply, her mind racing between old fear, new fear, and indignation at being talked about as if she were not there.

Their gazes left her and she huddled down on the floor, soaked through by freezing rain and exhausted by the adventure, and still uncertain whether the plan would work, whether it would draw the English from the hills.

The rest of the voyage was in silence. Bethia did not know how long it took. She only knew she was miserable and yet . . . she had *done* something. Right or wrong. She had stopped letting fate turn her one way, then another. Even if she failed, she had acted on behalf of her countrymen.

They landed north of another small cluster of dwellings. They pulled the boat up to the shore, then used axes to destroy it. The boat had been meant to betray one

of their own, after all. A mile down the beach, a lad
awaited them with her horse. She and the innkeeper would
both ride it back to Buckie. He would then attempt to
find his brother. She would return the horse to Anne, reclaim her own, then hurry home as quickly as she could
with some tale of being lost or waylaid by a bandit.

It was just after dawn when they reached his inn. The
streets were still, and he led them through back ways.
They tied the horse a street away from the Flying Lady,
then he sauntered back into the inn. Finding no one watching, he went to the back where she waited and signaled
for her to come inside. She changed to the ragged clothes
she'd worn before, then quickly took the food he offered.

"Ye are a brave lass," he said.

"And you are a fine braw Scot."

He grinned, the hole between his teeth quite prominent. "Ye want tae be telling me yer name?"

"'Tis best none are exchanged."

"Sick in soul."

She looked at him quizzically.

"It is the words to identify the Black Knave and his . . .
couriers. 'Tis the way we all feel about Scotland and wha'
is happening. Ye might be needin' it."

"Will you do something for me?"

"Aye, lass."

"Please donna tell anyone I am a woman. Ask the others to do the same."

"Aye, they will no' be objectin'. None will tell of this
night's work. 'Tis too dangerous."

She thought about asking him to tell the Black Knave
that someone needed him, that Bethia MacDonell, now
the Marchioness of Braemoor, needed him. But if the
name got into the wrong hands, her brother might suffer
for it. She would have to take care of her own needs later.
Bethia reached out and took his hand, tightening her much
smaller one around it. "Thank you."

"If my brother lives through this, 'tis we who be thanking ye. Away wi' ye, now. We both ha' journeys this day."

Several minutes later, Bethia was riding Sadie out of town, her necklace still in the left leg of her breeches. Still running on the excitement of the night, she pushed back the weariness in her. She had to get back home. She had to get there before anyone alerted Cumberland, and he used her brother to punish her.

Rory rode into the courtyard of Braemoor.

He had stopped by Mary's and changed again into the costume he had worn the morning he had left Braemoor. Eight days. He had been gone eight days, had almost lost his life. Had it not been for the interference of a lad who had pretended to be him, he might well never have come home again.

He wanted to thank the boy, but no one knew his name or where he had come from. No one knew anything about him.

Kerry's brother had met them halfway down the trail, and had told them what had happened. Together, they had concocted a story that Kerry had been employed by a mercenary to take him high into the Grampians to try to find the Black Knave. They had found nothing, and the man had never even paid him. It was a good enough story, since it was known he had gone into the mountains when the Black Knave struck at Geordie Grant's.

The English had looked like fools, which had not improved their temperament.

Now all he wanted was to get home to Bethia, to his wife. He had wanted her every second of every minute of every day, and particularly when he was in that damnable cave.

Drummond was safe now with the same family who had taken in other refugees. He should be safe until the French ship arrived. And hopefully he would have Bethia's brother then, too.

He had not realized until the last trip how he'd been courting disaster. And now he owed it to Bethia to get both her and her brother out of Scotland. Then he, too, would flee the country that ran red with blood.

He would have to plan well. He might even tell Cumberland that his wife was with child, settled now, and they would like her brother to come live with them. If Cumberland believed there was no more chance of her fleeing . . .

But first he needed sleep. A lot of it. He no longer trusted his judgement. One reason he'd not noted the spies at the Flying Lady was the fact that he'd been so bloody tired. He'd made mistakes he had never made before.

He tried to put a bit of jauntiness in his shoulders as he approached the stable and threw the reins to young Jamie. He slid down from the horse, hoping to escape his cousin's too-keen eyes. A few hours sleep and he would be ready to face both Neil and Bethia.

But such was not to be. Someone had apparently alerted Neil, because he met Rory just inside the door. His cousin's shoulders were stiff and his eyes cold. Colder, in fact, than Rory had ever seen them.

"The marchioness is ill," he said sharply. "She disappeared for five days, then reappeared, saying she had gone to see her brother but that the horse bolted and she became lost and some other preposterous tales. She dinna bring your horse back."

But he heard nothing but the first words. *Ill.* His heart nearly stopped, and breath caught in his throat. "What is wrong with her?"

"Trilby says she has a fever."

Rory frowned. "How bad a fever?"

Neil shrugged. "Trilby said she does not think it serious."

Rory made himself slowly relax. Still, anxiety ate at him, but he did not wish to show it. Not to Neil. "Does Cumberland know about her absence?"

Neil's jaw jutted out. "I do no' tell tales, Rory. It is your business, but I would advise you to stay here more and tame your wife. If Cumberland hears of this, there will be hell to pay."

"He will hear that I gave her permission to go," Rory said. "I should have made it clear that she was to take an escort, but I imagine she was eager to see her brother."

None of the disapproval faded from Neil's face. Instead, he turned around and disappeared inside.

Five days. Where had she gone? He should have realized that she would be restless. Especially after the way he had left her that morning.

Ill.

All his own weariness gone, he took the steps two at a time.

He paused at the door to her room and knocked, then impatiently strode inside without waiting for a reply.

She was in the huge bed, looking slight and small, merely a small bump under the feather comforter. Jack, the puppy, cuddled next to her.

Bethia's face was flushed. Her hair was down, flowing over the pillow like a waterfall. Rays of light filtering through the windows sent wine-colored ribbons through the strands. She looked vulnerable and young, and yet her eyes flashed fire.

Anger and defensiveness battled in her eyes. One hand curled around the dog; the other crept out from under the cover, and he saw her fingers knot into a fist.

"I heard you were ill," he said, striding over to the bed. He put a hand to her forehead. It was warm, but not dangerously so. Still, she looked drawn. Exhausted.

"I am surprised you care."

The retort stung. Mainly because he deserved it. And much more. He had not had time to see her before he'd left. At least, he had told himself that. In reality, the extent of his feelings for her had astonished him. And more than a little dismayed him.

"I was called away . . ."

"To your mistress." She turned away from him. "Will you please leave?"

"I think not," he said. He knew he was not handling this well, but he had no experience at this sort of thing. He did not know how a husband acted, nor even someone who cared for someone else. He had never seen a happy relationship at Braemoor, nor at the English household where he fostered. He'd seen cruelty and brutality, lies and deceit, and he'd watched them poison everyone and everything around them, including his brother.

He had never wanted to be cruel; yet to protect her, and himself, he knew he had been just that. He did not know how to remedy the matter without endangering the both of them.

And so he responded with the indifference and even arrogance he'd perfected to protect a heart too often wounded. Even with Mary and Alister, he had difficulty expressing feelings. He could only hope they knew how he felt, that they knew how grateful he was to receive their friendship.

He had expressed his feelings that night he'd spent with his wife. He had opened his heart for the first time, and had lost himself in the feelings of warmth and affection and tenderness. They had scared the bloody hell out of him.

Just as they did now, as he watched her sink further into the bed. Anger could not hide the hurt in her eyes, the exhaustion in her face. Because of him?

"I was not at Mary's," he finally said.

She regarded him steadily, waiting.

"I had business elsewhere," he tried to explain. He wasn't used to explaining, and he was not very adept at it. Even he thought his explanation weak.

"'Tis just as well," she finally said. "I had business of my own."

"I heard."

"I expect you did," she said as she moved up from the bed, sitting rather regally but making sure she was covered well. Her back was all defiance now. If he expected an explanation beyond what he'd just received, he knew she intended none. That she expected approbation was quite obvious. It was also quite obvious she was ready to confront it.

"You did not see your brother?" he asked uncomfortably.

"Nay."

"I told you I would get a letter to him."

She looked at him with narrowed eyes. "A letter is not seeing with my two eyes that he is well."

"No," he agreed. "But it is the best I can do. I will send Alister." He hesitated, then added, "I would suggest two. One for inspection, one that could be more private."

"How do I know I can trust you?"

"You do not. You have to make that decision yourself. I am just offering a small suggestion."

"Could Alister get a letter to him privately?"

"Aye. I believe so."

"Why do you offer it?"

"'Tis time for a little trust between us, madam," he said. "I have no interest in preventing you from seeing or communicating with your brother."

"Trust?"

"A wee bit, mayhap. Which reminds me. Neil said you lost a horse."

It was a question, not a comment. Was that what his "trust" was about? Trying to disarm her?

Her jaw set stubbornly. "I will repay you."

"And how will you do that?"

"I will beat you at cards." There was humor in her voice. Just a little, but he felt encouraged.

In those few moments, the room had warmed from the frigid chill that had permeated it when he'd first arrived. "I would not count on that," he said with mock competitiveness.

Her eyes seemed to waiver a bit, some of the anger fading from them. "What did Neil tell you?"

"What you told him. He did not send a message to Cumberland." He said the last with just a bit of the amazement he still felt. He had believed that Neil would do anything to gain Braemoor. He was slowly revising his opinion of Neil. Once free of Rory's father and brother, Neil seemed to be presiding over Braemoor with justice and fairness, rejecting what other large estates were doing: turning out the families who had farmed the land for so long. If he had, Rory would have stepped in and stopped it. But he realized that Neil was running the estate far better than he ever could. Neil had a true understanding of both the clan and the land. Rory had none.

Oh, he probably would like farming well enough. But he hated Braemoor, and he knew he would never feel differently. It represented rejection and hatred and failure to him. Braemoor would never be home.

Her eyes had widened, too. She, too, had apparently expected his cousin to run to Cumberland.

He went over to the bed and sat down. "Tell me what happened. How far did you get?"

"You wish to report to the butcher directly?"

It was the first time she'd used the Jacobite term for Cumberland. Rory knew it no longer belonged only to the Jacobites. A growing number of Scots, even those who fought with him and certainly all who were neutral, were becoming outraged by his excesses.

"I expect not," he said mildly.

"Why not?" she challenged.

"Because you are now my affair, not his."

Her lips thinned. "I am no one's affair but my own."

He had to smile. He admired her spirit. Bloody hell, he admired everything about her. The way she glared at him through her intensely blue eyes, the way her hair tumbled down the side of her face. The sprinkling of freckles and her wide mouth that could, on very rare occasions, curve into a blinding smile.

"What happened to you?" he asked again.

"I got lost."

"There are only two roads."

She shrugged slightly. "I took the wrong one. I have

traveled here only once before. For the wedding. When you were gone. As you are always gone."

"I expected you to be pleased by that."

"I am."

He reached over and took her hand, playing with her fingers, running his thumb over the palm of her hand. She tried to tug it back but he held on to it.

"Then what?" His gaze did not leave her eyes as he asked the question.

"I donna know what you mean."

"You were gone five days."

"A crofter's family took me in after I lost the horse."

"How did you lose it?"

"I stopped at a stream to water him. He heard an owl and jerked loose. It started raining, and I got sick, and a crofter family took me in."

"Why did you not send for anyone?"

"Who? You were gone." But her eyes had grown secretive, even as her tone held a note of accusation.

She was hiding something. That much was clear. Otherwise she would never have mentioned his absence, would never have gone so clearly on the offensive.

"What was the name of the family? I would like to thank them."

"I do not remember."

The momentary warmth, which flowed between them just seconds earlier, faded. She was withholding something from him, something important.

Something to do with her brother?

That possibility alarmed him. If she tried to get her brother, she might well spoil the Knave's plans. And get herself killed as well.

He had meant to soothe her, to tell her everything was all right. That she could go anywhere she wanted. He had never wanted to make her a prisoner. But now he did not know what she would do next.

He could tell her the identity of the Black Knave.

Would she believe him? Or would she let something slip that would get them both killed?

"Is that as much as you will say?"

"Aye. I dinna think I was a prisoner any longer."

"It is your safety I'm concerned about."

"Truly? Is it not your new estates? Your influence? Your own freedom?"

"Aye, all of that," he said, his gut hurting as he saw her eyes turn to blue ice.

"Are you going to lock me in the room?"

"If it becomes necessary. In the meantime, I will tell the grooms not to allow you a mount."

"I enjoy riding," she said rebelliously. "Are you going to take my one pleasure away?"

"You are responsible for that, not I."

"*Not I,*" she mocked. "You are truly despicable." She tried once more to disentangle her hand. Unsuccessfully. He held on to it.

"You have said that before."

"I said you were loathsome. Now you are despicable."

"Is that a step up or down?" he questioned.

Obviously stumped, Bethia glared at him. She was sitting straight up now, unmindful that the comforter had fallen from her upper body. A white linen nightdress outlined her breasts. It was all he could do to keep from kissing her, from allowing his lips to trail kisses down her throat.

"Not a very wifely welcome." He was resorting back to his old protective armor. Goading to provoke a response, goading to keep warmth at a distance. Goading to keep from taking her in his arms and telling her that her brother would soon be safe.

"You have not been very husbandly."

"I could change." But his tone was sly, challenging, not conciliatory.

She withdrew ever so subtly. Though her hand remained in his by necessity, since he didn't release it, she nevertheless moved away emotionally. Her hand turned cold as all the warmth seeped from the room.

"You are within your rights to take me any time you wish."

"I have no interest in a cold woman."

"That is encouraging," she said. "I thought that subtlety was beyond you."

It was exactly what he had wanted her to think. He just did not know it would hurt so much. "Then I shall leave you. Remember, though, what I said. You are not to ride unless I am with you."

"Then I should never ride again."

"So be it," he said flatly. "I will have guards at the stable to make sure you do not." His hand let hers go. "And I will see whether I can find that family to give them my thanks. I would think you would wish them rewarded."

"They do not like your branch of Forbeses."

"Nonetheless, I shall see what I can do." He was surprised at the streak of jealousy that suddenly ran through him. Had she been with a man? Someone she knew before Culloden? Had she tried to enlist help to rescue her brother?

She shrugged. "If you wish."

He turned to leave.

"My letters." Her voice stopped him.

"I'll send Alister Armstrong when he is free."

"Why Alister?" She'd wondered that before.

"He often works in that area," Rory said. "And Neil would complain if I sent one of our people. I like peace." He went to the door. "Have them ready this afternoon. I'll ask him to wait for a reply."

"Thank you."

"You are welcome, madam."

Bethia settled back into the bed and sighed heavily. It had taken all she had to keep tears from moving from her eyes down her cheeks. She did not want him to see her cry.

She had been so unexpectedly pleased to see him, even after all that had happened, even thinking he had gone from her bed to that of his mistress.

Though his eyes had been tired, he had looked so vibrant standing in the doorway. Even with a wig, he had a presence, a charisma that drew her to him. Her heart had somersaulted when she'd seen the worry, the concern in his expression. And when he'd said he had not been to Mary's, she'd felt an odd sense of pleasure.

She had enjoyed that one very brief moment of humor. But then he'd become as obnoxious and unfeeling as he'd been when she'd first met him. He'd questioned her, then made her position quite clear. She was a prisoner again.

How had she ever thought that something quite fine might lie under that colorful exterior?

And the letter. How could she dare write anything but inanities to her brother? The villain would probably read it. And why was he sending it now? So he could also send a message to Cumberland?

A tear found its way into her left eye and she felt it trail down her cheek.

She had been right. She *was* alone. Totally and absolutely alone. Any idea that the marquis was anything but what he seemed had been foolish. More than foolish. Harebrained.

She would not make that mistake and lower her guard again.

Eighteen

Cumberland was paying a visit.

The messenger arrived nearly immediately after Rory left Bethia's chamber.

Rory wondered what in the hell he wanted now. Nothing good, he was sure. Most likely to see whether there was a slight swell to Bethia's body.

But it would certainly hinder Rory's plans. He wondered how long the bastard would stay.

He planned to send Alister with Bethia's letters tomorrow. His friend could try to find some weak points in Creighton's security. He could judge the health and welfare of the lad, mayhap even talk with him.

Rory's most immediate need, though, was sleep. Sleep and more sleep.

Jesu, but he was tired. He should never have gone to her room when he was that tired. He said things, and felt things, that he usually had under better control. But he had been so concerned at hearing of her illness.

Where had she been?

He did not believe her tale for a moment. She was too capable a rider to lose a horse like that. She was too intelligent to take a wrong road. She was too good with people not to remember a name.

His first inclination was to believe her because there didn't seem to be another explanation. But she had not reached Creighton's holding. Evidently she'd not intended to go there at all. Otherwise, she and her brother would be long gone. Soldiers would be combing every inch of Braemoor. No, she'd had another purpose in mind.

There was but one other plausible explanation. A man. Not a lover. But someone who could help her rescue her brother. But who, what and when?

How far could she have traveled in those days? Who could she have met? Every Jacobite in Scotland was either dead or in hiding. There were a few clans who had remained neutral, but they had been disarmed and banned from wearing plaids.

Mayhap he might learn something from Cumberland. But God help him, he must get some sleep first. A few hours. Then he might be better able to puzzle out his wife's peculiar behavior, and ultimate aims.

Minutes later, he was sprawled across the bed, his wig flung on a table, his shoes scattered on the floor along with his purple coat with its gold buttons and trim.

Rory slept late into the night. When he woke, his head felt sluggish and his mouth dry. He felt he could have slept the rest of his life.

Rory groaned, then reluctantly put two feet on the floor. The log in the fireplace was down to embers, and his chamber was growing cold. He picked up a candle from beside his bed, lit it from the few glowing embers, then placed it in a holder. He then went to a window and looked out.

The courtyard was quiet. It would be crowded with horses on the morn.

He decided to ride out and see Alister tonight, before the Duke of Cumberland arrived. Despite his drugged feeling, he knew himself well enough to know there would be no more sleep tonight.

Rory opened the door, surprised to see that someone had placed a tray of food and tankard of ale outside. Now that had never happened before. He took it to a table and quickly consumed cold pheasant and a hunk of fresh bread along with some fruit. He had not realized how hungry he'd been.

Bethia? His wife? But she was ill. And she was not pleased with him.

Still, it was a wifely thing to do. At least he thought it was. His mother had never done that for her husband.

Hell, he was babbling to himself. She had reduced him to babbling.

He slammed down the now empty glass of ale.

He was the Black Knave, the scourge of the English.

So why did a slip of a lass so confuse him? Particularly a shrewish one?

An irresistible, shrewish one. And she was just two doors away.

His mind was babbling again.

Where in the hell had she been?

And why did he care so much?

He dressed in a pair of plain britches and white shirt, then selected a dark cloak. There would be few to see him tonight, and he was not up to his usual layers of clothing and tight neck cloths.

Rory left his room and hesitated for a moment outside Bethia's door. But most certainly she would be asleep. She was ill and should not be disturbed. He saw her, though, in his mind's eye. Her supple body, the dark hair spread over a pillow, the dark blue eyes that deepened with passion.

Stop that babbling!

He forced himself past the door and down the steps. Servants were cleaning the hall in anticipation of Cumberland's visit. Rory wondered whether or not Bethia knew of it, but supposed she did. Trilby would have heard everything. He knew his wife would dread it. She despised the man more, he hoped, than she despised her husband.

Why in the hell did she invade his every thought?

He moved quickly past their curious glances, through the door and down to the stable. Despite the late hour, Jamie was cleaning out stalls for the ducal visit on the morning. There was no sign of the lad's father. *He* was probably asleep.

Rory made a pledge to himself that he would speak to the father tomorrow.

"Do ye need a saddle, sir?"

"I will saddle my own horse," he said.

The boy's lower lip trembled. "I am very good at saddling."

"I know that well, Jamie. It is not that I think you will not do it well. But it is late and you should be abed."

"Fa—"

"Tell him I insisted." He looked in one of his pockets and found a crown. He tossed the coin to the lad. "That is for you. Not your fa. You keep it someplace safe in case you ever need it."

The lad's eyes grew large as he clutched the coin. "Aye, sir. Thank ye."

The Marquis of Braemoor probably never would have done that. But Rory was damned tired of being the selfish, arrogant boor. Which was a very dangerous feeling, indeed.

"Get on with you, lad," he said. As the boy scooted out the door, Rory quickly saddled his favorite mount, a flashy but steady gray. He never took him on the Knave's errands; he was altogether too memorable. He stepped into the stirrup, then swung himself up into the saddle and cantered down the lane.

The moon was high and bright. No fog or drizzle this night. 'Twas well past midnight, and he saw no other riders. He should be tired of riding, but now he needed to be away from Braemoor, away from the memories past and present.

He thought about leaving here, leaving the estates to Neil, the true-blood heir to Braemoor. And now Rory knew he would be a good custodian of it. 'Twas a small legacy Rory could leave; he'd wasted so much of his life in wanton disregard of others.

And Bethia?

He had given her the necklace for a purpose. Just as he would give her most of the Forbes jewelry. It should be enough for her and her brother to start a life elsewhere. He would seek an annulment or divorce so she could find someone of her own choosing. If, indeed, he survived to escape Scotland. If he did, he would have nothing except his gambler's skill and that was no' too steady an occupation. He wanted none of the jewelry or anything else that came from Braemoor.

He reached Alister's rooms behind his smithy. His friend would no doubt be querulous about his late-night visit, but in the last few months he had become used to Rory's nocturnal habits.

He knocked loudly enough to wake the dead, since Alister was a far better sleeper than he.

In a moment, a grumbling Alister opened the door. "Can you not ever do things the way ordinary men do?"

Rory grinned. 'Twas good to be with a friend again. "I see you made it back from Buckie."

"Did you have any doubts?"

"Nay, but I ran into a wee spot of trouble."

Alister raised an eyebrow.

"You got the warning there, but I fear I did not heed it strongly enough. Apparently someone was watching the tavern. They followed us halfway to Drummond's hiding place. Soldiers were all over the bloody place."

Alister gestured him over to a table, and he poured both of them some ale. "Donna keep me waiting. Since you are here, I sense you outwitted them again."

"Not I. Some lad posing as me."

"Who?"

Rory spread his hands in denial. "I hoped you would know. I would like to thank him."

"I know of no lad involved."

Rory shrugged his shoulders. "There are a number of mysteries. I suppose you heard that my wife disappeared."

"Aye. She was gone when I arrived. I was going to look for her when she showed up bedraggled and tired and wet. Did she tell you what happened?"

"A story I did not believe. It was a good tale, though. Almost as good as some of mine. She just is not as accomplished a liar."

"Damning praise." Alister yawned. "I suppose this visit has a purpose."

"Aye. I think she is up to something. I am particularly afraid that she might be planning to abduct her brother herself."

"All the more reason to tell her who you are."

"Nay," Rory said. "There are many reasons against it. The first being her lack of skill as a liar. And Cumberland is visiting on the morrow. He is far too shrewd not to detect changes in her."

"Cumberland? Here?"

"Aye. We received a message today."

"Could he know anything?"

"Nay, but they are becoming more determined to catch the Knave. We must be thinking about leaving Scotland. After we get Bethia's brother, and the two of them to France."

One of Alister's eyebrows arched again. "Bethia? Might you be going wi' them?"

"I have no love for France, either. They have been playing games with Scotland for centuries. I plan to go to America. I want you and Mary to go with me. I will have enough for passage for the three of us. A blacksmith is always wanted, and I will go where the cards go."

Alister peered at him. There was little light other than that from the fireplace which, like his own had been, was none too bright. "You will still be married."

"I will get an annulment or divorce."

"She is Catholic."

"We were not married by a priest."

"You have thought it all out, have you?"

"Aye."

"What about the lady?"

"She disappeared somewhere for four days. I suspect—"

"A lover?"

Not that. She *had* been virgin. Yet there could well be someone she trusted, someone she *loved*. He shrugged. "She never wanted this marriage."

Alister looked at him closely. "You care about her."

"Nay."

"Now who's not a good liar?"

"I would not expect her to honor something forced upon her. And I have nothing to offer her. When I leave, I will leave with nothing more than passage money."

Alister sighed. "Then what do you wish of me?"

"I want you to take a letter to her brother tomorrow. Look around. See if you can find a weak spot for the Knave."

"My absences are being talked about."

"An errand commanded by me. All think me an unfeeling lackwit anyway."

"Your problem, my lord, is you feel far too much."

"That is nonsense. You know I enjoy the game. Matching wits with Cumberland is supremely satisfying. He is an arrogant ass." He grinned as he took a last swallow of the brandy. "Almost as arrogant as the Marquis of Braemoor."

"You will miss the bright colors."

"Aye, like I miss a burr in my trews."

Alister grinned. "You thrive on discomfort, my lord. But Scotland will miss the Knave."

"I think he has done everything he can. It is becoming too dangerous for you and Mary. I would never forgive myself if you paid for my actions."

"You would be swinging with us," Alister said dryly.

"No' so much time to regret. And we both made our own decisions."

But Rory knew he had influenced the decision. "Can you go tomorrow?"

"Aye. If you promise to take no more trips for a week. You need some rest. You do not look like a fat, contented marquis."

"Are marquises ever contented?"

"Half-witted ones," Alister said. "At least I suppose so, never having been one."

"Half-witted or a marquis?"

Alister laughed. "I will leave the former to you, my lord. And now I need my sleep if I am to make a journey in the morning."

"I will have her letters ready. I want you gone before Cumberland arrives."

Alister nodded.

Rory went to the door. "Keep an ear out for a young lad masquerading as me. 'Tis a wee bit insulting, to tell the truth."

" 'Tis well known you are a master of disguises. I expect it is better to be a lad than an old woman."

"You can age yourself. You canna take it away."

"I did not know you were so vain, my lord."

Rory laughed. "Good night, my friend."

Bethia woke to a wet tongue swabbing her face.

She yawned. The bed felt good, warm, safe.

She giggled as Black Jack licked her ears.

"Lucky dog."

The deep male voice startled her and she sat up suddenly, spilling the puppy in her lap. Jack howled in protest.

He was sitting in one of her chairs, his legs stretched out in front of him. He was without wig this morning, and he looked devilishly handsome. But she would not be so easy to fool this time. "What are you doing here?"

"Visiting my wife."

"Your mistress is not available?"

"You do have a sharp tongue, lass."

"Not until I met you."

His lips twisted into a slight smile. "I doubt that. But I am here as a Good Samaritan. Alister will take your letters to your brother. He is down in the courtyard now."

"Oh." Why could he always disarm her so easily? She noticed his gaze lower, and she saw that her nightdress had gaped open. Warmth started at the point his gaze fell, then flowed inward. Her shoulders ached with a tension they'd never felt before, and her heart pounded against its cage. Lightning leaped between them, jagged and blinding, cloaking them with its intensity. A fierce urgency consumed her.

Why was her body betraying her?

Why were her thoughts doing the same?

He had stiffened also, as if the same urgency had seized him. His hazel eyes had a golden glow—a fire. Why did he not wear that infernal wig? Why did he look so sure and confident and masculine lounging in a plain shirt and leather breeches? Why couldn't she breathe properly?

But there was also just an edge of uncertainty in his eyes.

It was that uncertainty that always wound its way into her heart.

Remember that night. She repeated that warning to herself over and over again. *Remember the night when he loved you, then left without so much as a kiss. Remember how you felt?*

Why did that memory fade when he was so close to her?

"Do you have the letters, madam?"

"Aye," she said. Even she knew her voice sounded hoarse. "They are in the book on the table. The one with his full name is meant to be examined, the other is merely marked 'Dougal.'" Neither, in fact, contained anything damaging. She did not trust the marquis that much. But the plain one did have some words that might have a special meaning to her brother.

She watched as he picked up the book, studied the title, then put it down after taking the two letters and stuffing them in his coat. "You took up my offer on visiting the library."

"Aye," she said warily.

"I am surprised you had time, with all your adventures."

"I have nothing but time, since you have determined to imprison me again."

His eyes narrowed. "That was yesterday."

"It seems like forever."

"It is for your own good. I should not like to see you lose a horse again. You may not be so lucky next time."

"You care so much?"

"Cumberland would not be pleased if you were to disappear. Which reminds me: he plans to honor us with a visit today."

She felt color draining from her face.

"Is that why you came this morning? Not to fetch a letter, but to make sure I am well enough to meet your guests."

"His visit, in part, is responsible. I want the letters on the way before he forbids it. I think it would also be well that they arrive when he is not with Creighton."

Bethia did not expect that explanation. In fact, she could not remember when he had ever explained, much less apologized, for anything. "Why?"

"Cumberland might intercept it."

"Why do you care?"

"I dislike disharmony." He said it with such insincerity that she had to smile.

"There is already disharmony."

His brows furrowed together. "I hadna noticed."

Bethia could not tell whether he was serious or not. His eyes twinkled but his tone was . . . unctuous. He was either being very charming or very obnoxious, and it was disconcerting not to know which it was.

He rose gracefully. She had noticed that before. The

grace with which he moved, whether he walked or rode. It was even in the way he lounged in a chair, or stretched. Even in the lazy, sensuous way he'd made love.

She wished she had not thought of that. She wished that she could regard him with the same cool indifference with which he seemed to view her.

Cumberland. Some of her rage had waned, but none of her determination to do whatever she could to save others from him.

At least now she could look at him and know that she had done something, that she had acted to thwart him.

And to thwart her husband.

Unfortunately, she wanted to do something else with him, and that shamed her.

"Are you going to read them?"

"Madam?"

"My letters."

His look of utter astonishment surprised her. It was as if he had never even considered such a thing. But then he'd surprised her from the very first night when he'd not taken his husbandly rights. She'd thought then that it was because she was undesirable, but now she no longer believed that to be true. She'd too often seen the interest in his eyes. Warmth. Desire. Need.

"No, madam. I ha' no intention of reading your personal mail."

"You serve Cumberland. I would have thought such a thing a rather minor sin compared to your much greater ones."

His eyes grew cold. "Greater ones?"

"Treason to Scotland." Some demon was spurring her on. It always did with him. Perhaps because he always threw her off balance.

"Do you not know that the victor is always right, wife? It is the losers that are branded traitors."

He was opening the door, then turned back. "I expect you to wear your best gown. I wish the duke to see a felicitous couple."

If she'd had something other than the puppy in hand, she would have thrown it at him. She could not understand why she always reacted to him as she did. Why she allowed herself to be drawn to him. Why she challenged him. Why she cared at all what he thought. Every time he seemed to be kind, he followed it with some ulterior motive. Cumberland wanted a child. They were to look happy. He wanted a "harmonious household."

Yet she could not remove from her mind the image of him with that wry, attractive smile on his lips, and his unruly dark hair and enigmatic eyes that changed color so easily.

"What do you think?" she asked Black Jack.

He wagged his tail.

"That doesna help."

She put him down and rose, going over to the window. It was just past dawn, and the servants were beginning to stir. She looked down and saw Alister. He was standing next to a bay horse.

Bethia moved to the side of the window. The marquis stepped into view, said a few words to him, then handed him her sealed letters. She did not believe he'd had time to read them, and that pleased her. Then she studied the two men below. They appeared comfortable with each other, the marquis and the blacksmith. She had thought that odd before, but watching their ease together only deepened her interest. Several seconds later, the blacksmith mounted his horse and trotted down to the lane.

The marquis looked after him, then turned to look up at her window. She quickly darted away. She did not want him to believe she had more interest in him than she did. It was just that he was such a mass of contradictions.

She harnessed her curiosity and sat down in front of the mirror and started to brush her hair. She would play her part today. She would disarm both Cumberland and her husband. And then she would become the Black Knave again and rescue her brother. Perhaps then they could find the real Knave and get out of Scotland.

And away from the marquis's extraordinarily disturbing presence.

Nineteen

"To what do we owe the pleasure of your visit, Your Grace?" asked Rory in an ingratiating voice. He was wearing his most elaborate clothes—a long, coral coat with numerous gold buttons and trim over gartered red-and-black trews of finest wool.

He also wore his finest wig, the powdered curls falling over his shoulders.

His Grace, the Duke of Cumberland, did not seem impressed. He frowned. "How is the marchioness?"

"She is not feeling well at the moment."

The duke's face brightened. "Might she be with child?"

" 'Tis possible," Rory replied. Hopefully his wife would be long gone before such a boast could be disproven. Rory remained puzzled at the duke's intense interest in that particular part of his life.

Cumberland nodded with approval. "I want her to have the best of care. My own physician will attend her at birth."

"I am not sure that she is with child."

"We shall pray for God's blessing," Cumberland said piously. "You will receive ten thousand pounds when it is confirmed she is with child."

Rory could not conceal his surprise.

"I thought you would be pleased."

"I am, but I need no additional reward to serve you or the crown." He could be as obsequious as anyone.

"Still, I have been authorized to tell you this."

"I am grateful, Your Grace."

"As well you should be. Which is my second reason for coming."

Rory remained silent, waiting. He did not like the sound of any of this.

"This Knave fellow. I want him. I have doubled the reward. I am also asking every loyal family to patrol the roads and bring in any man—or woman—not known to them. I will not tolerate this man's impudence any longer. I will do what has to be done to bring him to the gallows."

"Aye, Your Grace. I will have men blocking the roads around Braemoor. Do you have a better description?"

"He is as slippery as an eel. The last report was of a lad. Dammit, a *lad*. Some of my men believe him a demon who can transform himself at will."

"And what do you think?"

"I think he has henchmen, nothing more. But the troops are frightened. And even worse, the Scots are making a legend of him, a symbol. He is becoming as dear to them as their damnable prince. He has to be caught."

"I will do what I can."

"You can become a very wealthy man, Braemoor."

"If he is within fifty miles of Braemoor, I will know of it," Rory replied.

Cumberland nodded. "I will spend the night here and be gone in the morning. I have others to see."

"We will be honored."

"Your wife will be at supper?"

"Aye, Your Grace."

"I will retire to a room now."

"I will send brandy to you."

"Ah, that French brandy. Are you smuggling, Braemoor?"

"Nay. I buy it from a smuggler."

"Do not be too clever, Braemoor."

"I try not to be clever at all."

The duke did not answer.

"Would you like me to accompany you to your room? 'Tis the one you occupied at the wedding. I trust it is satisfactory?"

"Most satisfactory." Cumberland was suddenly amiable. "And you need not trouble yourself. My orderly will take care of everything."

The interview was over.

Rory turned and saw Neil in the doorway. He was watching, but merely bowed when the duke passed him.

"What did he want, Rory?" Neil asked after Cumberland had ascended the stairs.

"He wants us to stop every traveler on our roads and apprehend anyone we do not know."

"Braemoor does not have the men. They have farms to till."

Rory sighed. "I could not say no. Have you ever tried to argue with Cumberland?"

"I canna say I have had that pleasure," Neil said dryly.

Rory fixed his gaze on Neil. "Then remember this. You canna cross the man. He will crush you and everyone here."

"You and he seem friendly enough." Neil's tone was hostile, and that surprised Rory. He had thought Neil tolerant of Cumberland.

Rory shrugged. "I have something he wants. But he despises all Scots, and I suggest you remember that."

He started to move, but Neil stepped in front of him. "Why do you care what happens to Braemoor? You seem intent on gambling it away."

"I care naught for Braemoor, and I ha' reasons for that," Rory said. "But I wish no one here ill."

"I donna understand you."

"That is not required. Just do as Cumberland wishes."

"And you? Are you leaving again soon?"

Rory grinned. "Do you miss me?"

Neil gave him a look of disgust.

"I plan to be here long enough to plant a seed. Cumberland's orders."

"Too bad you did not heed them at Culloden."

"So you would have the title at my death?" For some reason, Rory could not resist the jab. Although he felt that Neil was very capable of managing Braemoor and its properties, he could not forget those years when his cousin was Donald's ally. He thought he'd outgrown that pain. Apparently, he had not.

Neil sent him a thunderous look, then turned around and retreated back into the office.

Rory sighed as a door closed behind him. *It will not be long before you get what you want most. I just have to be sure that you are alive to enjoy it, that you are not blamed for the acts of the Black Knave.*

Bethia did not, as ordered, wear her best gown. But neither was it her worst. She was beginning to learn that honey might be a better weapon than vinegar. She wanted more freedom. She had to have it to do what had to be done. Obedience might win it for her. Still, she had not been able to force herself into the gown she knew her husband preferred.

Trilby finished dressing her hair, drawing up the sides to the back, fastening them with a jeweled clasp, then allowing the curls to fall down her back. "Would you like some powder?" Trilby asked.

For the freckles, Bethia knew. But they were part of her and she did not care if either Cumberland or her husband saw them. "No, Trilby."

"The necklace, my lady?"

"I think not," she said. She regarded that necklace as a symbol of imprisonment.

The door opened, then. No knock. The whiff of a

strong perfume assaulted her before she even saw her husband. Then he stood beside her.

It was, she thought, almost as if he could read her mind. "I want you to wear the necklace tonight," he said.

"I decided against it."

He smiled slowly, then looked at Trilby. "You may go, lass."

Trilby looked uncertainly from one to the other, then curtsied and hurried toward the door.

"You frighten her," Bethia accused.

"I do not think I am frightening," he said. "Now back to the necklace. You *will* wear it." He took a small box from a pocket in his coat. The coat was truly outrageous— a bright coral with enough gold trim to feed a family for a year.

When she made no effort to take the box, he opened it. A pair of magnificent emerald earrings lay nestled in the box.

"I note no gratitude," the marquis said.

"Possibly because I am blinded by your coat, my lord. 'Tis hard to see anything else."

He preened. "The color is the height of fashion."

"Do you think naught of anything but fashion and cards?"

He lifted an eyebrow. "Money, my lady. And it lies in the man about to sit at our table. Now the necklace. Where is it?"

Bethia went to the wardrobe and took out a box. She opened it and lifted the glittering gems. She thanked her heavenly stars that she'd not had to barter the necklace away.

"I will put it on you."

"I can do it myself."

"Aye, I ken that you can. But I prefer to do it."

It was the last thing she wanted. She did not want his hands on her. She knew how she reacted to his touch.

Even now, as he stood before her in what seemed all coral and gold, and draped in a dreadful wig, she felt the response of her body to him. It had warmed considerably.

He took the necklace from her hands. "Now be a good lass, and turn around."

She wanted to punch him instead. Good lass, indeed. Her eyes raged at him as she quelled her desire to do violence. *Freedom,* she warned herself. *You need freedom.*

Gritting her teeth, she turned around, though she knew her shoulders were arched in defiance.

She felt the cold stones against her bare throat, his hands at the back of her neck. Where the necklace was cold, his hands were warm. She knew when the clasp closed, but his fingers did not leave her skin. They were like embers, torching her blood. She felt his breath against her hair, and though the perfume he wore was stupefying, his breath was fresh and clean against her cheek.

She swallowed hard. How could she be attracted to such a dandy? But still she did not move away from his hands that kneaded the back of her neck, that fell and caressed her shoulders. She could barely stand under the onslaught of so many sensuous reactions to his touch. Her knees felt weak. Sensations crawled up and down her back. Warmth puddled in the center of her. *Damn him.*

Then his fingers left her.

"Now the earrings," he said smoothly, as if completely unaware of all the feelings he'd initiated. "Turn around."

A puppet. She was a puppet in his hands. She turned around, knowing her eyes were blazing at him. He had one earring in his hand.

She stepped back. "I can put them on myself."

"Of course, but I have a special expertise in such matters." A gleam illuminated his eyes, and his mouth crooked up in a half smile.

For a moment she almost succumbed to a charm that was not totally eclipsed by his extravagant adornments.

"Aye, I see you do," she said, a chill edging the words.

He apparently took that as assent, for his fingers went to the lobes of her ears and with a gentleness she'd experienced the night they'd consummated their marriage, he fixed first one earring, then the other, in place, his fingers lingering still.

The kernel of warmth inside her flamed to intense heat. She felt herself trembling. It took all the will within her to step away.

"You look very much the marchioness," he said. "You do honor to the gems."

It was prettily said, but she felt only humiliation at the way her emotions had bounced so out of control, at the way she responded to a man who was everything she despised.

She looked at him steadily. "'Tis a shame that you do honor to no one or no thing."

"It is," he said affably, "a character flaw. Now let us go, madam, and charm the Duke of Cumberland."

Indeed, he had not lied. He had some very serious flaws in his character. He had always known it, of course. He'd been told often enough.

But he had never quite been so aware of them as when he had touched her. He hadn't meant to. He had only meant to see that she wore the jewels and received his small gift, which would help her later escape. But any good intentions to keep his hands to himself faded when he saw her.

True, her gown was plain, but it suited her. It was a pale gray which made her eyes look even bluer, and her hair looked truly lovely tumbling down the silk. But even more appealing was the bare perfection of her neck. The gown was modest enough, but it still revealed enough to make his trews far more snug than they should be.

So he'd used obnoxiousness as a weapon the way he always had. He'd not been able to keep from touching her, but he could make sure she would withdraw from him.

He wanted her so damn badly. He ached for her. He ached to hold her, and make love to her. He ached to take the loneliness from her eyes, and turn defiance into passion. He yearned to have her touch him as he enjoyed touching her.

And Cumberland was waiting downstairs for them.

He took her arm, feeling her reluctance, knowing her hatred for the man who had destroyed everything she held dear. There was a gallantry to her that he envied.

They went down the steps together. He reached for her hand and took it. It felt small in his, and yet there was strength in it. There was strength in *her*.

The room was full. All of the lords from surrounding properties had been invited. By Neil, no doubt. Another glimpse of Neil's ability.

All eyes turned toward them. The men and women all stood while they entered. All except Cumberland, who sat at the head of the table. But when they approached him, he stood. "Marriage becomes you, my lady," he said to Bethia.

His wife curtsied nicely. "Thank you, Your Grace."

Rory, who knew his wife well by now, thought he might be the only one to detect the irony in her voice.

She sat and took a sip of wine.

Cumberland leaned over and stared at her. "I heard you were not feeling well. Nothing serious, I hope."

"How kind of you to be concerned," she said. "I would be much comforted by the presence of my brother."

"I believe he is quite content with Creighton," Cumberland said.

Rory took a deep swallow of his wine and listened to the duel between them. He was glad that, for once, he was not a participant and the recipient of Bethia's often-sharp tongue. He only hoped his wife would be wise.

"Then you would not object if I paid him a visit?"

"I believe your husband might object," Cumberland replied.

She turned to him. "Would you object?"

"I would have to think about it," he said.

The disappointment in her eyes hurt far more than it should have.

"You have duties here," Rory said. "And there is your health to be considered."

Her face fell, her eyes dulled. He knew he had failed her yet again, yet he could not risk incurring Cumberland's displeasure. Not now. Not tonight.

Cumberland nodded in approval. "A wife should be in her husband's home. Your brother is safe and happy." He looked down toward her midriff. "You might soon have children of your own to care for."

Her face flared red. But then, she often showed her feelings. Rory had been amazed that she had been as cordial as she had toward his royal guest.

"We hope to make a happy announcement soon, Your Grace," he said.

His wife kicked him under the table.

He turned and warned her with a glance.

Since Cumberland was in such an expansive mood, however, he decided to risk a suggestion. "My wife and I would like the boy to come for a visit."

"I am afraid that is impossible," Cumberland said. "He is well-settled now. We would not wish to disturb him. Now if you knew for sure she was with child, we might make an exception. Mayhap my physician should stop by."

Cumberland looked smug.

Another bribe. Money for him. Her brother for Bethia. Damn it, why?

Rory decided to change the subject. "We sent out men tonight, Your Grace. Not a man or woman will pass unnoticed on the road."

Bethia tensed. Her hand stilled. "Why is that?" she said.

"I have increased the reward for that bandit fellow," Cumberland said. "I expect he will be in our hands within a week."

"Would you like to make a wager on that, Your Grace?" Bethia's voice was silkily polite.

Cumberland looked at her disapprovingly, then turned to Rory. "Your wife needs some discipline."

"'Twas my husband who taught me the value of a wager," Bethia said impudently.

Rory could barely withhold a smile. She did indeed have courage. Good sense, no. Courage, yes. "Aye, Your Grace. I will see to it, and the other matter as well."

Cumberland nodded, then turned his attention to food and drink. Bethia sat frozen with disapproval. Rory frowned, trying to warn her not to push Cumberland too far, but she studiously avoided him.

"I hope you enjoy the meal," he said, trying to distract the duke. "It is my wife's doing. She is also doing the accounts and overseeing the cleaning of Braemoor."

Cumberland grunted. He was still obviously unhappy with Bethia's challenge. His attention focused on the jewelry Bethia was wearing. "The Forbes jewels," he commented. "They favor you, Marchioness."

He then turned to Neil who sat on his left, asking details of the number of men he would use to patrol the roads and lanes. Bethia's back was stiff with indignation, but she had the sense not to say anything more.

The first course of saddle of mutton, veal and sirloin of beef was followed by baked plum pudding and lamb fricassee, then a hot flan with chickens and spinach. A third course offered fried sole, roast fowl and sweetbreads along with green peas and artichokes. Almond custard and cherry pies concluded the meal. Decanters of fine wine were refilled constantly. Rory watched as the duke turned his attention to the food, emerging only once to comment, "Your table has improved."

It was, Rory thought, enough to feed an entire village. But Cumberland was correct. The food was far better since Bethia had joined the household. "As I said, my wife is responsible," he said. "She is competent in many ways. 'Tis a very felicitous union." His expression left no doubt as to what one of those ways were. Bethia kicked him again. He was going to have very sore legs.

"I told you it would be a suitable marriage," Cumberland said expansively. "Did I not?"

"Aye, Your Grace."

Rory leaned over and kissed his wife, disregarding her obvious displeasure. He made it hard and demanding, drawing the cheers of the men at the table. For a moment she resisted. Then she seemed to relax, only to bite down hard on his tongue. He could taste blood and he saw momentary triumph in her eyes.

Rory withheld any reaction, though it hurt like the blazes. His hand tightened on her arm, and though he closed his mouth, his lips savaged hers. After a moment, he was surprised to find her body reacting, her lips responding to his. Reluctantly. She tried to pull away, and this time he allowed it.

"I am lucky in many ways, Your Grace," he said, using a smirk to cover the blood in his mouth. She never gave up. The thought pleased him even if the lingering pain did not.

He took a sip of wine, and swallowed the bitter mixture of wine and blood.

Bethia pulled her chair back. "I am feeling unwell, my lord."

Rory looked at Cumberland, who nodded. Rory stood and pulled the chair back. "I will be with you soon, my love," he said.

She said nothing, just swept from the room.

"She does not care for public displays of affection," Rory said dismissively. "She reserves that for the bedchamber."

Cumberland nodded. "Marriage becomes her. So will motherhood."

There it was again: the man's obsession with his wife's childbearing abilities.

He decided to probe. "She said she has an English grandfather."

Cumberland took another bite of pie. "You do not have to worry about her pedigree. It reaches into royalty."

"Is any of her family still alive?"

Cumberland nodded curtly. "They disowned their daughter when she married a Scot." He couldn't quite keep the contemptuous outrage from his voice.

"She has English cousins, then?"

Cumberland turned cold eyes on him. "I would not take undue interest in the matter," he said.

A clear warning. It set all his senses tingling. He did not like it. He knew that Cumberland thought him none too intelligent. That kiss was meant to reenforce Cumberland's image of him as a womanizer, a bore, an ineffectual sycophant. Now he knew he was not to ask questions. He would have to get some answers from his wife. For the first time, he felt a chill of fear for her.

"As you wish, Your Grace," he said in an anxious-to-please voice.

The duke's frown faded. "Just do your duty," he said.

"Your wish is my command."

The duke nodded. Rory caught a puzzled expression on Neil's face. Why? He had always been servile to Cumberland in his cousin's presence.

Bloody hell, but he wearied of keeping so many balls in the air at one time.

He suffered through the rest of the supper. He waited, in fact, until Cumberland retired to his room.

Then he made his way up to Bethia's room. She would be furious. It was the third time he had publicly humiliated her. With Cumberland's men about, however, he did not believe this was a good night to go to his own chamber alone.

He did not bother to knock.

She was standing at the window. Her night robe molded her body, and he remembered too well how it had felt under him.

Bethia did not turn. She was holding the little terrier

and staring at the hills as if her heart were there, and only a shadow stood in the room.

"I am sorry," he said. "It was necessary."

"I know," she said. "When I got up here and thought about it, I realized what you were doing."

She had stunned him again. But why? He'd understood almost immediately that she was smart, intuitive.

"You were protecting me in your own way. You did not tell him about my . . . escapade."

He was silent for a moment. "Is that what it was? An escapade?"

"I wanted to get away from here. From you. I was angry because when I woke . . ."

He did not say anything. He wanted to take her in his arms. But it wasna right.

"Why did you not tell him?" she asked.

"It is a matter between you and me."

"I believe I know why he wants me to be with child."

Surprise flickered across his face. "Why?"

"You asked me once about my family. My grandfather is the Duke of Blandford. They had only two children, my mother and her brother. My uncle was ambushed and killed twenty years ago by Highlanders. He served with General George Wade when he tried to pacify the Highlands. He had no children. There is no direct heir now."

"There's your brother. And you."

"Nay. My mother was disowned, disinherited. They hate anything Scottish. My brother and I were both raised as Scots."

A muscle flicked in his cheek, and she knew he understood. A frown replaced the cool indifference he usually wore.

"Aye," she said quietly. "A bairn untainted by a Scottish past. One to be molded into a proper Englishman."

"But your brother . . ."

"He could try to claim the title. *If* he were still alive."

Rory stared at her. It all made sense now. Including Cumberland's demand that his physician be at any birth.

Would they just steal the baby, or try to convince Bethia that he, or she, was born dead?

"Why are you telling me this?"

"Because you did not tell Cumberland about my disappearance. Because you offered to deliver letters to my brother. Because perhaps you were right when you said we need a little trust between us. And because you are not the fool so many believe you to be. And . . ." she faltered, not finishing the sentence.

"Aye?"

"It would also be your child."

Rory could say nothing. She always surprised him, but never more than now. He thought honor had long left this country. It was disconcerting to find it in his wife.

"Why do you so often play the fool?" she asked.

"Why are you so sure it is playing?"

"Answers like that."

He shrugged. "Little is expected of a fool. I think I told you before that I dislike expectations."

Her gaze bore into his. "What do you want?" she finally asked.

"What everyone wants. To enjoy life."

"I donna know if I believe that any longer."

"Then you see only what you want to see."

She put the terrier down, and the pup fretted around the hem of her dress, obviously unhappy at being dislodged from the warmth of her body. Well, Rory would be, too.

Her body, in fact, looked inviting. Very inviting. Too inviting.

"Would you like to learn to play dice?"

"Dice?"

"I seem to be out of cards at the moment."

"I did not think gamblers were ever without cards."

He felt himself smiling. He always enjoyed their duels. He had from the beginning. He liked intelligent women, and he liked them as friends. Now that he thought of it,

two of his three friends were women. There was a strength
and loyalty in them that he had always admired.

"It happens," he said.

She tipped her head inquisitively. "Do you usually
win?"

"Yes."

"Fools do not usually win."

He raised an eyebrow. "You are acquainted with the
intricacies of gaming?"

"I listen."

"Aye, you do, Bethia." He wanted to say much more.
Which meant he needed to leave.

"You did not answer my question."

"Yes, I did."

"Not the important one. Fools do not win. And why
you pretend to be one. To disarm your opponents?"

"I would have little success wi' you, lass."

She gave him a look of disgust. She picked up the terrier again and carried him over to a chair, sitting down
and putting Jack in her lap. Then she turned her eyes on
him again. They had never seemed so blue, so . . . intense.
"Will you say anything to Cumberland about my family?"

"I like him little better than you do, lass."

"But you let him use you."

He raised an eyebrow.

"You wed *me*."

"I received much in return."

"Did you intend to wed only for material gain?"

"Does not everyone?"

"Nay," she said softly. "My father gave me a choice."

He said nothing. He could guess what happened to her
choice. He was surprised at how much that soft glow in
her eyes hurt. It wasna for him. It was for another man.
A dead man. And that hurt far more than any injury to
himself.

Dear Jesu. Was he falling in love?

"Do you love Mary?" Her voice was soft, compelling,
insisting.

He had no answer that. Mary was his bulwark against questions, against his disappearances, against any question about his character. He had not minded avoiding Bethia's questions; he did not want to lie.

"She is my friend," he said honestly enough.

"That is not what I ask."

"You ask too much, madam."

"You always do that."

"Do what?"

"Use that word—madam—when you do not wish to answer a question. Or want to create a distance between us."

"There is a distance. A chasm. You are a Jacobite. I am loyal to the king." He stood. "Since you appear disinterested in dice, I believe I will return to my own room."

She said nothing.

"Good night, madam."

"I would like to go riding in the morning."

"I will accompany you."

"Still my jailer?"

"Did you believe a few words would make it otherwise?"

"Go then," she said.

He went before he said, or did, more unwise things.

wenty

Bethia continued to play with Jack as the door closed behind her husband.

She was more puzzled than ever. Both at herself and at him.

Had she made a terrible mistake in telling him about her family?

But over the past several weeks, she was certain she'd seen a core of decency in her husband. Oh, he tried to hide it well enough. For some reason, he seemed to consider it a weakness. Too bad there was not more such weakness around.

He might be a gambler who had been naught but a wastrel most of his life, but she kept seeing hints of more, intriguing little bits and pieces that did not quite fit. She would have sworn he had not read her letters, and it had been naught but kindness, and wit, to suggest the two of them.

She had bitterly resented his possessive kiss at supper, but then she'd noted the approval on Cumberland's face, and recalled what her husband had said about sending the letters before Cumberland had a chance to forbid it. The kiss had all been an act for Cumberland's benefit.

And now she thought she knew why. He'd sensed the danger to her and her brother before she had. He hadn't known why, but he *had* sensed it. She would stake her life on it.

In truth, she just had.

If she were to bear a child, which was now possible, neither her life nor her brother's were worth a half pence. If she were right, Rory's child would be taken from him, also, and if he protested, he too might well meet with an accident. Cumberland would not hesitate to murder two more Jacobites, nor a weak noble with a reputation for cowardice. She supposed now that that was exactly the reason he *was* chosen.

Fear crawled around inside her. Fear and something more: a sickness that anyone, much less blood relatives, could plan something so ugly, so unconscionable. That they would literally steal a child, just because its parents were Scots.

She'd needed an ally, and none was available but her husband. She could only pray he would keep his silence. She could only hope he would relent on his orders refusing her a horse.

She must go to free her brother now. And she had to do it before she was with child, for then she would be too clumsy and possibly too well guarded to do anything. She could not pose as the Black Knave if she were with child.

Black Jack whined and fretted, and she thought he was probably hungry. He had grown an enormous appetite. She leaned down and snuggled him. She would have to take him, too, when she left. The pup whined again.

Bethia wondered if everyone was abed. She put the dog down, then went to the door and opened it. She listened, but there was only silence. Sconces along the wall provided dim light.

She thought for a moment. She did not want anyone to see her in the night robe. It was far too revealing. She went to the wardrobe and found a simple dress that was laced in the front so she could dress herself. She pulled on a chemise, then the dress, and fitted her feet into a pair of slippers. She took a candle to the door and opened it. Finding only silence, she slipped down the steps, Black Jack gamboling eagerly beside her.

A number of Cumberland's soldiers were sleeping in the great hall. She heard the snores, the restless sound of men, as she passed on her way to the kitchen area. It was dark now, but in a few hours it would be bustling with servants preparing a meal for their uninvited guests. She found a pitcher of milk and poured a healthy amount into a dish, then tore up pieces of bread.

Black Jack eagerly gobbled up the mixture as she stood by, waiting. Then she took him outside to tend his needs. He had been uncommonly quick at learning the difference between ground and carpet.

A sentry stood watch. Because of Cumberland?

She stayed outside only a short time, then called Jack. But just as they were about to enter the massive doors, she saw someone ride out from the stables. She knew instantly who it was.

Dear Mother of Mercy, she wished she had that freedom. She wished she could ride far from where the Butcher stayed this night. Her husband escaped so easily.

Her heart sank as she realized he was most likely escaping to the cabin in the woods.

She went inside and had just reached the steps where she heard voices and quenched the candle. The voices were soft, but she recognized one as Cumberland's. She picked up Jack and slid into the shadows.

"He will do as I ask," she heard him say. "I told him he will receive ten thousand crowns when she is with child. The marquis will do anything for money." Cumberland's voice was thick with contempt.

Jack wriggled in her arms, and she covered his mouth until the men passed her beyond her hearing. She felt a cold chill run down her back. Ten thousand crowns was a fortune, indeed. The marquis had said nothing to her about that. Nothing at all.

Neither had he made love to her again. Was she so repellant that he hoped that one time would accomplish his goal? And if it did not?

She took her hand from the dog's muzzle and ran upstairs, going into her room and shutting the door tight behind her. She found herself shivering. Not from cold, but now from something else. Fear. Apprehension. And an emotion even more powerful: a loss of faith so strong that it drained her until she felt like a cloth doll.

Bethia sat on the bed, clutching the dog, feeling more desolate than at any time since she arrived here. She had not thought that possible. But now she knew it was.

She still wanted to trust the marquis, but now doubt racked her again. How to contact the Knave?

Anne! She could get word somehow to Anne and ask her to send someone to the Flying Lady. She should have asked someone to get in touch with the Knave that night, but she had been so exhausted, so in a hurry.

She would call in the debt the Knave owed her. She was convinced of *his* honor. He would not refuse her.

She was sure of it.

All she had to do now was figure out how to get word to Anne. Her friend could send someone to the coast and pass word to the brothers at the Flying Lady that someone needed the Knave. She would not use her name, just ask that the Knave meet a fugitive at a specified place not far from the tower house. She would find some way to be there. She might have to drug the stableman, or . . .

Which meant another visit to Mary, pleading lack of sleep and the need for a potion that would help her. That prospect was painful. Humiliating.

But how to get a message to Anne? Since her husband was being so . . . agreeable, perhaps she could write in a code and ask him to send it to her friend.

Hope warred with a profound sense of apprehension,

of disappointment, even of loss. She did not want to think
of her husband. Yet she could not quite dismiss him from
her thoughts. And his presence still seemed to dominate
the room. Could she really have come to care for a char-
latan? Could he really be so devious?

   She could not chance it. Her brother's life depended
upon her being right, and as much as she wanted to believe her instincts, she could not put her faith in a man
she dinna wholly trust.

Rory fought the urge to turn back, stride into his wife's
room and tell her exactly who he was.

   But now it was more important than ever that he keep
his second life a secret from her. He accepted everything
she had said. Now everything made sense to him.

   He'd yearned to take her in his arms, but now it was
more impossible than ever. He just hoped like hell that
he had not already planted his seed in her. For if anything went wrong, and he were to meet his death before
getting the lass and her brother out of Scotland, they
would both be doomed.

   Damn Cumberland to hell, and let all the demons roast
him for an eternity.

   He urged his horse into a gallop over the hills dark
with heather and toward the loch four miles from Braemoor. It was surrounded on one side by high hills, on another by soft, rolling ones. He had often gone there as a
boy. It had been his hiding place, the one place where he
could go and be at peace.

   But now he wanted the cold wind biting at him. He
needed it to chill the longing in him, the heat that Bethia
always stirred in him. He had tried sleeping after retiring
from her room, but he couldna. His anger was too deep,
his need for her too demanding. He feared that if he ran
into Cumberland, he would skewer him then and there.
He needed this night to cool his rage. An angry man was
a careless one. His mask was already slipping. He had

become too involved, something he thought would never happen.

He'd debated with himself endlessly about telling her that he was the Black Knave, that he would help her. But he'd decided the time was not yet right. She had no reason to believe him. He certainly would have rejected the notion if he were her. And he still felt that he might be putting Alister and Mary in more danger. He knew now his wife would never consciously betray anyone, but Cumberland had ways of obtaining information, especially as long as he had her brother. And one wrong word, one wrong expression, one wrong gesture could kill them all. He simply could not risk it.

He would return to Braemoor, play the compliant fool for Cumberland, and do his bloody best to stay away from her. After tomorrow. He had promised to take her riding in the morning.

He had so little time before the French captain returned for a rendezvous. He would have to have the boy then, as well as Bethia. He would have to devise a plan to make sure the people of Braemoor did not pay for his own activities. And he would try to collect what remaining fugitive Jacobites he could. That would be his final revenge on Cumberland.

He wondered how Alister was faring. The journey would take him a total of four or five days, including at least one day at Creighton's stronghold. He could do nothing until then. He suspected the next week would be the most difficult he'd ever encountered.

And then?

He would lose the one person that lit all the dark, empty places inside him. He would miss her wit and courage and intelligence. He would miss that tentative smile. Yet he had to give her back her freedom. He had nothing else to offer.

At least he could build memories. He vowed to memorize each and every moment as a treasure to keep and hold in his mind, to pull out and relive when he was alone.

Bethia tried to be remote, cool. She had already decided she'd said too much.

Yet her heart fluttered when Rory arrived while she was eating breakfast. He looked the dandy, again. He wore a fine blue coat but without the gold trim he usually favored. He was wearing leather breeches today, too, not the trews that so outlined the muscles in his legs. His feet were encased in new, highly polished boots. His wig was not as elaborate as last night; in fact, it was actually quite modest compared to the others. Still, she much preferred the man without them.

Do not be thinking of that.

She had to be wary every moment. "I saw the Duke of Cumberland leave at dawn."

"Aye. He now has all our farmers and herders combing the countryside."

She looked up at him through thick lashes. She was flirting with him, and she cringed inwardly at doing so. She saw his eyes darken.

Did he really read her mind as she so often thought he was doing? How could he?

"Have you eaten, my lord?"

"Aye, with Cumberland before he left. He had a few last instructions."

She swallowed back the bile. She knew what some of those instructions were. Bed her. Produce an heir for the English nobility her mother and father detested—people who would do anything to take a child from its mother. Now she knew why her mother never spoke of her own family.

She lost what little hunger she had, and stood. "I will get my cloak."

"You look well this morning."

She curtsied. "Thank you, my lord."

"I speak only truth," he said solemnly.

She felt flustered. She was determined not to trust him, not to lower her guard, and yet when he spoke with that serious edge to his voice, she felt herself melt a little. She allowed him to help her put on the cloak, then her gloves. Black Jack panted heavily next to her, obviously afraid she was leaving without him.

She looked up at the marquis. "Can we take Jack with us? He does so love adventures."

"He takes after his mistress."

She decided not to reply to that. She just looked at him.

"He will stay out from under the hooves?"

"I will take him in the saddle with me."

"If that will please you."

Nothing but her brother's safety would please her now. But she nodded.

If he saw anything else in her eyes, he did not mention it. He only nodded. "The three of us, then."

The horses were already saddled, and Jamie was holding the reins. The marquis handed Jack to the boy. "Hold him until she is in the saddle."

He then helped her into the saddle, his hand remaining on hers a second longer than necessary, then handed Jack up to her. She noticed that his hands were gentle, that one hand ruffed the fur of Jack, as he lifted him up to her.

Then he mounted and they rode down the lane.

"Where are we going?"

"To a loch. I asked the cook to put together a meal. I thought you might enjoy getting away for a while."

Forever was more like it. But her husband was at his most likeable. Even though she did not trust him entirely, Bethia found herself caught up in a charm he used so effectively . . . when he so chose.

They rode for an hour, passing through one patrol before reaching the loch. Nestled between high heather-filled hills, it was a dark blue and lay shimmering in the sun. She could not contain a gasp of pleasure. She loved the heather and the wild hills, the plentiful lochs and streams and rivers.

She warned herself about her companion. He could turn charm on and off like a Highlands storm. He had listened to her, admitted that her concerns were most likely correct, but he had not offered to help in any way. The only thing he *had* done was keep her secrets.

Could she really expect him to risk anything at all for her? Especially when he had married an unwilling stranger for a fortune?

He helped her dismount under a birch tree, then spread out a blanket. She walked over to the loch. "It is beautiful."

"Aye, I used to come here as a lad."

She looked up at him. "I canna imagine you as a lad."

He shrugged. "I sometimes wonder if I was ever really one. I remember little except the yelling between the marquis and my mother. I was fostered to an English family and was grateful for the respite."

"When first did you come here?"

"My mother brought me here when I was seven. After that, I came every time I could. 'Tis the peace of the place. I would sit for hours and watch the deer come to drink. I thought . . ."

He stopped as if he were telling secrets that were to remain that way.

"Does anyone else ever come here?"

"An occasional shepherd with a flock." He looked toward a steep wooded hill sheltering the lake. "There are caves up there. I used to hide in them, play the part of Robert Bruce."

"And then you fought against all he believed in?" She could not stop the sharp retort. He always lulled her into a fantasy of safety. She had to do something to remind herself that he was no loyal friend. Yet a small voice suggested that perhaps he was suggesting a hiding place. Why was he always so oblique?

"That was more than twenty years ago, madam, before my family declared itself for the Hanover."

"Hanover?"

The Jacobites had called the king that with no little derision. She was surprised to hear the word from his mouth. But then he often seemed to have no loyalties, not to the side on which he fought, nor the other. He seemed to consider himself equally bemused by both sides, an uninvolved onlooker.

"Aye," he said with that curious smile that tipped only one side of his lips. "The Hanover."

"Why did you fight?"

"There are some that say I did not. That I ran at the first sound of cannon."

"Did you?"

He went to the rugged edge of the loch. He picked up a stone and flipped it into the water, watching as it skipped once, then twice, before sinking. "You are wanting to know the mettle of your husband?"

"Aye," she admitted wryly. "You so oft confuse me. I donna know what I think much of the time."

"I did not run, lass. I walked from the battlefield when Cumberland ordered no quarter. I had no taste for slaughter."

It was one of the first times she had heard real emotion in his voice. She was stunned by the depth of it, and even more that he shared it with her.

"Is that why you dinna tell Cumberland about my absence."

"Perhaps I just did not wish him to think how ineffectual I am as a husband."

She took several steps toward him and looked into his eyes. God's breath, but they were mesmerizing. Green and gold and gray. Always changing, always intriguing. And always secretive.

"Why do you allow everyone to think you are a coward?"

"I care not what they think."

And he did not. She saw that clearly enough. But strangely, he apparently cared about what she thought.

Her fingers started to tingle. She found herself moving toward him. A step, then two. He was also moving. A step. Then two.

They faced each other. Only a breath of air separated them. And that air crackled with emotion. Desire. Her limbs froze in place, then melted as his breath mingled with hers. His lips touched hers with a sweetness that contradictorily jarred every one of her senses. She felt his arms go around her, and she was pulled willingly against him, her cheek resting against his heart. She felt its beat, felt the warmth of his body.

Her body was responding to him again, in so many betraying ways. She felt the hunger, the need to have him become a part of her. She heard the gentle lap of the water against shore, the sound of birds rustling from trees. She heard all the music of the earth, and it was made more glorious by the melody in her body.

She also heard an unwelcome echo. *The marquis will do anything for money.*

He must have felt her instinctively drawing away, for he released her, his eyes at once curious and wary.

She did not want him to go away. Why did she always feel so safe with him, when she should feel the opposite? Feeling split in half by desire and fear of betrayal, she started to turn away.

Then she heard splashes. Frantic, panicked splashes.

She turned toward the loch. Jack was thrashing in the water. He must have tumbled from a rock into the lake, and in frantic efforts was moving away from the shore. She started to run toward the water.

He caught her. "The water is very cold and very deep," he said. "I will get him."

She watched as he pulled off his wig, then his coat, and finally his boots. 'Twas done in a matter of seconds, with more speed than she thought possible. Without hesitation, he plunged into the water, swimming with strong strokes to reach the pup, which had disappeared from view. Rory went down, too, came up, then went down again.

Her heart seemed to stop beating. Jack was *her* charge. How could she have not paid the proper attention? Just as she had not gotten her brother out of Scotland in time.

Then she saw a dark head surfacing. He held the dog. He swam back with one arm, the other holding tightly to the puppy.

He reached the shore, and stood. His body was shivering, and the pup was still.

He sat down and rubbed Black Jack, putting two thumbs at his chest and kneading it. Water dribbled from the pup's mouth, then it wriggled, emitting the little mewing sounds he had as a few weeks' old puppy. She took Jack from her husband's hands and bundled the pup in her cloak. She put a hand on Braemoor's drenched arm. It was freezing.

"We need a fire," she said.

He shrugged. "I have no flint." But he took off his shirt and put on the dry coat. His dark, wet hair clung to his face. She handed him the puppy and reached down, tearing off a piece of her petticoat. She used it to wipe the water from her husband's face. She was thinking of him more and more like that. *Husband.*

"Sit," she commanded.

Looking startled, he did. She used the cloth to try to dry his hair. She could do nothing about his wet breeches. She looked down. He was drying the pup in his elegant coat.

Her hands kneaded his hair, her fingers lingering to allow a clump to curl around them.

"You will ruin your coat," she said, distressed to find that her voice broke with emotion.

"He is chilled."

"So are you."

"But I know I will be warm soon, and he does not."

She stared down at the dark head, grateful he could

not see her face, nor what was in it. She did not want him to see the emotion, nor the fear, nor the utter gratefulness she felt.

Nor the surge of something more than gratitude.

"We had better ride back," she said.

"And miss our meal?" he said with mock horror.

"Is there somewhere warmer?"

"Nay. Naught but Braemoor, and I do not think I wish to go there. 'Twas the water that was cold, lass. 'Tis still summer. The sun is out, and I will dry out soon enough."

"Thank you," she said simply. "Thank you for Jack."

"Mayhap that will teach him to be more cautious about water." Despite his cavalier tone, though, she noted his hands tightened around the pup. His waistcoat had darkened with moisture. "And you, lass, are about to rub all my hair off."

Bethia suddenly realized she had been rubbing harder and harder. Embarrassed, she dropped the wet cloth from her hands. She stooped beside him and took the pup from him, cradling him in her own arms. He was still shivering and making piteous little sounds, looking up hopefully. "You are a little fraud," she said, yet terribly grateful that he was still among them.

She did not know how to swim. She knew she could never have saved him.

As one hand held the pup, she put another up to Rory's face. Her land lingered on his cheek. How could she have believed he would allow a child of his to be bartered away? But why had he not offered his help yesterday when they had talked? Why had he just listened to her?

He put on his boots, then started stomping around on the sun-warmed grass. She thought he looked a little like a bull ready to mate.

She giggled, and he looked over at her, a smile tugging at his lips. "Do I look so foolish, then?"

"Nay, you look quite heroic to me."

"You have small standards, then."

"I have high ones," she contradicted. "Jack believes so, too."

"Umm," he said dubiously. He resumed his stomping as she watched. She would always remember him this way. A wicked little demon made her wonder whether Mary saw him regularly like this, his dark hair freed from a wig, breeches clinging to strong legs. Pain rippled through her.

She looked away, toward the lake. Black Jack licked her cheek as if he suddenly realized she needed comfort more than he. But though she could no longer see her husband, every part of her was aware of his presence behind her. Every time she saw him now, she felt controlled by totally unfamiliar emotions, desires, feelings.

Even if he was a Scotsman who had fought with Cumberland, a man who at Cumberland's order married a woman not of his choice. Even as he kept a mistress nearby.

The pain grew deeper inside. She wondered what it would be like to be truly loved by the marquis.

Do not think of that. You canna hold on to something you have never had. Think of Dougal.

And did she really want a man who seemed to take nothing seriously, not death, not the proposed theft of a child, not loyalty?

Nonetheless, she would miss him. She would even miss the outrageousness of his clothes, the competence only she seemed to notice, the small kindnesses he either tried to hide or smooth over with some barbed remark.

She turned back toward him. He was still stomping back and forth. He looked irresistible in his dripping breeches and spoiled coat. Always before, even in his casual clothes, he'd looked elegant. Arrogant. Now he looked mussed and approachable and incredibly sensual.

The marquis will do anything for money. Remember Cumberland's words.

He might have drowned saving Jack.

Rory swerved and went toward the horses, untying a

bag from his saddle. He took a cloth from it, spreading it on the bank, then triumphantly placed a bottle of wine, two roasted pheasants, cheese and fruit on the cloth.

"I still think you should find dry clothes," she said.

"I do not," he retorted with the arrogance she remembered so well from the first few days.

She still wanted something from him, so she said nothing as he parceled out the food and poured wine into two silver goblets. She sipped it, and found it very good. She looked up at him. His hair was drying, the thick strands slightly curling. His coat was rumpled, but he paid no attention to it. Instead, he seemed immensely pleased with himself.

Bethia could not stop staring. Of all the Rory Forbeses she had seen, this one was the most appealing. He did not care about his appearance. He had unhesitatingly risked his life for an animal. Now he appeared uniquely pleased with what had happened this afternoon, despite his physical discomfort.

"You are not eating, madam."

"I am interested in you. You are enjoying this much too much."

"I have never been out on an excursion like this before."

Why not with Mary, if he'd wanted one? Why was he charming her so? And he was. She felt as if she were melting into a small puddle, just asking him to step into it.

But at the moment she did not want to bring Mary into the conversation. She wanted to learn more about this man who was her husband. Even if she did intend to leave him, to leave Scotland with her brother, to run far out of Cumberland's and her grandfather's reach.

Jack suddenly darted out of her arms and onto the cloth, snatching a piece of meat from the pheasant.

"You see," Rory said. "He will be all right. He's a braw lad."

She nibbled on the pheasant, sharing it with the dog

who had now seemed completely recuperated. Her hand ruffled his drying fur. She had come so close to losing him, and at the moment he was all she had. "Aye," she said. "He is that."

"As his mistress is a brave lass."

She looked up sharply. She wished she did not always wonder what he wanted.

"I would like to journey to the Innes land," she said, deciding to try his approachability. "Anne Innes is a friend."

"How good a friend?"

She tried not to show resentment at the question. Any husband would ask the question. "A fine one," she said.

A light quenched in his eyes. He shrugged. "I am aware of the family. She is Jacobite."

She sat, waiting, as his eyes seemed to study her thoughts.

"I think not," he said after a long silence.

Her heart dropped. For a moment, she had hoped he would agree.

"A letter then," she said. "She was betrothed to my older brother." She hated to plead for even that small privilege.

He drank some more wine before answering. She held herself very still. He was making it clear he was still her master, regardless of those few moments of warmth. "Aye," he said finally. "I will send someone with it this afternoon."

"Thank you." She should feel a moment of triumph, but she did not. She had to leave Braemoor, but now she knew she would leave with an empty place inside her. She wondered whether she would always look for that crooked smile.

She wished she could tell him everything, that she planned to ask Anne to find the Knave for her. Then she and her brother would disappear. But this was his home, and she was his wife, and everything he had recently acquired was dependent on her.

He rose, gathered up the food. Then he offered her assistance in mounting, but all the warmth was gone. He was cool. The arrogant smile was back on his lips. He was a stranger again and, oddly enough, she felt as if she'd just lost a friend.

Twenty-one

With Jack clinging to her feet, Bethia spent the afternoon composing her letter. Every once in a while, she leaned down and rubbed his back and he growled with pleasure. 'Twas a small, fierce rumble.

She could not put from her mind the different faces of Rory Forbes, Marquis of Braemoor. Wry. Thoughtful. Whimsical. Severe. Cold.

She tried to shake the thoughts from her mind and concentrate on the letter. She could not depend on the hope that he would not read it. And she had no idea what the marquis would do if he did read that, in essence, she was asking an enemy of the state to help her escape her marriage and her brother escape the Duke of Cumberland.

If his position and wealth were truly jeopardized, would he try to stop her?

So she very carefully wrote her note:

Anne,

I wanted you to know how much I miss you, and the friends we last discussed. I will always remember the journey to the sea. I wish I could go there again. Or that you could visit me at Braemoor. I would like to take you to Loch Maire. My

*husband took me there today, and it is truly lovely. We ate
on a finger of land that jutted out into the loch. It is an isolated spot, seldom used. I was hoping you could come, even
as soon as the new moon. We could ride out and watch it
shimmer under the moonlight. Tell our friend not to worry
about the debt. It can be repaid when we meet again. And
we can laugh together again about how last I looked.*

Your friend, Bethia

She sealed it, then gave it to Trilby to take to the marquis. She did not think she could bear seeing the marquis
again. He was far too dangerous to her emotions, to her
usual practicality. He confused her, and she knew she
could not afford to be confused.

Rory delivered the letter to Anne Innes himself.

He knew taking Bethia to the loch had been a mistake. He'd just thought she would enjoy it, and she'd had
precious few moments of enjoyment. He had not expected
the warmth that flared between them—or maybe he had.
He'd thought he could control his desire for her, his need,
and he'd been shocked when he'd discovered he could
not.

He knew then he could not stay at Braemoor, waiting
for Alister to return. He had to get away from the tower
house, from Bethia, before he destroyed all of them.

He would deliver the letter, then make a trip to Edinburgh. Two days' hard riding to get there, two back. That
should cool his . . . infatuation. Perhaps he could even find
an agreeable woman, one who would make no demands
on his heart or emotions. One that was free of loyalties,
just as he was. One that would just enjoy an evening of
lovemaking.

He'd liked Anne Innes, but he'd not tarried long. She
had greeted him with wariness and it was clear she thought
him something less than human. Still, conscious of the
Highland custom of hospitality, she'd invited him to stay

to sup with them. But he had already made enough mistakes; he needed no other person to see more than he wanted them to see.

The estate reeked of neglect, mainly, he supposed, because of lack of money, and the lady herself had a sadness about her. He quickly learned that her father was very ill, and had been for a long time. None of her relatives had fought with the young prince, which had saved them from the depredations suffered by other Jacobite families. Still, her cattle had been rounded up and sold for practically nothing to the Scottish Lowlanders who had supported the English crown.

Rory made a mental note to see that the cattle were replaced and that a sum of money would suddenly be repaid, a long neglected debt to her father. She'd given him no letter in return, but did ask him to tell Bethia that she missed her but understood everything.

"You will tell her that," she emphasized. "That I understood."

He assured her he would. Then he turned toward Edinburgh. He wanted to know whether Elizabeth had learned of any other Jacobites looking for safety, since this was likely to be the last voyage. He would also listen to what the English military said, whether there were any leads to the Black Knave. And, particularly, whether his usual coastal rendezvous was still safe.

Those were his excuses, at least, excuses to keep him away from Braemoor. Bloody hell, but he was drawn to Bethia like metal to a lodestone. She filled so many lonely places inside him.

He had to keep away from her.

Rory rode for two days straight, stopping only to rest his horse, and for several hours to rest himself. He reached Edinburgh late the second day.

English troops were everywhere. He wondered whether others felt the deep, visceral resentment that he did. He had not cared that much before Culloden. His father had been intrinsically linked to the country, and Rory had so

much simmering resentment for him that Scotland drew
precious little loyalty from him. But in the past few
months, he had witnessed fortitude and courage. He had
ridden the Highlands and passed through the glens and
over the gorges. He had seen the tears in the eyes of those
forced to leave, and that grief had transferred itself to
him. He felt their courage, their fierce loyalty to each
other, to their cause, and for the first time he had a sense
of place, and knew he would miss it.

The Fox and Hare was noisy and full, but he readily
found the innkeeper. "Ye ha' been neglecting us, my lord,"
the man fawned.

"Aye, some business at home."

"How long do ye plan to stay this time?"

"Only a day or two. I have need of clothes. The Duke
of Cumberland has told me of a new tailor."

At the mention of the most powerful man in Scotland
and the second most powerful in England, the man fairly
danced with excitement. "I will ha' yer rooms aired and
a fire prepared."

"A bath, too."

The owner was well used to his client's habits and
knew he would be well-paid for tending to them. "Aye."

Rory waited until long past midnight, until the tavern
was clear of the last customer. He told the innkeeper he
did not want to be disturbed. Then he changed to the
clothes of a beggar, put cotton in his mouth to change
the shape of his face, then pulled on a unkempt wig of
long, dark hair.

He dribbled some rum over his lips and onto his
clothes, then slipped out the door to a back stairs and
down the street. Rory kept to the shadows, sliding to the
ground and snoring loudly when a patrol passed. He finally approached Elizabeth's house, making sure that no
one else was on the street. He had not been able to warn
her of his visit. He could only hope that she had no male
guest this night.

He reached her rooms without problem, and rapped four times, waited, then rapped again.

No answer.

He started to rap again when he heard someone stir. Elizabeth had a maid that came each day, but did not live in the house. Discretion, she always claimed.

She opened the door and he slipped inside, taking one last look at the empty side street.

She started, then looked closer. "Dear God, but you should have been an actor," she said.

"I might just do that in the Colonies," he said. "I will ha' to change my name, though."

"You are leaving?"

"Aye, with the next shipment. My new wife will be aboard and, with the devil's help, her brother. I doubt the marquis of Braemoor would survive their disappearance. Cumberland would never understand."

"You are going to France?"

"Nay, I will take Bethia there, then find passage to the Colonies. Can you get word to the others that this will be the last shipment for the Knave? And to our people at Nairn that I need a dead body? About my height and weight. They are not to make one," he added quickly. "Merely to locate one already dead for one reason or another."

"What are you thinking?"

"I do not want blame to fall on the Forbeses. Rory Forbes must die trying to keep his wife in Scotland. Alister and Mary will be charged with helping her, but they, too, will be gone."

She smiled at him. "Neither of them are Forbeses."

"Exactly. My cousin should be clear."

"I did not believe you liked your cousin."

Rory shrugged. "He is a good manager. I wish no man to pay for my actions."

"I will miss you, Rory."

He took the cloth from his cheeks and kissed her.

"That was far too much a brotherly kiss," she protested.

He kissed her again, a kiss of memories and affection and good-bye. His lips lingered, but there was none of the exhilaration he felt with Bethia, only the sad parting of two good friends. "I will write you."

"And who should I expect to sign the letter?"

He thought for a moment. "What about Lazarus?"

She grinned. "Just make sure you do rise from the dead, my lord."

He started out the door. "If anyone knows of Jacobites, tell them to go toward Banff. Buckie might be watched now. Tell them to look for a farm five miles inland of the village; they will tell them where to wait." He gave her specific directions. "Tell them to be there within two weeks."

When he finished, he put the cloth back in his cheeks. "I must go before the inn starts stirring."

"Godspeed, my lord."

"Rory," he said.

"Godspeed, Rory."

"And you, love." He took a bag from his pocket and placed it on a table.

"No, Rory."

"In the name of all those you have helped," he said. "You might have to leave yourself. This can help buy your way." Then he quickly left before she could say anything more, before she saw the moisture in his eyes. He had too few friends. He knew he would not see this one again.

Upon his return, Rory went first to the smithy where he found Alister shoeing a horse.

"Your visit was successful?"

"Aye," Alister said. "I have a letter but I have not given it to her. I wanted to wait for you. I also have drawn a map of the castle where young Dougal is being held. He is a bright young lad, as quick as his mistress."

The boy was fine, he added.

Alister had arranged several moments with him alone

and had questioned him. The lad knew of a way in and out of the castle; apparently he'd charmed one of the serving girls into revealing a possible escape route. But he'd had no horse, no money. He was also locked in his room at night, and had a minder most of the time. "I think he has just been biding his time, waiting for an opportunity."

"What way?"

"A drain in the kitchen leads into sewers. The sewers dump into a moat."

"It would be a nasty swim."

"Aye, but the lad can do it, I think. He is well worried about his sister. He feels he needs to protect her."

"Ha. The lad needs to protect *me* from her wicked tongue," Rory said ruefully.

"I thought you had a truce."

Rory shrugged. "'Tis not easy being anyone's prisoner. I ha' been keeping a tight rein on her. She is more afraid than she wants anyone to know, and she might well do something foolish before I can work things out."

"'Tis said she had been ill."

Alarm filled Rory. "Ill?"

Alister looked at him curiously. "For three days. A physician was called. He apparently told Neil it was only 'female problems,' and naught to worry about. Young Jamie at the stable told me about it when I returned from Fort William."

"She is all right now?"

"Aye," Alister said. "It appears so."

Rory's stomach clenched. What if it were serious? What if she were with child? But then, would the physician not have revealed that? His child? If so, could he let her go? It was already excruciating to think that she might disappear from his life. Since that first crackling energy sparked between them, he'd felt more alive than he'd felt in his life. The sky was bluer, the air fresher, the moon brighter.

Bloody hell, but he was thinking like a lovesick fool. He would get them all killed.

He abruptly changed the subject. "The Frenchman is due soon. I want both her and the boy on board."

"And you?"

"All of us, I hope. In the meantime, I have to find a way that no blame will fall on Neil or the Forbeses."

"How do you propose to do that?"

Rory grinned. "I'm working on the details."

Alister's gaze looked upward as if praying. "Which means you have no idea."

"Exactly," Rory said. "Now about the boy. How can we let him know when we want him to escape?"

"A gift from his sister. His birthday is soon. The gift can be marked in some way."

Rory nodded. "Mayhap I will deliver that one. It is time I met my brother-in-law. I imagine he wrote a letter to his sister?"

"Aye. I suggested that he do as his sister did. Write two letters, one that Creighton would read. The other one is still sealed. It is inside my rooms. In the Bible."

"Perhaps giving them to her with the seal unbroken will reinstate some confidence in me. I fear that Cumberland or one of his men said something that has made her wary."

"How *was* Cumberland's visit?"

"Annoying, as always. He offered me ten thousand crowns if Bethia were to give birth to our child." He went on to relate Bethia's idea as to why Cumberland's interest in the MacDonells was so strong.

Alister whistled. "Damn me if you have not landed in the fire."

"That, my friend, is why we are all leaving."

Alister hesitated. "I received a message earlier today. It came from the Flying Lady. The lad that helped you is looking for aid. He wishes to meet you near Loch Maire."

"Maire?" Apprehension ran down Rory's spine. The

loch was far too close to Braemoor. Was someone suspicious of him? Was it a trap? For a moment, Rory wondered whether he had made a mistake.

"When?" Rory finally asked.

"The first night of the new moon."

"A week from now." Much too close to the time he and Alister would go after young Dougal MacDonell.

And why Loch Maire? Why not Inverness or Nairn? "Does anyone know who he is?"

"Nay."

Rory hesitated. It looked like a trap. It smelled like a trap. But how could he not help someone who helped him? "Can you get word to someone down there. See whether you can find anything at all about the lad. What he looked like? Whether he speaks Gaelic. If he does, he is a Highlander."

"Do you think he is a spy?"

"Cumberland has any number of them."

"But why would the lad save you, then?"

"They might have known we would suspect a trap. This would make the lad quite . . . trustworthy in our eyes. A spy in our camp? Cumberland might feel he could take the whole nest of us."

"Should I go myself?"

Rory shook his head. "You have been gone too much already. Do you have someone you can trust?"

"Aye. The lad who brought the message is staying in one of the caves in the hills. I thought you might want to send a message back with him."

Rory nodded. "Send him immediately. Tell him there's five pounds in it if he returns before the new moon."

"I will give him one of my horses," Alister said.

Rory agreed. Alister had three horses, all of which he had bought cheaply. They'd looked like nags then, but Alister had an eye for horseflesh. Under good care, they were sturdy and fleet.

Alister hesitated. "Are you sure about this, Rory? I do not like it."

"I know," Rory said, arguing more with himself than Alister. His sense of urgency had been growing greater each day. He could not tamp the feeling that Bethia and her brother were in terrible danger and that it grew every day. But neither could he fail to heed the call of someone who had helped him. "I owe him," he added simply.

"The message mentioned that."

"Bloody hell."

"Your instincts are good, Rory. Heed them."

Rory's instincts were all clamoring. They said run. They did not believe in coincidence.

"You have a week to decide," Alister said helpfully. "Hopefully, the lad will be back by then."

"And hopefully he needs nothing but passage himself. If he is who he says he is. Then I can get Dougal, and you can bring the marchioness. We will meet at the coast."

"Why do *you* not take the marchioness and *I* can get the boy?" There was an unusual twinkle in Alister's usually serious eyes.

"Because Creighton trusts me. He might not be so trusting of a stranger who comes twice within a month. And you must take Mary as well."

"Are you sure it is no' more than that?"

"Aye," Rory said. "No more than that." But there was. He knew it. He lost his objectivity when he was with Bethia. And that put them both into danger.

Alister regarded him skeptically, then shrugged.

Rory nodded. "I had best get back to Braemoor. I will go by Mary's tomorrow."

Alister nodded. "I will send the lad on his way tonight."

Rory nodded. The heat from the forge felt good. The smithy felt good to him. It always had. A place of warmth, even safety for him. He could even fashion a horseshoe. He would miss it. And Alister would have to start all over again somewhere. He and Mary.

"Have you asked her yet?"

Alister did not look at him. Neither did he need to ask what Rory meant. "Nay."

"Alister," Rory said with disgust.

"I ha' no right, no' until we are safe, and I have something to give her." Alister had years since picked up Rory's proper speech, but whenever he was worried he lapsed into his childhood dialect.

Rory shook his head, but he was no one to give advice. He had done a bloody lot of damage in his thirty years. Bethia was only the latest of his victims. He had not had the character and strength to stay away from her. He had indulged himself, just as he had indulged himself every day since he'd first escaped Braemoor. And now he'd made her a prisoner just as he had been one.

The one thing he could do now was give her freedom. And he had a letter for her.

"Mary's then, at noon tomorrow."

"Aye," Alister said and returned to his work.

Bethia tried to read a book she had pilfered from the library. Instead, her thoughts returned continually to the marquis. Although his absence aided her plan, she found herself looking for him, and not entirely apprehensively. He had been gone five days.

She'd also expected news of her brother by now. What was taking the blacksmith so long to carry a message?

Waiting. She felt as if she'd spent her entire life waiting. A woman's lot, her mother once told her when her father and brothers had ridden off on some secret raid or another. Bethia rebelled at that thought. She would be no tame wife, waiting for someone to rescue her. She would be part of any rescue. She just needed help. A *little* help. And the Black Knave *owed* her for her assistance.

She had already taken steps to escape. Once the marquis had left, she'd visited Mary, pleading sleeplessness. But the herb she'd received was not nearly strong enough, and the humiliating visit had been for naught. She then faked a stomach illness. A physician had been sent for, and at her request she'd been given a bottle of laudanum. She had secreted the small bottle in a pair of slippers.

She never could have managed it had the marquis been at Braemoor. He seemed to read her mind.

Jack barked.

Poor Jack, he'd had few adventures these last few days as she forced herself to remain in bed. Trilby would take him out occasionally, but the rest of the time he huddled next to her, unsure as to why his mistress was not playing with him.

Then she heard a knock at her door and she knew instantly who it was. No one else knocked with quite the same impatient authority. When had he returned? He must have just arrived or Trilby would have run to her.

He did not wait for her to invite him in, but strode in, filling the room with his presence. It always seemed too small for him.

"I have been told you were ill, madam?"

She did not stand, only looked up, hoping her face held none of the emotions he always raised in her.

"I was," she said icily.

"You are recovered?"

"Aye."

He hesitated, looking profoundly uncomfortable. "You are not with child?"

"It appears not," she said. "You will not receive your reward from Cumberland as soon as you probably hoped."

He sat down on her bed. Jack, the little traitor, dashed over to him, the tail waving like a willow in a thunderstorm. She wondered whether the terrier realized the marquis had saved his life. Whether Jack did or not, he obviously enjoyed the marquis's hands as they ruffled the dog's fur. Even from where she sat, she saw the gentleness in them, remembered those rare moments when she had felt a more intimate tenderness.

Her face blazed with heat and she very carefully closed the book and placed it on the table. "No reply, my lord?"

"You overheard something when Cumberland was here." It was a comment, not a question.

"Aye. A princely sum was mentioned."

"I told you that Cumberland wanted proof of consummation, that he would be pleased if we produced . . . a bairn."

"You did not tell me there was an extra ten thousand pounds involved. Did you know that when I told you about my family?"

He met her stare directly. "Aye, he had mentioned it earlier."

"Why did you not say something?"

"Why? It changed nothing," he said. "And if you remember, I did not force myself on you that night. In fact, I left before I was more than a little tempted. I did not particularly wish to father a bairn that Cumberland could use."

Bethia's breath caught in her throat. He was right. Had she just seized upon the overheard conversation because he had left so abruptly? Or had she been trying to find reasons to distrust him as a shield against her own growing feelings for him?

"Why did you leave?"

"I had business," he said shortly and stood. He reached into his waistcoat and pulled out a sealed sheet of paper. "Your brother sent this to you. Alister said that Creighton did not read it. And Mistress Anne sends you greetings and is sorry that you cannot come. She said she understood."

Her heart stopped. There was still the chance that Anne hadn't understood the note, that she was just exchanging a pleasantry, but Bethia didn't think so. She took her brother's letter, holding it for a moment, all too aware that he was standing so close. Too close. Tension radiated between them. But then, it always did. Her gaze lifted and settled on him. He wore a wig. And a startling vivid green cravat with a royal purple waistcoat and lilac-colored vest. And yet all she saw were his eyes, the dark brows that perched so provocatively above them and the sensuous lips that twisted just enough to make it appear he laughed at the world.

His hand tipped her chin. "I am sorry you did not feel well," he said.

"It was nothing."

"They said you were abed three days. That does not sound like you."

The observation both surprised and warmed her. It certainly disconcerted her. "It might have been something I ate." The words sounded false even to her.

"Did you complain to the butcher? The meat butcher," he added.

"I am not sure it was the meat."

"What did the physician say?"

"He thought it a woman's weakness."

He suddenly grinned. "But it wasn't that, was it, lass?"

It was not then, but it might well be now. She was feeling hot, dizzy, uncertain.

His hand was still on her chin but one of his fingers was stroking her cheek. A question was in his eyes, but it was a question she could not answer. "I missed you, lass," he finally said.

"Then why do you always leave?" She had not meant to ask the question. She should not care where he went, or how long he might be gone. She herself would leave in a few days. The question, though, just tumbled from her lips.

"You wished a message delivered to Mistress Anne Innes."

He leaned over. His lips touched hers, raising prickling sensations. Everywhere. Then his lips played with hers, his breathing quickening. Her hand had moved up, stroking her cheek in infinitely tender fingers. The air left the room.

His kiss turned hungry, as if he had been starving and she was the first food he'd had in weeks. She felt his intensity, his need. It matched her own. Her body was no longer hers to control; instead, it moved instinctively into his. He held her there, his lips nibbling hers until they opened, and then his tongue invaded her mouth with a sweet seductiveness. Her body arched and she felt a now familiar tightness.

Her body echoed with memories, pulsed with a need she'd so recently learned. She moved her arms up, and the letter fell from them.

Her letter. How could she have delayed reading it?

He must have sensed her sudden withdrawal. He straightened, though his fingers stayed on her cheek. He gave her a rueful grin, then took a step backward. Then he saw the letter. He leaned down and picked it up and handed it to her.

"I dropped it," she said as guilt washed over her.

"Aye, I see. I will leave you with it, lass."

"Thank you," she said. She prayed her voice did not tremble, but she feared it did. She did not want him to leave. She wanted to put her hand in his and keep him with her.

But he broke the spell with his next words. "Alister said the boy told him that his birthday is soon. I thought you might like to send him a present."

"I would like to see him," she said wistfully.

"Alister said he looked well."

"I am afraid for him."

"Creighton will make sure he keeps well."

"Because he can control me through him," she whispered.

He sighed, seemed to hesitate, then took her hand in his large one. "He will be safe, lass. I promise you that."

"How can you?" she whispered.

"I will find a way." He reached the door, then turned around, his gaze searching hers. "Just do not do anything foolish in the meantime."

Bethia's back stiffened. Her eyes narrowed.

He grinned. "You are very bonny when you get your ire up, lass." He took the few steps to the door, then turned back toward her. "I *am* pleased you are feeling better."

Her face grew hot again. She felt as if he knew everything she thought, everything she planned. Could he possibly know she had a bottle of laudanum hidden away?

But he said nothing more.

And as the door closed behind him, she felt as if all the warmth in the room left with him.

Twenty-two

The marquis escorted her to supper the next night, but first he handed her a necklace of perfect pearls. It was one of the most beautiful pieces of jewelry she had ever seen.

She could only stare at it speechlessly for a moment. Her family had never had anything quite so lovely. Then she looked up at him. "More family jewels?"

"Aye."

"Who do you want me to wear them for this time?"

"For me," he said quietly. There was none of the usual flippancy in his voice.

She turned toward the mirror while he fastened them around her neck. His hands lingered even as they had the night Cumberland had paid his unwanted visit, then kneaded the back of her neck, his fingers caressing her skin as if they were playing a beloved instrument.

One of her hands went involuntarily to touch the pearls. They shimmered against her skin and they felt as smooth as silk to her touch. Her gaze lifted, meeting his in the mirror.

"I wish you to understand one thing, Bethia," he said in the same quiet tone that was void of the usual amusement. "That any gifts I have given you *are* yours. I do not care whether they stay in the family. I do not care if you need to sell them. They are, and always will be, yours alone." His voice was huskier than usual and if she did not know better, she would have said he was trying to say good-bye.

She turned around then, because the mirror kept her from seeing his eyes. But they were no more clear than they had been through the mirror. His hands fell from her neck.

"Thank you, my lord," she said.

His eyes suddenly glinted with amusement. "You are welcome, madam. You will heed my words about them?"

"Aye," she said.

He then gave her a black velvet pouch. "This will help them keep their luster," he said.

It would also make it easier for her to take them with her. A shiver ran down her back. Did he know what she intended? Was he giving her his blessing?

She lowered her eyes. He turned, leaning over to scratch Black Jack. The dog was making a lackwit of himself, rolling on his back and sticking all four feet in the air, his tail snaking out to waggle eagerly. But, she had to admit, probably no more than she had just done, when the marquis had placed the pearls around her neck. Not because of the pearls, but because of his rare earnestness in presenting them.

But that was to be the last tender moment of the evening. Without informing her, he had apparently invited a number of the clansmen of various stations to supper. Once at the table, he drank steadily, directing his attention toward everyone but her. 'Twas as if she had ceased to exist.

She noticed that Neil watched even more carefully than usual, and she wondered whether they'd had a confrontation about his absences, his extravagances or even the pearls she wore. That made her wonder. Neil rarely left Braemoor except to visit Braemoor's now many properties. He had no wife and she had never heard him talk of a woman.

If she had intended to remain at Braemoor, she would try to engage him in conversation, perhaps even in match-making plans. He was so somber, so serious.

He had tried to avoid her since she had been here, though he'd not shown any hostility after the first few weeks. He had even expressed some gratitude when she'd seen to the transformation of the tower house. But she had never seen him smile. Their meals, except during large gatherings such as tonight, were mostly taken indi-vidually, even in the morning when they chose food from a sideboard. Neil apparently ate very early and the mar-quis was usually absent. At noon and at night, Neil ate at odd times; her husband was usually gone and she ate in her room. It was an odd, estranged household.

But now Neil sat next to her. He was even more quiet than usual when Rory was in residence, and he had not said more than a sentence since they had sat down to eat. Rory had so riveted her attention that she had not even noticed until now.

She turned to him. "Does the food please you?"

"Aye," Neil said. "Your coming has enhanced the kitchen."

"Just the addition of a few herbs," she said.

"Nay, I think not," he said. "The butcher sends us bet-ter cuts, the cook takes more pride because there is some-one to thank her."

It came as close to a compliment as he had ever paid her. "Rory says you are an excellent manager."

"Of fields, my lady, not of kitchens."

"Have you thought of taking a wife?"

His dark eyes clouded. "I have little to offer a wife," he said.

"Nonsense. You run Braemoor."

"But I do not own it, my lady, and that is what mat-ters to fathers and guardians."

She had nothing to reply to that. She knew, better than

most, that he was right. With no title, nor any property of his own, he was very limited in his selection of brides. But at least, he would not be forced into marrying a lass he did not want.

As she had been forced into marrying someone she did not want.

She turned back to the marquis. He was drinking from his glass again. His wig was slipping askew, and he had a stain on his coat. His voice was getting louder. He acted, and looked, like a bore. She turned back to Neil and caught an odd expression on his face. It was puzzlement rather than disgust. But then, just as quickly, it faded and he turned away to say something to another clansman.

Bethia had never seen her husband like this before. Oh, he had played the fool before, but she had never seen him drink as he was doing now.

Just then, he slammed down his tankard and wine sloshed over the table and onto her dress.

"My 'polgies, my dear," he said.

All eyes were on her. She tried to smile. "I had better change the gown before the stain sets."

"Leavin' my table, love?"

"With your permission," she said in a voice laced with disapproval. Her appreciation of the pearls was gone; it *had* been a thinly disguised ploy to show off his wife, and his ownership of her. She wondered if he had really meant what he had said about selling them. But he *had* said it.

She saw a sudden gleam in his eyes that belied the drunkenness, but it disappeared so swiftly she wondered whether it was her imagination.

"You 'ave it, lass. You might as well get in our bed, too. I will be there shortly."

Her face flamed red as the clansmen guffawed. She shot an angry look at him. He rapped her on her back-side.

Then she fled.

Hours later, she lay awake in her bed. He had not

come, and now she did not think he would. He probably lay in a drunken stupor someplace. The pearls were on the table next to her, their luster glowing in the candle-light.

They are, and always will be, yours alone.

How could he be so kind, then turn into a drunken boor? She had watched drink do terrible things to other men. He had, in fact, been more than a little boorish on their wedding night, but since then . . . since then, she'd thought that an aberration.

She quenched the candle. He had just made it easier for her to do what she planned to do.

The next day passed excruciatingly slowly for Bethia. She tried to avoid her husband and finally decided the library was the place to do it. She hoped fervently that a book would help pass the hours before her meeting with the Black Knave.

But just inside, she saw her husband, lounging in a chair, his booted feet on a footstool. He wore only his breeches and a linen shirt with the neck open and full flowing sleeves. No wig. No cravat. When she had appeared at the door, he'd looked up with lazy eyes, then seemed to unwind from the chair.

"Madam," he said the word lightly, but his gaze was intense. Dark. Sparkling with curiosity. Without the wigs, he looked sensuous and confident and . . . irresistible. She tried to think about his drunken performance the prior night, but her resentment faded as her gaze met his.

Her heart hammered against her chest. He looked well. Rested. No sign of dissipation. She wondered whether he had gone to Mary's, whether he was still spending time there. It was, she scolded herself, none of her business. None at all. Good riddance.

Jealousy made a tight ball in her stomach. He had never promised her anything, nor had he ever said anything indicating more than the hollow marriage between them. She told herself she felt these things because of pride. Only pride. Yet she felt a terrible betrayal that he preferred his mistress to her. His unexplained absences had made that clear over and over again. "I did not know you were here."

"I have some business with Neil. He should be here shortly."

"I see you recovered from last night."

"Aye. A night of debauchery is beneficial from time to time." The amusement was back in his voice, a glint in his eyes.

She wanted to run from the room, from him, from all the feelings he evoked in her. "I will go then."

"I have some business with you, too, Bethia."

She looked up at him. "I canna imagine what it would be."

"Your brother. I took the liberty of having a warm cloak made for him for his birth date," the marquis said. "I suspect he, too, had few clothes when he was taken from his home."

The knot of anger, of jealousy, unwrapped itself. The gift was a kind gesture, one that he sometimes threw at her just after she had relegated him once again to the regions of hell. It was uncommonly maddening. Disconcerting.

"Thank you," she said, lowering her eyes so he would not see the conflicting emotions that must be there.

"I will take it myself on Monday," he added.

That was two days after she hoped to meet with the Black Knave. She wished he would leave. Today. This moment.

She knew she should ask to go with him. She always did. What if, for once, he agreed? With luck, she would already be on her way to Rosemeare to fetch her brother. If not, if the Black Knave failed her, then she could talk to her brother, work out an alternative plan.

"May I go with you?" she finally asked.

He regarded her with those quizzical eyes. How had anyone ever thought him bland or inconsequential? He might be many things, but inconsequential was not one of them. Careless, perhaps? Self-indulgent? But she doubted even that, despite the evidence.

"We will talk of it later," he said and then he'd walked out toward Neil's office, leaving her to ponder exactly what had just transpired.

She still did not know two days later. She puzzled over that as she waited for nightfall—and her rendezvous with the Black Knave.

Bethia had seen little of the marquis since that afternoon. He seemed as intent on avoiding her as she was in avoiding him. He didn't even appear to care now whether the servants—or Neil—suspected he was not making trips to her bedchamber. She could only suppose that he was spending most of his time with Mary. He certainly made no effort to explain his absences to her. She only knew that tonight was her one possibility to escape Cumberland and all the troubling emotions that swirled around the Marquis of Braemoor. . . .

And now if everything went well tonight, she might never see him again.

She did not know where he was now. Sometimes she thought he was more a jack-in-the-box than a marquis. She never knew when he would pop up. She had already prayed several times that he would not do that tonight.

She looked out the window at the moon. 'Twas only a tiny slice. A new moon. Clouds drifted in and out between the stars. It would be dark, and the ride would be difficult and dangerous.

Please God, let him be there. How many times had she uttered that prayer? How many more times before this night would be over?

She wore a comfortable gown that laced in front, one she could easily change. Underneath it, she wore a pair of breeches that she had found rummaging around rooms in the tower house. She had abandoned Jamie's clothes prior to reaching Bracmoor a week earlier. She'd had to cut these, and sew, but now they fit her, albeit loosely. But that was what she wanted. She then pinned a dark-colored shirt inside the cloak as well as a small bag to fit Black Jack into. She was not going to leave her dog here.

Not knowing whether she would return, she had also sewn the pouch of jewels into the lining.

It was after midnight when she left her room. She had the small bottle of laudanum with her, and she went to the empty kitchen. She poured a measure of ale from a small barrel into two tankards, along with a good dash of laudanum.

With Black Jack beside her, she walked out to the stable. Her husband had posted a guard there, and on several occasions she had offered them cider or ale.

Both were sitting inside, playing some card game. Both almost tipped the table to stand when she entered.

"I could not sleep, gentlemen," she said. "And I went down to get some cider. I thought you might enjoy some ale."

They would. They took a drink, then another.

"What are you playing?" she asked.

"Casino, Marchioness."

"Will you show me how to play?"

They looked at each other dubiously. But then, how could they deny a marchioness? " 'Tis complex, my lady."

"I will try to concentrate," she said dryly. It should be far easier to beat him than the marquis. But she would keep that information to herself for the moment.

The two men exchanged disgusted looks, then took another draught of ale.

A half hour later, their heads were on the table. She had a few more coins, and now a horse.

Rory readied himself for the night's rendezvous with the mysterious lad. He'd debated over whether he should appear. He did not like the coincidence of the nearby location. And yet he could not fail to help someone who had assisted him.

Unfortunately, they had not heard back from the courier.

He used a cave in the hills above Braemoor to change. He did not want to go near Mary, in the event this . . . meeting was a trap. He planned to stay well away from the cottage, and he had different sets of clothes already here in the cave. Tonight he would be a sleepy shepherd.

He tried to keep his thoughts on tonight. But Bethia's face continued to intrude, as did her look of disappointment and distaste at his obnoxious performance at supper several nights earlier. The disappointment had hurt the most. He had not liked what he'd done, but it had been necessary on several levels. He wanted her to have the pearls, and he wanted to reenforce his image of a man who considered his wife property. Her reaction had been crucial to the play. He wanted no doubt that his wife was fleeing from both him and his home, and that he would chase after her. It had been cruel and bullying and yet he had seen little alternative to it.

The devil take it, but he would be glad to stop this playacting.

He heard a soft whistle, then a rustling as Alister pushed aside the brush conveniently growing outside the cave.

His friend strode in, a peculiar look on his face. "The courier returned. I gave him the reward."

"And?" Rory prompted.

"Your protector was not a lad at all, but a lass."

"A lass?" Rory was incredulous.

"A lass," Alister confirmed. "The innkeeper was reluctant, but finally admitted that the lad was no' a lad at all, but a lass. She'd asked that no one reveal that fact, and they were all so awed by her that they agreed. It was only the urgency of the request that produced the admission. They are not at all sure she wasna the true Black Knave."

"A lass masquerading as me?"

"Humbling, is it not?"

Rory shrugged. "It is no worse than an old woman." He could not help grinning. "But such information would really infuriate Cumberland were he to learn of it. Mayhap, if it were not for the danger to the lass, I might well like word to spread. His Grace outfoxed by a lass. He would be thoroughly humiliated."

"But what would she want with the Black Knave now?" Alister asked.

"Help of some kind. Or mayhap to join us in a more official capacity? Was any more said about what she looked like?"

"She had long, dark hair. It fell out from under a bonnet. 'Twas how they learned that they were following a lass."

Dark hair? A suspicion dawned in Rory's mind. "Was she well-spoken?"

"It was not mentioned."

Rory swore as his thoughts tumbled over each other. They all led, however, to the same startling conclusion. *It could not be. And yet . . .*

Bethia had disappeared for five days, exactly the amount of time necessary to reach the coast and return. *No. It could not be.*

Alister was staring at him. "What are you thinking?"

"That perhaps our other Knave may be closer than we ever thought."

"But who and why?"

"A brother, mayhap?"

Alister's eyes widened.

"My wife was gone for five days. She stayed with a crofter whose name she canna remember. She would not forget something like that."

"But the ride to the coast would be too much for a lass."

"She sent a letter just a week ago to the Innes lass. Their land is near the coast."

"And the request came from the coast," Alister said.

"Aye, and how many know of this loch?"

Alister's eyebrows bunched together in thought. "That is why it was selected. Its proximity to her. Not because anyone knew the identify of the Knave."

Rory lounged back against the side of the cave. "And I thought *I* was going to rescue *her.*"

"We canna be sure, Rory," Alister cautioned.

"Nay, but I would bet my last pence on it."

"But not your life."

"Not *yours,* Alister. It may not be her at all. Or it could be a trap. Which is why I will play out this little masquerade."

"How would she get a horse? You said yourself you posted guards."

Rory grinned. "If she made it to the coast, talked some rough fishermen into trusting her, stole a boat and returned back here in a week, I wouldna think a mere guard or two would stop her now."

Alister started laughing. "I knew there was a reason why I liked her."

"Probably more like a dozen, my friend."

"Are you speaking for yourself, my lord?"

"Aye. But I swore to myself I would let her go once I got her out of Scotland. She has a right to find a man she can love."

"I would no' so easily preclude myself, were I you," Alister said.

"She dislikes me," Rory said.

"Because you have been actively fostering that attitude."

Rory shrugged. "I will have nothing after this. I plan to make my way as a gambler in some place where the English will never find me. I have no taste for France, and that is the place for Bethia. She will be among friends there, among her own kind."

"What about the marriage?"

"She can get an annulment based on desertion. Some

would not even consider it legal, since we were not married by a priest."

Alister hesitated. "When she learns you are the Black Knave . . ."

"She may be grateful, but I do not want gratitude. I want her to be free."

Alister regarded him skeptically but did not reply. Instead, he changed the subject. "We still cannot be sure that tonight is no' a trap."

"For that reason, I do not want you anywhere around me tonight. If I am wrong, and it is a trap, collect Mary and Bethia. Get the boy, then head for the coast. Drummond is with the Harris family."

"Aye," Alister acknowledged.

"The French captain will be at the rendezvous at two hours past midnight on the fourteenth day of the month. He has already been paid."

Alister nodded.

"See Bethia and the boy settled in France. She has enough jewels that they will have an income for a long time." He hesitated, then added, "If I am taken, do not try to rescue me. You must look after Mary and Bethia and the lad first."

Alister said nothing.

Rory used his trump card. "I do not want Mary to pay for our crimes, Alister. She will not go without you. And Bethia's safety is far more important to me than my own. Swear to me you will see to the three of them first."

Alister hesitated, then nodded. "I swear."

"I could never ask for a better friend, Alister."

"Nor I."

"And that is enough of sentiment," Rory said. He felt awkward with emotion. "'Tis time for me to go. Help me look like a shepherd."

Bethia wondered whether she would ever reach the loch. The road was even steeper than she remembered. Fog had crept over the hill from the lake, and she finally dismounted and led the horse, afraid he might break a leg in a hole or go too close to a side that fell abruptly off down a hill.

A thousand things might prevent the Knave from appearing. Mayhap Anne hadn't understood the message. The Knave may not have received it. He could even be in another part of the country. He might well have thought a lad not worth his time. The English might have captured him. Was she completely a fool to make this trek?

Two hours now. She had only four more before dawn.

The fog seeped into her cloak and mud into her slippers. Step by step, her doubts grew, her optimism waned. 'Twas a fool's errand. And if she were caught, her brother's life would be forfeit. She was sure of that.

If only she could have rescued Dougal herself. But she would not be allowed near him. Especially without her husband, and he had refused to take her. She was well known at the castle since she'd stayed there several days before being brought to Braemoor. No, she had to have help.

She finally reached the nob of the hill that looked down on the loch. She could not even see the loch, though, because of the fog. She only knew it was below her. Bethia continued to walk down what was only a narrow path. Then in the silence, she heard the quiet lapping of waves against the shore. She started taking her steps even more cautiously, not wanting to end up in the loch as Black Jack had.

He whined in the small bag she had made for him and tied to the saddle, just as if he knew her thoughts had gone to him.

"Nay," she whispered, as she stopped to rub his ears reassuringly. "I do not want you to take another swim."

"Nor do I," came a voice out of the fog.

A voice full of amusement. A voice she recognized only too well. Deep-pitched, sensuous, seductive. A voice like no other's.

𝒯wenty-three

Bethia froze.

Black Jack barked excitedly and wriggled under her hands.

But *she* remained frozen. Had the marquis followed her? Had someone deciphered her note? Was it a trap for the Black Knave?

Hands reached out and took Black Jack. Strong hands.

She looked up. A shepherd had materialized in front of her. In the dark she could barely make him out in old clothes and a scraggly beard and white hair. But she could not mistake his stance, his height, the way even the air warmed when he was near.

The dog snuggled into his arms. *Traitor.* She had always heard dogs had instincts about people. Now she wondered.

"What are you doing here?" she demanded.

He was so close, she felt his breath.

"I might ask the same of my wife."

"But you are not asking," she said, suddenly very aware of the omission. "You know."

"Aye, you are looking for a traitor of the state."

Pompous words from a figure who had little pomposity. He looked every inch a shepherd, a lone, isolated man.

No. It could not be.

Her husband could not be the Black Knave.

Yet now she could not dismiss it. He was either the man she sought or he was something far more sinister. She had to proceed on the assumption of the latter. And silence was a far better defense than lies. Let him continue, even though she wanted to punch him in a place it would hurt the most. "You did not answer my question."

"You summoned me, lass. How could I refuse the request of someone who once helped me?" His voice held that mocking amusement she knew so well by now.

"You?"

"Aye. You are looking at the Knave, such as he is."

Her head was hurting. Her heart was beating much too rapidly. Her breath sharpened, became painful. She wanted to murder him. Instead, she managed to spit out, "The *true* Knave?"

"Aye," he said simply. "For better or for worse."

She could barely sputter, "Why did you not tell me before?"

"It would have changed your attitude toward me. No matter how hard you try, my lady, you have never been a good liar." He hesitated, then added, "There was something else. Your brother was being held hostage. I did not know in the beginning how far you might go to free him."

She stared at him incredulously. "You believe I would have betrayed you?"

He shrugged. "I know now you would not. I was not sure when I first met you. Then it just seemed the safest—"

Bethia had never been so angry in her life. She recalled all the fear, the anger, the desperation she'd felt in the past months, all of it unnecessary. The fury knotted in her stomach. She did not think. She only reacted. Her hand went back and she punched him in his stomach as hard as she could. She heard his breath go inward, the startled "omphhhh" as he stepped back.

She reached out and jerked the puppy from his arms. She felt as if she were breathing fire.

Then she heard him laugh. It started with a chuckle, then he nearly doubled over, and she did not know whether it was because of the blow or because he was laughing so hard.

Stiff with indignation, she weighed the option of hitting again. This time in the chin.

He seemed to sense the danger. He straightened up. "I was no' laughing at you, lass, but at myself. We have been at cross purposes, it seems." Still, the chuckle rumbled on. It had a warm, comfortable, vibrant sound. It echoed within her, settling around her heart.

Some anger remained, though, enough to keep her from joining in. "You knew it was I asking for help? Why did you force me to come up here?"

"I received the message saying only that a lad who assisted the Knave on the coast needed my help. I had no idea that it might be you until I received word just hours ago that the lad was a lass. Even then I could not be sure it was you. The only clue was your . . . unexpected journey and sudden lapse of memory about your Good Samaritan. It could well have been a trap. I can say with all sincerity, madam, that the sound of your voice scolding Black Jack was a bloody relief."

She continued to glare at him through the darkness. She could not see his eyes but she suspected they were full of merriment. That irritated her, too. If only he had trusted her, so much anguish could have been avoided, including this nightmare ride.

The Black Knave.

The realization was just beginning to sink in. Her husband. The dastardly marquis. The coward. The fool. The . . . drunk.

"You were not drunk the other night, were you?"

"Not altogether," he admitted. "It would have been un-wise."

"Why did you want to pretend otherwise? The Butch . . . Cumberland was not present."

"There were good reasons, lass."

"But you do not intend to explain them?"

"I will." He paused, then leaned over. His lips just barely touched hers before he straightened. "At least now I can thank the mysterious young lad. We were well-trapped until you lured the English away."

The anger in her dissolved like a lump of sugar in a hot drink. His voice no longer held amusement but a warmth that seeped through the chill and indignation she'd felt so strongly just seconds earlier.

But she felt a certain reserve. He had been her husband for months, and now she realized she still knew nothing about him. She believed he was indeed the Black Knave; she had no idea of the motives behind his . . . masquerade. Adventure? Principle? Honor? Or simply a game?

She wanted him to take her into his arms. She wanted him to kiss her doubts away. He did neither of those things, however, and curiously, she felt a greater expanse between them than ever, even when she had thought the worst of him. She'd thought she knew him then, but she had never known him. Not even during those few close moments. He'd only been a shadow.

"Bethia?"

She liked the sound of her name on his lips. But she was too shaken at the moment, too unsure to respond to it. "Did you enjoy your game?" she said bitterly.

"No. I did not like deceiving you. I thought—"

"You thought you could not trust me. That I would act the fool, that I would betray you on my own behalf." She was humiliated to feel tears begin to fill her eyes. She'd had such hopes, such expectations of the mysterious Black Knave. Now all she felt was a kind of defeat.

"Bethia, I will get you and your brother out of Scotland. The plans are already made."

"And when were you going to tell me? When did you feel you could trust me?" Hurt words came tumbling out. "But now *you* think I should trust you. Well, my lord, I do not." Now the shock was gone; it was replaced again by anger and, even more damaging, by a wound so deep and wide that she wondered whether it would ever heal.

"Lass . . ." He reached out for her, but she jerked away, keeping a whining Black Jack in her arms. She moved blindly toward the horse and tucked the dog into the little bag she had made for him.

The she swung up into the saddle, grateful that she had not taken a sidesaddle. Bethia needed no assistance to mount astride, and she did not think she could stand his touch. She turned the horse back toward the trail. Despite her best intentions, she turned back. Her few steps had taken her away from the marquis, and he'd disappeared into the fog like the phantom he was and always had been.

Rory heard the clip-clop of hooves as she moved away from him. His heart hammered as he berated himself. He obviously knew far less about women than he'd hoped. He did not know what he had expected, but he certainly hadn't expected her rage. Bloody hell, but she had a powerful punch. His gut still hurt. He was grateful she had not attacked a more vulnerable part of his anatomy.

He also stood stranded. His horse was a good half mile away. Shepherds did not have horses, but he had secreted one not far away in the unlikely, but possible, event that this had been a trap.

He had to catch up with her. He did not want her wandering into a patrol. And how in the hell had she obtained a horse, anyway? He was not surprised, merely curious. There would be some very unhappy guards in the morning.

Rory broke into an easy run. He hoped Bethia had enough sense to walk the horse on a night like this one.

But then caution, it was clear, was clearly not one of her strengths. Nor timidity one of her flaws.

Bethia seethed. The fact that she had other emotions only increased her fury. All these weeks of worrying about her brother, of trying to find the Black Knave.

She was also angry with herself. Why had she not suspected? All the absences when the Black Knave struck, his dexterity with cards, his bewildering changes in character. And the jewels. Now she understood why he had said what he had. If anything were to happen to him, she had the means to escape.

Curse him.

He had tried to protect her, he'd claimed. She was not a good liar, he'd protested. Well, she had been a good enough liar to save his skin. And despite what he'd said, it came down to the fact that he had not trusted her to have any intelligence or loyalty or honor.

Curse him.

It was all she could do to keep from digging her heels into the mare and sending her galloping across the hill and into the glen. He had plans. *He* had plans that he intended to keep to himself. Perhaps she *would* become the Black Knave herself.

Her hero, she thought derisively. She wished she had not saved his sorry hide.

Her mare pranced nervously. Bethia tried to calm her rollicking emotions before she entirely spooked the animal.

He had probably shared his plans with his Mary. Perhaps the woman had even been involved.

That sat even less well with her. That the marquis had slept with her, made love to her, then did not trust her while he trusted his mistress.

And Alister? She had always thought the marquis's relationship with a blacksmith strange. The night the marquis had been wounded, supposedly by the Black Knave— she recalled every moment now. Alister had kept everyone but Mary away. The Black Knave had reportedly been shot about that time. He must have had a gunshot wound, not a sword slice.

So Mary was a part of it all. Her husband must truly love her if he trusted her so completely. He was obviously a man who did not trust easily. Her rage gradually left, leaving a huge empty place inside her.

The Marquis of Braemoor was so much more than she had ever thought, than she had ever suspected. He had repeatedly risked his life to save others. He had risked everything he owned. She had no right to be so angry just because he had not risked other lives to soothe her own feelings.

But she *was* angry. Angry and hurt and jealous. 'Twas as if she had experienced a great loss rather than discovered a truth. Or were they inseparable?

He could get her and Dougal out of Scotland. Away from any danger from their grandparents. Was that not what she wanted this night? Was that not what she had wanted so badly?

An insistent voice, however, told her that was not all she'd wanted. She had never understood the attraction between the marquis and herself, nor how she could come to care for someone as careless and indifferent to human suffering as he'd appeared to be, someone whose main concern was a successful wager or a bright orange waistcoat. Now she knew the why of it. She must have sensed the honor and courage that he tried so hard to hide. It hurt badly that he had not trusted her. It hurt even more to think she would now lose him.

She wondered what time it was. Whether the guards at the stable had awakened yet, or whether anyone had found them. Black Jack whined and squirmed in the little cloth carrier.

Bethia blinked back tears. She had hoped . . .

She had no idea what she had hoped. It had been wild and romantic and ridiculous to believe the Black Knave would have a plan this night. Now she realized all the flaws in that dream. If she had gone missing this day, then someone would immediately have ridden to Rose-meare to secure her brother.

Mayhap the Black Knave had been right in not trust-ing her.

She was within a short distance of Braemoor when she heard the sound of hooves. She knew instantly who it was, but she did not slow nor turn her head as the rider slowed and fell in beside her.

Bethia ignored him.

The fog had dissipated as she left the hills, and though the night was dark, she knew she would see more of him than she could bear.

After what seemed an eternity, he spoke first. "I am sorry, lass. I truly thought to protect you by keeping silent." He seemed to hesitate, then added, "And to be honest, 'tis not easy for me to trust."

It was one of the few honest things he had ever said to her. At least, she thought so. But he had so many masks, so many facets.

Silence fell between them. One of the horses snorted, pulling on the reins to get back to the stable.

"How did you get a horse?" her husband finally said.

There was no reason for lies now. He would find out soon enough, in any event. "I asked them to teach me to play cards, and drugged them with laudanum. The ale was sour enough to disguise the taste."

"How did you intend to explain that away?"

She was silent again.

"You expected to leave with him tonight?" Indignation laced his words. "And your husband? You were going to leave without a word?"

"What was I supposed to say?" she replied waspishly. "Excuse me, but I am running away with a traitor tonight?"

"That would have been suitable."

His tone was so stilted and correct, she had to laugh. She tried not to show it. She tried to contain her mirth inside her stomach but it kept bubbling up to the mouth and finally exploded in a fit of coughing.

She finally turned and looked at him. He was no longer a ragged shepherd but her charming marquis in breeches, shirt and cloak. "How did you do that?" she asked.

"I learned long ago to change my appearance quickly. 'Tis remarkable what a wig can do. Take it off, pull on a pair of breeches and a shirt." He flung out an arm in the fashion of a courtly bow. "Here I am."

He was at his most charming now. But she knew that, too, was a veneer.

"Why?"

"Why what, my lady?"

"How, then? *How* did you become the Black Knave?"

"That is a long story."

Braemoor was ahead, its walls looming against the gray of dawn. She stopped her horse. "I have time."

He stopped then. "I told you I had no taste for killing."

"You dinna say you had a taste for rescuing Jacobites."

"It seemed to be an acquired taste, lass. I tired of the bloodletting at Culloden. I turned away from it and on the way back ran into some King's soldiers molesting a group of women and children. I dinna like the way they wore their uniforms."

There was sufficient light now for her to see his face. He was using humor again to disguise his emotions. But there was no masking the gleam in his eyes. "And . . . ?" she persisted.

He shrugged. "We were able to get them to safety, then someone else needed help. It . . . well, it became complicated. And I dinna like Cumberland," he said defensively. "It suited me to tweak his nose."

But now she knew it ran far deeper than that. She now remembered his small kindnesses, the gift of jewels, the gentleness with the dog. But she knew he would deny any noble motives until the day he died. The thought pleased her.

"We?" she said. "Who is we?"

"Now that I canna tell you, lass."

"Alister," she said. "And your Mary." The name burned her tongue, but she wanted to know.

"And now you are guessing, lass, and I willna be helping you in your games." He started to move ahead.

"You said you had plans to get my brother and me out of Scotland."

"Aye, and the lot of us. The game is becoming too risky, especially once you are gone. The fault could be tracked back here."

"When?"

"I leave tomorrow with your brother's birthday gift. He has found a way out of Rosemeare if I could but meet him outside the gates. We sail from the coast in six days."

She could only stare at him. *Six days.* Her throat grew tight.

"But you, madam, will have to be very careful."

"I am to go to Rosemeare with you?"

"Nay. I go alone."

They were almost to the stables when a number of men came riding out of the stable, Neil at their head. He pulled up his horse and trotted over to them, a frown on his face. "We've just discovered that the marchioness was missing." His gaze raked over Bethia, suspicion glowing in his eyes.

"I took her out to the loch," her husband said easily. "I thought she might enjoy the new moon. 'The new moon wrapped in the old moon's arms,'" he recited an old adage easily. "Unfortunately the fog came unexpectedly and we were delayed."

Neil frowned. "The guards say they were drugged."

"Is that what they claimed? When I went to find the marchioness at the stable as we agreed, they looked drunk. I was intending to take them to task this morning. Drinking on duty. Tsk, tsk. You need a tighter hand, Neil, but we will say no more about it this morning. The marchioness and I are weary, are we not, my love?"

Bethia had to fight to keep the smile from her lips.

What a marvelous liar he was. 'Twas never a quality she thought she would admire, but admire it she did.

Neil's sharp gaze moved from her to the marquis and back again. He did not quite believe, she knew, but neither was he in a position to ask questions. He nodded curtly. "If you would but let me know next time you plan a midnight expedition, I willna ha' all of Braemoor looking for you."

"I will try to remember that, Cousin," Rory said lightly, then slid down from his horse and went over to hers, holding out his hands for her to slip into. As she did, he held her a moment longer than necessary, a look of lusty anticipation on his face. She did not know, though, whether it was real or merely another of his acts. She wondered whether she would ever know the difference.

He took Black Jack from his bag and set him down on his feet. The young dog barked and darted after a leaf flying along the ground. Bethia looked backward and saw that Neil was still frowning, a puzzled look in his eyes.

Rory ignored him. "Have someone see about our horses. They've had a long ride tonight." He did not wait for an answer but took her arm and ushered her toward the door. Having captured, and subdued, the leaf, Black Jack followed.

Her husband said nothing else. He stopped in the kitchen and ordered food and ale to be brought to his room. The cook nearly fell off the stool where she'd been cutting vegetables. Trilby looked as if she had been crying when they met her on the stairs.

"My lady," she said tremulously. "We all feared you had been kidnapped."

Before she could say anything, Rory smoothly inserted, "A romantic ride wi' my new bride, Trilby. I wished her to see the lake at night."

Since Trilby had probably never done anything quite as lackwitted, she could hardly challenge the allure of such an adventure. She merely bobbed up and down like cork on the ocean.

"You are excused from tending the marchioness this morning," he said. "I will take care of that."

Trilby curtsied. "Yes, my lord."

Holding Bethia's arm, he guided her up the steps and into his room. Then he released her and sprawled in a chair, his long legs stretching out. "It has been a long night, lass. Food and some sleep will do us both good."

She did not want sleep, though 'twas true she was tired. She did not want food, either. She wanted to know more of the Black Knave, more of his plans. She had question upon question upon question.

But looking at his eyes, now half closed, she realized she was likely to get few answers. She did not think he was as tired as he appeared to be. He seemed indefatigable. And yet there were tiny lines around his eyes that she had not seen before. His face was drawn, more angular than usual.

He closed his eyes as if aware she was trying to search inside his soul, and he was not yet ready for that. She just stood and watched him, her heart making jerking movements. Most of her anger had fled when he hesitantly told her that it was difficult for him to trust. Her emotions were still raw, her pride still wounded that he had not thought her worthy of trust. But she knew a sense of well-being, even of safety, that she'd not known before.

She wanted to touch his cheek, to run her fingers through his thick hair. She wanted him to hold her close. But there was someone else. A woman he *did* trust.

A knock came at the door. She hurried over to open it, hoping that he would not wake. He obviously needed some sleep. But when she opened the door, she heard the chair move behind her and when a young lass entered, Rory was sitting up straight, his eyes alert. They followed the movement of the servant who placed a tray on the table. It was laden with food: scones and fresh butter and jams, cheeses, fruit and roasted chicken. There was also a pitcher and two tankards.

"Thank you, lass," he told the girl, who looked at him curiously then hurriedly left.

Her husband looked toward her, his brows arching lazily. "Are you going to stand there all day?"

"It feels good after riding all night."

He grinned. "You have a point. *I* was walking part of the night. That is the problem with posing as a shepherd. Usually I do better as a British officer. I am afraid I have a certain natural arrogance."

"Aye," she said. "You do."

"You do not have to be so truthful."

"You said I was not a good liar. I thought not to try."

"Good choice," he said, taking a chicken wing and consuming it in less time than she thought possible.

Her stomach rumbled. She had not realized how hungry she was herself. She still had a million questions, but the food came first. She took a scone and bit into it. Her tongue wiped the crumbs from her lips.

His eyes grew darker. Intense. Vivid. The gold in them looked like the flickering color of flames. He dropped his gaze, but his hand had stilled as it lay on the table, like a statue.

The air grew close. And warmer, though there was no blaze in the fireplace.

There was only a blaze between them.

"Ah, lass," he said. "You are a mighty diversion."

"I thought you liked diversions."

"On limited occasions."

Her fingers traced invisible circles in the table. She had not realized until now how much she'd enjoyed dueling with him. How could she ever have thought him a fool?

She would trust her instincts more in the future. And Black Jack's. Of course, Black Jack was being spoiled shamelessly on the other side of the table, snatching up tidbits of chicken and sweets. His tail was switching so eagerly that she thought it might break off.

But then her gaze turned back to her husband. Her

husband. The Black Knave. She was still trying to absorb the knowledge even though she realized she felt no real shock. The truth was far easier to accept than she would have thought possible. There had been so many hints.

He leaned over and his finger touched her lips. "You have a crumb," he said, but his fingers did not leave, and she realized it was naught but an excuse. Her lips opened and she caught one of his fingers, nibbling on it.

He tasted fine.

His other hand went to her face, his fingers stroking her cheek, then pushing a wayward curl back in place. "You look enticing," he said.

She was suddenly aware of how she really must look. Her face was probably dirty, her hair windblown and untidy, falling from the braid she had so carefully entwined in preparation for her meeting with the Black Knave. She had not had any sleep for a day and night, and her eyes were probably bloodshot. And yet she believed he saw her the way he had just described.

He certainly looked enticing. A tendril of hair had fallen over his forehead. As he had done with her, she lifted her hand, giving her fingers the luxury of pushing it back. Emotions swelled in waves, each one different but growing in strength. Her chest tightened, and her breathing became more difficult. She wanted to touch him everywhere. She wanted him to touch *her* everywhere. She wanted to go to sleep in his arms.

Her gaze shifted to the bed. So did his.

He took a draught of ale, then stood, offering her his hand. She took it, and their fingers intertwined. "You must be weary, lass," he said in a husky voice.

"And you."

He leaned down and kissed her. It was a strange kiss, poignant and even . . . sad but filled with a tenderness that made her legs want to fold under her. She wanted him to ask her to stay. She wanted it with all her heart.

He did not.

Instead, he released her lips. "We had both best get

some sleep, lass, and we canna do it together. I have to leave this afternoon for Rosemeare."

"I want to go."

"'Tis best if I go alone. Cumberland was quite insistent that you not see your brother until you are well with child. If he hears you have left Braemoor, he will send out all his hounds. 'Tis best if you stay for a day. Alister will bring you and Mary to the coast where a ship will meet us."

Mary.

"She is going, too?"

"Aye. 'Tis too dangerous for her to stay."

Bethia tried to stop her next words, but she could not. "Why did you consent to our marriage?"

He did not let her finish the sentence. "I agreed because the Marquis of Braemoor would most certainly have agreed. Rory Forbes is a greedy, selfish, self-indulgent man. Do you truly think Cumberland would believe he would decline such a prize? And it was clear he intended to marry you to someone. I could try to make it not quite so onerous."

"It would have been far less if you thought you could trust me," she said, that reality still gnawing at her like a rat through a piece of cheese.

He said nothing, but the mask was back on his face, and she realized she still knew so very little about him, or what compelled him to do what he did, or what he liked or did not like. She did not know him at all. She only knew he did not trust easily, but that he obviously did trust Mary.

"Will I see you before you leave today?"

"Aye, lass."

Her teeth played with her upper lip for a moment. There was still so much she wanted to say, so many questions to ask. But he was right. They were tired. She did not want to say something she would regret.

"I will see you later, then."

He still held her hand. He brought it up to his mouth

and his lips caressed it. "The Knave thanks you again for saving his life," he said.

"The Knave is welcome," she said. She knew she should go, but she could not. She was as unable to move toward the door as statuary in a garden. The other direction, however, was entirely possible. She found herself standing on her toes, her mouth reaching for his.

He opened his mouth, obviously to say something, but instead his lips met hers, moved passionately down on them. Swirling eddies of desire enveloped them.

He loves someone else.

Her mind kept telling her that, but it was chaff in the wind, disappearing in the blizzard of her other feelings. She wanted to touch and press and explore. She wanted to feel him close to her. She wanted to prolong every dizzying, warm exciting feeling before he disappeared again.

When she felt the intensity of his own passion, she knew momentary triumph. He seemed so aloof, so completely alone and obviously pleased that little touched him. But now she put her arms around him and felt him tremble, and she knew he was not as indifferent to her as he tried so valiantly to be.

She responded to his every movement, to the sudden passion in his kiss, to the swelling inside his breeches. The feel of him next to her renewed the gnawing need inside her, a need so recently awakened. As his tongue invaded hers, she savored each new jolt of sensation, of thrilling gratification. She felt the tension in his body, the barely restrained passion in his hands that now moved around her back. Warm, irresistible feelings flowed through her like a warm breeze on a fine Highland day.

His kiss deepened, his lips hard and demanding against her now tremulous ones. She wanted him more than she'd ever wanted anything, God help her. *He is your husband. His loyalty should be to you, not Mary.*

He groaned. His arms wrapped tighter around her, fusing her body to his, and she felt his manhood pulsing in

need. Her breasts strained against her dress, and her body
was alive with sizzling fires dancing up and down her
spine.

"Ah, lass," he said with a whisper of defeat. Then he
picked her up and carried her to his bed. Impatient hands
stripped her garments from her and ran reverently down
the sides of her body. She found herself reaching for the
laces to his breeches, undoing them as he stood in the
white, flowing shirt. Her hands touched his throbbing
shaft, now full and rigid, and she watched spasms tear
through his body.

He sat and leaned over, his tongue trailing fires over
her body until her hands reached up for him. He moved
into her then, his manhood probing gently at first, then
filling her completely as her body reacted with shuddering movements, grasping him.

Loving him. . . .

Twenty-four

She was gone when Rory woke several hours later. He reached out for her and found the pillow cold. He missed her more than he thought possible to miss someone, especially for such a short time. He told himself it was for the best that she'd thought better of laying abed with him.

He wished he had been stronger. But he had ached in every place a man could hurt. He had longed to hold her, to go to sleep with her in his arms. It had taken every last ounce of his will to *try* and send her away. He had not had enough strength to actually *do* it.

The sun was streaming in. He struggled to a sitting position. So much to do today. He had to talk to Neil, and that would be the most difficult of all. He needed all his wits.

His wits, however, seemed to have left him the day Bethia came to Braemoor.

Still, he held in his mind the images of last night, Bethia trying so hard to quiet the dog in the fog, the courage it must have taken her to travel the poor path at night. It pleased him to think of the risks she had taken days earlier to save him. Well, the Black Knave.

Then later, the way she had looked at him, her blue eyes shining as if he were the finest man in Scotland.

He realized, though, that she was looking at the Black Knave, not Rory Forbes. She must have realized that sometime this morning. She must have regretted her moments of gratitude.

Even if she did admire the Black Knave, the fellow himself was a sham. No one noble or brave. He was naught but man who enjoyed games and would be sure to disappoint.

Bloody hell, but he felt empty. Empty and, God help him, so damnably alone. Now, however was not the time for self-pity.

He poured water from a pitcher into a bowl. It was cold, and that was a good thing. A few splashes wiped away the cobwebs lingering in his head. He shaved carefully, as the fastidious marquis would do, and chose one of his more subdued sets of clothes. A shirt with a ruffled front, dark blue breeches, a bright blue waistcoat and finally a cravat of gold silk. A man of expensive but very dubious taste. He had rather enjoyed being outrageous.

He was a man of position. Of wealth. Of pomposity. And in a few days, they would all be gone.

As one last touch, he tucked a frilly handkerchief in his pocket.

Neil regarded Rory suspiciously as Rory held out a sealed document to him. He took it as Rory sprawled into a chair opposite him..

"I donna understand," Neil said.

"'Tis a will," Rory said. "It is witnessed by two people and dated six months ago, when I became the marquis. It leaves everything to you in the unfortunate circumstance of my demise."

Neil's brows furrowed together. There were no direct male descendants. He would have no more claim than a dozen others. "Why?" he asked bluntly.

"Why *you*?"

"Why any concern about something that is not likely to happen?"

"These are unsettled times, Cousin."

"Then why me? We have never been friends."

"No," Rory admitted. "But I have admired the way you have managed Braemoor."

Neil stared at him. "I thought you cared naught about Braemoor."

Rory shrugged. "I have not your talents, Cousin. I am smart enough to know that. And I think you will find I have not done undue damage to Braemoor."

Neil's eyes narrowed. "What are you planning?"

Rory leaned back with what he hoped was an innocent expression. "It amuses me to surprise people."

Neil dropped the papers down on his desk. "These are meaningless. You will outlive us all."

"I think not, Neil. If I were you I would keep those papers handy. It includes not only Braemoor but all the property I recently acquired through my marriage. It does not, however, include the jewelry. That belongs to my wife."

"You are not telling me something," Neil said, rising from his chair.

"As I said, these are precarious times. I do not want anyone at Braemoor to pay for mistakes I have made. You have an instinct and affection for Braemoor. A love I do not have nor ever will."

Neil put two hands down on his desk, leaned forward and studied Rory carefully, then sighed. "Why do you trust me? I was no' your friend when you were a lad. I ha' often regretted that."

"You were a lad, too, Neil. You were dependent on my father and brother, as I was. But now you have become a better man than either of them. Better than all three of us."

Neil's gaze sharpened. "Wha' is going on, Rory?"

Rory unwound himself from a chair he had settled into and stood. He grinned. "I could have died several weeks

ago when that dastardly Black Knave struck me. It reminded me of my mortality. I should hate to go to my
grave with Braemoor's future uncertain or, even worse,
falling into the hands of Cumberland. There *must* be a
lawful heir."

"Why?" Neil asked again. "You never seemed concerned with more than what coat you would wear."

"I have taken a liking to some of the people," Rory
said carelessly. "And I detest Cumberland. His greed
knows no bounds. He might well come after Braemoor
if there is no clear heir. That is reason enough."

Neil nodded. Nearly every Scot, even those who fought
with Cumberland, detested the duke. That had become
even more true as Cumberland continued his barbarity
over months. His excesses and his demands on clans loyal
to the English king had alienated all the country. "I fear
he would dispossess every mon and woman here."

"Aye," Rory said. "And hand the land to an Englishman who would clear it. I do not wish that to happen.
My quarrel was with my father and brother." He moved
toward the door. "I ask only that you swear you will look
after my wife . . . and Mary if misfortune wanders my
way." He made his last few words light. "And Jamie at
the stable. His fa is a bully."

"Aye," Neil said. "I will do that. But I expect you will
outlive us all."

"Mayhap," Rory said. "But I want you to have Braemoor in any event. You care for the people. My father
did not. Nor did my brother."

He left then before he said any more. He had already
said too much. But his instinct told him Neil would not
betray him, and he'd relied on his instinct this far.

Now for Dougal.

Bethia paced the room. She had awakened in the marquis's arms, had snuggled further inside them, seeking the
wonderful warmth of his body. Then, afraid that she would
waken him, she reluctantly slipped away. He needed sleep.

He did not need her. He had not even wanted her. She had made the overtures. *She* had seduced *him.*

He had made it clear earlier that she should go. He obviously felt loyal to Mary, and she had forced him into betrayal. 'Twas a fine reward for what he had offered.

And so she had quietly padded over to her clothes, dressed silently and slipped through the door to her own room. She did not want to hear apologies, or make them. She did not want to see guilt in his eyes.

Tears slipped soundlessly down her cheeks. She picked up Black Jack and hugged him until he'd whined, then she'd sat on her own bed. She would remember everything. The way he looked. The way he felt. The way he made *her* feel. She had never believed in this kind of love, the kind that shook her world, that broke her heart and made her soul cry. She had never believed she could love someone this hard, this painfully, that she could love so much she was willing to give him up to someone he cared about more. Someone he *trusted.*

Damn it, but the tears would not stop falling.

Black Jack licked her face anxiously, whining again.

"My own little Knave," she whispered.

Bethia finally forced herself to get up, to change clothes. She chose a simple gown that laced up in front. She undid her messy braid and brushed her hair until it appeared to shine. Then she pinched her pale cheeks to put some color into them.

She could not let him know how she felt. She would not give him that burden. The next few days would be dangerous enough without his worrying about some lovesick woman.

Then she gazed at herself. Did he think Mary bonnier than she? She was certainly brave. *Trustworthy.*

That knowledge burned in her.

And made her restless. Had he wakened yet? Had he missed her?

She left her hair loose, put on a pair of slippers, then

opened the door to take Jack outside. Instead, she saw the marquis standing there.

She was almost blinded by his clothes, then noted they meant he was probably leaving Braemoor. She backed away, allowing him to enter.

His green eyes were cool, his face expressionless. It was marred by a small black patch, an affectation he'd also used at their wedding.

Wedding.

"You are leaving?" she said rather stupidly.

"Aye, lass. I thought you had better write a note for your brother. He must trust me."

"You are going now?"

"Aye. I will reach Rosemeare tomorrow and hopefully get him out tomorrow night. You will leave tomorrow night with Alister. You both must disappear at the same time. Otherwise, if Cumberland learns one is missing, he will send men to guard the other."

"I still want to go with you."

"You canna. But we will meet not far from Rosemeare. I will have to return here shortly. Long enough to find you gone, swear to find you and the Black Knave and kill the bloody fellow."

She stared at him. "Why?"

"Rory Forbes must die, love. He must never be suspected of being the Knave, or all of Braemoor will pay for it. I think this coat and wig will be readily identifiable." He took out a couple of cards from his pocket. "A few jacks of spades," he said. "You must leave one on the table. We want Cumberland to believe the Knave assisted you. You might need the others for one reason or another."

She nodded, grateful he did not tell her to hide them somewhere. He was beginning to trust her a wee bit.

"Now the letter," he said.

She sat down and took a quill pen, dipping it into ink and quickly wrote her brother, wishing him a happy birth date, then adding that he could trust the bearer of the letter. She blotted it, then sealed the note.

The marquis took it and placed it carefully in a pocket inside his waistcoat. He then reached out and fingered a curl. "You have bonny hair," he said. "What did you do with it when you played the hero?"

"I braided it tight and pinned it on top of my head, then put a loose cap over it."

He hesitated. "Could you bear to cut it?"

"Aye," she said readily.

"You will be Alister's apprentice if stopped."

"And Mary?"

"His wife."

"I could be his wife," she offered.

"Too many attended our wedding, love. You might be recognized in a dress, but not as likely as a lad."

She would miss her hair, which fell nearly to her waist, but he was, and had been, risking far more. She nodded.

"Sew the jewels into your clothes," he added.

Her gaze met his. Her lips trembled. She owed him so much. She wanted him so much. And yet he stood there coolly, his eyes expressionless as if last night had not happened.

"If anything unexpected happens, lass, Alister has the name of a farmer with whom you can take refuge. As I told you, a ship will pick you up. The French captain has been paid and is reliable."

She nodded. She did not trust herself to say anything.

His hand reached her and cupped her chin. "You and Dougal will make it, and you can live quite happily in France. There is a strong Jacobite community."

"And you?"

He shrugged. "I am a wanderer, Bethia. I have already been here too long. You can get an annulment and be free of a bad bargain."

He was not a bad bargain at all. He was a very fine bargain.

But she could not say that. He cared about another. "Thank you," she whispered. "And Godspeed."

His gaze searched her face for a moment, then he turned abruptly, bowing with great courtliness. "I will meet you soon, lass."

Then he backed out the door.

She went over to the window. She watched until she saw him mount a waiting horse. She followed his image until he disappeared down the lane and out of sight. She would not see him again at Braemoor. When she saw him once more, they would be racing toward the coast. And Mary would be with them.

I am a wanderer.

Would Mary wander with him?

He had made it clear that he did not want his wife, that he had married her only to avoid detection and, God help her, because he feared for her. She did not want pity. Not ever. And yet he had saved her from what could have been a truly terrible marriage.

Dear God, keep him safe.

Rory hated to punish a horse. He had no choice, though, but to push the animal to his limit. He did not have much time.

He did not try to be careful. He took the main roads. Creighton would report his visit anyway, particularly after the boy disappeared. Rory would have to be long gone from Rosemeare when that occurred. He could not avoid the coincidence, but he could try to control the impressions made. He planned to be particularly obnoxious. God knew he had enough practice.

Rory took with him his last image of Bethia. Damn it, but she was a gallant lass. Not many women would agree without argument to ride through nights, to risk her life for a brother. Bloody hell, probably none would agree so readily to cut her hair.

Damnation. He still remembered last night, how she felt under him, how he felt in her. He'd known peace for the first time in his life. He'd felt loved, and he had loved, and that was unique to his life. It was truly magnificent, something he had never thought would happen. He could live with that fact alone the rest of his life.

He rode until deep into the night, passing by a total of three patrols. He stopped to chat with each, asking whether they'd had word of the Black Knave, whether all the Highlands were still filled with patrols. If so, they most certainly would capture the fiend and make the roads safer and far more comfortable to traverse. He discovered they were moving as blindly as ever.

He stopped at an inn to sleep, though he took only four or five hours to do so before leaving at dawn. He reached Rosemeare before noon.

Rory had met Creighton before. He had been an English general who had been given Jacobite property. He was arrogant, supercilious and twice as obnoxious as Rory had ever thought to be.

"His Grace did not tell me you would be coming," he said when Rory, freshly groomed, paid his compliments.

"'Tis a sudden journey," Rory said. "'Tis the boy's birth date and my wife was quite insistent on giving him a gift. You know how women can be when they are with child. I would ha' no peace unless I brought this to the lad," he said, holding out the cloak for inspection.

Creighton immediately became more hospitable. "With child, you say?"

"Aye. She believes so. She is ill in the morning and . . . well, I am sure you know more of women than I."

Creighton was rubbing his hands together. "Now *that* is fine news. His Grace will be most pleased." He took the cloak. "I will give it to him."

"I would like to see the boy myself. He *is* my brother-in-law now, and my wife would like a report of his well-being. I, however, am well pleased he is in your care and not mine. I am not fond of children, particularly children who are not my own." He took a snuffbox from his coat and held it up to his nose, taking a deep sniff.

"He is an arrogant little Jacobite," Creighton said. "I would not mind ridding myself of the little bastard, but His Grace insists he stay until a child is born, though I cannot fathom the reason."

Rory shrugged. "Better you than me. I will just take a moment, and then I plan to travel on to Edinburgh. Have a mistress there. I find that mistresses are far more sturdy than wives. Do you not find the same?"

The man blinked once, then gave him a knowing smile. "Aye." Then he cleared his throat, before speaking again. "Do you have a letter for the boy? I am to read them."

"Nay," Rory said carelessly. "I think 'tis best if they do not communicate. The cloak is sufficient. I would not have even consented to that but I feared the marchioness might do something that would hurt the unborn bairn."

Creighton nodded. He turned toward the hall and called, "Ames." In seconds, a man dressed all in black appeared.

"He is locked in his room for insolence," Creighton said as he turned back to Rory. "Ames will take you."

Rory followed Ames up four flights of stairs to a tower room. He waited while Ames unlocked it, then he sauntered inside, waving the man aside. "You may go."

"I am not supposed to leave him with strangers."

"I am not a stranger. I am the Marquis of Braemoor," Rory said in his most haughty manner. "And I wish a glass of wine. I have had a very long journey. I can well look after the little brat."

The man hesitated until Rory raised an eyebrow. "Do you wish me to ask your master?"

Ames shook his head and started down the stairs. Rory closed the door.

The room was cold and nearly bare except for a rough bed and a table. A small slitted window gave little light.

A lad with Bethia's dark hair and blue eyes turned toward him, every fiber of his being radiating defiance. A deep scowl marred a face that otherwise would be handsome. Eyes blazed at him. "Who are you?"

"Your brother-in-law, lad." He closed the door and

leaned against it so it could not be opened without him knowing it. He took Bethia's letter from his pocket and held it out to the boy. "Read it quickly, Dougal. We have little time."

The boy looked at him suspiciously but took the few steps necessary to snatch the letter from his hand. He broke the seal, then read it quickly. "I do not understand."

"It asks you to trust me, does it not?"

"Aye, but I see no reason to do so."

"Did you trust Alister?"

Dougal's chin stuck out so far Rory could have chopped it off. He waited.

"I am taking you and your sister out of the country. Alister said you had a way to get out of here."

"I might," Dougal said cautiously, obviously not yet sure about trusting him.

"Can you be outside the walls on the west side of the moat two hours past midnight?"

The lad hesitated.

"Your sister said you could trust me."

"She might have been forced."

Rory laughed. "Do you really believe that possible?"

Dougal suddenly grinned. "Nay. And aye, I do know a way out. I would have used it, but your man said to wait."

Rory nodded. "When Ames comes back, I am going to have to hit you. They have to believe we detest each other. It's important to the safety of other people. I canna be connected to your escape."

"Aye," the lad said, then grinned. "I will give you reason."

He was, indeed, Bethia's brother. Rory handed over the cloak. "A gift for you. My reason for coming."

"Why did they allow you?" The lad was suspicious again.

"I said Bethia was with child."

The lad went absolutely still. "Is she?"

"No."

Dougal sighed gratefully, which was a little insulting, then he became alert again. "Why are you doing this?"

"Have you heard of the Black Knave?"

"Aye. The servants have talked of him."

"He will be waiting for you tonight. I swear it. Now hand me back that letter."

Dougal did so and looked at him searchingly. "Are you really her husband?"

"Aye. I do not have to ask if you are her brother. You have her eyes."

The lad swallowed deep, and Rory was reminded of all the lad had lost: his home, his brothers, his family.

Then he heard steps outside. "Remember, you must get out tonight."

Ames came in just as the boy stepped back and glared at him. "English lackey. Traitor. I willna take anything from you."

Rory slapped the lad. He tried to hold the power, but the boy went back, falling against the wall.

Dougal's eyes blazed. "Bastard."

Rory turned to Ames, who had a tray with him. He took the tankard on it, and drained it. Then took the cloak that lay on the floor. "The brat said he dinna want it. I will take it with me. Ungrateful little wretch." He turned and left the room, leaving Ames fumbling around with keys.

He went down the steps two at a time. He looked for Creighton, who came out of his office. The man raised his eyebrow. "Jacobite dung," Rory said. "He lacks the barest of manners. I will have to tame him as I tamed my wife."

Creighton nodded. "I will be glad to be rid of him."

Rory grimaced.

"I will tell His Grace you looked in on the boy."

Rory shuddered. "I shudder to think of ever having the little barbarian in my home."

He took his leave then. He walked out into the courtyard, mounted and rode out the gates. Unlike Braemoor, this keep was fortified. The boy seemed sure he could get outside the walls.

If only the boy believed him. His eyes had most surely blazed hatred at him.

Rory sighed. He could do nothing now but gather up the other horse. And wait. . . .

Bethia visited Alister on the afternoon before she was to leave. She'd invited Jamie to ride with her, though it was no longer necessary. The marquis had issued orders that she could ride wherever she wished.

Her husband had apparently verbally castigated the guards on duty for their negligence. There was no need for guards, he'd said, when the ones they had were so derelict in duty.

Jamie had overheard the marquis and repeated the words with enthusiasm. The marquis had become his hero when he'd ordered the boy's father to allow him sleep during the night and had also told the man that any bruises on the boy would be repaid on the father's body.

Once in the village, Bethia gave the boy a half pence for a sweet from a woman who sold bakery goods. She then went to see Alister. He looked up from the forge with a slight smile on his lips. "My lady."

She remembered how he had tried to reassure her on her wedding day, how she thought that strange for a blacksmith. Now she looked into his intelligent brown eyes and saw so much more. The marquis's friend. His confidant. His trusted ally.

He straightened.

"I dinna think you would be working today," Bethia said.

"I ha' no' been working enough," he replied with a grin. "I want no suspicions, particularly today."

"You have been close to the marquis," she said. "Will that not cast suspicion on him when you disappear?"

"You know of the friendship, my lady, because of our

conversation on the wedding day. Few others do. We have been careful. 'Tis always been business."

"There is a . . . warmth between you."

"Only because you look closer than most," Alister said. "Now, can you leave the tower house an hour after midnight?"

"Aye," she said. "The marquis said I should cut my hair. Should I do it before leaving?"

He shook his head. "Nay. I will be waiting for you with horses. We will go to Mary's cottage where you can change clothes. Leave one of the cards Rory gave you on the table in your room. We want everyone to believe the Knave stole you away in Rory's absence." She was startled at his use of her husband's given name, rather than the formal "my lord." Then she reasoned it was indicative of a friendship far closer than she had ever imagined.

"My dog?"

"You will have to keep him quiet. Rory told me you would insist on bringing him."

She nodded and started to leave.

"My lady?"

She turned.

"Rory plans well. So, it appears, do you. I would not worry overmuch."

'Twas approval in his voice, and it lightened her heart. She nodded and left.

And now it was time. Apprehension had settled like a rock in her stomach. It was as much for the idea of meeting with her husband's mistress as it was of fear of Cumberland and his soldiers. She brushed her long hair for the last time, then laced it into a long braid.

She then put on a clean, simple gown and bundled up two others. After carefully placing all the jewels into the pouch the marquis had given her, she tied it to her wrist. She added needle and thread, intending to sew the jewels into whatever garments Alister had for her.

Black Jack whined at her feet. He was obviously nervous, sensing that something was out of the ordinary. She picked him up and held him close to her face. "I would never leave you," she whispered. "Never." She found the little traveling bag she had made for him.

She was ready. Bethia took one more look at herself, at the hair her mother had often called her best feature, at the room that had almost become home. She placed a single playing card on the table and slipped out the door, down the silent corridor, and past the great hall where her wedding feast had been held.

No one was in sight. There was no reason to keep guards on duty. She moved quickly toward the stand of trees located beyond the stable. She heard the neigh of a horse and she made for the sound. Alister was standing beside two horses. He was dressed in leather trousers and leather jerkin, his hair covered by a dark bonnet. He said nothing but helped her into an ancient saddle on a small, decrepit-looking mare. She looked down at the animal dubiously.

"She is far more fit than she looks," Alister assured her. He then handed the dog up to her.

They rode swiftly. The moon was still naught but a pie sliver, and stars were visible as they rode up into the heather-covered hills that led to the forest and the mountain beyond. Neither said anything. Alister occasionally glanced up at the sky, which was just beginning to fill with clouds. He hurried the pace.

Bethia's heart pounded as they neared the cottage. She did not know how she would feel facing her husband's mistress. She had not loved her husband the last time she had made this journey out of curiosity. Now she did, and it was like an open wound on her heart. How could she bear to see them together, work together, conspire together as they had done for months?

The sky darkened. Clouds layered the sky, blocking the stars and what little moon was out this night. Yet Alister moved swiftly. They reached the cottage and she slipped down, not waiting for his assistance. The door opened as if Mary had been standing next to it, waiting for her.

Mary was dressed in a dull brown gown made of rough wool and a kertch cap that hid the lustrous brown hair that Bethia remembered. She smiled at Bethia, ushering her in and indicating a pile of clothes on the table. "Do you need help?"

Bethia shook her head and Mary turned away from her, obviously to give her privacy. Despite the jealousy that still lingered dangerously inside her, she knew she would probably like Mary very much. There was a dignity to her, an instinctive warmth that Bethia knew would appeal to the Rory Forbes she was coming to know. Bethia tried to suppress the emptiness she felt at that knowledge. Instead she dressed quickly, wrapping a cloth around her breasts to make them flat before donning a dirty shirt, ragged wool trousers and an oversized, poorly stitched wool jacket. When dressed, she quickly sewed her jewels into the hem of the jacket. Then she faced Mary. "The marquis said my hair should be cut."

Mary's eyes were full of sympathy. " 'Twould be the safe thing to do."

Bethia swallowed hard, then nodded. "You will do it?"

"If you like," Mary said gently.

Bethia sat. She saw the shine of the knife, heard the sound as it sawed through the great, heavy braid and felt the weight drop from her head. She flinched as more tendrils fell around her face. No tears, though, for this loss. She had known too many greater ones. And hair grew back.

Mary looked at her critically, then placed a plaid bonnet on Bethia's head. Bethia did not ask to see a mirror. She did not think she could bear it, especially when Mary rubbed some smelly substance into her skin. "Your skin is far too fine for a blacksmith's apprentice," she said.

Mary was finally through and Bethia stood. She watched as Mary finished the last of the preparations. Mary pried a board up from the floor and took out several pistols and two knives, handling them with an ease that belied her modest dress. She tucked one last pistol into several blankets, then looked at Bethia. "Can you use one?"

"Aye," Bethia said without blinking. And she could. As the lone sister in a family of men, she had begged and teased her brothers into teaching her. She had never thought, however, to use one against a person. "Have you ever fired one?" she asked curiously.

"Not against anything larger than a target on a tree," Mary said. "But I donna intend to end on a gallows or be sold as an indentured slave."

Bethia wondered how Mary had ever become involved in the marquis's plots, but now was no' the time to ask questions. She merely nodded toward the knives. "And those?"

"I ha' never used those on anything larger than a loaf of bread or a side of meat," Mary said. "Rory has always been very cautious, but aft tonight I fear every English soldier will be after us."

Rory. Such an easy use of his name. Her stomach bunched up again as she watched the competent Mary roll up the second pistol, then handed her one of the knives. "Tie it to your ankle," she advised.

Bethia nodded and quickly did so with a piece of cloth she tore from a discarded petticoat.

Mary added one more bundle to the growing pile on the table, this one apparently food, from the smell of it. They divided the bundles between them and carried them out where Alister held three horses. Bethia took the reins of the horses while Alister tied the bundles securely to the saddles.

When he finished, she did not wait for his assistance. She was a lad now, able to mount his own horse.

She did notice that he helped Mary, however, and she noticed his hand lingered on hers, just as the marquis's had remained on Bethia's longer than required. Imagination? Wishful thinking? Hope?

She did not know.

Twenty-five

Bethia stared out the window of the abandoned hunting lodge. She had been doing it for hours.

Mary was asleep on the floor. She had urged Bethia to do the same, but she could not. Dougal and Rory hadn't appeared yet. Alister was out somewhere, keeping watch.

The three of them—Alister, Bethia and Mary—had ridden more than eight hours to a point east that was nearly equal distance from Braemoor and Rosemeare. Most of the ride had been in a driving rain, which was both a curse and a blessing. They had easily skirted—unnoticed—two patrols huddled around sputtering fires.

Alister had brought them to this long unused hut that was falling apart. Rain fell through holes in the roof, and there was no furniture. But it was hidden well. There might once have been paths leading to it, but now they were all overgrown. The three riders had fought their way through brambles and branches.

Mary had found a dry place for them to eat, then she had covered herself with a blanket and miraculously had gone to sleep. But Bethia could not. She wanted to wait for Dougal, for Rory. She had berated herself for letting the latter do what she thought she should have been able to do: rescue her own.

Bethia did not know how long she had been peering from the window. The driving rain had subsided to a steady drizzle and a mist obscured the trees beyond a limited vision of a few feet. Restless, she pulled her own blanket about her shoulders, wishing mightily for her warm cloak. She was fortunate that Alister had thought to bring blankets for them all. They, too, however, were still damp from the rain despite the fact that he'd packed them with oilcloth.

Her eyes started to close but she forced them back open, then she heard a shrill whistle. Alister had already told her that a series of short bird calls meant they should run away fast. One long sustained whistle meant Rory approached.

She hurried to the door, the blanket still clutched around her. She did not want to think how she appeared. She still had not seen herself since the shearing of her hair. But she thought only of her brother. Her husband. Black Jack followed her, barking madly, and she wondered whether he knew the newcomer was one of his cherished people.

Bethia stood in the rain as two riders approached. Both were wearing cloaks; bonnets protected their heads. A tall figure. A smaller one. She ran over to the smaller one as he slid from the horse and clasped him in her arms. "Dougal," she whispered, her breath catching in her throat.

His arms went around her as well. Her brave young warrior brother buried his head in her jacket. Twelve years old and he had lost everything dear to him. Her nose twitched at the odor of him, but she still held him tight.

Then, obviously embarrassed at his emotion, he pulled away, and Bethia turned her gaze upward.

The marquis stood easily, relaxed, though she knew he should be far more tired than she. He'd had a longer journey. And a more dangerous one.

"My lord, you are safe." 'Twas an obvious observation, and she felt foolish making it. Still, she was rewarded with a grin.

"Aye, though odorous," he grinned. "Your brother made his escape through the castle's sewers after charming one of the servants. Even the rain hasn't washed the stench. I had to ride a fair distance from him." His eyes softened as he looked at her. One hand went out and caught a curl, pushing it back. "I will miss your tresses, lass, but you make a bonny lad." Then he took her by the shoulders. "You should get rest. You will travel by night from now on. I imagine there is a hue and cry by now."

Her heart thumped so loud, she thought he must hear it. *You.* Not *we.*

"You are not coming with us?"

"Nay, I have to go back to Braemoor. I must be properly horrified at your disappearance and vow to find you and that villain, the Knave."

"You are tired."

"I am used to going days with only a few hours' sleep."

"I want to go with you."

"We have gone over that, lass."

She decided not to argue the point. Not now. "Will you get some rest, first?"

"Aye, an hour or so."

"Thank you for fetching my brother."

"He did it mostly himself," her husband said. "He most definitely *is* your brother." Approval laced his words, and she felt warmth fill her. In fact, not even the rain could cool the sizzle between them. It pleased her that even though he knew Mary must also be here, he lingered with her.

"Come, lass," he said, putting his arm around her. "Let us get you and the lad out of the rain. As well as this young fellow," he added, reaching down and picking up Black Jack with one hand. The dog was embarrassingly grateful, struggling valiantly to reach up and lick an already wet face.

Her brother was staring at them with undisguised interest, but his eyes softened at the sight of the dog. He had always loved animals, and it had broken his heart when Cumberland had forced him to leave the dogs at their old home.

The marquis obviously saw the same thing. He handed the pup over to Dougal. Black Jack immediately snuggled against his chest. Dougal smiled, and Bethia's heart jumped. It was the first time she had seen him smile since they had received word about their brothers' deaths.

The marquis guided them toward the door. *The marquis.* Calling him that protected her. He was still the man who had married her, infuriated her, rescued her. She had only called him Rory rarely, and each time had been a mistake. It made him part of her life, an *intimate* part of her life, and he did not want that to be.

She shivered and his arm tightened around her. It would have tightened around Mary as well, she knew. She kept telling herself that.

They walked inside. "Where is Alister?" she asked.

"He is still keeping watch. Your brother should get some sleep, then he can relieve him until you are ready to go to the coast."

You again.

Not if she could help it.

They went inside, and she saw him glance at Mary, who was still sleeping. He smiled. "At least someone has some judgment." The words were little more than a whisper and they bit right into her.

"Any food?" he asked before she could make a retort.

"Aye," she replied and went to a corner where a piece of oilskin covered Mary's cache of food. She tore off several pieces of bread and handed one each to the marquis and her brother, as well as hunks of cheese. Both ate as if they were starved, and she noticed the easy comraderie between them.

She feasted her eyes on Dougal. He seemed years older than the last time she had seen him months ago. He was twelve years old and he appeared a man. She wanted to

go to him, place a hand on his hair and ruffle it. But she
knew he would resent it now. She was lucky that she had
received a hug. So she merely watched the man and lad,
the latter feeding Black Jack's mouth as often as his own.

When they finished, the marquis said something to
Dougal, who nodded. Her brother lay in one of the drier
corners of the room and soon was snoring. The marquis
gave her a wry smile. "I think we would both do well to
follow their examples."

Now that he was safe—at least for the moment—she
could do so.

When Rory woke, he looked about the room. Mary was
gone, probably to take food to Alister. Both Bethia and
her brother were sleeping. Her hair reached just below
her chin, and its length made her look more like a pixie
than a marchioness. Mary had rubbed something on her
face to make it look less delicate, and a smudge of dirt
decorated her nose.

He had never seen a face that touched his heart as this
one did. She looked small and vulnerable and yet he knew
her strength, her tenacity, her courage. He would rank
those over long tresses of hair any day. The joy in her
face when she saw young Dougal had been more than
enough reward for him.

Rory had come to truly respect the lad in the last few
hours. He had apparently charmed one of the servants
into getting him an extra key to his room, then had used
the sewers to escape, meeting Rory exactly when he'd
promised. He had been uncomplaining during the long,
wet ride through the night. The brother and sister had
much in common.

His gaze returned to her. He had remembered the joy
with which she'd greeted her brother, but he also recalled
the grateful way she had looked up at him. He'd felt as
if lightning had struck him. He knew he had . . . cared for
her. He had not known until that moment that he loved
her.

He should have known. But he had always been mistrustful of that word. He had never thought it truly existed.

He watched her for a few more moments. He did not want to leave, and yet he knew he must. One more step before he could head for the coast and meet them. He knew the roads would be swelling with soldiers now. Both his cousin and Creighton must know that the MacDonells had disappeared, and that the Knave had something to do with both. The hunt would be furious.

And he knew he was risking a great deal to return to Braemoor. Cumberland might well have suspected him and ordered his arrest. And yet he had to do what he could to avoid suspicions falling upon Neil and others at Braemoor.

He stood, took some more bread and thrust it in the huge pocket of his cloak. His majestic appearance of yesterday was sorely tarnished. His peacock clothes were wrinkled, weather stained, and his wig must look as if Black Jack had taken a romp in it. Hopefully, he would look like a man cuckolded, desperate to reclaim a valuable wife.

At least the horses should be rested. He would take Alister's gelding, which would have even more rest. He took a last look at Bethia. He wouldna see her again until they reached the coast. Dear God, how much he wanted to touch her.

He resisted and went out the door. 'Twas late afternoon and the hills were clouded with a Scottish mist. Fine weather for nefarious business.

Rory quickly saddled the gelding, which had been secured under a heavy oak for some protection from the rain. He was just about ready to step into the stirrups where he was aware of another presence.

He whirled around. Bethia looked even more vulnerable than ever, but there was a determined glint in her eyes. "You canna go alone," she said.

"I thought you were asleep."

"I wake easily."

He reached out and touched her hair. A tendril curled slightly around it before he pushed it back and readjusted the bonnet she wore. It had been so askew that she'd resembled someone who'd just left a pub after spending a half day there. "My bonny lass. I thank you for wanting to come wi' me, but you would slow me, and I want to know you are safe."

"Do you think that I can let you buy my safety with your risks?" she said. "And I would not slow you. I rode day and night when I went down to the coast."

"To rescue me," he said wryly.

"Aye. I would keep a distance from you, but if anything went wrong, I could go for Alister."

"And get him entrapped, too, lass?"

"I will go with you," she said stubbornly.

He realized that she would do exactly that. The only way he could prevent it was by tying her up, and even then her brother might let her go. She knew where he was going, and he knew as surely as he knew anything that she would follow. He had learned that much about her. And if she followed, she might get lost in the rain and mist and fog.

She would hold some advantages if caught. Advantages he did not have. She remained her grandparents' only heir along with her brother. And with Dougal gone, her own worth increased.

He weighed all that, knowing that, in the end, he had little choice. If there had been another man along, mayhap he could place a guard on her. But there was only her brother, an exhausted Alister who'd had no sleep for two days, and Mary.

"Will you swear to do everything I tell you?" He asked the question against his better judgment.

"Aye, my lord," she said.

He detected some insincerity. "Bethia," he warned.

"I will obey your every word," she promised.

He was not comforted. He considered every other option and found none of them palatable. Pride with her filled him, though. She rode as well as any man, and certainly had the courage and wit that any man would want at his side.

No one, he thought, would recognize this dirty lad as the Marchioness of Braemoor. But they *would* be looking for a lad.

Bethia, at the moment, did not much resemble a young lord, but he would have to keep them away from roads and patrols. If she were stopped, she should be able to talk her way through. A groom taking a new horse to its owner. He would tell her exactly what to say. And he would never be too far away. Already his mind was thinking ahead, plotting.

"Your brother?" he said in one last effort to dissuade her. "Do you no' need to stay with him?"

"Nay, he has proved he needs no one. But I would like to whisper good-bye."

Rory nodded, following her to the door of the shelter. He watched as she went over to Dougal and stood there for a moment. Then she leaned down and kissed his dark hair so lightly he did not wake. He also noticed her hesitation. She did not want to leave him.

But she would. *For the Black Knave.* He felt humbled and wished he could dissuade her from coming. It was obvious, though, she had made up her mind, and he'd discovered that she seldom changed it.

After a moment, she came to the door. "I am ready," she said. "I know he will be safe with Alister. And if I were to say good-bye, he would insist on coming, too."

"No doubt," Rory muttered. He started toward the saddles that were sheltered under trees, but she shook her head.

"*I* will be doing it," she said. "If I am tae play a role, 'tis now I should begin." A burr roughened her voice.

She had been thinking exactly as he had. 'Twas uncanny.

He had no time to think further, though, because she

was saddling one of the horses. It was not easy. The saddle looked larger than she, and it took several attempts for her to throw it over the animal's back. Once she had managed landing it in the right place, she waited a moment before buckling the straps. He had to admit she knew what she was about.

Finished with the chore, she scrambled up into the saddle.

He mounted, and led the way. He whistled once. Alister appeared out of nowhere, Mary beside him.

"I am taking Bethia with me," the marquis said. "She can wait in the caves above Braemoor while I express my outrage at her disappearance. I will vow to bring her back, even if it means my own life."

Alister raised an eyebrow as if to ask the wisdom of taking Bethia with him.

"Do you want to try to keep her here?" Rory said.

"Nay," Alister grinned. "I think not. Should I head toward the coast?"

"Aye. The lad can relieve you shortly. Get some sleep. Leave for the coast at dark. Bethia and I will meet you at the farmhouse. I will tell her how to find it if anything goes awry."

Alister nodded.

Rory leaned down and reached for Alister's hand. "We had a good run, my friend. Thank you." Then he looked at Mary. "And you, Mary. I will see you soon, lass." He leaned down from his saddle and gave her a quick kiss.

Then he spurred his horse through the underbrush.

Biting down her painful jealousy, Bethia followed.

Neil carefully looked around the small cottage sitting at the foot of a rugged hill.

Nothing seemed out of place, yet the ashes in the fireplace were cold, and the interior had a look of abandonment. He muttered an oath to himself. Cold fingers walked up and down his spine.

He'd known two days ago that his cousin was up to

some mischief. He had felt it deep in his soul. It had been confirmed at noon today when Trilby had told him the marchioness was missing, and that a jack of spades had been found on the table in her room. Several hours later a messenger on a lathered horse appeared and announced the disappearance of the marchioness's young brother. He'd been told to keep Lady Braemoor within the tower house walls until Cumberland arrived.

Neil had said nothing about the fact that she had already disappeared. Nor had Trilby. No one else had been told.

At that moment, everything started to fit together in his mind. Rory's odd behavior, his will, his frequent disappearances. Neil berated himself as a fool for not seeing it earlier. Rory had been a feisty lad, always in trouble, always infuriating the old marquis when he took up one cause or another. But then Rory had been fostered and when he returned, his mother was dead and he'd had a terrible quarrel with his father. He had not returned until the call to arms.

Mayhap because of the reputation Rory had earned in London and Edinburgh as a gambler and womanizer, Neil had accepted the dandified version of his cousin without question. In truth, he had wanted to think the worst of him because Neil had honestly thought he should inherit. Neil had loved Braemoor with every fiber of his being, and Rory had made clear his disdain for it.

God had been unjust, and Neil had nurtured the envy and injustice that he'd felt. He would be such a far better caretaker than Rory. If only the dead marquis had made a will and disinherited Rory as he'd so often threatened to do.

Well, he had not. And Rory had inherited, and Neil had resented and begrudged it until he had become a man he did not recognize, like or admire.

And now he knew that Rory Forbes had been a far better man than he. He had fought for something he'd held dear.

Neil had not seen any of it until Rory had married the MacDonell lass. Then Rory had seemed to change. Oh, he had tried not to, but Neil had seen the keen intelligence in his eyes when Rory had looked at Bethia when he thought no one was watching. He had noticed Rory's kindnesses to young Jamie and other servants. He had finally come to feel that Rory had left the management of Braemoor to him not because he dinna care, but because he did. That last interview reflected that. So did the fact that despite all the new clothes and the proclaimed gambling, Braemoor never received any bills or duns or charges. Everyone thought the marquis was destroying Braemoor, when in reality he had never touched those accounts.

Most astonishing of all was his cousin's obvious intention to walk away without taking anything with him other than the jewels.

The cottage was cold. Neil picked up a couple of pieces of firewood laying next to the fireplace and put them inside, then found a flint box nearby. After several moments of trying to spark a fire, he finally succeeded. He did not know why he was doing it, why he did not want to return to Braemoor. He was still trying to work things out in his mind.

Mary. She must have been part of it. Otherwise she would be here. Rory's liaison with her had been rumored for years. Had it been merely a sham?

Neil realized one reason he lingered here was to delay sending a messenger to Cumberland. The longer the delay, the better chance Bethia and Rory had. He could always say he went out looking for the two before rushing to assumptions. The two of them had disappeared together before. Just the other night, in fact.

He backed up, his boots stomping on the floor as he waited for warmth to seep into the room. He heard a thud-like sound, and the beatened earth beneath him felt different. He stomped again, listening. Then he bent down, his hands running over the earth, his hands spreading away the dirt until they reached a board. He dug around it, until he could lift the board, then another.

A cache. Lined with oilcloth. He reached down into it and pulled up an old woman's wig, then two others. There were other items: dye, something that resembled a mustache, a large woman's gown, other clothing. Damning if found. He debated about throwing them into the fire, then hesitated. They might be needed.

You should tell Cumberland. You should tell them for the sake of Braemoor, for everyone who lived here. If Rory's identity were discovered . . .

He could not do it. He had fought for the English king because he had been loyal to the old marquis. But he was still a Scot. A Scot who had learned to detest Cumberland and his arrogance and his destruction of the clans that had once made Scotland great.

Could Rory be coming back here? Is that why the wigs remained here?

Neil carefully replaced the items, then the boards. He covered them with the loose dirt before stamping it down.

He looked outside. Dusk. He would send a message to Cumberland in the morning. He had heard the messenger say the duke was in Inverness, organizing newly arrived members of the Black Watch. The noose was tightening around Scotland. And around the Black Knave.

Mayhap he could give his cousin the time he needed. Mayhap that would in part compensate for the help he had not given him as a lad.

Rory passed through Cumberland's lines on two separate occasions, each time diverting the attention of the soldiers as Bethia skirted alongside.

He had muttered to himself more than once. The one thing he had in his favor was the miserable weather and the tired king's troopers. They knew who he was. Everyone knew who he was. The fact that he offered them a drink from his personal flask made them protective . . .

both of him and of themselves. Each one would be cashiered for such a weakness, and yet they stood shivering in a cold rain, bored beyond caring, stopping every farm wagon, every tinker, every traveler.

As he engaged them in conversation, Bethia passed in back of them and disappeared behind a hill or a stand of trees.

Part of him objected to her presence. The other was well pleased with her company. She would be gone before long, and he treasured the moments in her company. He loved her wit, admired her determination, reveled in the warm companionship they shared. Still, in the moments they were alone, they shared nothing of importance. He had noticed how quiet she'd been after he had kissed Mary. Part of that kiss had been natural, an affection he had always had for her. Another part, however, had been still another disguise. He couldn't seem to rid himself of them. It was both a disguise and armor, weapons he'd used to protect himself since a boy. A habit too ingrained to change.

He had used Mary as part of his armor. He did not know how to take it off.

Still, he had seen the hurt in Bethia's eyes, the set of her stubborn chin. But then they had never talked of love. They had made love, true enough. Passion . . . lust . . . need . . . loneliness. He had tried not to see more in it.

She would be far better off without him.

They reached the cave near Braemoor at dawn. He moved the brush protecting it and led the horses inside, taking them to the back. He helped Bethia dismount, then used a flint box to light a candle. He watched her eyes widen as she looked around. There were several boxes, some blankets and a neat pile of clothes, including a British uniform. He went to one of the boxes and took out a bottle of brandy.

Her eyes widened.

"This is just one of my caches," he said. "I have two others, including the one at Mary's." He handed her the brandy. "Here, drink some. It will warm you. And change your clothes. Pick whatever you like. I wish I could build a fire, but that might not be wise."

She took the bottle and tried a sip. Then she gave it to him. "You, too," she insisted.

He took a long swallow, then set it down on one of the boxes. "Get some sleep," he said. "You will be safe here."

She looked up at him. Her eyes were huge, with dark exhausted circles around them. Her face was streaked by rain and mud. "How long should I wait?"

"No later than noon, or you willna be making the coast in time. If I am not back, promise me that you will go."

He saw the stubborn lift of her chin. "Your brother will need you, lass. You canna forget that."

She looked so forlorn that he took her in his arms, held her tight against him. He felt her arms going around his neck, felt the shudders of her body. He felt her exhaustion. If only he had convinced her to stay at the hunting lodge.

His hand smoothed her hair. So short. He would miss those long tresses. But she would always be bonny to him. *Always.*

He leaned down and kissed her. He had not meant to do that, but an inner force was far stronger than his will. His lips played with hers for several seconds, and then he turned his cheek, and his now rough one simply lay against hers. Rory relished the soft feel of it. He loved her so bloody much, and never more than at this moment.

And he could not keep from telling her so. Not when he knew he might not come back.

His fingers caressed the back of her neck.

Then she looked up, and he saw more than warmth there. More than affection. More than gratitude.

He closed his eyes against the power of it. "Bethia," he whispered as his lips caressed her face. He tasted moisture and knew from the saltiness that it was not rain. "Ah, love," he said. To hell with his armor. To hell with a disguise of his heart.

Braemoor was dangerous. He knew that well. He also knew this trip was probably part of a recklessness he could no longer afford. Aye, he wanted none at Braemoor to be affected by his actions, but was he unnecessarily endangering Bethia by acting a role that had overtaken him?

He hesitated.

"Go," she said softly. The magic between them, the instinctive understanding that radiated between them, seemed to have grown with every day. Her fingers touched his face.

"You are so bonny," he said.

"I am not," she said. "I must look like a drowned rat."

He chuckled. "I donna think so, lass. A mouse, mayhap."

She pinched his ear.

He needed to go. They did not have much time. They had seen far too many patrols, and he did not doubt that there was one at Braemoor. He needed to get in and out before Cumberland put in an appearance. And the duke would. He had too much at stake.

His lips came down on hers. Hard. Fierce. Protective. Even desperate. He felt her mouth opening to him. He could not say the words. He knew, though, that he was telling her in another way.

He could not see her eyes. He wondered if they were filled with the same hunger that he felt. It was a wild, uncontrolled thing that shook him to the core. Somehow, she had become a part of him, as vital to him as breathing. Their bodies melded together, clinging together, just as their lips did.

He finally released her lips, but he could not yet let go of her. He clung to her for a moment, saying nothing. His voice would give him away. He would be stammering like some young lad.

In the end it was her strength. "Go quickly," she whispered, "and return quickly."

"Aye, lass," he managed.

And he was gone.

Twenty-six

Lights were visible at Braemoor. Horses were tied outside the tower house, and Rory knew they had visitors. But not Cumberland, not yet. There were not *that* many horses.

He strode in as if he owned the place, which, to his continued amazement, he did.

Torches in sconces dimly lit the hall, and he saw sleeping forms in the great hall. He went directly to Neil's room. He knocked loudly, and the door opened far faster than he thought possible.

His cousin stared at him. "I thought you would be long gone," Neil said softly.

Rory saw knowledge in his cousin's eyes, but he aped indifference. "Why?"

"Your wife is gone. Your brother-in-law is gone."

"Are they?"

Neil smiled. He was dressed in breeches and a shirt. 'Twas obvious he had not been sleeping. "So I hear," he said. "The boy was missing this morning, and Creighton sent a messenger to tell us to keep an eye on your wife. It seems he was too late. I sent word to Cumberland a few hours ago, just before the men you saw in the great hall arrived."

"Why did you wait so long?"

Neil shrugged. "She might have been with you some-where. I dinna wish to disturb the duke unduly."

"That was surprisingly judicious."

"I visited a certain cottage and found a few interest-ing items. I would suggest that either you, or I, destroy them. Or find a safer place for them."

"I am beginning to see that you have possibilities, Neil."

"I have missed too much too long," Neil replied. "I regret that."

Their gazes locked. "We both have regrets," Rory said. "But now I want to try to ensure that no harm came to Braemoor."

"Is that why you came back?"

Rory hesitated. But then he knew that Neil was al-ready aware of his other identity. If it was over, then it was over. "Aye. I had to receive the bad news about a wayward wife and go after her. I plan to chase the Knave and regain my wife. Unfortunately, I will be killed by the villain. No one then will suspect you or anyone remain-ing here of being accomplices."

Neil's eyebrows furrowed together. "Remaining here?"

His cousin was far more intuitive that Rory thought. But Mary and Alister were gone now. "Mary and Alister are leaving also. You might have to find an excuse for that."

"Aye," Neil said. "I dispossessed the wench when you met an untimely death. Alister went with her. Do you need any funds?"

"You have more than possibilities, Cousin. Thank you, but nay. I am a passing fair gambler and have managed to accumulate enough funds to get started. You need what is here. You might lose the estates Bethia brought."

"Where are you going?"

"I am not sure, yet. If you ever receive a deck of cards, though, you will know the sender."

Neil nodded. "You had better go. Those men downstairs were exhausted when they came in, but they will be combing every bush tomorrow. I imagine Cumberland will be here in the next several days."

"You will be all right?"

"Aye. I think I have learned a great deal during the past several weeks." He held out his hand. "I wish I had known you better."

"And I you, Neil. But I know you will take good care of Braemoor."

"I will try."

Rory grinned, then picked up a pitcher from the table and threw it against the wall. "The hell you say," he roared loud enough to wake the dead, much less soldiers used to sleeping lightly.

With one last rueful grin toward Neil, he went out the door, taking the steps three at a time, cursing loudly. He made enough noise to wake several regiments and kicked a sleeping man wearing sergeant stripes. "Hey!"

"Sleeping when you should be after my wife," he roared angrily, then disappeared out the door. He grabbed the best looking of the horses. His own, he knew, was exhausted. Before any of the soldiers could react, he was galloping down the road.

Bethia could scarcely breathe. Someone was chasing her and Dougal. They were running, and she knew they couldn't go much further. Then she heard the sound of horses behind them. She grabbed Dougal's hand and they went falling, slipping down a mountain into a black bog.

"Bethia." She heard *his* voice. Fear still pounded at her, though. A stark, terrifying fear.

"Bethia. Wake up."

"Rory," she whispered.

"You were whimpering," he said, taking her hand. "A bad dream?"

"We—Dougal and I—were being chased."

" 'Tis a natural enough nightmare," he said softly, his fingers squeezing hers.

"I've had them before."

"Now I am with you. And I will not let anything happen to either of you."

There was no candlelight in the cave, but she saw his comforting bulk. She sat up. "Is it time to leave?"

"Aye. I have just stolen a fresh horse and awakened a whole room of English soldiers. They will probably be angry as hornets, but I know every foot of Braemoor and the land around us."

She did not want to let go of his hand. The lingering fear from the nightmare was still too raw, too fresh. But she forced herself up. The moment she did, he lit the candle and she watched as he quickly changed from his fine clothes into an English uniform. He stuck pieces of cotton in his mouth, which completely changed his face and his voice. Then she watched as he very carefully rolled up the bright waistcoat and breeches he had been wearing and bundled them into saddlebags.

"Ready?"

Nay, she was not. She would be happy never to see a horse again, much less a saddle. "Aye," she said as enthusiastically as she could.

He grinned as if he realized the depth of her deceit. "In less than twenty-four hours we will be sleeping in a fine ship," he said.

"The horses cannot go that far."

"We will do a bit of trading along the way," he said. "The English always take exactly what they want."

"And me?"

"My prisoner, little one," he said. "*If* we are caught."

He helped her into the saddle this time. Then he led both horses out of the cave. Once outside, he swung up into his saddle. He urged the horse into a trot, then a canter as the first gray of dawn filtered through the lingering fog.

•   •   •

Bethia thought she would welcome even a nightmare. Her hands and face were scratched, her body ached in places she had not known existed. They rode four hours, rested for one, then rode four again. He led them through woods and across mountains, avoiding any roads, but both they and the horses paid for it. Branches had beaten against them most of the way.

At midday, the horses were exhausted. She and Rory dismounted. He found what he hoped would be a safe place for Bethia to rest. He left her there, taking the horses with him. He returned two hours later with two fresh ones.

"A matter of a small trade," he explained. "Since my horses were better than theirs, 'twas easy enough." They were immediately on their way again.

Rory slowed at midafternoon. A cold drizzle persisted, and mist shrouded the hills and then mountains. The terrain had become steep as he and Bethia traveled deeper into the mountains. At times they dismounted and led the horses, at others she clung to the saddle as they climbed narrow paths.

Only Rory's presence kept her going. At times she started to fall asleep and felt herself leaning forward, then would shake herself. He cast frequent glances toward her, giving her smiles of approval.

She almost fell off the horse when he stopped. He caught her as she slid off the horse and held her in his arms for several moments while she steadied. Her legs hurt so badly she dinna know if she could ever mount again. He seemed to understand. He thrust the reins of the horses in her hand, then picked her up as if she were no heavier than a piece of firewood.

He walked, obviously trying to find a place to rest. Finally he selected a piece of ground under an overhang of rock that would protect them from the rain. He gently lowered her, then unsaddled the horses, taking the blankets and spreading them out on the ground. He hobbled the horses so they could graze.

When he was through, he unbuckled his waist belt with its pistol, took the musket from its sling on his shoulder belt and sat down next to her. He offered some brandy from the bottle they had shared in the cave. The liquid burned all the way down, warming her. He then offered her some damp bread.

He watched as she ate, shaking his head. "I should no' have brought you, lass."

"I can keep up with you," she said indignantly.

"I have no doubt of your courage. You have proved tha' over and over again. But God's truth, I am tired. We both need rest. There is a gorge ahead, the only way across this part of the mountains, and I am sure it will be patrolled. We will have to cross it in the dark of night."

She closed her eyes, the brandy's warmth dulling some of the aches. His arms went around her, and she was enveloped in them. He smelled of damp leather and horse, and it was finer than any perfume. She felt safe. So safe.

Bethia had reached the limit of her strength. He had been a fool to bring her, and yet he'd known she would have found one way or another to follow.

His arms tightened around her as he lay down under the overhang. It was dry here, but she was still damp. So was he. He was also hungry. His stomach growled angrily, but he still rationed their food. He had brought only one loaf of bread, and it had to sustain them for another day. He dared not go where he might be seen to fetch more. He'd already taken too many chances.

They still had thirty miles to go. And they would have to change horses at least one more time. That would be the riskiest part of the journey. Unfortunately they were not traveling close to the Innes property where they could trade horses; he'd judged that part of the Highlands would be saturated with English soldiers.

Bethia went limp in his arms, and he knew she was asleep. He felt safe enough here to risk some sleep himself. If all went according to plan, they should reach the coast tomorrow night in time for the French ship. His fingers touched one of her curls. Dear God, how he loved her.

'Twas his last thought as his eyes closed.

Bethia woke in his arms. For the fleetest of seconds, she felt terror. She could see nothing; it was as if she were in a bottle of ink. She could feel the cold wind, though, and feel the rain it blew under the overhang.

She was stiff. When she moved her legs, the agony made her gasp. Every bone in her body ached, screamed, moaned. When she tried to snuggle back in his arms she felt him stir, then wake suddenly, his voice sharp. "What is it?"

"Nothing," she said. "I just woke up."

His arms tightened around her. "Ah, lass. This has been a hard day for you, and I fear it will be a harder night."

But she was with him, and that was all that mattered. She wanted him next to her every day of her life. Her left hand found its way into his, her fingers intertwining with his. These past few days had been the most frightening, exhausting, and painful of her entire life, yet she would not have given up even one minute.

"Thank you," she said.

He chuckled. "For dragging you through ha' of Scotland in the rain?"

"For helping me. Dougal. For making me a part of it." Her voice broke. She wanted to say more.

"Ah, lass. I would hand you the moon if I could. Instead, I give you rain and danger and endless journeys."

"With the Black Knave."

"The Black Knave no longer exists. I wonder if he ever did."

"All the Highlanders believe he exists. He gave them hope."

"The Knave is naught but an illusion. Like a rainbow consisting of a few rays of sun and a little mist. Nothing solid, lass. Nothing that lasts."

And nothing that could be held on to.

"And Mary?" She could no longer keep the question to herself.

"A friend, lass. Nothing more. She was part of the play. She loves Alister and Alister loves her. I needed an excuse when I was away from Braemoor. I could not always claim Edinburgh since it was too far, and there were too many people who should have seen me. And so I found a mistress."

For a moment, she wanted to strike him again, just as she had struck him when she'd discovered he was the Black Knave. Instead, her fingers tightened around his. *He did not love Mary.* She was relieved and elated and puzzled all at once. What else kept him from her? She knew he cared about her, perhaps even loved her.

"There is far more substance to you than you want to think," she said.

"That is where you are wrong," he said. "I ha' never earned an honest pound in my life."

"You are a marquis."

"Aye, but I never earned it. It wasna even mine by blood."

"You did honor to the title, though."

"I think not," he said. "Pompous. Arrogant. Terrible taste in clothing."

His voice was so wry, she started to giggle. Or perhaps it was the exhaustion that made her laugh. And laugh. And laugh.

And he started laughing with her. His fingers tightened in hers, and then the laughter stopped when his lips claimed hers. Momentary tenderness yielded to raw hunger. His body rolled over onto hers and she felt his weight, and his warmth.

He groaned. Mayhap she did, too. Or perhaps it was a whimper. All her aches, all her exhaustion faded in her need for him. She would always have that need. She knew that. He had become as much a part of her as her own soul, her heart.

She no longer felt the cold, the damp chill of a Highland wind. She felt only the pleasure of his body, heard
only the sound of their heartbeats, which seemed to pump
in unison. She felt explosive, and wondered whether it
was because of the danger, or because of the intimacy
forced on him during the long rides. He had no way of
escaping, as he had so many times before.

He untied the laces of her breeches, and the warmth
flared into intense heat. Her entire body tingled and ached
in another way now. A hauntingly familiar way. Not in
protest but in anticipation.

She felt his intensity as his mouth moved away from
her lips, down toward her throat, lingering there, his breath
teasing and seducing her. But she needed no seduction.
Her body was already afire, already wanting him.

Her hands went to the laces of *his* breeches. Her fingers, in their eagerness, fumbled uselessly. He quickly untied the laces and was back over her. She felt the swell
of him, the hungry touch of his arousal against her most
intimate part. His breath quickened, and their bodies
moved closer in unspoken tandem.

Bethia closed her eyes as his body seemed to melt into
hers. Obsessed with a craving so strong it eclipsed every
other feeling, she arched her body in welcome. He moved
down on her, entering with a deliberate slowness that
made her cry out in exquisite need. She felt her own body
move against his in instinctive, circular movements, drawing him deeper and deeper inside her.

Waves of pleasure washed over her as he quickened
his rhythm, moving faster and faster in a sensuous dance
that became more and more frantic. Bethia felt she was
riding some incredible wave, a great force that was rushing them headlong to some splendid destination. Then he
plunged one last time, filling her with billows of bursting sensations, each one greater than the prior one. His
warmth flooded her, and she experienced a contentment
she'd never before imagined. This time, she knew he cared
about her. And cared more than he'd admitted.

He rolled over, his fingers touching her face, then his lips raining kisses on it. Soft, gentle rain. Life-giving rain.

Dear God, how she loved him.

They lay together for several moments, then he pulled up her breeches and wrapped the blankets around them both, their bodies still experiencing the aftershocks, the shuddering reminders of something quite miraculous.

She did not know how long they lay there, wrapped in a cocoon of their own wonder, despite the wind and rain and danger that existed outside.

"I love you," she whispered. They were words she could no longer hold inside. They radiated from her like rays from the sun on a fine summer day. They wanted to burst out in shouts of joy. Instead, it sounded to her like an uncertain whimper.

His arms tightened around her, his fingers caressed her cheek. He had said he loved her in every way but the way she needed most. She needed to hear it from his lips.

And after a moment, she knew she would not.

It had been the danger that prompted her words, Rory told himself. He had felt her fear, and it had made him admire her more. Anyone could be brave if they did not fear. It took a truly courageous person to feel it and continue on.

But he had never felt himself worthy of love, and he still did not. He reminded himself again that he did not even believe in love. He had never ever seen it, so how could he possibly accept it as a lasting, living thing? And he could not escape the belief that she would be far better off without him. She was grateful now, but one day the time would come that he did not live up to expectations. He'd *never* lived up to expectations. *Never.*

His father had thought him a wastrel and fool. It had been drummed into his head so long, it had become a part of him.

Even now he felt that he'd survived these past few months because of luck rather than skill. He was as much a gambler with his life as he was with his cards. And what kind of husband would that make him?

So he merely kissed her once more and held out a hand to her, bringing her to her feet. He dressed, then helped her do the same. He looked at the sky. How long had they lingered? It was still dark, but dawn could not be far away. Fear struck him like the thrust of a knife. Too long. He knew they had been here far too long. Damn him. He might well have endangered her because he could not control himself.

The rain had slowed but mountains were eclipsed in mist. He fetched the horses, helped her up into the saddle of one. "We are likely to run into a patrol," he said. "Alister had time to skirt this pass before the English learned of your escape. We did not."

"That's why you wore the uniform?"

"Aye, and why I am going to tie your hands. 'Twill be loose enough that you can get free when you need to."

Her hand caught his, and held it tight for a moment. His heart pounded against his chest. How he wanted to make her warm and safe forever. With as much gentleness as possible, he tied her hands with a strip of cloth he cut from his shirt.

Then he took the reins of her horse, mounted his own and started down toward the gorge. He had to go slowly, the horse picking its way in the fog and dark. He had no idea how much time passed, but it must have been hours. He was almost beginning to believe they would not be accosted when he heard the sharp challenge.

"Halt and be recognized."

He halted his horse and waited. Out of the mist materialized two English soldiers, one of them holding a musket on him, the other a lantern. Rory could barely see their faces, and suspected they knew of his approach only because of the noise of the horses. Now just to get by them.

"Yes?" he said in his most haughty voice.

"Your papers, sir?" the soldier said, holding up a lantern to shine light on him, then on Bethia.

"I am attached to His Grace, the Duke of Cumberland," Rory said. "I am taking this lad to him."

The light shone again on Bethia who ducked her face and slumped in the saddle. The lantern moved down to her bound hands.

"He the boy we've been lookin' fer?"

"Aye, I expect so. The duke is in Inverness and wants him without delay."

"I still 'ave to see orders."

"His Grace was in a hurry. He did not give me any."

"Then we will accompany you."

"And leave your posts?" Rory said with mock outrage. The lantern was back on him.

"I 'ave to 'ave yer papers," the man said stubbornly.

"It is your stripes, Sergeant," Rory said indifferently. "If you leave your post despite orders from a superior officer, then it will be your court-martial, not mine." He wished he knew how many were with this soldier. He saw one. How many more? Two? Three? Ten?

The sergeant hesitated, considering his own options. Then, apparently making up his mind, he said, "I will send two men with you."

"How many men do you have, Sergeant?"

"Ten."

Dammit, but he'd been right not to take them on. He shrugged. "'Tis said the Black Knave is in this area. You will be needing all your men, but I have no time to argue with you."

Some of the light from the lantern hit the sergeant's face. It was just Rory's ill luck that the sergeant looked more intelligent than most of the breed. He was going to obey his orders. No one was to go through the gorge.

The sergeant looked once more at Bethia, who had let what was left of her hair fall in her face. She looked sullen and defiant. "'E don't look like much."

"He thought to disguise himself," Rory said. "But I can sniff out a Jacobite anywhere."

The sergeant kept shining his lantern at Bethia's face. "Mebbe you both should get down."

"No, Sergeant. *I* will be court-martialed if I am not back before noon."

"You will not make it, Captain. 'Tis a full day's ride, maybe more."

"*You* may not make it, Sergeant. I will. Can your men keep up with me?"

The sergeant bristled at the idea that his men could not keep pace with an officer. "They can."

But he signaled his comrade to lower his weapon, and Rory knew he had won. Two men were one hell of a lot better than ten. And he *did* need fresh horses.

A half hour later, four riders emerged from the end of the gorge. Rory knew he had to act. Inverness was in the opposite direction of where he intended to go. When they got out of earshot of the sergeant and his patrol, he drew to a stop. "Our horses need a bit of a rest."

The two English troopers nodded. Rory's horses were lathered, their breathing heavy, and now Rory had an advantage. The sergeant had not been so easy to intimidate. These two troopers, faced with orders from one of Cumberland's officers, would be.

He dismounted, took out a flask from a bag hanging from his saddle and took a long swallow. Then he held it out in invitation. "It is a raw night."

The two troopers dismounted, and Rory winked at Bethia, who was still mounted. He tied the reins of her horse to a tree, then walked around to where the troopers would have her at their back.

One of the troopers reached for the flask and took a quick drink, his obvious disbelief at such largess from an officer fading in the glow of good brandy. The second man accepted the flask, greedily taking several swallows.

Reluctantly he returned the flask, and started to turn. Then they saw the lad holding a pistol on them.

One started for his musket in a sling across his back, but Rory moved faster. He slipped out his own pistol.

Then he bowed. "The Black Knave thanks you for your escort," he said.

Their mouths fell open. Closed. Then open again. Like fish trying to grab air. He turned to Bethia. "Come here, lad," he said.

Bethia slipped from the horse, keeping the pistol in hand. The two soldiers turned their gaze from him to the lad, then back to Rory, whom they obviously considered the most dangerous.

Rory waited until Bethia reached his side, then he put his pistol in its holster. "Shoot if either of them moves," he ordered loud enough for them to hear. He then went to his horse, unsaddled it and cut the blanket into strips with a dirk he'd worn inside his breeches. He tied both men's arms behind them.

"Come with me," he said, starting up a wooded hill. The two English soldiers struggled up the hill, slipping and sliding. Bethia followed several feet behind, the pistol still in his hand. When they reached a level, secluded place, Rory backed them each to a separate tree, and told them to sit. He tied each to the tree, then tied their ankles together. Finally he gagged both of them. "I will send word to where you can be found," he said.

Both men muffled protests, their eyes nearly frantic with fear.

Rory regarded them with contempt. "Unlike the English," he said, "I do not take life for the pleasure of it." He flipped a card next to them, then he took Bethia's hand, and together they went back down the hill.

Rory took the saddle from Bethia's mount, then the bits and bridles from the horses they'd been riding. He slapped the two weary horses, sending them off the path. Then he and Bethia mounted the soldiers' horses and trotted east. Toward the coast.

Twenty-seven

Alister paced the main room of the small stone farmhouse not far from the coast. Rory and Bethia should have arrived by now.

The Frenchman would arrive in less than two hours. The rendezvous spot was a thirty-minute ride from here. Mary and ten Jacobites, all members of families marked for extinction by Cumberland, were already waiting near the beach. Alister had insisted that Mary go ahead. She would, he knew, reassure the others with her calm confidence.

Dougal remained with him. He had flatly refused to leave without his sister. They were a stubborn family, Bethia and her brother.

He went out the door and looked out, listening intently for the sound of hoofbeats.

The farmer and his wife were gone as well, visiting her sister who was having a child. Rory had suggested their absence, just in case anyone might see something suspicious. If caught, Rory would say he had come upon an empty house and used it.

So they had no fire and no light. Through the long evening and longer night, Alister had told the boy a little about Rory, and some of the families he had helped escape, including the first small group of two women and three children who had started it all.

Dougal came to the door and stood next to him, Black Jack tagging at his heels. The small black terrier, obviously confused by the absence of his mistress, followed the lad wherever he went.

Alister looked out at the clear sky. A part moon hung in the sky and stars dripped into the horizon. He swore softly. "We could use a bit of fog tonight, too. It is too clear."

Dougal looked up the sky. "Still, I do not miss the rain."

"Nor I, lad." It had been a long, miserable ride the day before, but they'd had the whole of today to rest. Jacobites had been straggling into the farm for three days and had been told to wait up in the hills. This morning Alister brought them down.

Later in the day, a fisherman had brought a gift from the owner of the Flying Lady. He arrived with a wagon full of hay. Under the hay was a dead body. "The Knave ordered one," he said.

Alister had looked under the hay gingerly. The man was naked. He had been tall and had dark hair. Little else was obvious, for his face had been bashed in.

"We were told not to make it happen," the man said, "but this mon is a traitor. He be the one who informed on us. I caught him doing it again, asking questions about me and my brother. A spy for Cumberland." He spit on the ground. "It was us or him."

Alister knew Rory would not like it, that he would feel responsible for the man's death. His friend had no taste for killing. Alister had no such qualms, so he merely nodded, then unloaded the body and watched as the wagon turned away down toward the road. He found a blanket, wrapped the body in it. It was already foul-smelling and stiff, and he knew he would have difficulty putting it on a horse, but it would have to be done. He knew exactly what Rory had planned.

But none of that would matter if Rory did not arrive. God's breath, but where was he?

"Do you think the English have taken them?" The lad's voice quavered with uncertainty at finding his sister, then losing her again.

"Nay, Rory can outwit any of them. Something must have delayed him." He looked at the boy, trying to prepare him for any possibility. "I donna know how long we can wait."

"I will not go without Bethia."

"And how do you think that will make her feel?" Alister countered, his voice harsher than he intended. "She has struggled to see you free and continue the MacDonell name."

Dougal shook his head stubbornly. "She and the Black Knave risked their lives for me. How can I run away now?"

Alister took out a pocket watch and looked at it. "We have to go," he said, ignoring the boy's protest. "I will try to convince the French captain to wait for them."

"I will stay here and wait," the lad said stubbornly.

"Dougal," Alister said with as much patience as he could muster. "It is very late. Rory will take your sister directly to the rendezvous point. You do not want him to have to come back for you and miss the ship."

'Twas the one argument that would sway Dougal, and it did. Indecision spread over his face.

"I will go with you," the lad finally conceded. "But I willna sail without her."

That, Alister thought, would be another battle.

Alister thought to leave a note and hunted for a quill and pen and paper in the event Rory did come here first. There was none. Damnation. Nothing was going as it should this night. He would also have to take the body with them. He could not leave it where an English patrol might find it and blame the residents of the farm. He took

one last look at his watch, then went out to saddle the
horses. The lad could ride with him; the body would have
to ride on the other horse.

Where *were* Rory and Bethia?

Rory looked up at the sky. The part moon was riding
high. He knew he was late. They'd had to detour twice
because of heavy English patrols. He also took a precious
few moments to stop a farm lad and tell him to inform
the nearest magistrate about the location of the bound English soldiers. He gave the lad a half pence and made
him swear he would deliver the message.

It had been the best he could do.

Then they had ridden as if all the demons in hell were
after them. They were hours late. The urgency kept gnawing at him. He had been careless back where they'd rested.
They had lingered far too long. Because of his own weakness, he had been unforgivably careless. Not because of
what she had done, but because of the way she affected
him. If only he had not given in to her warmth last night,
to the comfort of her arms. His lack of self-control was
abominable because of one very real possibility: he might
have cost Bethia her life.

Guilt ate at him. Except for brief pauses to rest the
horses, he kept them moving. Mayhap they could make the
coast in time. But he knew he was driving her to the very
limit of her strength. He could not even stop long enough
to hold her, to reassure her. He was so angry at himself,
he was not sure he could do that anyway.

He could only hope that the Frenchman would wait,
because if he did not, Bethia would be in terrible danger. He had also added another danger when he'd given
the lad a message. It most likely would send English
troops chasing after them.

And he knew Cumberland would not rest until he had
the MacDonells back.

•   •   •

Alister saw several flashes of light from the sea, and returned the signal with a lantern he had brought from the farmhouse. He watched silently as a long boat approached the shore. The sleek French ship, its sails gray to blend into night, was barely visible as a few clouds began to build again in the sky. Thank God for the predictably bad Scottish weather.

Perhaps the Frenchman would agree to wait another hour or two.

He only prayed that Cumberland would not have time to alert the navy to increase its patrols along the coast.

The long boat reached the shore, and three of the six sailors manning oars jumped into the water to pull the boat closer. One of them approached two of the waiting men, one of whom pointed to Alister. Alister went down to meet him while the sailors loaded the waiting refugees. Dougal stuck stubbornly to Alister's side.

"We have two more coming," Alister said.

"*Non. Venez vite,*" the mate said.

"Tell the captain it is the Knave and a woman," Alister said. "There will be more money for him if he waits." Alister did not know if there would or would not be. He had no idea how much Rory had with him. But hell, what was a lie here and there? He'd learned well from the Marquis of Braemoor.

The Frenchman looked dubious. "*Venez vite,*" the Frenchman insisted again.

"Ask him," Alister demanded.

"*Faut partir,* must go," the mate insisted in French, then in English.

Dougal was already moving away from Alister. "We will both wait," Alister said, "and hope the captain agrees to stay. If no', we will take our chances."

The sailor shrugged indifferently. "I tell him, monsieur. One light, *non.* Two, *oui.*"

Mary stood in the long boat as if she planned to get out. Alister picked up the little black terrier and went over to her, giving her the dog. "Take care of him for the mar-chioness."

"I will stay too," she protested.

"Nay," Alister said. "Please go. I canna be worrying about you, too. If he is not here in the next hour, we will come aboard." Another lie. He and Rory had started this together. They would finish it together. But he had to know Mary was safe. He took a bag of sovereigns from his pocket. 'Twas everything he had saved. "Keep it safe for both us."

He leaned over and kissed her. "I love you," he said.

Emotions flickered across her face. Defiance. Uncer-tainty.

"For me," he said softly. "If you never do anything else, do this."

A tear snaked down her cheek. He had never seen her cry before, and his finger brushed it away.

"For our future," he said. He touched her cheek with his palm. "I will rejoin you. I swear," he said softly.

Then he stepped back and signaled the sailors to push the boat back in the surf. He watched as it slowly grew smaller.

He walked over to Dougal. He had been tempted to throw the boy in, but he knew the lad would probably jump overboard. They would wait together.

Several moments later as they watched intently, he saw two flashes of light. The Frenchman would wait, at least awhile.

Silently, the two of them leaned against a dune and prayed.

Bethia thought she never wanted to see a horse again when they approached the coast in the deepest of night nearly twenty-four hours after encountering the English patrol.

Every muscle in her body ached. Every bone screamed in agony. Several times she had thought she could never mount again after they had rested and watered the horses at a stream.

Rory had had to help her mount again the last several times. Her legs simply had not worked. And once in the saddle, she'd had to force herself to stay awake. Even then she had pinched herself or washed her face with cold water from a flask to keep from falling asleep. But when she saw his set face as the day hurried past, she swallowed any pleas to stop and rest.

More than her own weariness, however, she felt Rory's desperation. The mask had slipped back over his face, into his eyes, and he was brusque, even curt. No more pretty words. No more comforting ones. 'Twas as if she rode with a stranger.

When she thought she could not go another step, that she would fall from the horse and never move again, she heard his exclamation.

"We're there." But where there should have been excitement, she heard only defeat. It was then, and only then, that she knew he thought they had arrived too late.

"Rory?"

But he was trotting toward the sound of surf. Over the grassy dunes, she saw a great rock jutting out from the beach. She smelled the sea, heard the surf pounding against the beach and against the rocks. But the dunes kept her from seeing it yet.

She followed him at a trot, then he slowed as the horses started to stumble in the sand. At the top of the dune, he stopped and whistled, then waited.

A sharp whistle came in response.

Then she saw a light from the beach, reaching out to the sea. She realized it must be a signal that they had arrived! She peered through the dark, finally spying the faint outlines of a ship. Just ahead, Rory dismounted, then he helped her down. Quickly unsaddling horses, her husband then took off the bridles and bits. He untied a package from the saddle, put it over his shoulder. He reached out for her hand and started down the beach toward the sea.

She fell, her legs giving way under her. He stopped, leaned over and picked her up, then ran down to two figures standing on the beach, turning toward them.

Alister. Dougal.

Rory set her down, and she hugged Dougal, holding him close and tightly, uncaring of his manly pride. When Dougal finally struggled for freedom, she released him and turned around to look toward Rory. He was untying the package he'd brought with them.

He turned to her. "Take your brother down to the water," he said as he took off his heavy ring that was also the Braemoor seal.

She disobeyed the curt order and watched as Alister unrolled a body from a blanket. The two men dressed it in the bright waistcoat and other clothes Rory had worn at Braemoor. Rory then put his ring on the man's finger.

The two of them then rolled the body into the shallow water. The tide might take it, but not for hours.

"Who is it?"

"A spy," Alister said flatly. "The boat is coming."

"Bloody hell," Rory exclaimed. "I hear riders."

Then Bethia did, too.

The boat was nearing shore. None of them waited for it to come closer. Rory picked her up and ran into the ice-cold sea, dumping her unceremoniously into the boat. Alister and Dougal scrambled in after her. Rory catapulted himself into the boat as the oarsmen started back out to open sea.

A group of riders appeared on the beach. Musket shots rang out. The oarsmen increased the rhythm of their strokes as one musket ball hit the boat. But then they began to fall short.

Minutes later, someone helped her climb a rope ladder onto the ship. Responding to loud commands in French, seamen scurried to unfurl sails. The ship moved briskly away from shore.

• • •

Bethia found herself in a cabin with Mary. Rory had left her side the moment he had stepped on deck, joining the man who obviously captained the ship. A sailor showed her to what must have been the captain's cabin.

Mary greeted her with a hug. "I was so afraid for all of you," she said.

"Especially Alister," Bethia guessed aloud.

Mary's expression grew bleak. "And as much for my lord."

Bethia remembered what Rory had said, that Mary had been an excuse for his absences, nothing more. Now she wondered.

Mary must have seen her expression. "Not in that way, my lady. Did the marquis ever tell you about me?"

"No," Bethia said, leaning against the wall. She was so tired, and yet she knew she had to hear this. It was the first time anyone had been willing to discuss the relationship between Mary and her husband.

"I was fifteen when my mother died. I was permitted to stay if I continued to provide the herbs for the kitchen and for medicines. One day Donald paid an unexpected visit and tried to bed me. When I said no, he became angry and attacked me." Her slender shoulders trembled as she told the tale. "He came a second time. Rory had just returned after fostering with another family, and he had come to get some herbs for a poultice for a horse. He heard my screams and threw Donald off me. He almost killed him. 'Twas clear tha' Donald feared his brother, though I had heard that the younger son was considered worthless and a bastard. He told Donald tha' if he ever touched me again he would kill him. Donald never came close to me again, but he did spread the word that I welcomed his advances."

Mary bit her lip. "Rory told me he would give me money to go somewhere else and get started, but I loved my garden, the herbs. So he let everyone believe he was my 'protector.'" She looked at Bethia. "But he never was. I knew he had a reputation with women, but never once did he touch me. He knew I cared about Alister."

Mary hesitated, then continued in a low voice, "The marquis has always thought the worst of himself, mayhap because his father always told him he was worthless. But he saved me, just as he once saved Alister from Donald. Just as he saved you and your brother. He has always protected those who could not protect themselves, although he would deny it. He would call it a 'game' or a chance to 'tweak' his father's tail, or Cumberland's nose. In truth, he has a hatred for injustice. He would deny it to the day he dies, but 'tis there. Strong as the roots of an oak."

Bethia felt a wetness around her eyes. She was tired, so tired, and yet she saw him in her mind's eye standing like that oak, surviving storm and fire and drought, the drought of going without love or affection. She'd had so much of both. She had always had a feeling of belonging. He'd had none.

"Fight for him, my lady," Mary added in a soft voice, "for he will not fight for himself. He knows only how to fight for others."

"Thank you," she told Mary.

"You need never thank me, my lady. Not if you can make him happy."

"I will try," Bethia said. She would sleep, and think about what to say, then challenge him in the morning.

He seemed to like challenges.

Rory stood next to Renard, the French captain, who had taken the wheel. The wind was brisk, the sails full. They had seen no sign of a British ship, although Renard assured Rory that his swift sloop could outrun the much heavier frigates favored by the British.

They had been under sail now for eight hours, and Renard was beginning to relax. 'Twas still a long, perilous voyage to France, but the worst was over.

Though young Dougal was sleeping and Alister was

Patricia Potter

huddled somewhere with Mary, several of the Jacobite passengers were on deck. They had all given him and Renard their thanks.

He had not seen Bethia since they had come aboard. She was, according to Mary, still sleeping. And well she should. It was a miracle he had not ridden her to death. She had gone through hell because of him, because he'd not been able to contain his lust.

She would be far better off without him.

The thought was excruciating.

He turned his attention back to the captain. "I have not thanked you yet for waiting."

Renard grinned. "I am an admirer of the Knave," he said. "I would be most desolate to see him end his life at the end of the noose."

Rory studied him for a moment. "Regardless," he said, "I owe you a debt that can never be repaid. I hope you remember it."

"Oh, I will, my lord."

Rory narrowed his eyes.

"I finally tricked the fair Elizabeth into telling me who you were," he said. "She feared you might need some extra help."

"You and Elizabeth . . ."

"Plan to wed, my lord. We no longer have secrets between us. She wanted to wait until you got out."

Rory grinned. "Please call me Rory. The marquis just died, Captain. He is no more."

"Such tragedy," the captain said. "Still, I think the marchioness may be looking for him."

Rory followed the direction of the Frenchman's eyes. His wife stood at the railing, looking toward him. Her short hair blew in the wind, curling recklessly against her face. She still wore the lad's clothing, but the jacket flew open with the wind, and her plain shirt now outlined the curve of her breasts. Her eyes were on him, and her lips curved in a beguiling smile.

"Go to her," the captain said. "She is far prettier than I."

Rory agreed with that assessment. He thought he had never seen a bonnier woman. In any event, 'twas time for a talk, to tell her what he'd planned for her in France. Friends who would help a friend of the Knave. He also had to warn her never to reveal his identity. He had taken too much care to kill the fellow.

When he reached her, she held out her hand for his, lacing her fingers in his and looked up at him. "My lord," she said softly.

"The marquis is dead," he replied.

"I will miss his bright clothes."

"I will not," Rory said. "The fellow was ill-bred, loutish and ostentatious."

"I must like ostentatious."

She looked so incredibly appealing. The sun magnified the smattering of freckles across her nose, and her cheeks were pink with the sharp bite of wind. Her eyes sparkled and her hair danced around her face. God's breath, but how he wanted her.

He remembered what happened the last time he succumbed to temptation. *Do not,* he told himself.

But she apparently had no such compunctions. She lifted on tiptoes and her lips brushed his. "I love you," she said.

He started to shake his head, to deny any such great boon. "You are grateful," he corrected. "But you have the jewels. You owe it to Dougal to make a new life in France. He will be safe there."

"And you?"

He tried to smile carelessly. "I am off to America. I told you I am a wanderer."

"Then I am going with you," she said. "I have the jewels. I can follow you anywhere."

He was befuddled. He knew she would do exactly that. But why?

Her fingers went up to his lips, effectively quieting

them. "You cannot tell me who or who not to love," she said.

He meant to open his mouth to protest. Instead he found himself nibbling on her fingers. She was right. He could not tell her who to love and who not to. He could only warn her. He just bloody well did not want to. Not at this moment.

She smiled. "No protest?"

"Aye," he said. "I have no title. No trade. Not much money. I have a wanderlust."

"Mary says you have the roots of an oak."

He looked at her through narrowed eyes. "Mary says too much."

"She loves you. So does Alister. So, I think, do a number of other people."

He looked astonished, as if the idea had never occurred to him. His arm went around her, and tightened. "I can offer you nothing. In France, you could have your choice of gentlemen. I'll never be that."

"You, my lord, are the finest gentleman I've ever met," she said, putting her free hand to his face. "And I would wither away in France," she said. "I would wither away anywhere if I were not with you." She hesitated, then said, "Or are you like all the other men in the world, thinking you know what is best for a woman?"

He chuckled. "I would never say that of you, lass."

"Then I know that *you* are best for me." She hesitated for a moment, then said uncertainly, "Unless you do not want me."

"Ah, lass, how can you think of such a thing? It is only . . ."

"Only?"

"Ah, hell," he surrendered. He bent down and his lips touched hers, and then he lost himself in them. He lost himself in the grandness of her love, in the glory of her touch, in the splendor of her giving.

His arms closed around her and for the first time in

his life he felt he belonged somewhere. He felt loved and needed. He was wanted. All things to fight for.

His lips left hers and he nuzzled her ear, then whispered, "I love you."

The ship heeled then, and a spray of water mixed with rays from the sun and formed a rainbow.

She moved to his side, still holding his hand. Together they watched it.

"It is for us," she whispered.

An illusion. He had called it that days ago. But now he knew better. It was a promise.

His fingers tightened around hers. They belonged together. He knew it now. He did not know what the future held, but they were meant to be together. They belonged together.

"Aye," he said. "Forever."

Epilogue

The Piedmont, Virginia, 1751

Rory had never wanted to be a farmer.

And yet now as he sat his horse, he viewed the fur-rowed acres and green pastures below with no little pride and satisfaction. He had produced something fine, something of worth. He and Bethia and Alister and Mary. Something of his own.

He took his arms from around his three-year-old son, Gavin, and lifted him from the saddle and set him firmly on the ground where Black Jack, who had followed them, immediately started pulling at his trousers to play with him. The two were inseparable.

Rory dismounted, then took a basket from Bethia and she slipped from her own saddle into his arms. He held her for a second, long enough to convey his love for her.

It had become a tradition now. She could most certainly manage her own dismount, but they both relished those shining moments when their bodies met and they shared a moment of intimacy, a sudden fire that had remained with them.

Of course, they enjoyed a deeper, more intense intimacy in the privacy of their room, but after four years of marriage, Rory still couldn't get enough of his wife.

He loved looking up at her, watching her slide into his arms, and feeling the sweetness of her body.

He relished her smile as they watched Gavin giggle as the terrier leaped up and took a swipe at his face. "Ugh," Gavin said, even as he looked pleased.

Bethia had wanted to come here today. They had traveled to this corner of Virginia four years ago. Still unwilling to take anything from Braemoor, he had reluctantly sold two pieces of jewelry. As Bethia pointed out, it was *hers*. Therefore, *theirs*. He compromised by sending the pearls back to Neil. Rory felt it Neil's birthright, and mayhap he would marry one day.

He and Bethia, and Mary and Alister, had married in France. Rory had taken the name of Logan, a common enough name in England, yet one that also belonged to a nearly extinct but proud Scottish clan.

The Logans and Armstrongs pooled what else they had—Rory's winnings, Alister's savings—and added it to the sum they received by selling the necklace and earrings. It was enough for passage and the purchase of six horses, which Rory intended to breed. A few games in a Williamsburg tavern had produced more winnings as well as information about the country. None of them had fancied staying in a well-settled area with a heavy British presence.

A Scotsman, though, told them of a valley in the Virginia Piedmont that was just now being settled. Most of the settlers there were opposed to slavery as they were. Land was inexpensive and grazing fine. A blacksmith was being sought and would almost immediately have a thriving business.

Covey's Crossroads was new, small and raw. A man named Alvin Covey had built a small inn, and merchants had followed to cater to those going further west, always looking for a place yet to be civilized. There were several small farms, and beyond the village a large valley. Covey held title to the land but his two sons had died of fever, and he no longer had interest in farming it. He did have interest in a blacksmith.

Alister liked Covey and the area. The five of them—Rory, Bethia, Dougal, Mary and Alister—rode to the valley, approaching it from a hill. Bethia had exclaimed with pleasure. Framed by mountains that reminded them all of Scotland, the valley was rich and lush and green and fed by a clear, running stream.

Rory had had something else in mind. A trading post, mayhap, or a stable, and yet when he saw the hope in Bethia's eyes, he looked at it again. The grass looked fine for horses. Perhaps he could breed horses. A small farm would not be so bad, not with Bethia.

And it hadn't been bad at all. In truth, he had loved every moment. Everyone in town and within fifteen miles came to help frame and build a cabin, then raise a barn. He and Alister and Dougal cleared sufficient land to grow enough crops to sustain them through the winter. And then it simply grew. He found several fine horses at reasonable prices, traded some to those moving further west, keeping the best to breed.

He was afraid, though. Deep down afraid that he wasn't worthy of all this, that he did not deserve Bethia and that one day she would discover the fraud he really was. The valley still wasn't home to him, the ever after place that Bethia considered it.

When he found out Bethia was going to have a child, he added a room to the house, and he'd never known a greater joy than when he'd taken Gavin from his mother's arms and held him awkwardly. He'd only hoped that he would not disappoint this boy of his, this miracle. Mayhap that was why God had blessed them with only one child.

Bethia spread out a blanket and the feast she'd prepared. That was also a tradition that she'd started. Each year after completing the spring planting, they came to the hill and looked down on the farm, each time marking the newest field. Now they had two hired men, both indentured servants to whom they had given freedom. Both had chosen to stay.

He took her hand. She was even more beautiful now. Her skin glowed, her body had developed a few more curves with motherhood, and her dark blue eyes fairly sparkled with life and love and pride.

She had prepared a roast chicken and fresh bread with jellies and cheese. It was a fine, warm day with a breeze that caressed rather than a wind that buffeted. After they finished, she watched as Gavin tumbled with the dog, then went sound asleep with Jack sprawled in his arms.

Rory wrapped his arm around her, wondering how he'd ever scoffed at the notion of love. He was amazed at it daily, and humbled.

Bethia leaned into his arms and laced her fingers with his. "We might be thinking about adding to the house," she said lazily.

Since she had been the one to demur every time he'd mentioned the possibility, he looked at her with surprise and then he saw the slow, secret smile on her face.

Emotion swelled in him. His fingers tightened around hers.

"Bethia?" His hand hesitated at her stomach, then touched it with wonderment.

"Aye, my love," she said.

A lump grew in his throat as his fingers wrapped around hers. So God *had* seen fit to bless them again.

Then he looked back at the valley. The stream, sprayed by the rays of the sun, looked like a diamond necklace flung across a bolt of emerald velvet. Further north, newly turned earth formed neat rectangles that would turn to gold in late summer.

The valley—the glen—nurtured them and had become a part of his heart. All of it had. Bethia's unwavering faith. Gavin's childish trust. Dougal who had become a son to him. Friends who had risked everything for him.

Their love and warmth had made him whole. But always there had been a seed of doubt. He dinna deserve it.

But now . . . contentment filled him.

A bairn. Another new life. God's gift.

His family and the land. These were *his* jewels. They were real and solid and partly of his own making. No illusion. No dream to be abruptly shattered as he had feared for so long.

His heart contracted. He leaned over and kissed Bethia, his lips brushing hers with a tenderness so strong, so piercing that he thought he might break with it.

"Do you feel this is home yet?" she whispered.

So she knew. He should have known. She read his soul. And his heart.

"Aye," he said, reaching out and placing a hand on his son's sandy hair. And for the first time, he knew it was true.